A
LIKELY
STORY

A
LIKELY
STORY

A Novel

Leigh McMullan Abramson

ATRIA BOOKS

NEW YORK   LONDON   TORONTO   SYDNEY   NEW DELHI

ATRIA
BOOKS

An Imprint of Simon & Schuster, Inc.
1230 Avenue of the Americas
New York, NY 10020

First Atria Books hardcover edition March 2023

ATRIA B O O K S and colophon are trademarks of Simon & Schuster, Inc.

For information about special discounts for bulk purchases, please contact Simon & Schuster Special Sales at 1-866-506-1949 or business@simonandschuster.com.

The Simon & Schuster Speakers Bureau can bring authors to your live event. For more information or to book an event, contact the Simon & Schuster Speakers Bureau at 1-866-248-3049 or visit our website at www.simonspeakers.com.

Interior design by Kyoko Watanabe

Manufactured in China

1 3 5 7 9 10 8 6 4 2

Library of Congress Cataloging-in-Publication Data is available.

ISBN 978-1-9821-9924-1
ISBN 978-1-9821-9926-5 (ebook)

For my parents

Well, I've been afraid of changing
'Cause I've built my life around you

—Stevie Nicks

Fiction is the lie through which we tell the truth.

—Albert Camus

PROLOGUE

New York, 1989

Claire stood with her back to the bar and surveyed the pulsating mass of people deeply pleased with themselves for being exactly where they were at exactly that moment. The party was an unqualified success. She kept being congratulated, as if it took genius to send invitations, rent out a restaurant—even a hot one like Gotham—and tell her florist, *it's an avian theme, go wild.* The maple branches growing out of birdcages were something, but Claire did not take pride in floral arrangements. As she and her husband had grown wealthy to the point of rich, Claire was wary of becoming one of those Upper East Side types who mistook purchased goods and services for accomplishment.

Claire had not read the book. As she nodded and smiled, agreeing with everyone about what a special, *important* novel it was, this secret blasphemy twinkled pleasantly inside her. Several yards away, the author was in the crowd, holding forth. The noise of the room was too loud for Claire to hear the specifics. After a decade of marriage, Claire couldn't imagine there was a subject she had not heard Ward expound upon, but she studied him still. By his theatrical gestures and exaggerated facial expressions, he was drunk.

"Can we get these at home, Mommy?"

Claire turned toward Isabelle, who was sitting cross-legged on

1

a stool next to her. The bartender had given Isabelle open access to the tray of maraschino cherries, and she was now holding one aloft by the stem, swinging it talisman-like in front of her face. A viscous, chemical red dripped onto the smocking of her Laura Ashley dress.

"They're more of a special occasion treat."

Isabelle sighed. "I thought so." Isabelle had come with Claire to the hairdresser that day, and her daughter's blond tresses had been plaited and pinned on her head, threaded with baby's breath. The long evening had left Isabelle with loose strands and a halo of frizz. And after the cherries there was a subtle, almost clownish red ring around her mouth. Claire felt an ache of love for her only child.

"I took off my shoes," said Isabelle.

Claire looked down. "So you did."

Isabelle started to yawn, before stopping herself. "I don't feel tired at all." The plan had been to send Isabelle back uptown with a babysitter. But Isabelle had lobbied persuasively to stay. So it was the babysitter who'd left, and Isabelle who remained, now several hours past bedtime.

"Hmmm," said Claire, kissing her on her head.

"I think I should come to all your parties," said Isabelle.

"Oh do you?"

Isabelle was looking down, her fingers moving over the charm that hung from her neck on a delicate chain. "Don't you love my necklace?" she asked, thrusting forward the gold miniature replica of Ward's new book, custom-ordered at Tiffany's. God knows how much it had cost. Claire had not been consulted on the purchase.

"It's very nice."

Isabelle smiled and began to play with her mother's hair. A series of sharp pings broke through the noise. Ward's publicist was standing on one of the banquettes, tapping a knife on a champagne flute. Isabelle looked up.

"Daddy's going to talk now," whispered Claire.

Ward took the microphone and climbed onto the banquette, a move that elicited cheers from the audience. Ward raised his fist in triumph, before making a patting motion in the air, like a coach quieting his team. His newly graying hair sprang voluminously from his scalp in a wide circumference. He wore his signature red-framed glasses, cartoonish on anyone who wasn't arguably the hottest literary writer in America. It was becoming more and more difficult to conceive of the before, the time when her husband had not been *the* Ward Manning. But not so many years ago, Ward was just another guy with a pile of pages, hustling a manuscript. Once upon a time, standing on a banquette wouldn't have gotten Ward applause; it would've gotten him fired. Now the lavish book parties, the award ceremonies, the inductions, the famous-people dinner soirées bled into one another. Yesterday evening, *Nightingale Call* had debuted at number one on the *New York Times* bestseller list. Whatever Ward published, people would read it. The number of authors—*literary* authors—who could do that was small indeed. People recognized him on the street, approached his table in restaurants. Ward was mythical, a god of letters. Just as Ward once promised her, he had become very famous.

Ward smiled without speaking for a long moment, reveling in the hushed anticipation.

"Two years ago, I started this book," Ward finally said. "I wanted to give myself a challenge." He paused.

"I decided I'd write about a guy who goes to live with the birds. Try making that not fucking boring."

A big laugh.

Isabelle giggled. The profanity didn't seem to have registered. Like everyone else's in the room, her daughter's eyes had not moved from Ward. He went on to thank a list of people. Claire raised her glass and smiled when he said her name.

"And my daughter is here tonight."

Everyone turned to Isabelle and clapped. Isabelle blushed and put her hands over her face, which elicited a collective *awwww*.

"Come here, sweetheart," said Ward, beckoning.

Claire had not been alerted that Isabelle was to be part of the show, but she picked Isabelle off the stool. At seven years old, her daughter was almost too heavy for her, but not quite. Claire set her down and smoothed the back of Isabelle's dress before she took off toward her father. Ward, who'd stepped off the banquette, scooped her up and placed Isabelle on his shoulders. "Isn't she beautiful?" People whistled. Ward was blatantly using their daughter as a prop, manipulating the crowd with this heartwarming visual, as if he were father of the year. Claire looked at Isabelle, searching for the subtle signs of distress that only a mother would see. Instead she watched as Isabelle took the crowd on, bright-eyed, smiling coyly, her little stocking feet resting on Ward's chest.

Until that night, Claire was meticulous in shielding their daughter from her father's fame. And she'd believed that Isabelle was still oblivious. Ward was just her father. But seeing her child aloft at this grown-up party, Claire knew she had been kidding herself. Isabelle knew about her father. She understood what was happening in the room, and she understood the role she could play in it. Claire watched the two of them gamely mug for a photographer from the *New York Post*. For the first time, it was Claire who was on the outside.

When the applause subsided, Claire watched Ward put Isabelle down on the ground again. He was pulled away by his editor, leaving Isabelle alone. She was suddenly tiny in the sea of full-grown bodies. She looked up at adults carrying on their own conversations, no longer interested, as her smile fell and her brow creased slightly.

Claire bent down to pick up Isabelle's Mary Janes before pushing through the crowd. She took Isabelle's hand, put on her shoes, and, without bothering with goodbyes, led her out onto the street. In the taxi, Isabelle lay down with her head in Claire's lap and was quickly asleep. Claire gazed out the window, a roiling inside her.

Long ago, she had made peace with her bargain. She'd known what she was getting into. Going along with one version of the story, allowing certain truths to be hidden—it hadn't cost her much. Or so she'd thought. As she blessed the narrative, over and over, year after year, she had never anticipated how she would feel when it was her own daughter who believed in it. Claire longed now to undo what had been done, to make Isabelle understand what was left unsaid. But as she sat in the car, speeding up Park Avenue, Claire feared she was already too late.

PART I

1

New York, 2017

Isabelle

Isabelle had told herself this would be the easy part. The service was over. She had delivered her eulogy. She had been to the family plot that smelled toxically of lilies and manure. All that was left to do was drink and absorb the condolences of the dozens of family members and friends now occupying her parents' living room. But she understood now that this, this party with the missing guest of honor, would be worse than what had come before it. The mass of people around her only amplified the loneliness growing over her insides like mold. She did not want to hear from some off-brand cousin how wonderful her mother was. *A real class act*, people kept saying. As if Isabelle needed to be told.

"Here. Trade." Brian stood beside her with a fresh glass of white. He handed it to her, taking her nearly empty one.

"You read my mind."

Brian nodded. "Still a big crowd."

"Everyone looks a bit too comfortable," said Isabelle, shaking her head. The reception had started at four and showed no signs of stopping at a quarter to seven. The apartment was swimming with people, and Isabelle had decided she hated all of them. For her guests, this event soaked up a few hours of a Tuesday afternoon. Afterward they would return to their quotidian concerns and routines.

"Some people claiming to be your relatives just asked me when we'd gotten married."

Isabelle smirked. "What did you tell them?"

"That I'm just a side piece."

"Ha. That's good," said Isabelle. "I hope it was the Connecticut contingency—those constipated people over there." She gestured with her chin. "They need to be scandalized. My mother loathed them." Isabelle took a sip of her wine. "Secretly of course."

"Of course." Brian added, "I said we were just good friends."

"I know you did." Clarifying that they were not in fact engaged, dating, or even fucking, was something that both Brian and Isabelle did with regularity.

"By the way, this has solidified it for me. If I ever get married, I am not having a wedding. I do not need to see my extended family ever again."

"Noted."

Isabelle paused. "And, anyway, I could never have a wedding without my mother." This is what happened now. Isabelle would forget herself for a moment, a seemingly benign thought would slip through the grief filter, and then, the reminder would pop into her brain, beeping and vibrating, like one of those iPhone storm alerts: YOUR MOTHER IS DEAD.

The last few weeks still had a surreal quality. It had started with a freakishly early case of the flu, nothing some rest wouldn't cure. But then there was a secondary infection, and the string of ineffective antibiotics. Things quickly spiraled. High fever. Fainting. Hospitalization. Sepsis. More infection. Spreading. Nights spent folded into upholstered hospital chairs with slick spots like old, worn-over gum. But Isabelle had not thought this was *the end*. She dismissed Claire's urgent directives about what to do "after" as her mother's fear talking. It was only when her mother developed MRSA, an antibiotic-resistant superbug, and slipped into unconsciousness, her organs giving out one by one, that Isabelle understood. By then it was too late to say goodbye. For the last week, Isabelle had allowed immediate concerns, numbers, statistics, vital signs, and the beep and hum of machines to crowd out reflections of missed opportunities. But now all would be quiet.

Isabelle looked over the sea of heads to the living room windows. The third floor aligned with the tops of the trees planted along Fifth Avenue. It was the middle of September; the leaves were still green, but with a brown curdle at the edges. Summer had ended without Isabelle's notice.

Brian put his arm around her. "Want me to get rid of everyone?"

"Yes, please. But how?"

"I'll say that you need to rest."

Isabelle laughed. "That won't do it. These people are animals. We'd have to cut off the oxygen—stop serving booze."

"I'm glad you still have your sense of humor."

"I wasn't kidding."

"Want me to tell the caterer?"

Isabelle sighed. "No. Having people around is probably good for my father. He does best with an audience." Ward was in the living room near the bar, where he'd been for several minutes. Isabelle's ability to track her father while simultaneously doing other things was a skill she'd perfected in childhood when he was always about to jet off on a book tour or shut himself up in his study for the evening.

The front door opened, and a group of underdressed young people walked in, looking like they'd lost their way. Of course they were here.

"Who are they?" Brian asked.

"The MFAs," said Isabelle.

At another time, Isabelle would have gone over to greet them. She once reveled in the blatant stares of Ward's students, imagining them discussing her, the spawn of their idol, in hushed, reverent tones. She'd make a point to schedule lunch dates with her father on Ward's teaching days so she could pick him up at Columbia and feel the specialness of being Isabelle Manning at its most acute. But now she kept her distance. At thirty-four—nearly thirty-five!—she was older than most of his students, sometimes much older, and there was too little to separate their aspirational circumstances from her own. In their eyes she saw only the question that ran on a loop through her own mind: What the hell had happened to Isabelle Manning?

Ward

A phalanx of sheath-wearing women of a certain age stood between Ward and his second martini. By the teeth and headbands, he'd identified them as Claire's childhood friends from *the club*. It was unnerving to see these women in dark mourner's garb. They existed for Ward perennially in summer, gin and tonic in hand, tennis whites exposing pointy elbows and runny knees.

"Oh Ward, I'm so sorry," said a jowly woman holding a smudgy wineglass. She came close enough for him to see tributaries of lipstick in the tiny wrinkles around her mouth. She smelled of WASP, a stale, churchy mix of booze and Wheat Thins. Ward had once known the woman's name, but that information now existed in the vast landfill of the forgotten. He gave her the widower nod—eyes half-closed, lips flattened Muppet-like into a weary grimace. He was eager to get away from her, procure his drink, and return to the task of finding someone important to flatter him.

"And how is Isabelle?" the woman asked.

"She's holding up." Ward believed this was true, in as much as such a platitude could be true. Ward wanted to help his daughter during this critical moment. Of course. But he did hope that the maintenance of her emotional well-being—always Claire's expertise—would fall within someone else's purview. Consoler-in-chief was not a role in which Ward would excel. His daughter had others to support her. That boy who was not a boyfriend. And there was Glenda. Glenda was his best hope.

"You'll excuse me," said Ward, moving away from the woman and closer to the bar. The reception following the memorial had been Glenda's idea. "People need an outlet, Ward. To mourn," his wife's closest friend had told him. So Isabelle had hired the caterers, extended invites. And here they were. It occurred to him now, watching the inebriated hordes tucking into pigs in a blanket and bearing down on his upholstery, that perhaps Glenda's home, an even bigger spread several blocks south on Park, would have made a better "outlet." And no one was mourning. He'd seen Glenda going hard at the cheese table and doing what everyone else was doing: drinking. Real mourning could not be calendared in like a dentist appointment. It snuck up, occurring in pauses, the little empty pockets of life. Ward did not like to be snuck up on. The day before, he was standing in his kitchen when he'd spied a grocery list written out on a white pad in his wife's elegant hand. *Green apples, salad things, loads of seltzer, pistachios.* Before he realized what was happening, he was crying. Sobbing, really. He had not cried since he was a child, and it was a truly off-putting experience. Ward did not intend to be caught off guard again. Luckily, Ward would not have the time to break down. He was facing one of the tightest deadlines of his career.

Ward had barely written of late. The ostensible reason was his wife's sickness. But the real impediment could trace its origins to years, maybe decades, earlier. It had begun as a harmless guilty pleasure, an occasional indulgence that had given him a little boost now and then. But in the last several months—long before what happened to Claire—it had turned into something else. Something out of his control, verging on pernicious. But Ward had a plan. Today would be the last day of the letters.

Before the party, he'd hauled up a large sack of fan mail to his study in anticipation of one final bender. After all he'd been through, he deserved it. And then complete abstinence. He'd roll up his sleeves and get to work.

There was a tap on his shoulder. He turned and saw a tiny woman, wiry gray hair secured in a ponytail, in an oversized blazer.

"Ward," she said as she leaned in for a kiss on the cheek. She looked familiar, but the specifics evaded him. "I'm sorry—"

"Thank you—"

"—that we couldn't give Claire more space."

Ward nodded as if he knew what the woman was referring to. He'd gotten good at this pretending. The pretending was easier when someone else was speaking. The more vexatious was the sudden disappearance of words and entire phrases from his lexicon, the feeling that they were there, but just beyond his horizon. Trying to forcibly remember them, to muscle them back into the spongy matter of hippocampus, only seemed to make it worse. It had happened that morning at the memorial. He had gone off his notes. "Claire left all of us feeling more—" and he just blanked. He finished with "energized," but that was not quite right. It was not until after the service he remembered the word, coming to him like a clap of thunder. *Invigorated.* He had forgotten "invigorated." A simple, fourth-grade word, nothing special about it, but it had floated maddeningly out of reach. This was the kind of forgetting that ate at his soul.

"Some physicist had to die the same day," the woman continued in her husky voice. "I'd never heard of him, but sometimes I have to throw the science guys a bone."

"Right, right." Ward felt the pieces coming together like the first tickly breeze of a coming train. His mind churned for a moment, and then, click. Dale Horowitz, editor of the *New York Times*. Christ, he should have known. Especially since she was precisely the kind of person he'd been looking for.

"The obit was lovely, Dale." **New York Philanthropist Dies at 69** had been accompanied by a picture of his wife when she was young, not even forty. Isabelle must have given it to them. He'd spent time that morning staring at the photo. By the looseness of the smile on her face, he guessed the picture had been taken before Isabelle's accident. She still looked like the girl he'd seen walk into a restaurant decades before, his Claire Cunningham. The write-up was brief, focused on the reading program Claire had started at Mount Sinai. It took two full sentences before it mentioned she was the wife of Ward Manning. Claire would have appreciated that. She also would have understood that even with her blue-blooded, Mayflower-sailing family, even with her successful non-profit, she got into the paper because of him.

"Glad you liked it," said Dale, before leaning in with the back of her hand shielding the side of her mouth and speaking in a mock whisper. "Don't worry. Yours is in the can."

"Excuse me?"

"Your obit. It's done. I drafted it myself."

Ward raised his eyebrows. Dale smiled and looked at him expectantly.

"I hate to nitpick, but there's the small matter of me being, well, how shall I put this?" Ward cleared his throat. "Not dead."

"Come on. We have to write the big ones in advance."

Ward considered this. He wouldn't want anyone slapping together two thousand words on him overnight. He shuddered to think of all that could be inadvertently left out. And yet, Dale's information was unwelcome.

"Not everyone gets the editor of the whole goddamn paper, Ward."

"Hm." Ward felt a surge of melancholy that he would not get to read his own obituary, which he very much hoped would include the phrase "greatest novelist of our time" with the absolute minimum number of modifiers.

"And unless someone drops a bomb, I'll try for A1 placement."

"You speak as if this is imminent."

"Can't promise above the fold," Dale continued, as if she hadn't heard him.

Ward snorted. "My fingers are crossed."

A low, insistent moan began emanating from Dale's black leather bag. Dale retrieved her phone. Eyes locked on her screen, she punched the buttons, muttering before she looked up at Ward and said, "I gotta run. My condolences again."

Alone, Ward stood motionless for a moment, dazed. He was considering walking upstairs to his office, where a nice, thick stack of mail awaited him. But then he saw them. A gaggle of students loitered in the entry, their eyes widening at the massive apartment. He had to give Claire credit for that. Nearly thirty years before, when they'd moved above Ninety-Sixth Street, people thought they were crazy. The duplex facing the park was now worth many times what they'd paid. Ward decided it would be savage of him not to greet his students personally. He walked toward them, ready to be adored.

Brian

The Manning apartment had emptied out at last. Ward had disappeared upstairs, and Isabelle and Brian were camped out in the kitchen polishing off a bottle of wine and a leftover platter of pigs in a blanket. Isabelle sat cross-legged atop the island, and Brian below her on one of the metal stools.

"So who was the woman in full equestrian gear?" he asked.

"Oh god. My cousin Trudie. Really like third cousin or something, but whatever. She's completely insane, walks around Manhattan with a riding crop. Her parents were obsessed with birds and used to leave Trudie as a child for weeks at a time to go to the Galápagos. Trudie became unnaturally invested in horses."

"As one does."

"I'm telling you. My mother was the only one in the family who wasn't crazy."

"I can believe it."

"They're actually pretty good cold." Isabelle held up a mini hot dog before dipping it in mustard.

"Yeah, not bad," said Brian, though they were unsettlingly rubbery. They sat chewing, not saying anything. Brian intuited that Isabelle did not want to be asked how she was doing for the millionth time that day, even by him. She wanted to talk about anything but her mother dying.

"Oooh, is there cheese over there?"

Brian retrieved the platter from the counter by the stove, and brought over another of vegetables, too. This one looked barely touched. There were fuchsia heads of cauliflower, green tomatoes still attached to the umbilical vine, and something that might be called *Romanesco*. The carrots, mottled purple, the color of a three-day bruise, had a thick tuft of vestigial greens. Brian had grown up thinking carrots were the flavorless severed thumbs sold bagged in the grocery store, the ones that calloused and chafed in the refrigerator. He knew better now.

Brian watched Isabelle retrieve some takeout containers from a drawer. She wordlessly handed him a spoon, and they began emptying the platters into the Tupperware. He didn't pry about why Isabelle was hoarding prosciutto-wrapped figs, or offer to buy her dinner. She'd only laugh and tell him he had no money, while mussing his hair. She wasn't entirely wrong about the money. He was a public servant, if a glorified one. But he had some savings from the law firm he'd worked at before he became a U.S. attorney. And he could easily make more if he wanted. He could certainly afford dinner. True as they might be, when these arguments hit the air, they would turn defensive and sad. And he was acutely aware that few people would be permitted to witness Isabelle doing what she was doing, and that his inclusion in this private moment and others like it depended on his tact.

The Mannings and their money was a mystery Brian could not fully unravel. He'd grown up under the impression that people had as much money as they earned at their jobs. But with people like the Mannings, it was far more complicated. Ward was unquestionably a very rich man. In contrast, if the family jokes were to be believed, Claire's side of the family was nearly insolvent. And yet, Isabelle's maternal relatives lived in large—if crumbling—estates and possessed multiple sailboats. Isabelle's own financial situation was a tangle of contradictions. She owned a small one-bedroom on east Seventy-Fourth Street in a doorman building, and had beautiful things, clothing, furniture, art. But she was often strapped for cash, claiming she couldn't go out because she was broke, and he didn't get the sense she was being overly dramatic. She certainly couldn't be living on the articles she sold here and there as she worked on her novel. Brian didn't know how she got by. Perhaps leftover fancy cocktail appetizers were part of it. The only thing Isabelle reliably had in her refrigerator was a box of Triscuits. She preferred them chilled.

Brian stacked the takeout containers on top of one another, and then rinsed the platters and put them in the dishwasher. After a day spent loitering around Isabelle, offering inevitably meaningless expressions of comfort, it was a relief to have a task, a tangible way to be helpful. When everything had been packed up, Brian lifted the stack of containers and asked, "Do you want me to find a bag for these?"

"No, let's put them in the refrigerator," said Isabelle.

"Aren't you taking them?"

"Tomorrow. I'm going to stay here tonight."

"Oh." Brian paused. "Are you sure? I could walk you home."

"It's okay." Isabelle pressed the container of vegetables into his hands. "For you, Mr. Healthy."

Brian nodded, realizing he'd been given his cue to leave. He'd been expecting the night to gently taper off with the twenty-minute walk down Madison. He felt the sting of disappointment that he would instead have to say goodbye here before the long subway ride to the financial district alone.

They walked into the foyer. Before that afternoon, Brian had not been inside these walls in years, a decade maybe, but being in this apartment, inhaling that crisp, warm laundry smell, it felt like 2002 again, Brian camped out at the Mannings' during a school break.

It was in the guest bedroom just down the hall that he had learned what high thread count sheets felt like as he listened to the hiss and rattle of prewar building heat. He was a regular at Thanksgiving, where turkey never appeared, but a high-power mix of literati, artists, and theater actors he'd almost heard of did. All of Ward's friends were "very famous," sometimes for things Brian didn't know you could be famous for, like lyric poetry or glassblowing. It was a far cry from the Thanksgivings Brian had grown up with, a bunch of his extended family in Lands' End turtlenecks tucking into marsh-mallowed sweet potatoes. Ward usually ignored him, or called him "Byron," but Claire was different. She was warm, remembering what he liked to drink and asking after his parents by name. She made a point to roll her eyes across the table at Brian when Ward or one of his friends said something pompous, which happened a lot. If there were teams, Claire had chosen Brian for hers. Claire had to know her daughter well enough to realize her obvious endorsement might not sway Isabelle's affections in his favor. But Brian could never feel anything but gratitude toward Claire after what she had done for him. Claire Manning had changed the course of Brian's life. He owed her a debt he would now never be able to repay.

◆　◆　◆

Brian often considered how differently everything could have gone if he hadn't met Isabelle one of his first days at Brown. His new roommate Beckett, a sardonic, backward cap–wearing, rap-lyric-reciting graduate of an all-boys prep school, brought Brian to a party in an upperclassmen suite. It was there that Isabelle was nestled into a beanbag chair, passing a joint back and forth with an-other girl. Her bare legs were crossed, the top one swinging gamely. Her long blond hair was parted to the side, curtaining her forehead sexily. He would later learn that the style was purposeful, the way she hid her scar, faint and white, but still visible. But in that mo-ment, he couldn't imagine Isabelle having a single flaw. Brian only knew that there were no girls like this in Minnesota.

Because he had played football in high school, because he was written about in the town newspaper when he got into Brown, because he had dimples and a six-pack, and because he didn't yet understand that he was from the wrong place, with the wrong parents, and ate the wrong kind of carrots, Brian approached her. He couldn't remember what they talked about. But he did remember what Beckett said afterward.

"Dude. That was *Isabelle Manning.*"

"So?"

"So? Her dad's like super famous. Ward Manning?"

"Who's that?"

Beckett doubled over in laughter, mock spitting out his Pabst Blue Ribbon. "Ah, I love it, dude." He patted Brian on the shoulder as if consoling him from major embarrassment. Beckett then explained who Ward was, and that Beckett knew Isabelle "from the city." Brian came to understand this was a euphemism for a rarified sect of Manhattan society, those whose lives had been woven together since infancy with the sturdy threads of common privilege: music lessons at Diller-Quaile; summers on Lily Pond Lane, Putney France, Tennis Europe; schooling at Chapin, Brearley, Collegiate, Trinity, before matriculating at Harvard, Princeton, Brown, Yale, Duke. To these people, "the beach" meant the Hamptons, and "Florida" meant Palm Beach. It was a world Brian had not known existed until Brown, but he decoded it slowly, layer by layer, like a new language. It fascinated him. And he was its consummate observer. But he knew that no matter how he studied, how granular his acquired level of proficiency, he would never pass as a native speaker. He would always be on the outside, looking in.

Isabelle was not, however, turned off by Brian's outsider status. She seemed to get a kick out of it. When they ended up in the same Engine Nine class, they often got coffees afterward. Brian kept Isabelle company while she smoked cigarettes outside the library. Sometimes she'd laugh midconversation seemingly at nothing, and say, "Oh Brian, you're so wholesome." They watched hundreds of hours of *Law & Order* reruns together in their dorm rooms. And yes, he had a hopeless crush on her.

He wanted Isabelle because she was beautiful, but that was only part of it. Even by then, just out of high school, Brian had been with beautiful girls, girls with rosy cheeks, Christie Brinkley smiles, and perky tits; girls even prettier than Isabelle, who could look sharp and horsey from the wrong angles. Isabelle had something more potent than beauty, a kind of supreme confidence. She walked the earth radiating certitude that it did not get better than Isabelle Manning. When he was with Isabelle, he never wondered what anyone else was doing. He never worried maybe there was something cooler going on. For Brian, Isabelle was that thing.

The chemistry was not one-sided. In the intervening years, Brian had often questioned this, wondering whether he'd made more of Isabelle's feelings than they really were. But Brian had kept a journal all through college—he still did, writing down his thoughts, and some other ideas too—so he could actually go back and read about all the times Isabelle had quietly linked her arm in his as they walked around campus; the many, many hours they spent snuggled up together in an extra-long twin; how Isabelle got jealous when Brian hooked up with anyone else. The evidence was overwhelming.

Brian would've been happy at any point in college and most of his twenties to be her boyfriend, but Isabelle was fickle, never able to give into the feelings that seemed to simmer just beneath the surface. She was complicated, her very own Rubik's Cube of carefully designed walls and hard angles, devilishly difficult to wrestle into an organized shape. The question of who Isabelle Manning really was had dogged him since college. He had a feeling it had dogged Isabelle far longer.

But aside from a brief period sophomore year when Isabelle was recovering from a failed affair with a TA, and then again seven springs later at an unexpectedly hot and heavy five-year reunion weekend, they had always been just friends. Best friends. Brian had long accepted their platonic state. He honestly didn't even think about Isabelle that way anymore. He dated other girls. Obviously. He hadn't had a girlfriend in a while, but that was because of work. Brian was preparing to prosecute a high-ranking member of a powerful and murderous drug cartel. Even leaving the office to attend the memorial had required a Jenga-esque logistical shuffling that would be paid for in early mornings and late nights for the rest of the week. Brian could not afford to mess up. Not now.

◆ ◆ ◆

Brian waited for the elevator in the private vestibule, as Isabelle stood at the entry to her parents' apartment, a long, sinewy arm holding the front door open. He still saw in her that confidence from their college days, but it had been clouded over, like a beautiful window in need of cleaning. She'd been wounded by the disappointments of her career. And beneath the banter about her relatives lay the unfathomable devastation of losing Claire. Isabelle and Claire spoke every day, often multiple times. Claire was Isabelle's first point of contact whenever anything remarkable happened, from a funny conversation she'd heard on the subway to the food poisoning she'd gotten at a hip restaurant. It was silly, but Brian had sometimes felt jealous, knowing he got information second in line.

Brian knew that later, as he lay in bed, reconstructing the narrative of that evening, there would be words he wished he'd said to Isabelle in these moments, but all he could come up with was: "What's your plan for the next few days?"

"I have no idea," said Isabelle, then added, "I need to go out to the house at some point. Clean out closets and such."

Brian nodded, knowing she was referring to the Manning outpost in Sag Harbor. "I could go with you."

"No, that's okay. It'll be a hassle." Isabelle opened her mouth to say more but shut it again. The elevator came and Brian had no choice but to step in.

"I'll call you tomorrow."

"You better." Isabelle smiled and then stepped out of her doorway, closer to him, holding her arm in in the elevator sensor. "Thank you, Brian."

"Any time."

Isabelle moved back. Brian held up his hand in a motionless wave as Isabelle disappeared back into the apartment. Even on that sad day, departing a house of mourning, he felt the familiar deflation of leaving Isabelle's world to return to his own.

Isabelle

Isabelle closed the apartment door and twisted the lock, relieved to no longer play host, even to Brian and his sweet, puppy-dog kindness. She was exhausted in a bone-aching way, though she suspected sleep would require pharmacological interventions. With or without sedation, she knew she would dream the dream. Her dream. It had come nightly the past few weeks, more menacing than ever. She'd wake up, sweaty and filled with panic, convinced for a moment it was real, that she really had lost her voice, that she actually was shouting into a canyon, the wind ripping away her words, or submerged deep underwater, unable to produce more than a waterlogged moan. At some point in the dream, the person she was calling for crystallized into her father. Going back to sleep was nearly impossible.

Isabelle went into the kitchen and poured the remainder of the bottle of white into her glass, then turned out all the downstairs lights. The house was quiet, nothing to suggest what had just occurred, save a doughy alcohol smell and a subtle vibration that hung in the air like a bell recently rung. She walked up the stairs to the second floor of the duplex and saw a light emanating from the door of her father's study. Ward often read over his work late into the night. It was both ridiculous and completely unsurprising that her father would maintain his routine today.

When Isabelle was growing up, her father stayed in the office all day, the methodical click of the old-school typewriter the only proof of life. Long ago, he'd added a bathroom, and he'd outfitted the room with a bar and a mini fridge so that human needs would not draw him out of his private world. Her mother warned Isabelle not to make too much noise or knock, or, god forbid, try to enter. So Isabelle would leave her father "books" she'd made with crayons and folded paper outside the door for him to find. The next day at breakfast, Ward would give her his critique. He'd always taken her seriously as a writer. He'd even had one of Isabelle's crayon books framed and hung at Quatorze, a French bistro that displayed the books of local writers (Ward had his own section). "A placeholder for your real book," he'd said. Isabelle found it amusing until her real book never came and was secretly relieved when the restaurant closed.

Isabelle paused at the top of the stairs before gingerly approaching her father's door. The study had a hallowed vibe, and still a forbidden-fruit element. One night in high school, Ward and Claire away in Sag Harbor, Isabelle invited a group of friends over. Feeling the evening was taking a turn toward boring and noticing a lot of people checking their beepers, Isabelle suggested they all take a tour of her father's office. Luckily—or unluckily—the door was unlocked, and Isabelle blithely walked in like she did it all the time. She showed off pictures of her father and his famous friends. Tina Brown. Julian Schnabel. Patrick McMullan. They all made themselves comfortable underneath Ward's life-size old master rendering of Napoleon charging into battle. But quickly a choking feeling took hold of Isabelle, as if there was not enough air in the room. She attempted to usher her friends away. But having gained entry into the sanctum, they would not be lured back out. Instead, they took books from the shelves and left them strewn all about the room for Isabelle to clean up later. A boy from Collegiate, one Isabelle would later take to prom and have regrettable sex with, started a discussion about who was superior, Ward or Tom Wolfe. It was just jokes at the beginning, but then her friends, coddled budding intellectuals, started arguing seriously, ignoring Isabelle, as if her father's fame made him fair game for a no-holds-barred academic discussion in front of her. When the group came down on the side of Tom, Isabelle clearly intuited that it wouldn't be cool to be offended. And she realized she wasn't, exactly. Surprise morphed into secret, dangerous pleasure that her father did not universally reign supreme.

◆ ◆ ◆

Now Isabelle strained to identify a noise coming from the study. When she did, her whole body stiffened, resisting the sound. She listened motionless to her father crying. She had never seen her father cry. The very idea sickened her. She stood there paralyzed. After a few moments, Isabelle realized she was mistaken. Her father was not crying at all; he was laughing. Chuckling really. Presumably at something he'd written. Isabelle was flooded with a mix of relief and revulsion alongside the familiar feeling that her father was not like other people.

Being Ward Manning's daughter was a central tenet of Isabelle's identity, as was the idea that she was close to her father. Of course she was. Since she was a little girl, she and Ward had gone out to dinner just the two of them, once a month or so. Though lately it had been increasingly infrequent. Their conversations tended to focus on the particular flaws of various overrated writers, a topic on which both of them could expound fluently. Ward would often leave her voice messages along the lines of, "It's your father. The latest [insert bestselling author] is pure shit. Call me." Ward treated Isabelle as an equal in these conversations, a generosity considering every author they discussed had done something Isabelle had not. Being with her father was always a little bit exciting. But when Isabelle interacted with him, she felt an oppressive pressure to be interesting, charming, to live up to the genetics he'd so generously bestowed upon her. And it created a certain formality between them. Isabelle had never questioned this, because she had Claire, the parent she could unload to about her bad dates or her broken air conditioner, the parent she could be herself with even if that self was an unpublished wannabe with increasingly dire prospects. But now things were different.

Isabelle paused at the door, her eyes suddenly hot and a constricting feeling around her throat. Her body tensed, steeling itself against the rising tide of her misery. Isabelle raised the back of her hand to knock. She and her father were alone in the house, both of them navigating the aftermath of Claire's death. There had never been a time more conducive to drawing them closer together. But then Isabelle heard the clicking of keys. She lowered her fist to her side. She didn't want to interrupt his work. Perhaps writing would be good for her, too. Isabelle backed away and walked down the hallway to her old room.

"911, what is your emergency?"

I opened my mouth, but the words were lodged in the back of my throat.

"Hello? Is someone there?"

"Yes," I managed.

"What is your emergency?"

"My husband."

"What about your husband?"

"He's . . . he's—" There was no way to put this delicately. "He seems to be dead."

After giving our address on the Upper West Side, I hung up the receiver. I shook my head and let out a noise somewhere between a sob and a giggle. It was just so ridiculous that Aiden had done something as pedestrian as dying. He was only forty-six, and had been well enough at breakfast to monologue energetically about the complex flavor profile of hand-churned French butter—as opposed to the supermarket Land O'Lakes I'd dared to serve him.

"Look, you can't even spread it," he'd said, making a show of laboring his knife over the baguette. "You understand that uncultured butter is junk?"

I nodded, but what I really understood was that Aiden's refined tastes in dairy products, as with everything else, were increasingly at odds with our financial realities. Aiden had made some money in his time, but he was a painter, not a bond trader.

After breakfast, I'd found his misplaced reading glasses between the couch cushions and decided to bring them to the studio, a preemptive gesture of largess before the uncomfortable money talk that was brewing. That's when I found him.

I still couldn't believe it. Maybe I was imagining things. Or maybe my secret bedtime Halcion habit was catching up to me. I peeked out of the studio's galley kitchen where I stood next to the phone. There he was, just as before, splayed out on the floor, knee bent at an unnatural angle, a paintbrush cradled in his palm. I walked toward him and knelt down, feeling again for a pulse. Nothing.

Was it possible to change the future with wicked little daydreams? If so, I had fantasized about this moment far too often for comfort.

Well, here I was. Free at last. I sat beside him and waited for the people who would take my husband away.

2

Sag Harbor, 2017

Ward

The fresh air filling his lungs was just what he needed. Ward walked up John Street toward town. The weather had finally turned, and it was one of those crisp fall days, the sky cerulean and the air with just enough bite for a scarf. He'd arrived in Sag Harbor yesterday, the plan being to sequester himself out east with his manuscript that was not more than a quarter written and due in six months. His agent and editor—no doubt in cahoots—had begun launching flares over email, "just checking in." What they wanted was an update on a book that had fetched a two-million-dollar advance without a single word written. Ward had successfully abstained from reading his fan mail following a multi-hour bender the night of Claire's memorial. He had canceled all other obligations and taken a leave of absence from his teaching duties at Columbia. He assumed that with a few monk-like weeks he could emerge triumphant with a polished draft. He'd begun tinkering with the beginning the week before. It was building a nice sense of foreboding suspense. But as he read further once he got to Sag, things unraveled. His focus waned. He caught himself calling out to Claire, as if she were just downstairs. Several times, he could've sworn he'd heard Claire sounds—her quick, syncopated footstep, the scrape of pots on the stove and the hiss of a lit burner, the rustle of an opened newspaper, the little yelps of crossword puzzle satisfaction. But when he listened in, there was nothing. With each hour, the silence intensified until it was no longer a lack of noise, but an atmosphere so thick and stifling he could taste it. He needed to escape.

Ward walked past the Cove Deli, reaching the corridor of stately old houses once owned by the captains of whaling ships. These blocks were a tiny bastion of quaintness in a town where, all summer, Range Rovers—black, shiny, and plentiful as cockroaches—jockeyed for parking and women stalked the streets in stilettos, eating ten-dollar frozen yogurt. Though he technically was one himself, Ward loathed the second-home people. He was glad that it was off-season when the worst of the worst had left town and he could venture out of his house again, his hamlet returned to him.

In town proper, Ward opened the door to Wharf Books with a jingle. He looked around the store but saw only a slight woman with dyed black hair, college-age if he guessed, behind the counter.

"Hello there," he said.

"Hi." The girl did not look up from the books she was scanning.

"Is Mira here?"

"She's away."

"She's away," Ward repeated, as if by some strange, inverse logic he could make the statement untrue. He ran his fingers over the new hardcovers on the front table. "Will she be here tomorrow?"

"No. She went to visit her sister in Boston."

"I see." Ward walked around the store pretending to browse. Mira, the octogenarian owner of the bookshop, was a devoted fan. For several years she had run Ward Manning "theme" nights. People would come in character, and they'd act out scenes from the books. Everyone got very into it with costumes and rehearsals. Ward had made a surprise appearance at more than a few of these gatherings. The crowd always went nuts.

After rereading his manuscript, Ward needed space to digest the task that lay in front of him. And he needed something to help get his mind back in the game. He was looking for a little boost to get him going, but he'd sworn off his letters. Mira would have been the perfect fix. But now a thick lump of disappointment rose in his chest that this trip had been in vain; he would not get what he wanted.

Ward circled back to the front table, relieved to see that his book still held its rightful place in the center. *Whalers* traced the extreme gentrification of the Hamptons, a searing indictment of the entitled leisure culture that was laying waste to the East End. Ward had insinuated himself into the community of Montauk fishermen, getting them to trust him, open up, introduce him to their wives, brothers, children. The process took up the better part of a year, but Ward did not put pen to paper until he was sure he had mastery of the subject. Because mastery was his thing. Roth had Newark. Updike had suburban sex. But Manning had details, the ability to paint a whole world and nail it. His books—as critics mentioned again and again—were transportive. *Whalers* was no exception. The book should have turned him into a hero of the locals. He envisioned guys getting out of their pickups to shake his hand, saying, "Just wanted to thank you, sir," with cigarettes dangling from their mouths. He'd start getting invited to locals-only bars and secret swimming holes. Maybe he'd run for mayor. None of this had happened.

"And how's this one selling these days?" he asked, winking as he gave a little pat to *Whalers*. There was a Post-it Note on his hardcover reading in Sharpie lettering: *Signed Copies Available!* Mira hadn't asked him to sign anything in months.

The girl stared at him blankly. She had one of those nose rings through the septum, like a bull. She shrugged. "Eh. Not great. It's, like, two years old. I don't know why she still keeps it on the table."

Ward was pierced through with the understanding that this girl—this girl who worked in a bookstore in his own town!—did not know who he was. Nearly simultaneously he decided that now that she'd insulted him, it was imperative that she not be made aware of her mistake.

"Can I help you find something?" she asked. "I could make some recommendations."

"No. No, I'm fine." Ward wound his scarf around the lower part of his face and headed for the door. Then he stopped. He turned around, made his way to the table, and grabbed his book. "I'll take this one," he said through his scarf, plunking the book on the checkout table.

The girl shrugged. "Cash or credit?"

"Cash," said Ward, adding, "And you know what, I'll take the rest of the copies in the back."

The girl looked at him skeptically. "You want to buy all the copies of this one book?"

"Yes. All of them." When she returned with a stack, Ward fished out two hundreds from his wallet and tossed them on the counter, not bothering to wait for change.

◆　◆　◆

Ward settled himself on the deck at exactly five p.m. with a large drink. He had not written that afternoon but trolled Amazon, reading five-star reviews of his previous nineteen books (which were technically not fan mail). He looked out at the water, a large cove that pooled off the bay, admiring the view they'd bought the house for. It was Claire who'd picked it. Sag Harbor was unfashionable then, a no-man's-land for the moneyed set. But Claire wanted nothing to do with Southampton, where she'd spent summers as a child. And she was prescient in believing Sag Harbor would have its day. There was no one who had a better eye than his wife; no one with taste like her. The down payment had come from his advance for *American Dream*, his first book, a semi-autobiographical novel about a boy who escapes the dismal poverty of rural Missouri. He and Claire had sat out on this deck hundreds of times, drinking vodka. The perimeter of the cove was populated with other artists and writers. When Ed was alive, Claire liked to take the dinghy over to the Doctorows' so she could come back and tell Ward what a marvelous book Ed was working on and what a rare genius he possessed. It drove Ward crazy, but thinking of it now made him miss Claire with a physical ache running from his chest down through his coccyx. It was not right for him to be alone this way.

Ward was still smarting over the scene at the bookstore. And he'd definitely pulled something in his neck carrying all those goddamn hardcovers home. Ward had successfully convinced himself that the store clerk was simply a moron. With his boisterous hair and signature red glasses, Ward Manning was recognized by *everyone*. One negative word to Mira, and the girl would be fired. But she was not the real problem. The real problem was that the store still had *Whalers* in stock. Ward was, of course, wildly successful. All of his books were bestsellers. But he was well aware of the thing that his publisher danced delicately around. His last four books had each sold fewer copies than the one before. And none of his books had ever sold as well as the first three. It was an unsettling trend, with the obvious implication that he had peaked long ago; his writing behind the times. But Ward Manning would not go quietly. He was eager to show everyone with a big, gigantic, multiple reprinting, bestselling hit. He wanted his "fuck you" book.

And he needed this new book to be just that. Ward's publisher had been on him to change things up, leave "his comfort zone." The industry was crowing for "strong female characters," unreliable narrators, and eerie plot twists. If Ward wanted to stay relevant, his editor had made very clear, he needed to get with the program. So he and his agent had hashed out an idea and sold it. Ward had made the protagonist a woman, which, to be honest, he really hated doing. To compensate, he made her shifty, not entirely trustworthy, and shrouded her in satire. Yet Ward did not feel in control of the fictional person he was creating.

Over the last few years, a pressure had begun closing in around him like the tight, stale air of a descending airplane. In recent days, the pressure had crystallized into a question: *What if this book is my last?* The vexing part was that this was not a ludicrous idea, a paranoia that could be easily swatted away. He was seventy-four years old. Dale Horowitz was circling.

With no conversation to break up his sips, Ward drank his vodka wolfishly. With his empty glass, he stood up, slid open the screen door, and went inside. He poured himself a second drink, realizing for the first time that he had not had dinner. The house had never been restocked since the summer, the refrigerator offering only a few condiments well past their prime and a bottle of seltzer. He opened the door of the pantry and rummaged around, finding a package of Stoned Wheat Thins. He began eating them, two stacked together. Their prim saltiness only made him crave something more pungent. He opened a jar of pimento-stuffed olives, pinching them out with his fingers, the juice running over the backs of his hands. When he'd had his fill, Ward abandoned the open sleeve of crackers and half-empty olive jar on the counter and ascended to his office.

Ward turned on his computer and spent several minutes flipping through videos before settling into a teacher-student scenario. As the female "professor" cajoled the pants off the initially reluctant student, Ward unbuckled his own. Quickly impatient with contrived play-acting, he fast-forwarded to when the guy was doing the girl roughly from behind. Ward climaxed efficiently but unremarkably. As soon as he'd come, the vulgar, manufactured screams of gratification displeased him. He shut off the monitor. He sat for a few moments staring into space. The house was so still that new buzzes and hums emerged from the quiet. He got up. There was nothing to do but go to bed.

3

New York, 2017

Isabelle

Isabelle stood at the desk unnoticed as she unwound her scarf and removed the oversized shades she'd been using to disguise her puffy eyes. "Hello, Margot."

The librarian let out a yelp, her hands drawn to her mouth as the book she'd been holding dropped with a smack on the marble floor.

"Isabelle! You startled me!" Margot resettled the glasses that had been knocked askew and picked up the hardcover. If she lived in a previous century, Margot was the sort of person for whom smelling salts would've been frequently deployed. She was around Isabelle's own age, tiny, barely five feet, with long hair she wore over her shoulders in two ropey braids. She favored old-fashioned dresses and blouses decorated with cats and horses. Margot checked members into the Metropolitan Library Association, reminding them to lower their voices and confirming that there really was no Wi-Fi. Isabelle had seen her nearly every weekday morning for the past four years.

"What have you got there?" Isabelle leaned over the desk to look in Margot's lap.

"Oh. Just this." Margot turned over a copy of *Fifty Shades Freed* in a plastic library dust jacket.

"Steamy. Haven't you read that one before?"

"I've read them all a few times."

"They say a good reader is a rereader."

"That's true." Margot spoke so softly and breathily that Isabelle sometimes had trouble catching what she said. And Isabelle didn't think it was just because the accident had left her with only partial hearing in her left ear.

Margot bit her lip. "I'm so sorry about your mother." Margot's face flushed red. The two had never discussed anything more intimate than the latest bestsellers. For a moment, Isabelle feared Margot might start to cry, an outcome she could not handle. This morning marked two weeks since Claire had died. It was the first day of a new month—October—and Isabelle was making her inaugural attempt at a normal day, but holding it all together was a tenuous situation.

"I got the note from the library," Isabelle said quickly. "Margot, are you responsible for that marvelous card catalog stationery?"

Margot's face brightened. "Yes."

"I had a feeling."

"We didn't, um, expect to see you so soon, Isabelle."

"Routine will be good for me." Isabelle nodded as if to underscore her point. This was probably true. But she did not share the more urgent reality that had driven her out of bed and to the library that morning.

She inhaled the scent of musty books mixed with Pledge furniture polish. "Nice to be back," she said as she walked to the elevator. Margot waved, and looked relieved when Isabelle disposed of her deli coffee cup without needing a reminder of the strict ban on food and beverages.

The Metropolitan Library Association occupied a double-wide limestone just a few blocks from Central Park. For three hundred dollars a year, one could come read the newspaper in what looked like a beautiful nineteenth century living room, hole up in the stacks that snaked up the back of the building, take your toddler for puppetry hour, or, as Isabelle did, toil at your novel in the fifth-floor study, a bright, sunny space with wooden tables, antique desk lamps, and Aeron chairs. The library offered private study carrels on reserve, but Isabelle preferred to work among the people, mainly older, cantankerous types with definite opinions about personal space and noise-leaking headphones. When she became frustrated with a sentence, Isabelle needed the potential of shame to keep her from opening Solitaire in front of her tablemates.

Today, Isabelle found a seat at a central table, giving half smiles to a few of the other regulars. She powered on her laptop and opened Word, reading over the beginning chapters of her latest endeavor. Isabelle had chosen to examine the sudden end to a fraught marriage. The wife—wry, incisive, and tremendously fun to write—attempts to find her footing after a traumatic event and is forced to take a hard look at herself and the questionable choices she's made. She had fallen in love with her main character. And the topic was no doubt a rich subject matter that had been mined to great effect by multitudes of authors. But something felt slippery, as if she was afraid to get too close to it. Still, Isabelle had already told her agent, Fern, she had pages to show him, and she believed this book would finally be "the one."

If there was a time before Isabelle wanted to be a writer, she could not remember it. She'd learned to read at four—or at least her mother claimed. Isabelle had always loved imagining what other people's lives were like. Her father encouraged her to carry a notebook, eavesdrop aggressively, and note even the smallest of details. In middle school, a short story she wrote about a lonely woman who fantasizes hosting a lavish dinner party won an award. Isabelle remembered sitting on the squeaky gymnasium floor, her sneakered feet tucked into her skirt, at the assembly where her prize was announced, and the pure elation she felt when her name was called. In high school, she ran the Chapin literary magazine. At Brown, she majored in literature with a minor in art history. Her thesis on the secondary characters of Jane Austen received high honors. Everything was unfolding just as it should.

When she graduated, Isabelle became a junior editor at *Town & Country*, where she wrote up debutante wedding announcements, and authored a feature on her mother's family's crumbling compound near Shinnecock Bay. After a well-received review of the MoMA's Richard Avedon portraits retrospective, Isabelle did a regular art roundup. She stayed at the job for seven years, becoming senior accessories editor. And it was fun. She liked her work, along with the perks and the parties of magazine life. But her goal had never been to climb the ranks of Hearst or Condé Nast. While Isabelle worked at *Town & Country*, she wrote short stories, submitting them to various literary magazines. She got some published here and there, mostly at publications read by a few hundred people with MFAs. But then she got lucky.

Since she was a teenager, Isabelle had had the same dream. There were many variations, but the dream always began with her having something urgent to communicate, but being unable to. Sometimes she couldn't dial a phone; sometimes she'd lose her voice. Isabelle sat down one day and wrote a story based on the dream. She had a feeling this writing was different, better. But when she sent it in to the *New Yorker*—something she'd never dared do before—she expected precisely nothing to come of it. And then a few days later, an editor called her up and accepted "Wrong Number." If Isabelle had to choose the pinnacle of her life, it would have been the ninety seconds of that phone call.

She took her success with "Wrong Number" as a sign. Isabelle had squirreled away enough savings, so she quit her job and spent the next two years writing *Invite Only*, the story of a young, idealistic woman who moves to New York for a job at a WASP-y fashion magazine and becomes entangled in and then corrupted by Manhattan's materialistic, cutthroat party scene. Emulating her father's punishing work ethic, Isabelle labored mightily over the manuscript.

When she was done, she submitted it to one of the agents at the literary agency that represented her father. The manuscript was snatched up by Fernando Ramirez-Clement. Fern was well-established, but still hungry and eager to represent a budding novelist with an inherited literary pedigree. As Fern sent the book out to publishers, Isabelle braced herself for the calls to come rushing in, setting off a lively bidding war. She sat at home, staring at her phone and refreshing her email day after day. Nothing came. Still, Isabelle was calm. At that point, life had generally unfurled itself like a giant red carpet; bad outcomes were not part of her repertoire of experience. Well, except for the accident. But that was a fluke. Then the first rejection came in. And then the next. There was little explanation in the denials, just *not for me* or *couldn't connect.* The no's piled up. Once ebullient, predicting Isabelle's future in florid detail, Fern became fatalistic. Word got out. There were whispers in gossip sites about Isabelle's failure. The manuscript was tainted. After a few months of shopping it, Isabelle had to acknowledge that the book was dead and she would have to move on. But that was easier said than done. Isabelle floundered. She made a half dozen starts, only to abandon them. One hundred pages in, the premise that seemed so promising bore down on her like bad gambling debt. It had now been over two years of frustration.

The obvious person to go to for help was, of course, her father. Ward had been on the faculty of the Columbia MFA program for three decades, after all. But Isabelle never let her father read her work. For one thing, the thought of Ward Manning finding so much as an errant comma made her stomach turn. Isabelle wanted to do this on her own. She wanted the gratification of presenting her father with her trophy, a hardcover, weighty and smelling of glue. Ward seemed to respect Isabelle's choice. Claire had read bits and pieces and was always effusive with praise. It was in fact Claire's enthusiasm that sustained Isabelle. Her mother could pick up on exactly the sentence or phrase Isabelle was proudest of, and she laughed at exactly the places Isabelle wanted readers to laugh. Claire made her feel that there was reason to forge on. But Isabelle resisted her mother's pleas to read the whole book. Claire's love for Isabelle would prevent her from making the kind of incisive critique that Isabelle needed. Now she wished she'd shared more of the book with Claire.

Isabelle felt a familiar welling in her eyes. She inhaled and looked up, a trick that Claire had taught her decades ago when Isabelle had badly skinned her knee during someone's seventh birthday party and didn't want to look like a baby in front of the other girls. "Keep your head straight and look at the ceiling," Claire had counseled as she wiped away the gravel from Isabelle's pulpy knee with a damp paper towel. "Deep breaths." Isabelle did as her mother said, and her tears dried up. The trick had worked many times over, and recently, Isabelle had been employing it on a nearly hourly basis. A full-scale breakdown seemed dangerously possible, and this was why Isabelle needed to finish her book before she went out to Sag Harbor, where further emotional devastation awaited her.

Two days before she died, in some of her final moments of lucidity, Claire had given Isabelle specific instructions to go to Claire's dresser in Sag Harbor and retrieve items she'd left for Isabelle. "You must go yourself, Isabelle," Claire said. "Your father will save my jewelry, anything with monetary value, but I don't trust him with these things, sentimental things. Everything in there is meant for you."

Isabelle agreed and thought that was the end of it. But a moment later, Claire took hold of Isabelle's wrist and looked at her intently. "Do not count on your father for this. Promise me?"

Isabelle had promised. Now this trip to the house loomed over her darkly, what awaited her in the dresser filling Isabelle with a bone-level dread. It was just like Claire to have discreetly saved up a perfectly curated selection of Isabelle's childhood mementos. Whatever artifacts awaited her, Isabelle was sure finding them would unlock a secret compartment of unimaginable grief, and she would be undone.

Isabelle could not afford to be undone. Literally. At this point, selling a book was not just a matter of personal fulfillment, but of financial realities. Isabelle Manning was flat broke. Contrary to common assumption, Isabelle did not live like an heiress or anything close. Her parents had bought her the apartment—a lovely shoebox of a one-bedroom with a view of Lexington Avenue if you stood at the right angle—when she turned thirty. But this gift, as generous as it was, was to be her only inheritance. Ward did not believe in trust funds and had already committed his estate to the construction of a wing bearing his name at the New York Public Library. When Isabelle left *Town & Country*, she had expected to support herself on savings for only a year or two. For the last few years, Isabelle had subsisted on the occasional freelance check—most barely enough to cover dinner out in New York—selling her designer clothing and bags to an online consignment website, and periodic cash infusions from Claire, which her mother discreetly provided without Ward's notice or permission.

But Isabelle's closet was nearly cleaned out of anything with a recognizable label, and there would be no more rescue funds from her mother. She could put her apartment on the market, but it had taken so much goading from Claire to get Ward to give it to her in the first place, Isabelle feared that selling it would make her father irate, his generosity perverted to underwrite his daughter's flailing career. And divesting the apartment would be too poignant an admission of her failure. Of course, Isabelle could just get over herself and start reading the classifieds. Refusing to get a day job when writing did not pay the bills was wildly entitled. Her awareness of this was why she did not let anyone know of her financial trouble. But she feared that if she got a different job now—in her mid-thirties—that would be it. Her writing career would go the way of so many others, subsumed by the minutiae and exhaustion of daily life. And Isabelle was not ready to give up. Despite everything, in a defiant knot underneath her sternum, Isabelle continued to believe that her real life was the one where she was a published writer, the rest just a bloated preamble.

So, though her psyche felt as raw as her once freshly skinned knee and thinking about anything but the absence of her mother felt utterly ridiculous, Isabelle set her hands over the keyboard, and she tried.

DRAFT

Aiden worked in an apartment two floors up from our own. We had a spare room at our own place, but this complete physical separation was increasingly vital to our survival. In recent years, something had chilled between us, and we had no children to force us to pretend otherwise. I rarely visited the studio, but in the days after Aiden died, I had this nagging feeling behind my eyes like when you can't remember if you turned off the oven. Something in my lizard brain kept telling me to go back in. Finally I did.

I had in fact remembered to turn off the lights, and, with the curtains pulled close, the room was full dark. Aiden preferred to work in shadow so that the photographic projection would be visible on his easel. The technique involved overlaying a grid atop a photograph before painting section by section.

Soon Aiden's agent would descend, scavenging through what was left. It would be good to know what was here before he did. I had a few minutes before I needed to collect my mother for yet another doctor's appointment. So I walked to the windows and parted the heavy velvet drapes. In Aiden's space, this simple gesture of authority felt illicit.

Sun flooded the room. Aside from his workstation, his bookshelves, and heavy, metal filing cabinets, the only furniture in the room was a massive black-and-white cowhide couch. Aiden had it custom-built for an obscene sum so it would be worthy of the asses of very famous people. He insisted upon working from his own photos, and celebrities were happy to pose for him. An Aiden Connors portrait was perfect feeding for an A-lister's ravenous ego. As time went on, Aiden adopted the proclivities of his subjects, a taste for ostentatious displays of wealth.

I could now see Aiden's half-finished painting of John

42

Cusack. After his breakout as the adorably awkward Lloyd Dobler, and the highly anticipated *Grifters*, Cusack was the get of 1990. Aiden was expecting significant buzz and a heady payday for the portrait. That wouldn't happen now unless anyone was interested in what the man would look like with one eye and half a face. *Domage*, as the French say. Still, even in its half-finished form, the work was exquisite. Aiden's talent had never been the problem.

Next to the easel, in an old Folger's tin, was a bouquet of brushes. Aiden special-ordered his from a workshop in a tiny village in India. He was particular; some might say obsessive. It was one of the things I'd found most attractive in him in the beginning: He took every element of his craft so seriously.

Plucking one of the smooth wooden handles from the can, I held it to the light, admiring the hundreds of tiny mink hairs hand-nestled into a perfect point. It had been a long time since I'd held a paintbrush. I closed my eyes and ran it against my cheek.

After I replaced the brush, I stood staring at the canvas. I reached out and touched its surface, coarse with paint. Then, impulsively, I took hold of the portrait and removed it from the easel. The cellular matter of a plan had been forming since I confirmed my husband's nonexistent pulse. I carried Mr. Cusack across the room and stowed him behind a filing cabinet, a place where only I would find him. Then, I left.

4

New York, 1975

Claire

Claire stood in her slip at the mirror over her dresser. She examined her face, trying to diagnose the problem. Claire was twenty-seven. She was still young, but now old enough to conceive of a time when she would not be. Her face looked ever so slightly saggy and bereft of color. Maybe she was getting a cold. But Claire turned to the side and saw clearly that what she looked was bored. Her forehead looked bored. Her cheeks looked bored. Even her chin had a resigned quality. Claire sighed. She went to her closet and selected a dress: black, capped-sleeved, appropriate. As she pulled it over her head, Claire wondered if there was any way she could get out of this dinner. She was deeply involved with *The Woman in White* and desperate to get in bed and finish it. At the moment, there were few things in Claire's life that could compete with a hot bath and a delicious book. Perhaps she could claim a last-minute date? A headache? But no, she'd begged off two previous engagements. She would go and then not have to see them again for a nice, long stretch.

Claire sometimes tried to feel bad about not liking her parents. But all she could muster was relief that she no longer lived under their roof and that her interactions with them were limited to quarterly dinners at the University Club. Meals with Robert and Kitty Cunningham, stale, jacket-required affairs, followed the same script. Conversation centered on backgammon and tennis, and if either of her parents were still cogent enough after drinking a quantity of gin that would kill a normal human, they'd move on to sympathizing with Richard Nixon. The Cunninghams were relics. Claire's father had a pristine lineage, one that he often recited in detail with little or no provocation, speaking about relatives like prized show poodles. But the grain distribution business that had made them one of the most prominent families in the country had long been sold, and the once stupendous fortune depleted by descendants like her father, who had a PhD in Norse mythology but had never actually worked in the sense of going to a job and earning money. The family survived on name and real estate holdings, the fumes of great wealth. Her parents rarely dined outside their clubs, places where meals could be charged and there were gentlemanly grace periods on monthly bills. Their Park Avenue apartment and Southampton house looked like Miss Havisham lived there, if Miss Havisham was very into taxidermy.

Claire had known for a long time she wanted a different kind of life. She started off by getting an actual job, one in the prints department at an exclusive auction house. She reasonably believed the work would be about art, which excited her. But she quickly realized that for the other female employees, the position was just a placeholder, a way to gild their résumés before they were plucked for marriage and could quit to raise children. With their headbands, pastel prints, tapered fingers with exquisite nailbeds that cried out for a cushion-cut diamond, these women were familiar to Claire. How willing—eager!—they were to tread carefully inside the well-worn tracks of the previous generation. It wasn't that Claire didn't want to get married and have children. She did! But Claire did not want to replicate her own experience as much as reject it. She longed for a do-over of her childhood, a string of long afternoons alone in her room, playing with her dolls, realizing as the sky darkened that her parents had forgotten about her. As the parent, Claire would be the warm, nurturing figure she had craved. She would cocoon her child in affection, not allowing them to forget for even one minute how much they were loved.

Claire did not think her co-workers, consumed with news of the latest engagements and real estate purchases, would understand this deep longing inside her. So instead of joining in the office banter, Claire kept to herself, wandering the galleries during her lunch break, sitting on a bench by the East River and reading a book, feeling that she was looking for something she did not know how to find. She'd begun to entertain the idea of quitting her job, going away somewhere, maybe Paris or Rome. She'd thought about it so much it no longer seemed ridiculous. Of course, this was not the kind of thing she could bring up at dinner with her parents. Claire put her wallet and keys in her handbag, along with a lipstick, and then, on impulse, grabbed *The Woman in White*.

• • •

"The shrimp cocktail," said her father.

The waiter stood at the table expectantly. "And?"

"And nothing."

The waiter scratched his head. "That's just three shrimp."

"I know that, sonny, I've been eating here since before you were born." Robert Cunningham viewed a single freezer-burned shrimp as an entirely sufficient meal. When they hosted guests, her parents never offered more than the few bowls of musty nuts that always sat out in their living room. It wasn't only that they were cheap—which they were—but that food was unimportant to them.

"All right," said the waiter, looking at Claire with raised eyebrows. Claire smiled and gave a little shrug. He must be new. He was young, maybe a few years older than her, with a noticeably large head and a halo of unruly dark hair. All of his features were large; his nose and mouth putty-like, with round, almost bugging, blue eyes.

And yet, he was still somehow handsome. Claire watched him walk away, noticing that his jacket was too tight over his shoulders.

When her attention returned to the table, her father was re-counting an incident in a duck blind that resulted in an octogenarian relative getting shot in the foot. He banged the table with his palm, his wheezy laugh bouncing him up and down.

"Yikes, Dad, is he okay?"

"Oh sure. It'd take more than that to take out old Weymouth."

Claire looked at her mother, who was staring off into the middle distance. Kitty came to when the waiter returned with a martini, raising her arms to take it directly from his hands. After tasting it, Kitty Cunningham's lips pursed and her brow creased. "Is this vodka?"

"Yes," said the waiter.

"No, no, I want gin."

"You said vodka."

"I didn't."

The waiter sighed, openly rolling his eyes. He reached to take the mistaken drink, but her mother jerked it away. "You can leave this one while you make another." The waiter pulled back his hand at the same time Kitty raised her glass to her lips. Their arms became tangled and in the process of detangling, the waiter knocked Claire's mother's ice water into her lap, causing Kitty to shriek loudly.

"What in god's name?" her father muttered. The waiter took Claire's napkin and handed it to Kitty.

"As if this will do any good," Kitty said. "There's a lake in my lap."

"You're fine, Mother." Claire began wiping with the napkin. The waiter returned with several dish towels. As they both wiped at Kitty's dress, Kitty blithely sipping her vodka, Claire's eyes met the waiter's, both of them stifling laughs.

When the drinks had been drunk and the shrimp eaten, Claire determined they were sufficiently blotto for her to slip her book into her lap and read undetected. After the plates were cleared,

Claire believed she was about to be released from the evening, but the maître d' himself approached their table carrying a Baked Alaska.

"On the house, Mr. Cunningham," he said. "For your troubles."

Her father nodded as the giant, flaming dessert was placed on the table. "Thank you. But I think you better do something about that waiter. Not up to snuff."

"Certainly, sir."

Claire took a few bites of the cloying meringue with cherry ice cream before she excused herself. She walked through the restaurant and into the ladies' room. When she re-emerged into the dark vestibule by the bathrooms, she heard his deep voice before she saw him. "Is there a villain more sublime than Fosco?"

Claire started. She looked up to see the waiter.

"Fosco," he said again, fixing her with a piercing stare. "I saw you're reading *The Woman in White*."

"Oh. Yes, of course." Claire shrugged and then said, "Don't tell."

The waiter raised his eyebrows. "One condition."

"What's that?"

"Have dinner with me."

"What?" Claire laughed.

He smiled. "Have dinner with me."

"You think I'll go out with you because you knew about Count Fosco?"

"That. And you want to." At closer range, he was taller than she'd realized.

"And why's that?"

"You like me."

Claire almost guffawed. She wasn't used to anyone speaking like this. In her family, true meaning had to be excavated from under layers of politeness and euphemism, like a fossil.

"I'm a writer," he said.

"Oh. What is your name? Have I read any of your books?"

"Ward Manning. And not yet."

"Well, Ward Manning, I hope you are a better writer than a waiter." Claire turned to go, but Ward caught her arm.

"I am," he said, adding, "I'm going to be very famous."

Claire laughed, but stopped when she realized he was not joking. "Well," she said, "good luck to you."

"Come on. What do you say? I went to Harvard, you know."

"Good for you," she said. "I have to get back to my parents."

◆ ◆ ◆

Thankfully her father had signed the bill by the time Claire returned, so there would be no more awkward interactions with Ward Manning. Claire made a mental note to insist upon a different venue for their next dinner. Her escape from the restaurant was stymied at the coat check as Kitty loaded herself into her ancient mink and a couple from her mother's bridge club appeared. Kitty, her voice slightly slurred, made introductions.

"This is my daughter," Kitty said to the wife, a woman with a floral headband and rabbit teeth, "Claire Cunningham, Vassar graduate."

Claire flinched. Kitty had done this many times before, and Claire knew her mother was reciting her undergraduate institution out of pride. It had always bothered Claire. She realized, as she stood there with her parents, what she hated about this addendum to her name. Her mother was not just telling where Claire had gone to school, she was implying a beginning, middle, and end. *Vassar graduate* was Claire's whole story.

Outside the club, her father stepped out into the street and raised his hand for a cab. "We'll drop you off."

"Thank you," said Claire. But as the car pulled up, Claire suddenly felt that if she got into that cab, her fate would be sealed. She would be the woman her mother described. She heard herself saying, "I'm sorry, Mother. I seem to have left my keys in the restaurant."

"Your keys?" asked her mother, swaying slightly.

"Yes, I have to excuse myself. Don't wait on my account. I'll walk or catch my own cab." She kissed her mother on the cheek. "Really."

Claire watched her parents drive off, then she turned and marched back into the club, and up the stairs to the dining room.

She found the maître d'. "Is Ward still here? Ward Manning?"

He looked at her, worried. "We've already spoken to him, miss."

"No, no, it's not that."

"Is there something I can help you with?"

At that moment Claire saw Ward at the back of the dining room, removing glasses from a tray. "No, thank you," she said as she sped off.

"Hi," she said, once she'd reached him.

Ward looked up and smiled at her. "Hi."

Claire plucked the order pad out of Ward's front jacket pocket along with the pen. She wrote quickly and handed it back. "Here's my number."

He looked, nodding, as if the specific series of seven digits held hidden significance. "Good choice," said Ward, finally.

Claire smiled. "I hope so."

5

New York, 2017

Isabelle

Isabelle took the phone into her hand. It was an eighties-style cordless, junky gray plastic with retractable metal antenna. She punched the on button and listened for a tone. Isabelle poised her fingers over the keys to dial the number she knew by heart. That's when the trouble started. Sometimes she got the first few numbers, but then she would make a mistake and have to start over. Her hands began to swell and lose feeling, as if shot up with Novocain. The heat of panic began rising from her chest. "No, no, no," she breathed, her voice growing shrill, as her fine motor skills failed her. Numbness seeped farther and farther up her wrist until there was no longer strength to hold the phone. It fell to the ground, the back panel breaking off, the battery springing out and dangling on its red and yellow wires. "Mom!" Isabelle tried to scream, but nothing came out, only a vibration, a straining at her temples and neck. "MOM!!" Her voice had been sucked up inside her, her body turned soundproof chamber against the outside world. Her ears buzzed, all sound replaced by the low whirr of the water that had filled the space around her. Her voice emerged a deep, whale-like howl. The water, briny and stinging, rushed in, filling her mouth and nostrils, just as it had that day so many years before. She was back there again, sputtering, choking, losing consciousness.

Isabelle opened her eyes. Her heart was racing and her skin was slick with sweat. She looked at the clock. Six a.m. It was her thirty-fifth birthday.

Isabelle had had this version of the dream before, the retro plastic phone, the drone in her ears, the water, always the water. But this dream had a twist; instead of trying to reach her father, it was her mother. And now the dream was not just a dream; she would not reach Claire again no matter how many times she dialed.

Isabelle was thirsty and had a dull headache. She walked to the bathroom and filled up her water glass. She was dismayed to find that the Advil bottle in her medicine cabinet was empty. She vaguely remembered intending to recycle it but not wanting to walk into the kitchen, so she'd left it on her shelf. Isabelle sighed. She was essentially middle-aged and not even responsible enough to keep a fresh supply of ibuprofen.

Isabelle had told herself for weeks that this threshold was arbitrary. Why was thirty-five any different than thirty-four or thirty-three? Maybe it wasn't. But she had been an adult for a very long time. For years after college it had felt that adulthood was "new." She was grown up, but adolescence—childhood even—were right there, so close she could reach back and touch them. Now those times felt like the receding shoreline of a tropical paradise separated by a vast, un-swimmable expanse of water. When she was in her twenties and she'd meet a woman in her late thirties or forties, Isabelle would think, *How does she even get up in the morning?* She viewed age as almost a failure of will, something she could avoid with sheer determination. But this had not spurred Isabelle into action. She occasionally took herself to a yoga class, but she abhorred exercise. Isabelle's only skin care routine was the thick cream from Bigelow's that Claire swore by, sojourning every few months to the Village to procure it. By now the safety net of her favorable genetics holding her against the abyss of aging had to be going threadbare.

Isabelle walked to her vanity to retrieve her laptop, taking it back to bed to begin her morning ritual. She'd told herself the night before that she was going to skip it today. But Isabelle was not very good at keeping promises, especially to herself. She opened the computer, navigated to Publishers Marketplace, and checked out the new deals in fiction, ogling which people who were not her had sold their manuscripts to publishers. She then googled these authors to find out their ages, specifically whether they were younger than her or not. If an author with a big deal turned out to be in her twenties, Isabelle would be despondent until her obsessive tracing of the writer turned up some nugget of information, usually relating to their physical appearance, that she could use to feel better about herself. She was not proud of this.

As Isabelle scanned the announcements, she felt her pulse quicken. Of course, today of all days, he would have a deal. *Bestselling author Darby Cullman's dystopian fantasy of a world following a catastrophic nuclear event . . . to Eastwick House . . . in a major deal.* Isabelle knew that was code for north of $500,000. And Darby already had a book coming out the next month. Before she could stop herself, Isabelle navigated to Darby's own website, where he'd already posted news of his latest publishing conquest. "Humbled to announce that my next book, *Nuclear Cowboys*, will be out next spring. Looking forward to getting this baby into the world with the all-star team at Eastwick and sharing it with y'all." Isabelle felt bile rising in her throat. Y'all? Y'ALL? Darby was from fucking Connecticut. And Darby Cullman, a boy who had walked the Brown campus in a smoking jacket over a bare chest, was not humble about anything. Especially the fact that he'd bedded nearly every comely girl to carry a Louis Vuitton pochette around Max's bar. Isabelle Manning included.

Well almost. They had not actually had complete sex. Darby's erection had faded that night in the face of the massive amount of drugs coursing through his system, including a bad batch of psychedelic mushrooms. Or at least that's what he'd told Isabelle the next time they ran into each other. Isabelle hadn't been sure she was interested in Darby. He had a brooding handsomeness, a cocksure way about him, and was definitely an asshole—a prerequisite for Isabelle—but there was something ridiculous about him. He made a show of parading around with a book of Thoreau poetry. A Sanskrit symbol hung on a thick silver chain around his neck. But when Darby seemed similarly uninterested in pursuing her, Isabelle decided he was a complete buffoon, worthy only of derision and contempt. Which is why it was so deeply wrong that he had become a bestselling author instead of her.

So far Darby had published three novels, described in the—glowing!—critical reviews as "literary suspense." Isabelle thought they were ill-written, with trope characters and cheap, alarmist plots, and she did not miss an opportunity to air her views to any potentially sympathetic listener. Every new triumph—of which Isabelle kept careful track—fed her hatred. She'd figured out exactly where Darby lived in Brooklyn: in an amenity-rich luxury condo in Williamsburg, which, given all the pictures of him on Instagram brewing his own kombucha, concocting sourdough starter from wild yeast, and biking around town with canvas shopping bags overflowing with local produce, seemed the height of hypocrisy. She regularly fantasized about ways in which she could expose him as a yuppie poseur.

Last year, she'd run into him at the *Paris Review* Halloween party. Darby acted like he didn't remember her from Brown, and then finally said, "Oooh, right, Ward's daughter," as if *that's* how he knew who she was. And calling her father "Ward" like he and her father were besties, as if breaking onto the *New York Times* bestseller list gave Darby permission to refer to her father this way. Had Isabelle been slightly drunker, she might have reminded him about his flaccid penis circa 2003.

Isabelle's phone began buzzing. She swiped to answer. "Don't even say it."

"What? Is today something special?"

"Ha, ha."

"What are you doing?" Brian asked.

"Oh you know, just sitting in bed being masochistic."

"Uh-oh."

"It's nothing. Darby Cullman has a new book deal."

Brian groaned. "Isabelle, you have to stop. That guy is the worst. Remember the smoking jacket?"

She sighed. "Yeah."

"And the Birkenstocks with his really disgusting feet?"

"What was wrong with his feet?"

"The nails were too long, like curling around his toes. And they were filthy."

"Ew. You were really paying attention."

"They were hard to miss. So. Am I the first call?"

"Obviously. It's not even seven a.m."

"Niiiiiice. I don't like to break a seventeen-year streak."

"*That* makes me feel ancient."

"What are you doing today?"

"Glenda is making me have lunch with her." Isabelle had agreed to this because it was easier in the moment to say yes, and Isabelle planned to cancel. But she hadn't gotten to it when her godmother had called her last night to confirm their reservation at Barneys. It was too late and too rude to bow out now.

Isabelle had always been a birthday person. When she was little, her mother did something elaborate every year, toting Isabelle and her friends to tea at the Plaza, setting up stations in the apartment where twelve little girls decorated their own hats, a garden party where everyone took home a newly potted bulb. Her mother was excellent at things like this, and Isabelle remembered the specific sense of deflation she felt as a child on the day after her birthday. When

Isabelle was older, she and Claire had a tradition of lunch at Serafina and a walk around the Met. Claire would give Isabelle amusing gifts from the Eli's store on Madison, RBG socks, a composition-notebook-patterned canvas tote, an umbrella that spouted pointy cat ears when opened. Isabelle would host multiple celebratory dinners with various groups of friends, and on bigger years, a genuine party. But on this day, she wanted none of that and could hardly conceive of once being a person who did.

"Can I take you to dinner, or is your father doing that already?"

"My dad is in Sag," said Isabelle. "That's really sweet of you. I don't know, I may not be able to take candles in a piece of chocolate cake."

"No candles of any kind. Can't make that kind of guarantee on chocolate."

Isabelle hesitated. "All right, deal. Thanks."

Brian said he would look into restaurants. After they hung up, Isabelle felt slightly icky. She'd predicted that Brian would ask her about dinner, and she had planned to refuse. She knew that she held Brian back. And her old therapist had strongly suggested the reverse was also true. "He fulfills too many emotional needs for you," was how she put it. But Isabelle didn't want to be alone. Isabelle had other friends, of course, but most of them had children and were rarely available for impromptu get-togethers. Besides, she didn't want to admit to anyone else that she was actually completely planless on her birthday.

Isabelle had always said she'd back off if Brian ever got serious with anyone. But who was going to get serious with him with Isabelle around? No one would believe that they weren't sleeping together, especially since Isabelle had in fact slept with Brian. A handful of times in college, and during a nostalgic turn back at Brown for a reunion. And the sex had not been bad. Not at all. Especially the last time, when Brian had seemed to have picked up some new skills. But that was all ages ago. She'd been twenty-seven—young!!—the last time they'd slept together. She and Brian were just friends.

He'd always been the opposite of the guys she usually went for.

In her youth, Isabelle tended toward tortured trust-fund types. Guys who thought they were rebels because they stopped washing their hair and smoked American Spirits, but who were only too happy to be parentally subsidized, living in grand NoHo lofts or flying first-class to a family ski chalet in Gstaad. They were never traditionally handsome. They were sarcastic, they were moody, they were emotionally unavailable. Isabelle liked her love affairs jagged and dramatic, all cigarettes and tear-streaked mascara. Fragile egos and heavy drinking made excellent kindling for the bonfire petty mind games set ablaze. More recently, she went on a lot of dates with men in their late thirties and early forties that she met online or through the occasional setup. They were all, in some fundamental way, the same. Usually they referred to themselves as "entrepreneurs," running start-ups that were invariably described to her as "the Uber" of whatever industry. In the last year or two, a lot of the guys she'd been set up with were divorced. They had tricked-out bachelor pads in new, soulless high-rises, lots of giant TVs and Hudson River views. Swanky, but undercut with the loneliness revealed in refrigerators with nothing but beer and molding-over takeout, the smattering of loose cutlery rattling in a drawer, a cheaply framed picture of the kid they saw Wednesday afternoons and every other weekend.

It didn't really matter since Isabelle's priority had never been to get married. Her book had to come first, then she would worry about a husband and a family and all that. She knew she could not have a child until her career had been set in motion. But time was no longer on her side. If Isabelle had any money to spare, she would've frozen her eggs. But she didn't, and she was just going to have to risk it. She could live without becoming a mother, but she was not sure the same was true for being a writer.

◆   ◆   ◆

Glenda was waiting when Isabelle got off the elevator on the ninth floor at Barneys.

"My darling girl!" Glenda opened her arms but waited for Isabelle to come to her. She was dressed in leather leggings with a gray cashmere crewneck. Glenda had a sturdy build but dressed like a much thinner woman. She was so self-possessed that she could pull it off. Isabelle embraced her godmother, almost tripping over the giant shopping bag at Glenda's feet. Isabelle's present. At least there would be that. Glenda was one of those rich people who wielded their generosity like a saber. Isabelle was hoping for a good designer bag; a new Celine or Bottega was consignment gold. And it could not come at a better time.

"How *are* you?" Glenda asked.

Isabelle let out a muffled "fine" from Glenda's bosom. Her godmother stepped back and sandwiched Isabelle's face between her hands. Her dyed jet-black hair was pulled into a tight bun, showcasing the two-plus-carat emerald-cut diamond studs that sparkled on her ears, and the matte-red cemented on her lips. "You look good, all things considered."

"Thanks."

"Well, you're a little wan. Wan can be cute in your twenties. But we're way past that now, aren't we?"

Isabelle sighed.

"Maintenance, darling. It's all about maintenance from here on out." Glenda patted Isabelle's cheek and laughed. "At least you didn't inherit your father's overgrown forehead," Glenda concluded. She took Isabelle by the arm and picked up the shopping bag before moving them both into the restaurant, calling back, "Van Dorn" to the hostess. The crowd at the tastefully taupe restaurant didn't vary. Aside from a few older men on business lunches, it was populated with wealthy women, older ones like Glenda, with well-preserved faces pulled like circus tents, and those closer to Isabelle's own age with blown-out hair, scalloped Chloé flats, and teeny wrists dripping in Cartier and Van Cleef.

"Happy birthday," said Glenda when they were seated. "Did I say that already?"

"No. But we can just ignore *that* altogether."

Glenda had turned her attention to the waiter at the table offering bread. "Oh, this one has a sense of humor," she said, pushing the basket away roughly. "Bring us two glasses of Dom Pérignon as fast as your little legs can carry you, and a reasonable amount of time after that come back with two Madison Avenue salads—that's what you want, isn't it, Isabelle? Unless you've lost all willpower and are having *pasta*, which frankly I wouldn't blame you, given the run you're having."

"Salad's fine. As long as I have my champagne, I'm good."

"Quite right."

Isabelle felt surprisingly glad to be with her godmother. Maybe this lunch had been a good idea. Glenda had always doted on Isabelle, the daughter of her best friend. Glenda had married later in life, to Jonathan, a jolly little man who found Glenda adorable, and had no children of her own, so Isabelle had been her surrogate. Glenda came from a massive publishing fortune, and her family still owned dozens of newspapers and magazines. When Isabelle was little, Glenda would have her over for tea in her palatial Park Avenue penthouse with her set of Bordeaux mastiffs. Places would be set for her giant dogs, who were very good-natured about being dressed in brocade ruff collars like Tudors and had been trained to sit calmly on silk-upholstered chairs. After tea, Isabelle would be permitted to play dress-up in Glenda's enormous closet. Proof of one of these afternoons hung in a hallway in her parents' apartment: a black-and-white photograph of a six-year-old Isabelle swimming in a cap-sleeved, full-skirted Oscar de la Renta gown. Held high in her right hand between her first two fingers is an Audrey Hepburn–style cigarette holder, and on her lips is a smirk that is at once joyous and defiant.

Glenda took a sip of her champagne. "Hm. Could be colder, but I'm not going to be difficult."

"You? Difficult?"

"Ha."

Isabelle had only eaten half a croissant all day, and she could feel the fizzy liquid zip straight down her throat to her empty stomach.

"I still can't believe it," said Glenda, shaking her head. "Every day I forget and pick up the phone to dial your mother. I'm devastated. Just completely devastated. And what rough shape you must be in. You must feel utterly lost." Glenda laid a hand adorned with a paperweight of a sapphire on top of Isabelle's.

"I'm sad," said Isabelle, maintaining composure. This was certainly true. She felt abysmal. But she had the feeling that her grief was onion-like with many layers, and she was just at the papery outer skin. "And I'm probably about to be a lot sadder."

"Oh?"

Isabelle cleared her throat. "My mother said she left me some sentimental things—you know, stuff from my childhood." Isabelle couldn't put off going to Sag Harbor forever, but every day she found a reason not to board a Jitney.

"Ah, sounds like Claire." She waited for Glenda to say more, hoping Glenda knew something of this dresser-drawer trove and might give her a clue, anything to help Isabelle blunt the emotional impact of what awaited her.

But the other woman just sipped her champagne. "Well," Glenda said finally, "if there is anything you need, Isabelle, please call on me. Day or night. *Anything.*"

Isabelle nodded.

"I mean it."

She was sure that Glenda wanted to mean this. Lots of people had made similarly well-meaning statements to her in the weeks since her mother had died. But no one wanted to be taken literally. No one really thought she would call up at two a.m. for a heart-to-heart. And of course she wouldn't. That's why they offered.

"What are you doing tonight?" Glenda asked.

"Having dinner with Brian."

"That farm boy is still following you around?" Brian was from a suburb of Minneapolis, but nothing could convince Glenda that he hadn't spent his childhood milking cows and rotating crops.

"We are still friends, and he's a U.S. attorney now."

"A government lawyer?" Glenda brought a hand to her chest. "He enjoys penury, does he?"

"Glenda . . ."

"He's quite adorable—I'll give you that. I've thought frequently of the afternoon he came to the compound in his swimming trunks." Glenda shivered slightly at the memory of Brian and Isabelle once visiting her in Southampton. "But come on, Isabelle." Her godmother cocked her head, and with her eyes said everything Isabelle did not like to admit.

Isabelle loved her friend, and god knew he had been there for her. But sometimes she found him just a little too down the middle, a little . . . lacking in sophistication. Once, in college, he told her his two favorite things were football and ice cream. Football and ice cream! His social effort was sometimes too obvious. He overused people's first names and did a double-handed handshake. For special events, he wore heavy cologne. He drank protein powder shakes and sometimes said he was going to "lift" without irony. He came from a family that wore matching personalized T-shirts on vacation. His mother was a tiresome, meddling woman whose conversational currency consisted of mass product recalls and freak accidents, especially those involving small, white children. And Isabelle was pretty sure his dad had voted for Trump.

Claire diverged dramatically from Glenda on the matter of Brian. Her mother had thought Isabelle was entirely mad for dismissing Brian as a romantic prospect and was uncharacteristically blunt in advocating for him as a match. Claire wasn't wrong: Brian was smart, he was kind, he was funny, he was almost laughably good-looking, with abs that had no business on anyone with a law degree. When Isabelle's book didn't sell, Claire had insisted Isabelle come out to Sag Harbor to recuperate. Claire secretly invited Brian to join them, strolling him into the house like a gift, the grand antidote to Isabelle's disappointment. Isabelle felt blindsided, annoyed her mother was using her professional crisis to push a suitor. Isabelle turned cranky and aloof. She spent the weekend in front of the TV while Brian and Claire played Scrabble. Now Isabelle hated herself for believing she had the luxury of being a shrew, because she had limitless opportunities not to be.

"Still writing?" Glenda asked now, squinting her face up as if the subject was too painful to face dead-on, pronouncing the word "writing" like it was a contagious skin condition.

"Yup." Isabelle caught the eye of the waiter and tapped her empty champagne glass. She had sent the chapters to Fern last week and was now compulsively hitting refresh on her email for his reply. The draft was shaping up. She was slowly sowing the seeds of conflict. The elements were there. Fern had to see its potential.

Glenda nodded. "Oh your mother was so angry about your first book. She was beside herself. I think she felt the pain as if it was her own wound."

Isabelle nodded. Claire had kept her cool in front of her daughter, but Glenda was probably telling the truth. And the thought of her mother's empathetic sorrow forced Isabelle to once again turn her eyes to the ceiling, blinking until the heat receded.

The salads came, and they picked at the lettuce mixed with onion and red bell pepper cooked to a limp, wormy consistency while discussing Glenda's most recent Sardinian cruise. When the plates were cleared, Glenda slapped her palms on the table and declared, "Time for the gifts."

"Gifts?" Isabelle smiled and raised her eyebrows.

"Yes, gifts. Plural," said Glenda.

"What could they be . . ."

"Isabelle," said Glenda, straightening up in her seat and looking at Isabelle intently. "I know that your mother was helping you."

"Oh. Well, yes." Isabelle had not known Glenda knew this.

"So *I* am going to help you get through the next few months."

"Wow, Glenda, I don't know what to say, that is so generous." It had not occurred to her that Glenda might just give her straight up financial support. This was completely awkward, and Isabelle knew she ought to refuse, but her desperation lit up a spark of hope inside her.

Glenda reached into her bag and pulled out a check, which she slid across the table, smiling magnanimously. Isabelle looked down. At first she thought she must be misreading the decimal point. But she stared at the check, and it was indeed written out for three hundred dollars.

"I can see how relieved you are," said Glenda.

"Uh, yes." Glenda was very purposeful, so Isabelle doubted this was a mistake. Perhaps Glenda was so rich that she had completely lost touch with the value of money. Maybe she didn't understand that three hundred dollars wouldn't come close to covering any real expenses. Not in New York City. Maybe to her—three hundred, three thousand, thirty thousand—was all the same.

"Don't get used to it," Glenda warned her. "This is the last check I will provide. Your real birthday gift is in here." Glenda pushed the white shopping bag toward Isabelle's chair. "Go on, open it."

Isabelle peeked in the bag and saw that it was not one present but several. She fished one out. It was not a bag. By the size and weight, it was unmistakably a book. She undid the plain brown paper.

"Oh. James Patterson. Wow. Thanks?"

"Isabelle, you can give a man a fish and feed him for one day, or you can *teach* a man to fish . . ."

"I don't think I follow."

"I bought you a copy of every book on the *New York Times* bestseller list. You can read them, and then," said Glenda, her tone turned gleeful, eyes sparkling, "you can make your writing more like those writers, who clearly have more of a handle on what they're doing. And then you'll write a book that will be successful too!"

"Ha. Very funny, Glen." Her godmother looked at her, full poker face. This little prank was quirky, even for Glenda, but well within her godmother's wheelhouse. She took particular joy in playing the eccentric. But Glenda did not break, continuing to stare at Isabelle expectantly.

"Oh—you're serious?"

"Of course I'm serious. Why wouldn't I be serious?"

Isabelle saw that not only was her godmother not at all joking, but Glenda believed she'd just handed over the keys to Isabelle's happiness. Three hundred bucks and a dozen police procedurals.

"You should pay particular attention to this Patterson." Glenda pounded the hardcover with her red lacquered finger. "Have you read him?"

"Maybe a long time ago . . ." Isabelle was not sure, but Patterson was one of those writers so ubiquitous, so ingrained in the culture, his books were less read than absorbed.

"He's fabulous. And he sometimes has more than one book at a time on these lists," said Glenda, adding, "I don't think even your father has done that."

"Maybe not . . . But James Patterson writes more like crime, thriller-type books. Not really my style."

"But this is my point, dear," said Glenda, softly now, as if Isabelle was a deluded inmate at an asylum. "Your style—whatever it is— isn't really working, is it?"

"Not yet. But I'm not going to just copy someone else's."

"Oh darling, don't be naïve," said Glenda. "Everyone's copying someone. Everyone. You just need to find the right person."

"Well, I don't think he's it."

"So you don't want to be successful?"

"Yes but—"

"But nothing. I'm trying to *help* you, sweetheart."

Isabelle looked at her godmother with the sinking realization that Glenda was going to make her unwrap every single book in the bag until Isabelle agreed that this was a great idea and Glenda felt she had been properly appreciated. "You know," said Isabelle. "You're completely right. I should look closer at his writing."

"You must."

"I will. As soon as I get home, I'm going to read this."

"That's my girl," said Glenda. "You know, I almost got you a Birkin or some serious earrings. But then I thought, instead, I'd give you the gift of self-sufficiency. Much better than some coveted handbag or an iconic piece of jewelry, don't you think?"

Isabelle drained the last of her champagne. A Birkin would've kept her afloat for a year.

Even though it was rude, since Glenda was clearly paying, Isabelle signaled for the check. Downstairs, she helped her godmother into her chauffeur-driven Bentley, thanking her profusely. She waved to Glenda as she pulled away from the curb, holding up her shopping bag and giving a thumbs-up.

When Glenda's car was out of sight, Isabelle started lugging the bag of books toward the nearest trash can. She would dump the books and walk uptown. The day was glorious, fifty-five and sunny. Everywhere she looked, New York vibrated with color, the trees flush with yellow leaves, the domes of red, auburn, and orange mums filling the tree planters. When she reached the garbage, Isabelle considered whether she could really trash fifteen brand-new hardcovers. Recycle maybe. But it felt wrong to just send them to a landfill. Isabelle saw that up a few feet there was a vendor selling the typical fake Louis Vuitton totes, sunglasses, and scarves with cats on them.

"What do you want to buy?" the man said to Isabelle when she stopped in front of him.

"Nothing. I want to make a donation to your business."

"What's in there?"

"Books."

"Books? I don't know, my friend."

"I felt the same way," Isabelle mumbled.

The man started pawing inside the bag, and his expression changed.

"James Patterson?" He held up one of the hardbacks. "I love James Patterson!"

Isabelle sighed and nodded.

"This will sell," he said.

"Of course it will."

6

New York, 2017

Brian

Brian sat down and took in the scene: low lighting, exposed brick walls, crisp white tablecloths upon which little fists of red roses sat next to tall taper candles burning suggestively. He winced. Brian had been to the restaurant once before when his parents were visiting New York. He did not remember the place striving for romantic quite so literally. The other patrons had clearly gotten the memo, all of them dressed up in a blatant, unselfconscious way, like middle-aged prom-goers, which felt jarring in New York. Because, of course, they weren't New Yorkers. When Isabelle arrived, Brian would have to play it off as if he'd known, titrate a very specific amount of mockery to show her the pick was a joke, not a genuine attempt to please her.

"Special occasion?" A pony-tailed waiter was at the table pouring ice water into goblets.

"Nope." The last thing Brian wanted was to be fawned over, get the hard sell on steak for two or the pre-order soufflé, this guy treating them like lovers from Ho-Ho-Kus. Despite their long tenure as friends, Brian still took care that his words, actions, and physical gestures could not be misconstrued. He was mindful not to disturb the carefully constructed scaffolding of platonic friendship. Isabelle did not feel burdened by the same restraints. She was happy to carelessly rest her head on his shoulder or throw in a sua sponte, *I love you, Bri*. And because of dynamics established before either of them was of drinking age, she could do this.

"How lovely," said the waiter, "just out to enjoy each other's company."

"Yeah," Brian mumbled. "Something like that." He and Isabelle did enjoy each other's company. They always had. Isabelle was one person—maybe the only person—he did not get sick of. Brian knew that tonight, as with many other nights, it would be Isabelle's stories, her anecdotes, the article she'd read or the podcast she'd just heard that sustained the conversation. This was okay with him. His fascination with Isabelle's rarified universe had not faded from bloom. No detail of hers was too tiny or immaterial to digest. At this point, Brian knew New York's intellectual elite better than they knew themselves. And if he played his cards right, Brian's attention would one day—maybe soon—be rewarded.

It wasn't that Isabelle ignored Brian's life. She asked him questions about being a lawyer, a job she found about as exotic as snake charmer. She loved prosecutor stories, like the ones about "Rooster," the colorful Russian mobster Brian tried last year. But Brian preferred to keep his cards close to his chest. He had his own plans, goals that burned inside him. Some of them might surprise Isabelle. The two of them were more similar than Isabelle realized. But Brian's ambitions were like mating plumage, tucked away for the opportune moment. Until then, it was best to keep his striving under wraps.

Brian looked up just as Isabelle walked in the door, wearing a cobalt-blue dress and bright red lipstick. He watched her taking in the room, a smile creeping onto her face. He waved from the table, and Isabelle came toward him.

"What's cuter than this?" she said.

"You wanted to celebrate thirty-five at the one non-ironic restaurant left in the city, right?"

"Obviously." Isabelle leaned in and kissed him on the cheek before sitting. "Oooh, I love tall candles. You never see them anymore."

"Very retro."

"When I was little, my mother used tapers at dinner, even if it was just the three of us—or the two of us. I got to use this copper thingy that looked like a pilgrim's hat on a long handle to snuff them out."

"Why not just blow them out?"

"Wax drippings." Isabelle took a sip of her water. "Anyway, you'll never believe what Glenda pulled today."

"Tell me."

The paparazzi were already staked out in front of the funeral home on Madison Avenue, primed for the parade of Aiden's former subjects. When my taxi pulled up, they lunged like pigeons at a crust of street-cart pretzel.

"Save your film, gentlemen," I said, giving a wave as I got out, "it's just me."

Inside, Aiden's agent, Sebastian, was placing dozens of enlarged replicas of Aiden's work down the center aisle of the chapel. It was, I'll admit, an impressive sight. But all together like that, the disparity in male versus female subjects was comical. The men were fully dressed, for one thing. Most wore a look of deep contemplation or a sly, in-on-the-joke smile. The women were captured scantily clad, dazed and disheveled with bedheads and Parliaments hanging from their mouths. This overt sexualization was an Aiden signature. It had sold a lot of paintings. And it was one idea for which my husband deserved full credit.

"Too bad Aiden wasn't able to finish the Cusack in time." Sebastian shook his head. "By the way, I've left a few messages on your machine. I need to get into the studio."

It had been more than a few. I told Sebastian I'd call the next day, and then took the opportunity to excuse myself when I saw my mother being wheeled in by her aide, Gloria. After two falls and once leaving the house with the kettle on, she needed round-the-clock care, and I hired Gloria right away. Even if it would bankrupt me, I couldn't let my mother end up in one of those pea-soup-smelling homes shuffling around in a bathrobe.

"Livi!" my mother said when I'd reached her. She looked at me and laughed. "Sweetheart, what are you wearing?"

"A dress?" I'd managed to pour my forty-four-year-old body into a Kenzo knit sheath.

My mother clutched her throat where Gloria had jauntily tied a silk scarf, a smile still playing at the corner of her lips. "Black on your wedding day? I know you like to push the envelope, but it's a bit much!"

"Oh, no, Mom, it's not my wedding." My mother had been one of the first stewardesses on commercial airlines. She was sharp, fearless in a way I'd grown up desperate to be. Now she was slipping into senility. "Aiden passed away, Mom."

"Aiden?"

"All the medicine makes her groggy," Gloria said, knowing I knew better.

. . .

After all the celebrities oozed into their seats, and some kind of religious person did intros, I was up. It had taken me most of the night to formulate what I would say. Aiden had not always been the Aiden he was when he died. He once had self-awareness and a sense of humor. After all, he only asked me out after I made a searing critique of his work during our first year at Cooper Union. I'd been having one of those mornings, spilling coffee on my blouse, snapping a heel on subway stairs, and I unleashed my frustration on Aiden's gigantic splatter painting. Instead of hating me, he invited me out for a beer and told me he liked my "fire." And what made me like him was that he admitted I was right. But that Aiden had died long ago. And no one wanted to hear about the magic of our early courtship. So I told a true, if incomplete, anecdote about the very first Aiden Connors portrait, the one of Christopher Walken.

Back then, Aiden didn't have the clout to get Walken to pose for him, and he was using an image of Walken crossing the street near Central Park. Aiden grew frustrated that he couldn't get the right sense of movement from someone else's photo, so I posed as the actor, stuffing up my hair into a

Mets cap like the one Walken wore. And we tramped around New York City, Aiden snapping pictures of me as Christopher Walken.

After me came the big-deal artists, Eric Fischl and Julian Schnabel. Within their lavish praise, Aiden would've detected some whiff of condescension, real or imagined. Aiden had become a kind of celebrity himself, captured the zeitgeist of the eighties, but his dream had not been to have his images silk-screened onto baby tees sold at Urban Outfitters. Aiden blamed me that he was not a Pollock or Rothko. He never got that other types of art could be just as meaningful. And if he hadn't been such a decadent spender, he could've made other choices. But, really, cry me a river. Perhaps, in the end, we all get the careers we deserve.

7

Sag Harbor, 2017

Ward

Dear Mr. Maning,
  Big fan of your books. A few things though.

Oh brother.

  On page 241 of "Suburban Saint", there's an error you need
to correct. The street is Pinewoods, not Pinetree. And also
later, you talk about a 60-foot boat at the Halsey Marina,
but Halsey's too small for that kinda vessel. Can you please
contact your publisher about these things? I'm going to review
your other books and see what else I find and I'll let you know
ASAP. —Don

Ward shook his head. "Hey Don, why don't you check the spelling
of my last name? Idiot," he muttered to the empty room. Everyone
was an editor. The downside of choosing to read his fan mail was
enduring notes like these. But they had not deterred him. Ward
Manning could not unconvince himself that somewhere in the pile

there would be the one, the letter that contained some new, previously unvoiced praise, a perfect little phrase that would tuck itself puzzle-like into an empty crevice of his psyche. And while he once was able to put the mail pile aside after finding a good letter or two, the missives were like an opiate, and he now needed three or four times that many to feel satiated.

Ward was off the wagon. And his consumption had never been quite so gluttonous as it had become since the afternoon at the bookstore when he'd bought up all the copies of his own book. At his direction, his housekeeper Astrid had gathered up the letters that came to the apartment and had sent them out to him in a big envelope. Ward called up his agent's assistant and told him to forward messages sent to the generic inquiries account to his personal email, "for research."

He'd spent two weeks in the country, struggling to get into a flow. He was not in control of his protagonist. Ward had made the mistake of trusting her, letting her lead him in unknown, unsettling directions, getting him lost in the deep, dark woods of a novel. And a novel is a terrible place to get lost. Now she was in charge, leading the story as she pleased. And as much as he tried to expose the perfidy in her character, she still came out empathetic. He was, despite fervent efforts, setting her up to be the hero. This was not what he wanted. To combat his disorientation, Ward had begun to hold on too tightly. But nothing good was ever written with a death grip on the keyboard. Writing a worthy novel required a focus at once steady and loose, an ability to nimbly expand and contract the aperture.

Ward was increasingly convinced that there was something wrong with him. Gravely wrong. He now spent a significant amount of time on the internet, researching his symptoms. Fatigue. Mental cloudiness. Forgetfulness. His reading did little to console him, but he could not help but avail himself of the infinite rabbit holes the web was gracious enough to provide. He was on a roller coaster, convinced of the worst—the big A, or at least the big D—and then thoroughly persuaded by one website or another that he just needed more exercise or to go vegan like Bill Clinton. But surviving on kale and seitan was a hell he was not willing to endure. He would not be the jackass who ordered the portobello entrée at a steakhouse.

Not that he was going to restaurants. Ward did not leave the house much. He'd stopped shaving or getting dressed in the morning. He padded around in his bathrobe and slippers, surviving on canned goods, powdered Lipton noodle soup, and Conca D'Oro takeout. The situation only gave further credence to the idea that he was becoming a doddering old imbecile. And yet, it continued. The problem, Ward could see clearly, was that he had no one to take care of him. He could staff up. Bring Astrid out to the house to make his meals and clean up after him. Or hire someone to stay with him full-time. But Ward hated interacting with help. Nothing made him feel like an asshole more than explaining how he liked his egg prepared or his shirts ironed, like one of those people he loathed as a young man, when he was waiting tables, poor and striving, stinking of garlic and broiled steak. But the fact remained that Ward was not going to do these things for himself. He was an artist. He couldn't create while bothering about buying dish detergent and toilet paper. Claire had always acted as the buffer, the lubricant between him and the help, making sure things got done without him having to be made aware of the transactions. But he'd have to figure something out before Isabelle came to the house.

That reminded him. Ward needed to call Isabelle for her birthday. He assumed that would fulfill his obligation. Or was he still supposed to purchase gifts? Surely that silliness could be done away with by now. Did he need to orchestrate a dinner when she came out to visit? Was this what fathers did for adult children? Christ, he didn't even know how old his daughter was turning.

Ward had never planned to have children. Too much work, too distracting. Claire had won that standoff, quite cleverly as he remembered. But she had gone in understanding that he would not be one of those fathers who constructed a crib or carted a diaper bag.

He'd loved Isabelle from the start. She'd been a beautiful, charming, and intellectually superior creature since birth. But his love for his daughter had not been the type that compelled him to crawl around on the floor, to partake in Play-Doh and finger painting, or to endure cacophonous cartoons. It was easier later. Their relationship began in earnest when Isabelle was old enough to sit across from him at a restaurant and wield an appetizer fork. Starting when she was eight or nine, he'd take Isabelle out to Vico or Quatorze, just the two of them. They'd share clams oreganata or a crisp mound of baked goat cheese atop arugula; he'd magically turn her water pink with a spoonful of red wine. They'd talk about what books she liked, and which ones she didn't. Isabelle always had definitive opinions. He began to think that his daughter might be like him.

Ward knew that he could have been more present for her. But writing could not be done with a wandering focus. Not the kind of writing he did. Ward could not pollute the pristine reservoir of his mind with the particulars of child-rearing: the schedule for all the overindulgent extracurriculars; the names of friends, pediatricians, teachers; the ever-shifting list of snacks, clothing, equipment needing to be purchased. Even thinking of such things felt to him like being slowly smothered by packing peanuts. And he felt serene knowing Isabelle had Claire to mother her. As a writer, Isabelle would understand this now. She'd been smart enough to have put her own writing before personal matters. And he believed he'd given his daughter something else, a keepsake far more valuable than coaching soccer or making her peanut butter and jelly. Or knowing exactly how old she was. Ward Manning had given his daughter the legacy of being his. Having him as a father was a biographical sparkler bright enough to light up the rest of her life. Even if she did nothing.

• • •

Sitting at his computer, still in his bathrobe, Ward sensed the familiar disgust he felt every day around three p.m. when he had not done a whit of writing. He turned away from his computer to his trusty typewriter. He'd used it to write the first draft of every book since *American Dream*. The machine was an artifact and continued to function only due to the costly and laborious efforts of a nonagenarian in the far East Village. But Ward would never trust another instrument with his ideas in their most nascent and delicate form. Ward flexed his fingers, then wiggled them over the keys. He made a deal with himself: He'd write five more pages, and then he would call Isabelle.

Just as he was about to start, the phone rang.

"Ward? It's Herb."

"Hello, Herb," said Ward, cursing himself for not screening the call. Their estate lawyer had been stalking him with a torrent of irksome demands. Claire did not have many separate assets—her fancy, blue-blood family the victim of "WASP rot"; the money was gone, but the pretensions remained. Herb still found reasons to lecture Ward about the minutiae of New York testamentary jurisprudence. Ward had a hazy memory of being appointed the executor of Claire's estate, but at the time the idea that his wife would die before him was a contingency bordering on ludicrous. Claire was five years younger, for one thing. Not a gaping chasm, but it had always seemed enough of a cushion for him to avoid the exact situation in which he now found himself. He had assumed he would go first and that Claire and Isabelle would soldier on, devoting a substantial part of their remaining time on earth to the preservation and maintenance of Ward's legacy. He was especially counting on Claire, with her taste and eye for detail, to oversee the construction of the Ward Manning Wing at the New York Public Library, where his future estate had already been pledged.

"Herb, I'm just in the middle of working here."

"This will only take a minute," Herb said, launching in. "There is a provision that was inserted into Claire's will directing 'any future earnings to be paid out to Isabelle.' We've scoured our files and cannot determine what this part is referring to."

"Didn't your office write the will?"

"We did. But this clause was added by Claire, and somehow, I am sorry to say, it missed our review. I'm hoping you can shed some light?"

"It beats the hell out of me."

"Claire never had any business ventures?"

"Business ventures? No." He was fast losing his patience. "Look, my wife's biggest concern was always Isabelle. And, as you know, we disagreed on matters of inheritance." The tenor of Isabelle's upbringing had been a source of strain between Ward and Claire, and never more so than over money. Claire had begun lobbying for a trust to be set up when Isabelle was a child, right after the incident in Jamaica. She continued to bring it up every few years, but Ward always shut it down. The only thing a trust would give Isabelle was a sense of entitlement. His daughter had experienced far too much privilege as it was. And if she wanted to be a writer—a real writer—she needed to earn it. No good writing came without personal struggle. A young writer needed hunger and the wiliness of a prairie dog. If she would learn anything from Ward, it was that. Isabelle was talented, maybe very talented. But talent was a tiny percentage of it. The way she just got that story in the *New Yorker* was luck; it wasn't the way this industry worked. Isabelle needed to learn that. She would look back with gratitude on her initial struggles to publish—maybe even fondness. Ward hoped his daughter was capable of focusing on the long game. Well, after what he'd done, he was counting on it.

"Perhaps this was some misguided attempt to funnel funds to Isabelle," Ward said now to Herb.

"Yes. Fair enough," said Herb. "Just puzzling."

"I really have to run."

Once he'd hung up, Ward got up from his desk to close the window where a draft was coming in, the October air turning chilly. That was another thing about getting older, he was cold all the time. The Ralph Lauren cashmere cable-knit that had once been his uniform was no longer plush enough to keep him comfortable. Only Loro Piana made a knit substantial enough to please him these days. Something about special looms in Italy. Or maybe it was the wool of infant sheep. Whatever, they were well worth the four-figure price tags, and Ward made a note to stop by their Madison Avenue boutique to buy a few more the next time he was in the city.

Ward turned to his keys. In two hours he'd completed just five pages. Writing this protagonist felt like wading through molasses. He couldn't remember a struggle quite like this one. He walked downstairs, the sun already setting. That was all the permission he needed to make himself a drink. Ward paused as he perused his wine inventory. He was sure there'd been some task to complete, a call to make, but what it was had left him. It could not have been too important, Ward thought, as he took a first sip of merlot and looked out the kitchen window to the water. The cove was a steely blue gray, framed by the burnt umbers and ochers of autumn. He could almost hear Claire admiring the quality of light, the view that never ceased to delight her. This was the moment they would have gone out to the deck with their drinks and a good, sharp Gruyère from Cavaniola's in town. But instead he remained inside, still, watching the slow, steady progression into darkness.

8

New York, 1975

Claire

Ward called the day after the dinner at the University Club and gave Claire the address of a jazz club downtown, instructing her to meet him there at ten p.m. It struck Claire that the late hour was probably purposeful, so he didn't have to buy her dinner. Claire would have to make clear she wasn't a girl who cared about things like that. If this turned into anything more, that is. But the late hour created a torturous expanse of time in which Claire changed her clothes no fewer than five times.

She arrived at the tiny space down a set of stairs in a dilapidated brownstone and settled at a table. She'd expected the place to be packed, but it was nearly empty. As she waited for Ward, Claire had plenty of time to inspect the other patrons, a couple who looked as out of place as Claire did, and a scruffy guy who seemed as if he'd been sitting, smoking, at his table for a very long time. At ten fifteen, Ward finally appeared, casually sliding into the seat next to Claire and giving her a kiss on the cheek, as if they saw each other all the time. "This place doesn't really get going before midnight," he grunted.

"Oh, sure," said Claire, realizing that Ward's plan to impress her had been thrown off by the sparse crowd.

"I usually go to another place, but I didn't want anything too loud," said Ward. In jeans and a white T-shirt, Ward was decidedly more handsome than he'd been in his waiter uniform. He looked freshly showered and smelled pleasantly of soap and something muskier, like firewood. They sat drinking whiskey sours, listening to the mediocre music in an awkward silence. Ward bounced his leg and Claire's impression that he was eager to leave was confirmed when he said, "Do you want to get out of here?"

"Sure," said Claire.

"Let's go to my apartment," he said. "You can read my book."

• • •

Ward led Claire a few blocks away to a tenement building snaked by fire escapes. As they walked up the four flights of stairs, Claire had time to wonder if she had made a ghastly mistake. Who was this guy? And how much of a fool was she that she'd been lured back to his apartment? Was there any way this was anything other than a ploy to get her into bed? He probably had never even written a book. But she had come this far, and she might as well confirm that Ward Manning was full of it.

The apartment was a single room with a tiny table and chairs by the stove, and a mattress on the floor. There was a desk in the corner and on it a sleek black typewriter. The window looked out onto the street, the full moon shining through, and Claire could see the space was spare, tidy, not unclean. Claire stood awkwardly, waiting for Ward to make his move. But instead of putting his arm around her or something sleazier, Ward went to the desk and turned around with a stack of carbon paper pages, cradling them protectively, like a firstborn.

"Here," he said, presenting them to her. "For you, Claire Cunningham."

"Oh," she said. "You want me to read these now?"

"Yes."

Claire sat down at the table. She thought Ward might busy himself with something, giving her privacy to read, but he sat across from her and stared.

Claire read the first dozen pages, then stopped. She looked up at Ward. "How long have you been working on this?"

"My whole life."

"It's good. It's really good."

Ward grinned. "See? I told you."

The book was about a struggling cartoonist who leaves rural Missouri for New York to seek his fame and fortune. Not an earth-shattering premise, but Ward's prose was rich and nuanced, like a stew of complex flavors. He picked up on that small, elemental detail that made her think over and over as she read, *Yes, that's just it.*

Claire continued reading, remarking on sentences here and there, which made Ward bob up and down in his seat with pleasure. Ward uncorked a bottle of wine. They talked about books they loved. When Ward leaned over and kissed her, she did not resist. Claire was so wildly turned on by his writing that she drew herself closer to him, straddling him on his chair. It was she who pulled off his T-shirt and unbuckled his pants. Ward slowly undressed Claire, seeming to savor her like a long-awaited reward. He moved deliberately, decisively. Most of the men—boys, really—she'd been with were boarding school drips, boys who rowed college crew and then suited up for jobs at Solomon Brothers their fathers had arranged. Sex had always felt like a favor she was doing for them. But with Ward, it was different. He was only five years older than Claire, but he felt like a man in an entirely different way. And he displayed a generosity, seeking out not just his own pleasure, but Claire's too.

"So is this your thing?" Claire asked, propped up on her elbow.

"Is what my thing?" asked Ward, tracing a finger from Claire's bare hip up to her breast.

"You take women home and seduce them with your book?"

Ward shook his head. "You're the first person I've shown it to."

Claire was skeptical, but she asked, "Why me?"

Ward turned to face her. "You seemed like a woman of refined literary tastes, Claire Cunningham," he said with a smirk.

"Come on."

"Am I wrong? Look, I've waited on a lot of girls eating with their parents. But never one reading Wilkie Collins."

"Fair enough."

"And, Claire Cunningham, if you don't mind me saying so, you possess a truly stupendous behind."

Claire laughed. "Why do you keep calling me by my whole name?"

"It's a great name." Ward lay back down and closed his eyes. "Tell me more about what you liked about my book."

"I think I've given you enough praise for one night. You'll have to let me finish it."

Ward's brow creased.

"Have you shown it to publishers?"

Ward shook his head, then leaned over for a pack of cigarettes.

"Why not?"

Ward fumbled with the matches as he got his cigarette lit. He exhaled slowly before he said, "It's not done."

"What do you mean?"

"The ending. It's not right."

"Oh."

"I cannot show it to anyone until it's right." Ward's words came out in a halting way, a vein pulsing in his temple, suggesting this had been a long and difficult struggle.

"Sure, of course," said Claire. Ward lay faceup, smoking as he gazed at the ceiling. Claire felt as if she'd inadvertently thrown a damp cloth over them. Was she meant to leave now?

But she did not move. She suspected once she left, she would never return to this scene again. She liked Ward. She did. But he was a fantasy, a mirage of beautiful otherness. She would leave her night there, not forcing something to continue that should remain enclosed. And Claire had no illusions that this man was ever going to call her again.

Ward put out his cigarette and then pulled Claire to his chest, kissing her with intention. But tonight was not yet over, Claire thought, as she kissed him back, rolling on top of him.

• • •

Claire woke up in Ward's bed with a start. Out the window it was still dark, but light was bleeding upward into the sky. She sat up gently, not wanting to wake him as she peeled the covers off and stood. Before putting her clothes back on, Claire walked to the table. There had been a passage in Ward's opening chapter that was not quite right. In it, the protagonist lies down in the yard of his meager house, staring up at the vast universe. It was a good image, but it did not pack the punch it should. As she slept, the question of *why* swirling in her subconscious, an idea had come to her. She leafed through the pages until she found the one she was looking for. In her neat, Vassar-girl hand, she crossed out several sentences, drew an arrow and wrote out replacements, using the blank back of the page to insert sentences showing the mother watching from the window, mixing in a poignancy that was missing. Perhaps it was a bit presumptuous to edit Ward's work. They'd just met, after all. But it was Ward who'd made his book the showpiece of their date. And her edit was right.

Claire dressed quickly and let herself out of the apartment without Ward so much as stirring. It was nearly six, enough daylight to walk the streets. She had barely slept, but she felt more awake than she had in months. She smiled to herself at the thought that maybe, if he got it together to finish the book, someday she'd tell her grandchildren about her one-night stand with a well-known writer. Or, more likely, no one would've ever heard of Ward Manning, and no one would care.

9

New York, 2017

Isabelle

Isabelle walked into the cramped, ill-lit lobby of the nondescript building on Madison Avenue where a security guard was slumped on a stool next to a well-worn visitor log. Riding up in the creaky, metallic-scented elevator, Isabelle liked to think about all the literary heavyweights who had stood exactly where she was. Lorrie Moore. Michael Chabon. Robert Caro. And, of course, her father. Ward's agent was Irving Kennedy, the owner of the agency that bore his name. A blown-up sepia photograph of Irving and Ward sitting at Park Tavern on Nineteenth Street, their ties loosened, all sloppy grins and shaggy 1970s haircuts, graced the office entryway. Supposedly the photograph had been taken right after Ward signed his deal for *American Dream*. Maybe it was, though it had always seemed to Isabelle a little too staged.

Isabelle's agent had summoned her to his office. This was unusual. She and Fern had always met for salads at Bilboquet or sashimi at Hatsuhana. Once upon a time, when everything still sizzled with possibility, they got giggly on midday pinot grigio or sake. But it had been a long time since either had ordered anything harder than a Diet Coke. Fall was a busy season for books, and today Fern probably couldn't get away from his desk. The anticipation of the meeting had lived inside Isabelle like an intractable case of hiccups. The only acceptable outcome was that Fern wanted to move forward with the book—and fast. Isabelle was subsisting on Triscuits and Laughing Cow as it was, and Glenda's three-hundred dollars had been absorbed by an overdue electric bill. She had done some calculations, and Isabelle only had enough savings to get through three months, maybe four if she was truly monastic, before she would be flat out of money. But if Fern liked the book, she could get it in shape for publishers and conceivably be paid the first installment of an advance in that window. That is if everything went perfectly, which, Isabelle knew, was highly unlikely.

Isabelle was circling the conclusion that no matter what, she was going to have to ask her father for money. The thought was made slightly less abhorrent by the fact that Ward had forgotten Isabelle's birthday. Isabelle had been waiting for his call all day, but when it hadn't come by early evening, she gave in and called him while she was getting ready to meet Brian for dinner. Ward pretended that he had been "just about to call," and it was easier to let this fiction sit between them than acknowledge he would have let the day pass unremarked. Without Claire's prompting, Ward was entirely incapable of being a parent. Isabelle should have known this, but the reality still jolted her. The only upside was that Ward's mistake might make him more amenable to floating his daughter, at least for a little while.

◆　◆　◆

"Hi, Isabelle!" said the receptionist cheerily after buzzing her through the glass doors. "Fern's just finishing up a call. Can I get you anything?"

Isabelle demurred and sat on a modular Design Within Reach love seat beside the reception desk, absently picking up one of the books displayed on the coffee table. *Eat Dessert First*, a cookbook with a beautiful woman—presumably the author—pictured on the cover, wearing a cleavage-exposing gingham dress and holding up a rainbow-sprinkled birthday cake. Not all the agency's clients were literary powerhouses. Sometimes when Isabelle held a book in her hand, felt the weight, ran her hands over the cover image, she thought, *What's the big deal? It's just sheets of paper condensed between two covers. What is so magical about a book?* But Isabelle could never convince herself that a book was not the most magical object in the world. And thoughts quickly jumped to *Why this writer and not me?* It seemed to Isabelle as she sat there waiting for Fern that, at this point, she had earned it. Surely after the last few months, the universe could just give her this, let her have this thing it had already given to so many other people, including this sexpot whose primary hope for her readers seemed to be a diabetic coma.

"Isabelle."

Isabelle looked up from the book. Standing above her, Fernando Ramirez-Clement looked dapper as usual in a slim-cut suit and lavender shirt with a white pocket square.

"Wonderful to see you, doll." Fern kissed her on both cheeks.

"You too."

"Come on," said Fern, turning back in a mock whisper to add, "I've heard that cake is murder."

"Please. Baking is for masochists as far as I'm concerned."

"Preach."

Once in the office, Fern settled himself behind the desk, and Isabelle sat across from him. Behind Fern was a window with a view of the backs of the buildings on Twenty-Eighth Street. The built-in shelves on either side were filled with books by his authors as well as several silver-framed photographs of Fern and his husband, Craig, in various fabulous locales: matching tuxes in front of the Louvre, riding an elephant in Morocco, swinging on a lamppost in London. Craig Clement was a prominent Upper East Side plastic surgeon, and both he and Fern were meticulously maintained. Fern was probably a good ten years older than Isabelle, but with his creaseless brow, it was impossible to say for sure.

Fern sat looking at Isabelle, as if waiting for her to speak.

"Oh, I don't know if I thanked you for the orchid you sent after my mother . . ."

Fern batted his hand. "Please, please, it was nothing."

"It's huge."

"Oh good," said Fern, his eyes lighting up. "When the florist told me she'd send something 'tasteful,' I said 'forget tasteful, honey, I want a fucking Texas-sized orchid.'"

"She listened."

They both let out small almost-laughs for a moment.

"So . . . come on, what did you think of the pages?"

Fern folded his hands on the desk and cleared his throat. "I read them."

"Okay . . ."

"And the writing is good. Of course, your writing is always good."

"Right."

"And I'm into this protagonist."

"Great!"

"Yeah. But there was something . . ." He paused, closed his eyes, and rubbed his thumb against his first two fingers as if checking the thread count of the guest linens. "Something a bit off."

"Oh?" Isabelle struggled to sound breezy, detached, as if she were one of those writers who could discuss their work on a purely intellectual level. As if that kind of writer existed.

"Your woman is a little opaque in these first chapters, isn't she? I want her motivations to have more of a presence from the outset."

"I think you'll see what I'm aiming for after I get further in," said Isabelle. "It's meant to be a bit mysterious at the start."

Fern seemed to consider this. "Maybe."

It felt as if the temperature in the room had risen ten degrees. "Can you show me what specifically? I'm sure I can fix it if I know what it is."

"Well . . . I could. But I'm not sure I am the right person to help you mold this one."

"What?"

Fern looked at Isabelle for a moment and cleared his throat. "Isabelle, I am just going to say it: I think we've reached an impasse, doll."

"An impasse? What does that mean?" Isabelle's heart was racing now.

"You could use some new blood looking at your work."

"Wait." Isabelle held up her hand. "Wait. Wait. What is this?"

"It's nothing—"

"—are you breaking up with me?" Isabelle suddenly understood why she was not at that moment sitting with an iced tea and a leather-backed menu; Fern did not want to endure a meal with an ex.

"No, no, not at all," said Fern, laughing awkwardly. "I'm saying it might be more productive for you to work with another agent at the agency."

"So more pawning me off, then?"

"Isabelle." Fern pursed his lips. "Let's not get ugly. I'm trying to do what's best for you."

"Does Irving know about this?"

"Yes. He's offered to help you find someone else to work with."

"Who?"

"Perhaps Kendall."

"Kendall? Who's Kendall?"

"You know Kendall, Isabelle."

"Are you talking about that anorexic who fetches coffee? You cannot be serious."

"She's now a junior agent."

"I don't care. Kendall is seven years old."

"She's at least twenty-six and very intelligent. And she knows how to reach Gen Z."

"Forget Kendall," she said through clenched teeth. In the space of five minutes, she had come to hate Fern. "My mother is dead."

"And I am very sorry for that."

"Yes, I know. The orchid."

They sat in silence for a moment, Isabelle glaring at Fern as he rubbed his temples. She wanted to storm out of his office, to tell him to fuck off. But the most horrible thing was that she was trapped; Isabelle needed him.

"Let me ask you a question—and I need you to be honest with me," she said. "Brutally honest."

"All right."

"Do you think I have talent?"

"Isabelle—"

"Because if the answer is no, then just tell me, and I'll find something else to do with my life—I don't know what, but something—and stop torturing myself. Stop torturing you."

"Yes," said Fern tiredly. "Yes, yes, I do think you're talented, Isabelle." Fern put his palms together and rested his chin on his thumbs, his lips on his forefingers, and closed his eyes. "Honestly, I never agreed with—" He stopped and shook his head.

"Never agreed with what?"

"Nothing. I am sorry that we find ourselves in this position now."

"You and me both."

"Let's keep perspective here. You want to come up with a book that's going to have editors going wild to buy it, not something we can manage to squeak through and sells, like, two copies. That won't do you any good—it'll be even harder to sell the next one. You can only be a virgin once, my dear."

Isabelle snorted.

"So if it takes more time to get it right, so be it."

"More time? More time? It's already been so much time, Fern," Isabelle shouted, more forcefully than she'd meant to.

"Maybe you need to take a breather. Take yourself to a beach, get an umbrella drink. A massage. Decompress."

"An umbrella drink? That's what you think I need?" The rage that churned through her, throbbing at her temples, vibrated in her voice. "I can barely afford an umbrella drink at the corner bar, much less some Caribbean getaway."

Fern winced perceptibly at the reference to money. He probably thought she was being hyperbolic. No one believed that Ward Manning's daughter could be strapped.

"Look," said Isabelle, trying to recompose herself. "We need to figure out a way to make this book work."

"Isabelle, I don't—"

Isabelle put up her hand. "Fine. What if I turned the next draft into something much more commercial? The pages I already have could trend in that direction, I think, with a little finesse. Something like, maybe, I don't know, James Patterson?"

"What are you talking about?"

"Maybe I could write a thriller. Add an element of crime, mystery."

"Isabelle." Fern looked as if he'd eaten something sour. "Come on."

"What?"

"This is unbecoming, sweetheart."

"Clearly what I'm doing is not working."

"You want to write like James Patterson? Murder investigations and political conspiracies? Well, great, but please enlighten me on your experience with these topics."

"I'd figure it out."

"I don't think this is your bag, doll. Let's not grasp at straws here."

Isabelle looked down. "Please don't give up on me."

"Isabelle . . ."

"Fern, you know as well as I do what dumping me will do. Everyone assumes that being Ward Manning's daughter gives me this huge advantage. Ha," she spat. "If you dump me—because let's call a spade a spade, that's what you plan on doing here—it's even worse. 'She's Ward Manning's daughter. Ward Fucking Manning. She had every advantage and couldn't even keep an agent. She must be a freaking idiot.'" This was the rub of being who she was. Anything good that happened was because of her connections; anything bad was in spite of them.

Fern looked down and massaged the back of his neck.

"If you leave me, it's not just leaving me, it's ending my career, you know that, right?"

"Fine, Isabelle. Fine," he said. "Let's try this one more time."

Isabelle closed her eyes. She had convinced him. But in place of relief, she felt the paltriness of her victory. She'd expected to leave this meeting with a plan to finish and sell her manuscript. Instead, she'd been put on probation, groveling to keep an agent who'd once pursued her with the ardor of a fairy-tale suitor. She had gained nothing. She had only not lost everything. At least, not yet. So Isabelle swallowed and said, "Thank you, Fern."

Fern nodded. "Do not attempt any James Patterson. Please."

"Okay."

"All right. But." Fern raised a finger in the air. "If your revision isn't something I feel I can sell, we'll part ways. No more of this."

"Deal."

"All right." He sighed heavily, his face tired. Their conversation had made Fern look suddenly badly in need of fillers. "Well, doll, you better get to it."

Brian

Brian took a sip of his lukewarm deli coffee. He'd spent two nights at the office this week, and his body was becoming inoculated to the effects of caffeine. That morning he'd had two double espressos before he got to the office, and three empty blue-and-white deli cups now sat on his desk, which was a complete and total mess. Brian hated that. Some lawyers—a lot actually—could work amid a tangle of binders, filings, and loose sheets on their desks. He knew a few whose offices looked like something out of an episode of *Hoarders*. The scene repulsed him, but he'd also wondered if an ability to think in such conditions was a sign of genius, a mind that could cut through chaos like a hot knife through butter. He'd wondered if his brain was inferior because it needed organized piles, a workspace free of clutter, pristine and Clorox-wiped, in order to function properly. Brian had a conference with the judge in two hours, and no time to get all Marie Kondo, but he stood up and began tossing things into the recycling bin under his desk and shuffling his papers into order.

The trial for which Brian had been preparing for over a year was set to start next week. Brian was prosecuting members of a sprawling drug cartel who'd orchestrated the smuggling of a massive quantity of cocaine into the United States and ordered the killing of dozens of people in the process. The case had been built on a web of cooperating witnesses, and it was part of Brian's job to wrangle and manage them so that they did not end up poisoned or kidnapped and were kept relatively content while sequestered in prison or small border towns near Canada until trial. The case had gotten a lot of publicity—it was juicy, with good characters. In the right hands, it could make a great book.

His desk clean, Brian began reviewing his arguments for the evidentiary hearing, mouthing out the words in a barely perceptible whisper, when his cell phone buzzed. He glanced at the number and considered ignoring it—he really had no time. But he picked up.

"Hey, can't really talk."

There was a long silence in which Brian could hear the hum of street noise and the beep of a car backing up, and then what sounded like a shuddering sigh.

"Everything okay?"

"Um, no."

"It's loud where you are. What's going on?"

"My agent tried to dump me."

"What? Fern?"

"Yes. He's tired of working with me, watching me fail." Isabelle's voice cracked.

"Oh, Iz, I'm sorry. Forget him, okay? This is just a hiccup. You are an amazing writer." Brian believed this, but in all the years of their friendship, the only piece of Isabelle's writing Brian had ever been allowed to read was the *New Yorker* story, the one that they were no longer permitted to talk about because it made Isabelle too sad. But even from that single piece of writing, he could see that Isabelle was the real thing. Brian admired how Isabelle could turn some peripheral almost-thought into words, a detail that his own outcome-oriented mind would zip past, but which he nevertheless recognized immediately as true. Like the burnt paper smell of takeout rice. He thought about that every time he allowed himself chicken and broccoli at work. She had taught him that it was the details that matter in writing.

"Hey. Don't take it so hard," Brian said now. "It's going to be okay."

"Can you come meet me?"

"Now? Where are you?"

"Yes. In midtown. At a bar. Or outside of a bar. I've been drinking. And I just had a cigarette."

"I'm at work, Isabelle."

"Brian, please."

"I have to be in court in two hours. I have no way of leaving."

"But I have no one else to call. My mother . . ." Isabelle trailed off into sobs.

"I know, I know. I am so, so sorry. If there were any way for me to be with you, I would, Isabelle. You know that. But I have to be in front of a judge. I would get fired if I missed this." Brian had dropped everything so many times for Isabelle. He'd once flown home early from a bachelor party because Isabelle's first book had not sold and she'd needed him to sit on her couch, watch *Law & Order: SVU*, and eat ice cream with her. And there were all the nights he'd spent in his twenties at Doubles or some pretentious benefit, enduring her friends with names like Tantivy or Halstead. He could not blame Isabelle for expecting that he would once again be at her disposal. And, ironically, the one time he could not acquiesce was the time she needed him most legitimately.

"Look, how about this?" he said. "I can't leave right now. I can probably get out of here by eight. I might have to bring some work with me, but I could come over to your place, we can order in, and talk this over. How does that sound?"

Isabelle breathed in. He could picture her, looking up, trying to stop crying.

"Why don't you get a cab? I can stay on the phone with you while you ride home." He really had no time to do that, but he'd manage. "Then you can get into bed and take a nap."

"Take a nap? A nap? Like a toddler?"

"You just sound like you could use a rest."

"You think *rest* is going to fix this?"

"No. I just—Isabelle . . . I'm sorry, I'm just trying to help." There was a long pause. "Hello?"

"It's fine." Isabelle's voice was suddenly closed and sharp.

"Don't be like that. Work with me here. Maybe I can get out by seven if I hustle."

"Forget it," she said. "I'm just going to go to Sag Harbor."

"Huh? Where did that come from?"

"I keep putting it off, but I'm just going to go now. You know, since you're busy." She was punishing him, pulling away because he couldn't be what she wanted at the exact minute she wanted it.

"Isabelle, really? Do you want to do that?"

"Yes. It's fine. I'm going to go."

"I could come if you wait—"

"No thanks. Talk to you later."

Brian heard the click of the phone, and she was gone.

Sebastian was displeased.

"There's barely anything here," he said. "And how could the half-finished Cusack have just disappeared?"

"It may turn up."

Aiden's agent regarded me for a long moment. The man always had a particular leering way about him.

"Look," he said, "I know Aiden left you in a bit of a bind financially."

I snorted. "That's an understatement."

Aiden had bequeathed me a level of debt beyond my worst fears. The credit cards, many opened without my knowledge, the charge accounts all over town, added up to more than the sum of our paltry nest egg. My income as an art consultant would barely cover the interest. My lawyer had mentioned the word "bankruptcy" and he was not even considering what I would need to support my mother.

"Anything we find now—even a little sketch," said Sebastian, "would be worth a lot now that he's . . ."

"Dead?"

"Yes, dead." Sebastian looked at me and cocked his head for a long moment. "Livia, I'm sure you know where the secret hiding places are. And I bet if you looked, looked really hard, you would discover something." Sebastian continued to stare, his raised eyebrows like a lengthy ellipses.

"Yes," I said finally. "I might."

Sebastian smiled for the first time since he'd entered the studio. "Like you said, something may turn up."

I let Sebastian out and stood alone in the room, inhaling the familiar mineral fume of paint undercut with rubber cement. I would list the place, but not just yet. Sebastian had given me the impetus—and, if I read him right, the green light—to do what I'd wanted to do. Yet fear tightened around my throat. This self-doubt was what had separated me from Aiden. He never questioned his genius; the world was always the problem in his eyes. But for my own preservation, for my mother's, I needed to be like him and stop being afraid.

10

Sag Harbor, 2017

Ward

Isabelle was set to arrive in ninety minutes. It was just enough time to prepare for her surprise visit, especially because there was little chance that the Jitney was running on schedule. That bus was never, ever running on time. Isabelle had little choice in transportation. Ward's daughter hadn't bothered to get her driver's license until she was nearly twenty years old, and she used it almost exclusively to tool around the local roads of the Hamptons. She avoided highways, any drive that involved merging or changing lanes. This was one thing that bothered Claire more than him. She scolded Isabelle about being "one of those women" who can't drive, but without measurable effect. Enduring the indignities of the Jitney—the smell of heavy, synthetic deodorizer mixed with urine that wafted from the restroom, the dwarfish little bottles of water, the entitled women using seats for their handbags—seemed reason enough to just buck up and get over it, but his daughter dug in. She was stubborn that way. And stubbornness wasn't a bad thing. It was why Isabelle kept at it with the writing, why she—like him—did not quit. It was, in fact, Isabelle's stubbornness that would make the little gamble he made years ago pay off.

• • •

When Ward had gotten rid of the obvious mess in the kitchen and living room by stuffing the old newspapers and takeout containers in the trash and dirty clothes in a closet, he returned to his office. He closed the window, turned on his monitor screen, and opened his email. There was a new one from his editor asking for chapters, "anything he had to show." Ward responded he was deep in the draft and preferred to wait until he had a more finished product, probably sending the poor man into paroxysms of anxiety. Not unwarranted. Ward was still thrashing about on the page. He felt at times he was writing his own nightmare, an alternate future without him in it. And he was forgetting words again. Silly, nothing words. Something wasn't right. It terrified him. Perhaps this was why Ward had been so amenable to a pleasant distraction.

Ward heard the ding of his Outlook and felt the now familiar accompanying zip of serotonin. He turned to his screen and saw this was indeed the one he had been waiting for. He double-clicked on the subject "Re: Hi."

Dear Ward,

Receiving your reply was the highlight of my year—maybe my life! Lol! I wished I reached out to you years ago—I just never thought that you would respond! I'm so flattered you think I "got" your books. Wow. I might frame your email. Seriously!

You asked what my favorite was. Gosh, that's a tough one. Probably American Dream. I could read that over and over.

Can you tell me about what you are working on next?? I CANNOT WAIT to read it!

And, I hope this isn't too personal, but I read about your
wife passing away. My sincere condolences. I hope you are
holding up okay and you've got someone looking after you.
You mentioned you're in Sag Harbor, so I've sent something to
your house (not a stalker ☺, just in real estate). I think you'll
like it.

I just can't get over it. Is this really you?

Sincerely,
Diane

Diane Dunmeyer's initial email had reached him through the batch of messages forwarded by his agency. She'd written months ago to tell him how much his books had meant to her, how she'd found one at a hotel she'd been staying at, and it had changed her life and gotten her through her divorce years before. Ward had never before responded to a fan's message. But he had never been in the position he now found himself. And just reading the words was no longer enough. Now he wanted engagement, discussion. More. More. More. When Diane wrote in her initial letter, "Your books make me feel feelings I didn't know I had," it made Ward feel like god. And that was Ward's favorite feeling.

He could not help but notice from the thumbnail picture next to Diane's name that she was probably mid-fifties, pert and blond, with a big smile and bigger hair. Ward had a weakness for women who had just a touch of floozy in them. You could take the boy out of the country . . . and all that.

Despite what most people assumed, Ward had never actually been unfaithful to Claire. Ward loved the way Claire looked, all Grace Kelly and Catherine Deneuve. He remembered the first time he saw her in that stuffy club, how refined she was, how flawless, how he'd eavesdropped intently to learn her name. Claire. Claire Cunningham. Even having sex with her felt highbrow. Nothing turned him on like making her—the elegant prom queen—lose it in bed. They'd had a spark that lasted well into their marriage. And it might have lasted longer if it weren't for what happened to Isabelle in Jamaica. After that, Claire never had the same abandon. And things between them were different. In the later years of their marriage, Ward had flirtations with many women, an attractive teaching assistant, a precocious student. Ward enjoyed his reputation as a tomcat, so he did nothing to squelch the rumors of his infidelity. But Ward knew he didn't have it in him to cross the line; even after all these years, a part of him still couldn't believe he'd ended up with a woman as classy as Claire.

Ward read over Diane's email again. This was where to let it go, his ego stroked, this nice little exchange complete. He rolled his chair away from his computer and picked up a section of the *Sag Harbor Express*. But he couldn't interest himself in any of the articles, even the crime blotter, which usually included at least one DWI of someone he knew. Ward checked his watch. Still another hour before he needed to leave to pick up Isabelle. Ward wheeled himself back to the desk. What the hell.

Dearest Diane,
You're not dreaming. It's really me. . . .

Isabelle

Sitting on the bus, the beers she'd downed after meeting with Fern now sloshed unpleasantly in her stomach, she smelled badly of cigarettes, and the itchy synthetic fabric of the seat had pricked up hives on the back of her legs through her leggings. Isabelle watched the highway exits count up, bringing her closer and closer to the house. The afternoon light was warm and golden over the trees that were beginning to lose their leaves. Going to Sag Harbor to find the keepsakes her mother had left for her would only devastate Isabelle further. But there was no going back. It would be better to get it over with, to bring on the misery herself rather than stew in anticipated devastation. And it wasn't as if things were going particularly well as it was.

Isabelle had packed quickly and forgotten to bring a book, which was probably some Freudian something. She reached into the seat pocket in front of her and took out *Hamptons Magazine*, an oversized glossy with articles about where to find a private Keto chef for your toddler or how to choose the right helicopter service to your East End manse. Isabelle flipped through the pages of party pictures, and then she came to it. A full-page photograph of Darby Cullman staring into the camera, chin resting on his hand, as he sat on a bushel of hay. Next to this idyllic farmscape was the headline, **Author Darby Cullman Finds Peace in a Refurbished Sagaponack Barn.** Several pages went on to describe how Darby had purchased and transformed his barn into his "place of zen" by using "reclaimed wood" and other "socially conscious materials." Further photos showed him in a cowboy hat standing in a field next to a mid-pant Raymond Carver. The article culminated in a picture of Darby in his signature plaid shirt and talisman necklace, staring off into the distance as he straddled a bright green tractor. Isabelle threw the magazine on the floor, got up, locked herself in the cramped bathroom, and vomited.

In the hours since her meeting with Fern, a thought had begun to circle, and it now descended upon her in all its glory. Despite all of her work and all of her desires, there was no successful novelist inside her. She was a middle-aged person who drank too much and puked on a midday Jitney en route to ask her father for money. This day was not an aberration, this was not a red herring. This was who she was. And this was her life. It felt sometimes to Isabelle that she was too late. Not just with her book, but in a deeper, more cosmic way. She had missed some vital connection from one life phase to the next. She was thirty-five years old, with no career and no children. What place does the world have for a woman like that?

The bus crawled along 27 until it hiccupped to a stop in Bridge-hampton, where her father always picked her up because the Sag Harbor route required a transfer. She used to love the car ride back to the house with her father. Something about sitting side by side, without the pressure of facing each other, allowed for some of their most effortless exchanges. But the beauty had resided in the inherent limit; once the ride was over, they would get out of the car and Claire would be there, diffusing the pressure Isabelle always felt around her father, a pressure to live up to his standards, his ideal of who his daughter should be. An entire visit, just the two of them, felt overwhelming, like staring directly at a bright light.

Isabelle could see him now, standing in front of the bench out-side the Bridgehampton Community House. She knew how this went. If they hadn't already, soon other people in the waiting crowd would start nudging elbows, motioning with their chins, mouthing, *Do you know who that is?* Braver souls would approach him, shak-ing his hand and telling him how much they loved his work. Ward pretended afterward to be put out, but these encounters were the reason he arrived early and never waited in the car. The reason he wore his red glasses and grew his hair. This recognition was her father's life force, the nutrient that sustained him.

Over the years, Isabelle had tried to imagine what it would be like to have a dad whom no one recognized, one who didn't have people lining up for a signed copy of his book, a hero only in the tiny confines of his family. Isabelle had always felt sorry for friends with normal parents, ones who were doctors or lawyers, boring people whose creative outlets consisted of evening pottery classes or needle-pointing throw pillows. Isabelle was the daugh-ter of a real artist, a famous artist, and she was of him, his genetic material tucked deep in the fibers of her own DNA. It was difficult to exaggerate how exceptional it had felt to be the only child of a world-renowned writer.

And how much it had fucked with her.

Isabelle had one particular memory of her childhood that lived permanently at the periphery of her consciousness. The book party for *Nightingale Call*. The room glittered with half-empty wineglasses and pulsed with the raucous purr of adults on third drinks. At the end of his toast, Ward had called Isabelle up to where he was standing and hoisted her onto his shoulders. Isabelle felt that tingling zip in her stomach she later came to associate with roller coasters, as everyone clapped and cheered. The day after the party, a picture ran on Page Six of Ward carrying a beaming Isabelle on his shoulders with the caption, **Ward Manning and the writer's daughter**.

It felt to Isabelle—never more acutely than as she lined up in the bus aisle and shuffled off the Jitney that afternoon—that the rest of her life had been one big, frustrating attempt to live up to the promise of that moment.

Ward

Ward's first thought when he saw his daughter walk off the bus was that Isabelle no longer looked young. She'd lost weight, and he could see her bony clavicle exposed in her wide-neck sweatshirt underneath her open jacket. She was still beautiful, striking, but there were circles under her eyes and the heaviness around her mouth of an older woman. She looked sad, but more than that she looked tired. It was hard to see the cherubic, rosy-cheeked girl who'd once run circles around the house. Well, she was thirty-five. Isabelle had informed Ward of that when she'd called him on her birthday. Thirty-five was not old. Christ, he'd kill to be in his thirties again. Even his forties! But it was not truly youthful, either. At that age, no one marveled at how precocious you were when you accomplished something. There were no thirty-five-year-old prodigies.

"So," said Ward as they sat on the deck with drinks and cheese. The Mannings had vodkas outside until it was truly freezing, layering up in coats and hats and piling on thick, woolen blankets. Tonight, mid-October, a jacket and scarf were sufficient. "What are you reading?"

Isabelle sipped her drink. "In between books. You?"

"Same."

They sat in silence for a few moments.

"So did Irving mention anything to you?" Isabelle's question came out with a pop, like it had been bottled up and uncorked.

"About?"

"Fern suggested I should work with another agent."

"Really?" Ward wondered if Irving had said something and he'd forgotten.

"You know Fern. He was just being testy," said Isabelle quickly. "If he doesn't think he can sell my revision, we're going to part ways."

"I see. Well, if Fern isn't right for you, then you'll find someone else." Ward liked Fern well enough. He had been cooperative. But maybe it would be better for his daughter to start fresh with someone who did not know quite so much.

By the shore, there was a rustling in the grasses before a blur of orange fur shot out. "Ah, the beast. She's been over here all day." The obese Abyssinian cat at the shoreline was Claire's feline bête noire.

The cat climbed up the steps attached to the bulkhead and sauntered onto the Manning lawn. When Claire repeatedly found feces in the grass, she thought it must be raccoons or even a dog. But then she'd seen the cat in the act, crouching in her geranium planter. Claire did not take kindly to the defiling of her property. The cat belonged to their new neighbors. Claire asked them to keep the animal—who'd been saddled with the unfortunate moniker of "Miss Muffins"—in their yard, or better yet, indoors, but the request went unheeded. Claire had gone so far as to purchase a cat carrier and plan a capture. After many near misses, Miss Muffins had become a kind of obsession. What exactly Claire planned to do with the animal once in hand was a question Ward had never asked. Miss Muffins had proved too canny, so now he would never find out.

The days with his daughter suddenly stretched out before Ward. How long would she stay? Even a day or two felt like a grand, echoing expanse of time. Alone in his house, he could feel like he was simply in one of his writing black holes. Not that he was doing much writing. But with Isabelle there, it was harder to pretend that their lives had not been upended, that Claire was not really gone.

"You still have the boat," said Isabelle, motioning with her head to the little motorized dinghy tied up to the dock.

"It seems to be sticking around." Taking the boat in, covering it for winter, was an item on an ever-growing checklist that Claire would have taken care of had she been alive. Like calling to have the dishwasher fixed and the pool serviced. And buying new towels for the bathroom. And grocery shopping. Ward's strategy thus far had been avoidance and denial.

Isabelle stared straight ahead as she asked, "Did you ever think of not being a writer?"

Ward coughed on his drink. "Is this about Fern?"

"I don't know. Maybe."

Ward paused before he said, "No." He had begun putting stories to paper when he was eight years old. At the time, he didn't think of this as "writing"; he thought of it as escape from the neighborhood of rotted-out houses with rusted farming equipment out front; escape from the dilapidated school with its dank, sickly gray classrooms full of kids who'd already given up; escape from the oppressive stench of too-lateness that blanketed the town. His parents, only in their mid-thirties, but already with booze-brined livers and the whiff of death on them. They lived—if you could call it that—depressed and angry that life had not offered up something more than grinding, smothering poverty. Ward could not accept such a life. He would not. He spent most of his time reading at the public library. In middle school, he found an old copy of Chekhov stories. And a light was lit within Ward Manning. He would be a writer. He decided this because he understood that he was talented with words, but even more, he understood that writing was how he would survive the balance of his childhood. As a writer, Ward could be an observer, a visitor merely gathering material. What he endured no longer identified him. It was no longer real.

So, yes, he had always known he would be a writer. If he hadn't had that supreme conviction, he would have stopped so many times. When his mother laughed at his plan to go to Harvard. When he had to work two jobs to pay for his tuition. When he had to wait tables at night, so he could write during the day. Of course, there had been the early troubles. The unmentionable period that Ward's ego was nearly successful in muscling into his subconscious. Nearly.

"I thought so," said Isabelle.

"That doesn't mean it's *easy*. Writing is torture. Pure and simple."

"You don't have to remind me."

"This profession is about grit. You'll be better for this."

"I don't think you know what *this* is like."

"Hm." And then, because something inside him was straining to reach his daughter, he said the thing that haunted him but had not yet been voiced aloud. "But I do know what it's like to be closing in on eighty years old, trying to write what may well be my last book."

Isabelle turned to face him fully. "Are you retiring?"

"Not willingly. But I'm old. I'd be a fool if I didn't hurry up and say what I have to say."

Isabelle scowled, her expression briefly flashing to what she'd looked like as a child. "Dad. Don't talk that way. Please."

Ward wanted to tell his daughter that he loved her. That he was sorry they'd been left alone like this, and sorry for a lot of other things, too. But the feelings were too big to convert into words. If he were writing the scene, it would be the kind that should build gradually. He would need to put together a specific structure to support the emotional weight or it would buckle on the page, coming out trite and meaningless. He had not "earned it," to use the parlance of an editor. So he said, "I'm glad you still wear that necklace."

"Oh." Isabelle took the little square book between her fingers and tucked her chin in to examine it. "Me too."

"Come, it's getting dark," said Ward. "Let's go get something to eat."

11

New York, 1975

Claire

Ward had to be starving, but he didn't touch the bread basket that had been placed on the table between them. He had not left his apartment for nearly three days, and Claire was sure he was subsisting on little but canned beans and coffee. He could not write the ending of his book. Or at least not an ending that pleased him. And he was going off a cliff. He'd gone two days without sleep and at least twice as many without shaving, and his hair sprouted off his head in unwashed spikes. His eyes had a feral quality, and they darted about now as he gulped his second vodka while he and Claire waited for the third guest to arrive.

Claire and Ward had been seeing each other for nearly six weeks. Barely a few hours after Claire had left Ward's apartment the morning following their first date, Ward had called her.

"I like what you did," he'd said when Claire picked up the phone. Claire had felt a flush of satisfaction in her cheeks.

"Good," she'd said.

There was a silence before Ward said, "Let me make you dinner tonight."

Claire had returned to the apartment that evening. He'd fixed them a crude spaghetti and tomato sauce on his little stovetop that they ate directly from the pan while nude. Had Claire really thought that she'd never hear from Ward again? Didn't she know when she'd taken her pen to his work that she was guaranteeing another meeting? Would he have called her if she hadn't made her edit? Maybe not. But she had, and he did.

Nearly every day since, Claire left work and headed straight to Ward's apartment. They talked about books, about art, but mostly about Ward's own writing. She liked how seriously Ward took her, how smart she felt during their discussions. She liked how Ward made her feel in bed, too.

Ward and Claire often made love multiple times a night and didn't bother to put back on any clothing. Claire had grown up in a house where no one showed anything more scandalous than an elbow. She'd never seen her mother in a bathing suit, or her father out of long pants. Her parents maintained separate bathrooms and she didn't think they so much as undressed in front of each other. But Ward seemed to view indoor clothing as superfluous. His bare body was solid, muscular, but not without a pouch here or there. And he was hairier than Claire found ideal. But the overall impression was pleasing. It felt odd to remain dressed when Ward was naked. And Claire had no reason to hide herself. She might not want to be a country club beauty queen, but she looked like one, with her lithe, tennis-player figure.

Claire's sudden unavailability did not go unnoticed. Glenda was dubious of Claire's rapturous love affair with a waiter.

"But he's a writer," Claire had protested over the phone.

Glenda sighed. "Aren't they all?"

Glenda had showed up their first day at Vassar in a chauffeured Rolls-Royce. Her family was a media dynasty, and they had actually hung on to their money. She'd grown up in one of those households where generations of extreme wealth had given way to wild eccentricities. Her mother bred a special type of miniature zebra in a private zoo she had built on their fifty-acre property in Bellport,

Long Island. Her brother was a contortionist with Barnum & Bailey. Glenda could play the snob, but she had a kind, giving side that saved her from being a bad joke. In college, Claire came down with a bad case of mono, and Glenda had brought her dinner from her favorite diner each evening and kept her stocked in mystery novels. When Claire made a passing reference to her love of Fairfield Porter, Glenda gifted her with a compendium of his work at their next meeting. She was thoughtful that way. When the affair with Ward continued, Glenda became curious, insisting upon meeting him, and refusing to be put off. So this dinner was arranged. Looking now at Ward with his head in his hand, seeming to doze off, Claire regretted it.

It was not surprising to Claire that Ward was moody. He was an artist. He had a certain manic-ness to him, especially when it came to writing. There had to be a flip side. She had come to believe that Ward had genius; it was not fully developed, and it often hid under layers of insecurity masquerading as bravado, but it was there.

• • •

Claire reached out her hand and touched the one of Ward's that was lying on the table. "It's going to be okay."

Ward raised his tired eyes. "No, Claire," he said. "It's not."

"You'll write your way through this."

Ward shook his head. "You don't understand," he spat out bitterly. "The ending is shit. No one will publish this book with an ending like this. And even if they do, it'll get canned in reviews. I won't put this out into the world. I'd rather make myself a hemlock cocktail."

Claire sighed. This type of hyperbole had become increasingly commonplace the last few days. "Can I take a look?" Claire knew the gist of the ending, but Ward had been cagey about showing her the actual pages.

Ward glared at her. "The book isn't working," he'd said quietly but with conviction. "I'm going to rip it up and start over."

"Let's not get overly dramatic," said Claire, but Ward had put his head on the table, not listening. It was at this moment that the door to the tiny restaurant opened, and a woman ensconced in an arctic-level of fur walked in. Glenda spotted Claire and surged toward them.

Claire nudged him, and Ward raised his head weakly. He offered nothing by way of greeting. Glenda looked him up and down, unimpressed. "Claire mentioned you were the ruminating type," she said.

Claire kissed her friend on the cheek, and the two women sat down. "Ward's been on a writing tear, not getting much sleep."

"Ah," said Glenda, beckoning the waiter over to order a drink.

Ward apparently felt very little pressure to uphold the social contract to converse with the people at the same dinner table. Glenda and Claire spoke to each other, while Ward stared into his drink. After a while Glenda seemed to forget he was there, chatting with Claire and getting positively orgasmic about her chicken scarpariello. They were just paying the bill, so close to the end of the meal, when Glenda turned to Ward and asked, "So. When's this book of yours hitting the shelves?"

Ward looked at her with narrowed, bloodshot eyes. "Don't hold your breath."

"Ward's just about finished," said Claire.

"I'll never finish."

Glenda did not pick up the cue to drop it. "Uh-oh. Writer's block? I hear that can be quite maddening."

Ward made a noise somewhere between a grunt and a growl. Claire stood up and said, "Shall we?"

Ward went outside while Claire and Glenda bundled up by the coatrack. Glenda raised her eyebrows. "This is who you're not going to Europe for?"

Before Claire met Ward, she had told Glenda of her desire for a trip abroad. But now the desire to flee, once a hot-burning flame, had dwindled to embers. "He's having a hard time with the book. He's usually not like this."

Glenda shrugged. "Have fun with this. Do your little rescue fantasy or whatever this is, and then cut him loose. You don't really want all that." Glenda gestured in Ward's direction.

Ward certainly was a diversion, but Claire liked not knowing exactly where things would lead. Besides, nothing had been set in stone. She had time to make up her mind about Ward. Claire put her arm around her friend. "Thanks for coming downtown, Glenda."

. . .

Claire and Ward walked back to his apartment, where Ward lay down on the bed without a word of apology for his dinner performance. He curled up into a little ball. By the way his shoulders moved, Claire could've sworn he was crying. She knew better than to try to speak to him. When he stopped shaking, Claire realized he was no longer awake. She got into bed but could not manage to fall asleep. At one in the morning, she gave up.

She went and sat at Ward's desk, where she found the ending pages of the book, the ones she was not supposed to look at. Reading through them, Claire saw the problem. While Ward was good describing struggle, he was unskilled when it came to writing about success. It was still too much a fantasy for him. The scenes where the protagonist triumphs came out slick and false. Ward was trying to fix the ending with long, flourishy paragraphs on accomplishment, an exegesis on contentment. Claire frowned; if this was Ward's plan, he was right: He ought to give up. Ward conjured success like a single, one-dimensional thing. He did not understand that success does not make anyone purely happy. Claire had lived among the moneyed, the prominent, the well-known long enough to understand that success fills most people with a festering and corrosive self-doubt, a fear they'll be exposed to the world as an imposter. Triumph hardly ever leads to lasting satisfaction. How quickly a new rung of accomplishment becomes a floor. With new ceilings in sight, fresh competitors to vanquish, peace is elusive.

When Ward published this book, perhaps he would learn this for himself. If he ever published this book.

Claire sat at Ward's desk in gray-blue moonlight. She felt suddenly and acutely that this was the moment to leave him, this brooding, mannerless man. Ward might well be a genius, but lots of geniuses died lonely and unfulfilled in sad little New York apartments just like this one. Glenda might be right. Claire could see Ward growing bitter and mean, raging at the world because he could not set his own talent free. There would be little help for a man like him, one drawn so easily into the sinkhole of his discontent. Claire would only end up pulled into the mire.

And yet, she did not move from her seat.

In less than twelve hours, Claire would be engaged to the man she had very nearly abandoned without looking back.

12

Sag Harbor, 2017

Ward

The night Isabelle arrived in Sag Harbor, Ward slept fitfully. At some point he'd gotten up to pee. Feeling his way to the bathroom, he'd tripped on the rug and fallen heavily on his right elbow, bumping his head on the side of the bed frame. His arm was bruised, and he sported a bump on his head. Luckily, he still had enough hair to cover it. But Ward was shaken. In the morning, he went early to his office before Isabelle was awake, trying to lose himself in writing. He kept at it for an hour before turning away from his typewriter in frustration. Ward had been making progress, but a sense of mastery evaded him. It felt sometimes that this fictional woman he created was having a laugh at his expense. And now he was stumbling around like some geezer.

Later in the morning, Ward told his daughter he was going to play tennis. She seemed to believe him; he often played this late in the season. Ward got into the car and started west. In twenty minutes, he was out of the Hamptons, driving north on Route 24. Close by there were vineyards, antique shops, farms offering hayrides and hot apple cider, but none of that was on Ward's agenda.

Until that day, a major impediment to seeking a medical opinion had been that going to a neurologist in the city, some Cornell MD with a side entrance off Park Avenue, was out of the question. At his age, doctors' offices were like Studio 54 in its heyday; full of everyone he knew. Ward Manning could not risk it. So he found a doctor in Riverhead online that morning and made an eleven a.m. appointment, at once relieved he could get in so quickly and dubious of the competence of any medical professional who didn't book up weeks in advance.

As he drove, Ward considered what he might say to Isabelle when he returned home. A feeling had been brewing since Claire died, and it had coalesced into a thought with Isabelle in the house. It was not good for him to be alone. And Isabelle seemed as if she could use the company too. Grief radiated from his daughter. He thought of suggesting that she move out here for a little while. He'd set her up with an office in the guest room and they would both work on their books. If Isabelle were in the house, he would surely become more disciplined. He'd sell it like a writing retreat. And perhaps it could be a new chapter for them.

Ward desired to be closer to Isabelle, but the idea also terrified him. Isabelle and Ward had their roles. Ward's was to be the celebrated writer. And Isabelle's was to venerate him. This was how it had been since she was old enough to talk. Isabelle probably didn't remember this, but in fourth grade, she'd been assigned to write a profile of someone she admired. Isabelle chose him. And in her opening sentence she'd written, "My father is a brilliant writer." Just stated it as fact, no embarrassment, no toning it down to be humble or polite. How he loved her for that. Ward still had her little report, typed up in Courier on her Apple IIGS. It was what he pulled off the shelf when he was in bad need of a boost. In all his reading of fan mail, he had never found a letter that topped Isabelle's.

If he and Isabelle were to have a more fulsome relationship, Ward would have to step down from his pedestal. But right now, as he struggled to hold on to the career that was slipping away, he needed someone to believe he was a superhero.

Ward turned onto Route 25 and saw signs for Splish Splash waterpark and Tanger Outlets. He'd entered a rough, junky terrain of big-box stores and strip malls. Ward pulled into a drab, beige shopping plaza. This couldn't be the right place. But as he cruised along, he saw the unassuming storefront and the name on the glass.

Dr. Schneider, Geriatrics

Ward parked the car but did not move. This was silly. Things weren't *that* bad. But instead of backing out, Ward opened the door, because he knew that, in fact, they were.

13

Sag Harbor, 2017

Isabelle

Over twenty-four hours in Sag Harbor had not given Isabelle the courage to go to her mother's dresser. Here, in the house, so close to what Claire had left for her, Isabelle's terror was only amplified. She kept hearing her mother say "sentimental" and knew this really meant excruciating. So, instead, she let herself become consumed with something else. Her father. Without Claire, he was changed. Tall, with his large head and unruly hair, her father had always loomed. But it was as if the house had grown bigger around him, and he was diminished inside it. He was soft, almost out of focus. And more human in an unsettling way. During the course of drinks the first evening, he'd had some brie stuck to the corner of his mouth that Isabelle didn't have the heart to point out. There was something lonely and heartbreaking in watching her father spoon takeout onto plates, as he had probably been doing alone all these weeks out here. And most upsetting, he'd come close to admitting he was having trouble with his writing.

Ward had left early to play tennis. Isabelle used the time to write, but her fears were compounded when that afternoon, Ward returned entirely morose, mumbling about a broken serve. He locked himself in his office, coming out only for a drink once it had gotten dark. At seven o'clock, Isabelle realized that there was no plan for dinner, and quickly made them a batch of spaghetti with garlic and oil. Her father had said he needed to work again and left her with the dishes. When he did not reemerge, she had retired to her own room in hopes of falling asleep.

Instead, she now lay awake, blinking her eyes in the thick country darkness. When she was a little girl, used to the unrelenting illumination of the city, she hated the dark of Sag Harbor. Her room in the house had to be lit up with nightlights for her to sleep. But the little Glow Worms and ballerinas had been thrown out ages ago, and Isabelle's room—converted to guest quarters—was pitch-black. Isabelle looked at her phone. Nearly eleven thirty. Brian might still be up, but after hanging up so rudely on their last call, she'd better not risk waking him. *Hey,* she texted, *I'm sorry about yesterday.* Isabelle waited hopefully for the undulating ellipses. Nothing.

She'd forgotten to bring up water, and her throat was dry. Isabelle got out of bed and walked out of her room. The house was quiet. But when Isabelle padded down the stairs to the kitchen, there was her father, standing in his pajamas at the counter, his back to her. From the fluorescent lights underneath the cabinet, she could see his head was bent down, focused on something. She stepped closer, but he remained unaware of her presence. Isabelle watched him methodically lay out pills. There had to have been a dozen. He took a few at a time, drinking from a large tumbler of water. In his slight profile, she could see his Adam's apple working as he swallowed.

After a moment, Isabelle coughed lightly. Her father swung around, using the counter to steady his balance.

His eyes were wide, startled. "Oh hi. Hi, Isabelle," he said, as he quickly scooped up the remaining pills like jacks. "Just having a little snack."

Isabelle nodded, choosing not to point out that there was no food anywhere. "I needed a drink," she said. She retrieved a glass from the cabinet and filled it at the tap. Afterward, they stood there looking at each other for a moment before Ward said, "All right, sleep well, darling," cuing her to leave.

"You too, Dad."

Isabelle went back to her room and got into bed. She pulled her covers up to her chin and stared into the blackness, her body shivering, though the room was warm. It all made sense now. The way he looked. Sequestering himself in Sag Harbor. All the talk of the book being his last. Her father was sick.

Isabelle should have suspected. Her parents were always this way; hoarding away private things, doling out information in bits and pieces, maintaining secrecy until it was no longer tenable. Ward thought everything was his own private business. And Claire was no better. As much as Claire disavowed the family she'd come from, a deep, WASP-y repression, tucked away from the prying gaze of self-awareness, sat at her core. She did not talk about her family. She did not really talk about her life before Isabelle at all. And she sometimes had an odd sense of what facts required disclosure. Claire had not bothered to tell Isabelle she had knee surgery while Isabelle was gone at summer camp. Isabelle got off the camp bus horrified to see her mother with a cane. And Isabelle had always assumed her paternal grandmother was long dead until Claire announced one morning that Ward had left for her funeral.

As Isabelle lay in bed, the narrative pieced itself together. Her mother had been waiting for an opportune time to begin letting Isabelle know—not all at once, little by little—that Ward was ill. But then Claire got sick herself. Fuck, of course. This was why Claire was so adamant that Isabelle find what Claire had left her. This was why Claire had told Isabelle, "Do not count on your father." It wasn't just that Ward was hard-hearted, fully capable of tossing away a cherished piece of third-grade pottery; Claire knew Ward was sick and could soon be impaired.

When Isabelle finally drifted off to sleep, she had terrible dreams. Her father shriveled in a hospital bed, Isabelle at his side sobbing. She tried to tell him over and over that she was sorry, sorry for something too large and profound to put into words, not an action, but her very being. Her voice failed her. Her father did not meet her gaze, looking straight ahead, his face wooden, skin grayed and waxy. If she had any doubt of what was happening, the dreams confirmed what she already knew. Ward was not just sick; he was dying.

14

New York, 2017

Brian

Brian heard the buzzing and saw the name but resisted, proving a point. Not grabbing at his phone meant that he had not been waiting for her to reach out since she'd hung up on him the day before. Brian finished with the paragraph he was working on before he allowed himself to open her text. Isabelle was sorry about yesterday. She did not address not responding to all the texts he'd sent checking in afterward. Brian was a little sick of the sorry-after-the-fact routine. And Isabelle's tendency to only shift her attention to him when it was convenient for her. Or when she needed something. Maybe he wasn't being fair. She was having a rough go. But he just couldn't avail himself to her that easily. Not yet. Brian breathed in, debating whether to send a curt *no problem* or not respond at all, which could seem peevish. Brian was always having these little internal standoffs when it came to Isabelle, as if he could somehow recalibrate their relationship with the right texting game. What Brian really aspired to was responding to Isabelle without a second thought, the way he interacted with every other human. He sometimes asked himself what he would do if it were Matt or Scott or any one of his bonehead friends. Then felt pathetic that sending a text to Isabelle required mental role-play. Nonchalance could not be faked. Annoyed, he put his phone down. Let her wait. Given the late hour, he could always say he'd been sleeping.

Though Brian was in bed, he was not sleeping. He was writing. And he had gotten a good rhythm going. With a few more hours, he could finish what he'd started. And he'd be one step closer to where he wanted to go.

I carried Aiden's heavy leather portfolio up the rickety elevator to Sebastian's SoHo office. I'd come on a Saturday, so the building was empty.

"Livia, darling," Sebastian greeted me theatrically, leading me into the office. "Let's see, let's see." He gestured to a cleared desk space. I removed the canvas from my bag and laid it out.

Sebastian's eyes widened. "It's finished," he whispered.

"Indeed." We both took in the rendering of an earnest John Cusack.

"What luck."

"Yes, what luck," I said. Sebastian smirked but said nothing.

"There's one more."

"Oh?" Sebastian arched an eyebrow. "Goody."

I made room on the desk, and carefully took the second canvas from the bag. Sebastian let out a genuine gasp. "Ann-Margret."

"Looks like about the time of *Bye Bye Birdie*," I said. "If I had to guess."

"Retro . . . A different choice from Aiden's usual fare."

"Do you think anyone will be interested?"

"We'll see, won't we?"

I'd just gotten the bill for my mother's latest ER trip—an overnight stay at Lenox Hill that cost as much as a week at the Four Seasons—so I hoped very much Sebastian could make something happen.

"I am so glad you found these, Livia," said Sebastian. "You always did have the magic touch."

When I got home it was only mid-afternoon, but I poured myself a glass of wine. After all my wondering whether Sebastian had understood from the very first portrait what had actually transpired, the role that I had played, I now had my answer: he had. There was a relief in confirmation. Along with no small amount of rage. He had known all along. And he had known what people would've said about me if I tried to tell the truth: *So Livia thinks she's the mastermind behind Aiden's success? Oh please, a likely story.*

And now, together, we were breathing new life into my deception.

In the weeks since Aiden was gone, I'd spent a lot of time wondering why I'd stayed with him. My life might have been easier if I'd chosen a different sort of man for a husband. I had been close to leaving once, but then my mother had a stroke. I'd been too scared to lose the income Aiden's portrait work was bringing in. But there was something else that had kept me from leaving.

As crazy as it sounds, I kept hoping that Aiden might one day decide to paint a portrait of me. He never did civilians, but I had this silly idea that if he painted me, he would look at me. And maybe he would see me again, the fiery girl he'd once loved. And what had been broken could start to mend. Of course, I never mentioned this to Aiden. And perhaps this was unfair.

My phone began to ring.

"Hello?"

"Livia, it's Sebastian. I have news."

"Pray tell."

"I have interest from multiple buyers. Big, beautiful buyers."

"You're joking."

"Nothing sells like death."

"Apparently."

"Find more, Livia," he said. "As many as you can."

15

Sag Harbor, 2017

Isabelle

The next morning, Isabelle and her father had endured an awkward breakfast before he said he was going for a walk. Neither had brought up what had happened in the night. Isabelle was not emotionally prepared to have that conversation and get confirmation of the worst possible scenario. She needed to reconsider her plans. Obviously she was not asking her sick father for money. That request would have been odious enough when he was well. She'd live on ramen. She'd go without internet. The only thing that mattered now was that she write her book and write it in time. It was clear to Isabelle that Ward pitied her; he was ashamed his only child could barely keep an agent, let alone publish a book. Why else could he barely look her in the eye? Why else did he keep fleeing whatever room she was in? He did not want her here.

Books were the exclusive medium through which she and her father communicated. The ones she wrote to him in crayon; Ward's own books; their critiques of other writers' work. If Isabelle did not publish her novel, she would never have the chance to speak to him in the only language he understood.

So she would fulfill her mission to gather up what her mother left her, then get on the next Jitney home.

Isabelle was on her way to her parents' room when the doorbell rang. "Argh," she said aloud. She peered out the kitchen window and saw that a FedEx guy was standing on the front porch. Isabelle took her coffee and opened the door.

"Sign here," said the delivery guy, offering her a touch screen and a stylus. The overnight box was addressed to her father and was crisscrossed with tape reading, *OPEN IMMEDIATELY.* A sweet, cookie smell wafted from the box.

"Do you know what this is?"

"I just deliver it, lady."

"Yes, sorry, stupid question."

Isabelle took the box into the kitchen and impulsively retrieved a knife from the wooden block. It said "immediately." She cut the tape and opened the box. Underneath a layer of pink tissue paper was a large Tupperware container. There was a note on pink stationary taped on top.

Dear Ward! My snickerdoodle pie fixes everything.
Enjoy! XO Diane.

Who the fuck was Diane? And what the fuck was snickerdoodle pie? Isabelle opened the Tupperware container and found a giant mound of pastry with white icing, like the kind on cinnamon rolls, on top. It smelled amazing. But she closed the container. "Diane" could be some psycho hell-bent on poisoning her father. Though Isabelle suspected she was not actually that. She put the Tupperware on the counter and walked up the stairs.

Ward and Claire's room sat perched on its own, comprising the entire third floor with a big window overlooking the cove. Inside her parents' closet, Claire's summer dresses hung, crisp and perfectly lined up like soldiers at attention. Her mother had good style, understated and conservative, neutral tones punctuated by patterned scarves or tasteful costume jewelry. Despite her lineage, no pastels or Lilly Pulitzer. Isabelle ran her fingers over the stacked sweaters, all cashmere and downy soft. Claire could wear the same sweater for years without it pilling. Her mother was magical in small ways like that. Isabelle would save all of it. Even if she discovered a secret Chanel bag, Isabelle couldn't stand to sell what belonged to her mother.

Isabelle walked to the dresser and opened the top drawer. In the front, her mother's nightgowns were folded wallet-sized and laid out in overlapping rows. Isabelle packed them away, and then peered farther back in the drawer for what she'd been sent to find. She pulled each item out one by one. A tiny, petrified ballet slipper. A cache of Isabelle's drawings of "fancy ladies," women in ball gowns, always standing slightly on the diagonal. A quilted pouch full of seashells collected on Long Beach, still musky with salt. A crude ceramic scarab glazed in turquoise that Isabelle had made the year she longed to be Cleopatra. A decade's worth of Isabelle's homemade Mother's Day cards, arranged in chronological order. There were two photographs. One of Claire and Isabelle ice skating at Rockefeller Center. Another of them, years later, outside the fountain at the Met. Isabelle felt heat in her throat and behind her eyes. The sense of nostalgia was near violent. Isabelle's gratitude toward her mother for this time capsule was undercut by the knowledge that Isabelle would have to take up a mantle she was unready to assume. What she and Claire had shared—so often just the two of them—was now Isabelle's alone to keepsake.

When she'd carefully packaged all of it up and was about to close the empty drawer, she noticed a bulge in the blue and white contact paper patterned like china. She tried to smooth the lump down, but there was something caught underneath. Isabelle peeled back the paper, which came up easily as if someone had recently loosened it, and pulled out a manila envelope. She opened the top and slid out a stack of typed pages. What she was holding was unmistakably a manuscript. A square of paper clipped to the first page was her mother's heavy card-stock stationery, cMc engraved in navy ink at the top. Written on it in her mother's even, graceful hand were two words. *For Isabelle.*

16

Sag Harbor, 2017

Ward

Ward had not run for years, decades probably, but the motion felt familiar, a long dormant part of himself awakening. It was reassuring. There was some life in him yet.

He'd run long-distance track in high school. Each evening before dinner he'd take off from his house and run seven, eight, nine miles, down dirt roads lined with farmhouses slumping into the earth. He ran as long as he could, every minute on the road one that he was not inside the home teeming with mess, overflowing ashtrays, and his mother's ever-brewing resentment at his father, at him, at life. Barbara "Bobby" Manning had always been poor, but she had airs, a desire to rise above her station. She was tall and blond, striking. She looked a lot like Isabelle. And Claire, too, in a way. Bobby had believed that her face was her ticket. And it might have been. But she was careless and fundamentally self-loathing. She got pregnant and married Jess, Ward's father, a mean and reckless drunk. The predictable happened. Bobby and Jess spiraled into alcoholism, fought nastily, slurred profanities, and hurled whatever hard object might be at hand. As a child, Ward spent many nights on his knees cleaning up the shards of a broken wine bottle or some worthless figurine.

Jess always had big plans that led to him squandering what little money they had into some scheme or another. His failure rate did little to deter him. Jess was a shifting, unreliable presence, disappearing for weeks at a time, forcing Bobby to look for house-cleaning work or take handouts from whatever family member she could. Any redeeming personality traits were choked out by bitterness. The primary recipient of her vitriol was Ward. Even through her rotgut whiskey haze, she could see that, unlike her, Ward would get out. Bobby never missed an opportunity to belittle him. She nicknamed him "the idiot," claiming his good grades must be due to cheating. When Ward didn't make varsity football, Bobby had a field day. Ward was a loser. A pussy. A shame to the family. Her parting words when he left for Harvard were the most cutting of all. *You'll be back.*

But Ward would never go back.

In fact, he had already left long before he went to Harvard. Late at night when his parents were asleep—or god knew where—teenage Ward would sneak outside to the yard. He'd lie down in the grass and look up at the stars, comforted by the great vastness of the sky. In this position, he understood on a visceral level how much grander the world was than this one, tiny patch of earth. Ward would stay in the grass, eventually closing his eyes, levitating into the universe—above his house, his town, everyone he knew—vacuumed up into blackness, and Ward alone, floating, rising among the stars, his very own solar system.

◆　◆　◆

When he was too winded, Ward slowed down, but kept walking along the back roads. He continued over the bridge to the tiny hamlet of North Haven. In this part of town there were mansions, big, Hamptons-style gray shingles. If anyone asked, he'd denounce them as boring, but his heart could not help but swell for such a naked status symbol. Maybe he'd buy one. Live out his last chapter ensconced in a final trophy.

Ward had not written since he'd been to Riverhead. Writing required thinking, analyzing, and he wanted nothing to do with either. Any moment of quiet reflection could lead to reliving the scene at the doctor, hearing the words the doctor had said in his grating upper Midwest lilt. So instead of writing, Ward had been corresponding with Diane Dunmeyer and avoiding his daughter. But he had decided that when he got home, he would ask her to stay. And maybe he would let her in on what was happening.

Ward wound his way back to the house. Not seeing Isabelle in the living room or kitchen, he called upstairs. There was a rustling from her room and a loud shutting of a drawer. Isabelle opened the door to her bedroom and appeared at the top of the stairs.

"Are you all right?" he asked as Isabelle descended the stairs.

"Fine." Her eyes were wide, and her mouth twitched.

"What have you been doing?"

"Nothing."

"Nothing?"

"Reading."

"Ah. Anything good?"

"Yes."

"You'll have to tell me about it." He started to move toward the kitchen for some water. Isabelle followed behind him.

"Did Mom ever do any writing?"

"Your mother?"

"Yes, my mother. Your wife. Did she ever write?"

Ward stopped and looked back at Isabelle. "No. What are you talking about?"

"Are you sure?"

"Yes, I'm sure. Your mother wasn't suited to writing."

"She wasn't *suited*?"

"She could edit a bit."

Isabelle looked at him intently. "What did she edit?"

"Not much, really. A little of my work, on occasion."

"Mom was your editor?"

"No, nothing like that. She cast an eye over the first few. No heavy lifting."

"No one ever mentioned this."

"Wasn't much to mention."

"Why did she stop?"

"She got busy with other things. You. The charity. And by then I had other people reviewing my pages. Professionals." Claire had been a solid editor in her own way. She was a sharp grammarian and a cold-blooded killer of darlings. And there had been what she did for the ending of *American Dream* that night in his little apartment. She'd contributed to the early books, too. More than he liked to admit. But he outgrew her. At some point, without any overt discussion, he had stopped sharing drafts with her, and that was that. Working à deux wasn't the kind of thing one did when one was trying to be the greatest writer of his time. And besides, this mantle took more than good writing. It took persona. It took a careful and meticulous presentation of information. Claire knew. She knew, and she understood.

Isabelle was silent, staring into space, her lips moving slightly as if calculating something, entirely somewhere else. But when Ward walked into the kitchen, Isabelle followed a moment behind.

"Oh," said Isabelle. "That came."

Ward turned around and followed her gaze toward a giant Tupperware container.

"It said perishable, so I took it out of the mailing box."

"What is it?"

"A pie."

"A pie?" Ward looked back at Isabelle.

She nodded, not breaking eye contact. "From Diane."

"Oh. Okay. Thanks." Ward coughed. "Diane is, you know, just a friend."

"Right."

"Shall we venture out for lunch? I thought we could go to the Hotel." The American Hotel was where Ward planned to order them both kir royals and ask Isabelle to stay.

"I need to go back to the city."

"Oh? Today?" A sting of disappointment ran through him.

"Yes. I want to get to work."

Ward nodded. They stood in silence for a few moments. The words to invite his daughter to stay with him, to write together like a little artist colony for two were right there inside him, but he could not quite push them out. "All right, sweetheart," he said, adding, "That's probably for the best—I have a lot to do, too."

17

New York, 1982

Claire

Claire was thirty-nine weeks pregnant and under instruction to take it easy, not lift anything, and be generally slothful. She had tried for a day or two, but gave up. And today of all days, as she and Ward prepared for the television crew to take over their living room, Claire would not sit still. So far, the baby had not made any moves. Perhaps the fetus's amenability to remaining in the womb until the launch of Ward's third novel portended a congenial nature. But really, Claire didn't care if the baby—she had not found out if it was a boy or a girl—came out a sputtering, shrieking tyrant. She was having a child. At last.

Ward and Claire had been married for six years. Ward had proposed the morning after Claire stayed up all night rewriting the ending to *American Dream*. Ward knew a good editor when he saw one. With her rewriting of the ending, the book soared. She knew it would. And that's why she had stayed that night instead of running away. She might've been able to leave Ward, but she could not leave his work. And Claire was heartened that Ward had taken her help. His ego had not prevented him from seeing reason. When he asked her to marry him, she'd said yes because in that moment of elation over the completed book—a book she viewed as theirs together even though it bore Ward's name—it felt completely natural.

With Claire's treatment, the manuscript received multiple bidders. Soon after the book sold, Ward and Claire eloped. Claire's parents were somewhat put out that their only daughter had married a lineage-less man with what they saw as extremely limited financial prospects. But their disappointment was tempered by the relief of not having to foot the bar bill for all their gin-guzzling relatives at a wedding. The only person who needed making up to was not a family member at all.

Glenda expressed her hurt at being excluded from the marriage trip to Niagara Falls by aggressively lobbying Claire to get an annulment. She even went so far as to entrap Claire into a meeting with the lawyer who took care of the capricious marriages in the Van Dorn family (of which there were many). When her efforts proved fruitless, Glenda saw the writing on the wall: If she wanted to keep Claire, she had to accept Ward. But after that disastrous first meeting, it was difficult to kindle any genuine affection. Glenda thought Ward was a loser, and Ward, sensing as such, made no effort to pander to her. Claire had told him several times that Glenda was incredibly susceptible to flattery and it would take very little to win her over, but Ward was uninterested in even that minimal effort.

Ward and Claire barely knew each other when they got married. The only thing they had discussed at length was writing, along with many long postcoital conversations in which Ward expounded upon the meaning of life and asked Claire detailed questions about her family, a topic he found endlessly fascinating and returned to with great frequency.

So while she felt that she knew something of her husband's innermost desires and had shared with him intimate details of her upbringing, they had never talked about practical things that would shape their life together, like children. Then *American Dream* came out. It was a breakout hit. Ward's literary career was no longer theoretical. And they were no longer broke. With the proceeds from the book, Ward and Claire rented a two-bedroom near Gramercy Park and bought a modest house in Sag Harbor. Suddenly Claire was almost thirty. Having a child seemed like a logical next step. But when she raised the idea of getting pregnant with Ward, he looked at her for a long moment and said, "Oh. I didn't think you were like that." Claire bristled. Though, what did she expect? He was a man who never mentioned children; he clearly was not interested. So she put it aside as Ward worked on the next book. Having left the auction house job, she toyed with the idea of applying for a job as an editor somewhere. But then there was the trouble with Ward's second book.

Ward had not let Claire participate in the first draft of *Urban Idols*, the follow-up to *American Dream*. She sensed he wanted to do this one all on his own. But after he submitted it to his editor, it came back with a searing critique and a threat that the manuscript would be rejected by the publisher as it stood. Ward would be a one-hit wonder. When Claire read over the draft, she understood why. Ward's sentences were overwrought; long didactic tangents appeared in each chapter. Just as Claire had predicted, success had made Ward happy, but it had also paralyzed him. The book felt like a massive, showy attempt to prove brilliance. It was unreadable.

If there was genius in Ward's work, it was Claire who would have to excavate it, cut through the fat of ego to get to the meat. She stepped in again. And there was no room for anything but the book. They lived and breathed *Urban Idols* for a year. Ward worked in the morning, Claire reworked in the afternoon, and they hashed it out together over drinks and dinner, often returning to the pages until late at night. All the effort was worth it. *Urban Idols* became a worthy successor to *American Dream*. The book was met with critical praise and commercial success. Claire had done it again.

Under Ward's contract, he was under pressure to produce a third book quickly. He said he wanted some time with the idea before Claire saw anything. Ward was eager to prove his independence on this score. He holed up in his office and, six weeks later, he emerged with the opening chapters of his new work. Ward handed Claire the pages without further comment, other than a provocatively raised eyebrow. It took no more than the first chapter for Claire to realize what book Ward was writing. She walked into the living room, holding the yellow-lined notepad.

"So?" Ward asked.

"So? Ward. It's barely even fictionalized."

"I took some bits here and there."

"Bits? There's a lot more than bits," said Claire, incredulous. All that she had divulged to Ward between the sheets, every tiny detail about her family, was right in front of her. The lost wealth, the drinking, the houses filled with the smell of mildewed chintz, and the incessant rattle of ice cubes against crystal. In her shock, she found room to be impressed with her husband's recall and how he had nailed the decaying WASP milieu. But even the plotline of a pedophiliac Latin teacher who trades on connections and money to secure employment at a series of prestigious boarding schools had been pillaged from Claire's family secrets.

Ward went over and put his arm around her. "Come on, you know this will be a great book. I'll make sure to disguise everyone enough so no one wets their pants."

"Oh they do that anyway," snapped Claire. Beneath her joke, however, she was furious. She was within her rights to tear up the pages right there, make Ward go find his own damn material. He'd used her as a crutch, one who could spin his plot, his prose, his structure. Now he was stealing his subject matter from her, too. Claire hated most of her relatives, but it was not Ward's place to skewer them.

"No, Ward, you can't use this."

Ward looked shocked, as if Claire's objection had not been a possibility he'd considered. But of course he had, which was why he had hidden the pages until he had enough so that asking him to stop would be a sacrifice.

"You can't just take my stories."

"Claire, come on. This is good. You know this is good." He was not wrong. The writing was the best she'd seen from Ward.

Claire and Ward regarded each other, assessing who had the greater appetite for slugging this out. And then she had an idea. She could give him this. But it would cost him.

"Fine," said Claire. "I want a baby."

Ward looked at her. "A baby?"

She watched as the scale inside his mind weighed parting with the pages with which he had already formed a deep emotional attachment against the obligations of fatherhood. Claire had him. "All right," he said finally. The pages had won.

And now, a year later, with much effort and anticipation, the twin offspring of that conversation were about to enter the world. Needless to say, Ward had not been one of those expectant fathers who escorted his wife, chest puffed out, to doctor appointments or toiled with a screwdriver and an instruction booklet to assemble the crib. Claire didn't particularly care. She found something slightly embarrassing about men who went around saying "we're pregnant" and enthusiastically massaged their wives' shoulders during Lamaze class. Ward would shift once the baby was out. Her husband was too narcissistic not to bond with a being carrying his genetic code. So Claire bore no resentment that the focus now was only on Ward's other baby. *Manifest Destiny* was just released, which was why Claire was waddling around the house, straightening the books on the bookshelves, turning the angle of the potted orchids, preparing for the reporter and crew who would shortly arrive to interview her husband for the local five p.m. news.

By now, Ward had been labeled as a talent, a new, hot author. He was certainly not a household name, but their lives were changed. Claire had become accustomed to seeing her husband's work discussed in newspapers, going to readings where he had actual fans. She and Ward had appeared in the *Times* society column. It was jarring. Growing up, Claire was used to people answering "Boston" and "New Haven" when asked where they went to college. Morgan

Stanley was a "little shop" and Cravath "a small firm." The bigger the success, the more contorted the euphemism. But to Ward, accolades were made to be worn like Boy Scout badges. Well, let him have his fun. How famous could someone who wrote books really get? And Claire wondered privately about the long-term sustainability of Ward's career. *Manifest Destiny* was Ward's best work. He was learning. She had gifted him compelling subject matter this time. But this book was no guarantee for the future. Ward was one set of mediocre sales away from obscurity. And he was not the type to bounce back from failure. Ward got dark and fatalistic, tunneling into black holes of bad writing, or he simply stopped working, without the tireless efforts of cheerleader Claire.

Perhaps Ward's own understanding of himself underlay his obvious nerves that morning. Ward tried to play it off as if it was just a matter of course, no more than his due, but he was uncharacteristically fidgety. He'd spilled hot coffee on himself at breakfast. Each time he came into the room, he switched out which books were displayed on the coffee table (he'd settled on the hardback Met exhibition catalog of old master paintings). Claire pretended not to notice that he'd worn at least three different jackets that morning, and even the big, red-framed glasses could not mask a certain deer-in-headlights expression.

"You'll be great," said Claire as they stood in the living room. Ward walked over and hugged her, no easy task at her current pregnant girth.

"You're the only one who keeps me sane," he whispered into her ear. "What would I do without you?"

Then he pulled away and exhaled loudly near Claire's face. "Does my breath smell?"

◆ ◆ ◆

The reporter was a brunette with a 1960s bob wearing a royal-blue, shoulder-padded suit. She was young, maybe twenty-eight, but with a layer of foundation thick as cement. Claire thought she recognized her, but it might have been that she was just such a perfect newscaster-type, with that big, toothy smile. She had heard people on TV put Vaseline on their teeth. Looking at Amanda, Claire wondered if it was true. Ward embraced the reporter like a long-lost friend. Claire could see a switch inside her husband had been turned on, the celebrity percolating inside him awakening. "Amanda, wonderful to see you."

Ward gave Amanda a tour of the apartment, pointing out where he liked to write, and the framed photographs of other famous people he knew. If Amanda found it anything but charming, she displayed no evidence. When they wound their way back to the kitchen, Amanda smiled widely at Claire and said, "So, how did you two meet?"

Claire and Ward locked eyes for a moment before he said: "I picked her up at a bar."

"Oh yes?"

"It was actually—"

"—yes," Ward interrupted Claire. "I was having a drink at the University Club and this beautiful blonde walked in." He put his arm around her. "Not very exciting I'm afraid."

"Aw, you guys are cute."

Claire raised her eyebrows at Ward but did not correct him. As a writer, surely Ward could see that the real story was far more interesting. She also did not care for being summed up as a "blonde."

When the crew had set up cameras and lights, Ward and Amanda sat in the two chairs facing each other in the living room to begin the interview. Claire situated herself off to the side of the room, along with Irving, Ward's agent, and several publicity people from the publisher who all looked to be about twelve years old. The recording began, Ward was smooth as silk, describing his loyalty to his typewriter, which he happened to have sitting on the table right next to him, presenting it as Napoleon might his cannons. He stoically explained how he worked continuously, refusing breaks or meals, until he'd finished a set number of words. Ward had always been able to channel his intensity into an ordinary story or anecdote and make it seem profound. In the right mood, Ward could imbue everything with an ineffable charm. Even after several years, she still found her husband a magnetic creature. Claire supposed she should count herself lucky she still felt this way. And, judging by what her friends told her, their sex life was nothing short of a miracle.

"It's going great," Irving whispered to Claire. She nodded.

"Ward, it's clear that you are incredibly driven," said Amanda. "But you must have people who read your work and edit you. Who are those people?"

Claire felt her breath catch.

"Well. That's an interesting question," Ward said, pausing to consider it. "First and foremost, I think a writer must be truly self-reliant and steel himself against influence."

The skin around Claire's cheeks and temples tightened.

"And I have taught myself to be a ruthless self-editor."

"I see," said Amanda, nodding.

"Look, maybe someone else can make superficial improvements, but the writer—the good writer—stands on his own."

"So another person's editing is like the icing on the cake?"

"I wouldn't even go that far," said Ward. "Maybe the sprinkles."

Amanda giggled. "Sprinkles, I like that."

The constricting sensation moved down around Claire's throat. Her head was on fire. Fibbing about how they met, fine. Ward was sensitive to his background. But this—this was a lie carefully constructed to cut Claire out of the picture. This was nothing short of betrayal. She had never asked for credit; she'd never told anyone the truth. She had kept hidden who she was to Ward, the way she molded his work, the way she managed him so the book even got written, the way she lent him her own family history. But she had always believed, even if the role she played was not publicized, it would be respected. Claire was not a fucking sprinkle.

Claire knew from Ward's delivery that this was not some line he'd thrown together spur of the moment. This idea was planned, honed, perfected. Ward had known he would say this, if not in this interview, then in another. He'd been waiting for his chance. Claire also understood that Ward had never been at peace with what happened with *American Dream*. Eclipsing Ward's gratitude was resentment. A part of him hated Claire for her role in his work— and hated himself for needing her. And now that he was a big shot, now that he thought he could stand on his own, he was taking his chance to edit their past, lopping Claire off like a pesky, run-on sentence.

She had woken up that morning grateful that the baby was still nestled inside her. She did not want the birth to interfere with the book's publication. Ward deserved to have his moment. The book deserved its day in the sun. And maybe there was something else, too. Maybe she did not want to know—at least so clearly and so early in parenthood—what Ward would do if he had to choose between his career and his child. But now Claire's feelings changed.

In that moment, hormones raged through her like wild stallions. She was gripped with a desire to walk into the center of the living room, get between Ward and Amanda, and, illuminated in the bright studio lights, go into labor. If Claire could have, she would have given birth right then and there, on television, for the pleasure of upstaging her husband. As she looked at Ward and Amanda's smug faces, she pictured her water breaking, gushing dramatically onto the floor, Claire squatting primitively down on the area rug, howling like a possessed wolf. By the end, the only thing people would remember about Ward Manning was his being covered in placenta.

♦ ♦ ♦

The interview ended to applause in the room. Ward walked beaming toward where Claire and Irving were standing. His face was noticeably fuller than it had been that morning, as if an extra pint of blood had been pumped into him. The trace of doubt she'd seen in him had been replaced by a pulsating aura of triumph. He held his arms out and folded both her and Irving into his broad chest. He smelled musky, as if he'd just taken a run.

"Phenomenal," said Irving.

"Bet you're pretty glad you picked me out of the slush pile, huh?" Ward said to his agent.

Irving laughed.

"And my beautiful bride? What did you think?" In his smiling face Claire could not find even a hint of awareness of what he had done. Perhaps Ward believed what he said. Perhaps her husband was so threatened by the aid he'd been given by his wife, he'd become delusional.

Ward continued to look at Claire expectantly. Blowing up at him right there would have only made her look absurd. The big, fat pregnant lady goes crazy. And besides, that wasn't Claire's style. So she smiled and said, "It was revealing."

Ward and Irving went out to celebrate, and Claire begged off. Neither of the men seemed devastated not to have a nine-months-pregnant woman in tow. A few hours later, alone in the privacy of her own bedroom, Ward still out, Claire felt the first piercing pangs of labor. The baby had waited just long enough. The next morning, in the maternity ward of Mount Sinai, Isabelle Eleanor Manning entered the world.

The Oyster Bar was pungent with shellfish and hard liquor. The hum of the crowd boomed off the curved, tiled ceilings. It was glorious. I wedged myself between bodies toward the bar. Not ten feet into the room, I came face-to-face with Sebastian.

"Oh, Livia," he said, puzzled. "I didn't expect to see you here."

Of course he didn't; I hadn't been invited.

That afternoon, I'd decided I'd played the shut-in widow long enough. My need for people, merriment, cocktail banter was urgent. And I didn't want to be alone. I kept having this creepy sensation, almost like someone was watching me. I felt it in the streets of my neighborhood where the same beefy guy with shifty eyes seemed always to be out when I was. At home I often picked up the telephone to a long silence on the other end before the line clicked off. Surely it was all coincidence, but nevertheless, I was keen to be around people. So I went to the credenza in the front hall and rifled through the invitations that inexplicably poured in for Aiden two months after his death. And, voilà, there was one for that evening, a soiree celebrating *Molded*, the memoir of a sculptor I'd almost heard of.

"Surprise!" I said now to Sebastian.

"I'm glad I saw you," he said, coming closer than felt necessary. "I have an idea—a show of the newly found works. Cusack and the rest. Several galleries are interested."

"Oh." I inched away from him. "That's interesting. Let's talk later. Or tomorrow." I continued on my way, trying not to dwell on this new information. Tonight was meant to be a break from all that. I got my Manhattan, took a long, slow sip, enjoying that first warmth of alcohol in the back of my throat when I heard a voice say, "Unfortunate homonym."

145

I turned to see a man with salt-and-pepper hair in an argyle sweater. He looked familiar.

"Pardon?"

"Molded." The man tapped his finger on the book. "Sounds like the story of the takeout in the back of the fridge."

I laughed. "Funny."

"Sam," he said, extending a hand.

"Livia."

"So how do you know the author?"

"I don't."

"That makes two of us," Sam said. "I got asked to cover this for an under-the-weather colleague."

"You're a journalist?"

"You could say that," he said. "I write the Ethical Studies column for *Vanity Fair*."

"Sam Stillman? I knew I recognized you!" Accompanying his column was a cute little thumbnail photo of Sam looking pensive in a sweater just like the one he was wearing. "The column is the best part of the magazine."

"You're far too kind."

"No, no, you're our collective conscience," I said, adding, because the liquor was already going to my head, "I've always wondered, though, isn't it difficult to be so *upstanding* all the time?"

Sam considered this. "Sometimes. But ethics got very personal for me after I fell in love with a pathological liar." He took a sip of his drink. "I had a bad divorce a few years ago."

"Ah." We both were silent as I thought of how to restart the conversation. "The column you wrote about that private tutor being paid to write college admissions essays was dynamite."

Sam smiled. "A dirty business, academics."

We kept up our flirting chatter. It all felt light and hu-morous, exactly what I had left the house for. I wonder now what would have happened if I had picked another invitation and never met Sam. How could I have known how complicated it would all become?

18

New York, 2017

Isabelle

Isabelle took a sip of the coffee that had turned bitter and cold, and looked up from the page, feeling a strange alienation from her own life. Since arriving back in New York from Sag Harbor that afternoon, she'd been holed up at Three Guys diner on Seventy-Sixth Street. Isabelle frequently brought her laptop to one of the booths, and, fueled by endless refills, overpriced tuna salad, and the low din of a coffee shop, she often did some of her best work. Her plan had been to dive in right away on the book she'd write before her father, too, was gone. Sitting there, she could see that this idea was straight-up insane. She was in no shape to write. Everything Isabelle thought she understood about her family, everything she knew of her mother—and perhaps her father—was wrong, or at least entirely incomplete.

The untitled manuscript, which she'd now been through twice, had no by-line, but her mother had written it. Though it was still unfinished, this story—this . . . book!—was the real gift that had been left for her. Her mother was a writer. A good one. And she'd had a hand in Ward's career. This was also news to Isabelle.

Given the subject matter, it made complete sense that her father knew nothing about the book. By making him an artist, Claire had done *some* to disguise Ward in "Aiden," but, of course, the character was her father. The depiction of Aiden shook Isabelle, poking at a juvenile, but very much alive, vision of her parents' storybook marriage. Isabelle knew—obviously she knew—her father was not easy. There were times Isabelle could sense Claire's frustration. Her mother had a particular way of speaking to him through clenched teeth. But Isabelle had believed that Claire, like herself, accepted Ward's temperament as part of the package. She thought her mother too had made the calculation that being related to Ward Manning was well worth enduring his ego, his lapses, even, at times, his complete disregard. This had certainly seemed true all those nights they sat shivering together with their vodka on the deck. But the person who'd written this book, the one who'd so enjoyed killing off the Ward character, harbored other, unspoken feelings about the man in real life.

"More coffee?" Alex, the waiter, appeared with the glass pot.

"Thanks, I'll take one more in a to-go cup."

He nodded, then returned with the coffee and the check.

Isabelle was rummaging around to find her wallet, hoping she had enough cash, when she stopped. "Actually, Alex," she called after him, and he walked back toward her. "Do you have a job application? Like for a waitress or something?"

The application for a waitress job consisted of a two-minute conversation with Nick, the manager, in which after some skepticism, he offered, "Dinner shift. You're not lunch material." Isabelle would start the following week. Dinner would be slow with few tips, but at least she was less likely to wait on people she knew, though complete evasion of her crowd would be impossible. Hopefully the pay would be enough to keep her going while she finished a book of her own.

Isabelle walked home, holding her mother's manuscript to her chest. She had never considered that Claire had creative aspirations. Her mother ran an organization that donated books to hospitals and sent volunteers to read to sick children, and that seemed Claire's life's passion. But Isabelle had spent much of her life so focused on her father—her big, famous father—that it left little room for curiosity about her other parent. Her mother existed in too close a range. It was difficult to see where Claire ended and Isabelle began. Thoughts of Claire conjured up the way her mother smelled like Lubriderm and honeysuckle, the freckle patterns on her shoulders where Isabelle had so often rested her head, the way she liked to sing the Supremes, and the satisfied *mmmmm* sound she made when eating crackers with really good brie. The fuzzy outline of Claire's face Isabelle saw when she first opened her eyes in that Caribbean hospital.

But, of course, Claire had been much more than just Isabelle's mother. Sitting there now, she knew there were questions she would spend the rest of her life wishing she had asked. Chiefly, why had Claire written this book? And why had her mother wanted to share it with Isabelle only after she was gone? Based on the cultural references to the 1980s and early '90s, Claire had likely written it a good twenty years before. And yet, Claire maintained her secret all that time, declining to say to her daughter as Isabelle struggled, *I get it, I've written too.* And why had she stopped? The book cut off after a hundred and eighty pages, Livia's fate still hanging in the balance.

But what kept striking Isabelle as she read over page after page, was that Livia, her mother's alter ego, was wry, subversive, unapologetic. Isabelle loved her. Claire's writing unveiled a part of her mother that Isabelle had never gotten to know. And because of this, underneath Isabelle's shock and confusion, was a deepening devastation. There was too much she was learning much too late.

19

New York, 1989

Claire

Claire paid for the taxi and carried her sleeping daughter into the lobby and up in the elevator. Her pulse had not slowed since they'd left the party at Gotham, and she could still feel the flush in her cheeks. She gingerly took off Isabelle's party dress, loaded her daughter into pajamas, dismantled her braids, and ran a toothbrush over her teeth. Isabelle remained mostly asleep, yawning occasionally, a dopey smile on her face, as Claire tucked her under her covers.

Claire smoothed a hand over Isabelle's forehead, got up, and was about to turn off the light when she heard, "Mom?"

"Yes, sweetheart?"

"Tonight was the best."

Claire closed her eyes as she inhaled. "Good night, love."

She walked downstairs to the main level of the duplex they'd bought two years before. In the kitchen, she put a few ice cubes in a glass and poured herself a vodka. Her mind circled back over and over to the image of Isabelle up there on Ward's shoulders. Claire had no right to be surprised. She had no right to be angry. It was Claire who had enabled all of this to happen. It was she who had created Ward Manning.

Claire had stopped helping her husband years before—after the TV interview, the night before Isabelle was born—but it had been too late. Her student had learned just enough. And it turned out that while Ward was a skilled writer, what he was best at was making himself relevant. Ward was everywhere. He became a literary touchstone, familiarity with his writing a necessary element of the pedigree for those who desired to be part of certain social and intellectual milieus. His books were aspirational, and their success self-perpetuating. All the while, Ward's own persona became his most carefully constructed piece of fiction. In the years since they'd first met, Ward had turned from bohemian to Caddy Shack character, carefully mimicking the habits and tastes of someone from generations of money. He'd turned into one of Claire's own relatives. Ward wore monogrammed dress shirts and herringbone pants underneath his Barbour coat, he drove a station wagon. He played good tennis. He had a vague lock-jawed intonation. Then there was his hideous collection of pretentious oil paintings of military leaders. Claire cringed every time she saw the gaudily framed portrait of Napoleon straddling his steed in Ward's office.

Ward distilled his meager background into a set of convenient half-truths to be strategically deployed. He liked to trot out a story about trying to sell unsweetened lemon juice by the roadside as a youngster because he was too poor to buy sugar—a complete invention—whenever the success of any writer who was born into a more comfortable setting came up. But even as he reached the apex of his career, his stint waiting tables had been omitted from his sparse narrative; the story he told the reporter in their living room became the official record of how she and Ward met. Over the years, lies told over again hardened around the facts like lacquer. That Claire knew the real story was a truth that simmered between them.

While all of this was tedious and maddening, Claire could handle Ward's manipulation of the masses. The necklace had been the first sign that the trouble was closer to home. Isabelle had been begging for weeks for an Elsa Peretti silver bean from Tiffany because some older girls at school had them. Claire was willing to indulge Isabelle and give it as her birthday present. Ward adamantly refused, bellowing about how she was much too young for "status" jewelry and if she wanted something like that, she'd have to earn it by scrubbing the toilets. As if that was an appropriate task for a seven-year-old. Then, a few weeks later, without telling Claire, *he* went to Tiffany and had a gold charm necklace made of his book, a bauble that probably cost twenty times what the damned bean did. Ward took no responsibility for the mixed message this sent. And it was such a ridiculous gift. Why would Isabelle want to wear a replica of one of Ward's books—an adult book she'd never read and had no connection to—around her neck?

Except Isabelle did; she loved it.

The vodka was not having its desired effect. Her anger was growing like a hurricane over open water. Maybe it was horrid of her to resent her daughter's love for her own father. But Ward was hardly there for Isabelle. He hadn't earned her love with fatherly affection or by performing the hard, unrelenting work of parenting. He had procured it the same way he got people to buy his books: convincing her to believe in his legend. Claire had been a fool not to expect it. Did she think that by being the parent who read stories and gave baths, who got into the sandbox herself, who sewed the elastics on ballet shoes, who always had Band-Aids and a secret lollipop in her purse, that Isabelle would prefer her? Did Claire believe if she did all of those things, Isabelle wouldn't notice her father was a big, fat cultural icon? The answer, ridiculous now, was yes. Without ever articulating it to herself, Claire had implicitly believed that because she was the one actually raising their daughter, she could decide who Isabelle was. Oh naïve hope!

Within Claire's fury was the understanding that the damage had been done. Already asserting itself into Isabelle's identity was the role of famous writer's daughter. If tonight was any indication, it was one Isabelle was only too happy to play. There was no putting the cat back in the bag. Claire would have to cope the way she had so many times before. But she needed to do something. If a channel to unleash her resentment was not provided, she would go mad. Claire looked at the clock. Glenda was no doubt still awake and would provide a vigorously sympathetic ear for Claire's complaints. But Glenda would want to transform Claire's upset into action. And she would never let Claire forget anything she'd said in anger. The last thing she wanted was to be accountable to Glenda. No, not an option.

Claire drained her vodka, grabbed a dish towel hanging off the oven, held it to her mouth and screamed. When she was done, she took a deep breath and smoothed back her hair, settling herself. She had an idea, one that had been percolating for weeks, maybe much longer. There was one thing she could do to save herself. There was a skill she had not yet put to use, an outlet she could create all on her own. Claire sat down to the desktop computer in their kitchen, opened up a blank page, and entered an alternate reality.

"He's wonderful, darling," my mother whispered as Sam and I gathered our coats. She was having one of her good days, now fewer and further between. Sam and I had come for tea, and my mother regaled us with tales of her flight days, like the time the steak had gone bad, and she'd served the first-class cabin pancakes whipped up on the tiny galley stove for dinner. "All I had to do was call them crepes and no one batted an eye."

In the elevator, Sam kissed my hand and said, "Thank you for letting me meet her."

This guy was the stuff of fairy tales. And I was a smitten kitten. I would've found the whole thing revolting if it were happening to anyone else. He was just so *nice*. He complimented me. He called when he said he would. I'd thought a sweet guy like him would've been a snooze. But the thing was, he wasn't. We were out all the time, taking the subway to tiny, hole-in-the-wall restaurants in far-flung outer boroughs. Holding hands on long walks around parts of the city I'd never been to. I know, gag.

Of course, in all our lovey-dovey conversations, I still had not told Sam the whole truth about me and what I was up to. And things were getting out of hand. Sebastian was relentless, insisting upon orchestrating a show of Aiden's found works. This public display seemed like asking for trouble. And I was ready to be done. I'd finished the Cusack and done the Ann-Margret because, after all these years, I wanted to know if I still had the stuff. And there was satisfaction in using Aiden's fame to get what *I* needed. Once upon a time, it had been the reverse.

Years ago, Aiden's career was spiraling. He could gain no footing as an abstract expressionist. Sebastian, at first hot for Aiden's paintings, had become aloof, telling Aiden to go in another direction but offering little in the way of specifics. I'd become an art consultant to support us. In my work, I saw a new hunger for realism, pop art. Aiden dismissed the portrait idea over and over, viewing it as beneath him. But, at his lowest point, I had convinced him. I found the photo of Christopher Walken. I showed him how to use a grid. Hell, I did a convincing turn as Walken himself. We worked together, a kind of husband-and-wife team. I thought we would continue that way. But as soon as Sebastian was interested in the portrait work, Aiden cut me out. Sebastian must've liked it that way—a photogenic male artist was more saleable than a husband-and-wife team.

Now, painting again after more than a decade, I'd remembered my own bona fides; I had no desire to impersonate my husband for the rest of my life. It was time to turn off the spigot. I would do enough paintings for the show, enough to set up my mother, and then I would stop. I'd start over, under my own name.

As we walked from my mother's apartment building on Second Avenue, I started to get that weird feeling again, as if I was being watched. I was increasingly convinced that someone had figured me out. A panic rose in my chest as I saw a now familiar figure. The man was huge, over six feet, with a hulky, muscular body. He had a shaved head, deep-set eyes, and was dressed in gray sweats. I'd seen him time and again near my apartment, but never all the way on the East Side. As we passed, he kept looking at me, masticating a toothpick with his lips. I wanted to believe his presence in this new neighborhood was happenstance, but his hard stare said otherwise.

"Are you all right?" Sam asked. "You keep looking over your shoulder."

"Oh yes," I said quickly. "I'm fine." But I was beginning to think I was not.

20

New York, 2017

Isabelle

Eight o'clock and the diner was empty save for two tables. Mrs. Coddmeyer, an ancient Upper East Side doyenne, came in every evening for a bowl of lentil soup and a glass of merlot. Isabelle knew by now that if she wanted a decent tip, she should fill Mrs. Coddmeyer's wineglass to the brim and not ask if she would like to remove her gargantuan patchy fur coat. The other table was two high school kids, a boy and a girl, who might be on a date or might just be two friends who liked to flirt with each other. Both of them were on their phones, periodically flipping their screens toward each other. They were typical for the neighborhood, smug and coiffed. The boy wore a downy cashmere cable-knit, and the girl had on those Golden Goose sneakers that cost hundreds of dollars. Isabelle studied the way the girl flipped her hair, the way the two of them leaned in close and whispered before bursting into laughter. Isabelle thought of her and Brian, who weren't much older when they'd met. The two kids barely looked up at Isabelle when she took their order for a plate of fries and seltzers "with, like, a lot of lemons." How horrified they would be to learn that she had once been just like them, an entitled private school kid with the world at her feet.

Since returning from Sag Harbor two weeks before, Isabelle had retreated into her own world. She communicated with no one outside the coffee shop. She let Brian's texts and calls go unanswered. The manuscript and the unsettling truths it had revealed about her parents were too delicate to divulge, even to her best friend. And the thought of trying to talk to him—or anyone—while pretending that her life had not been completely altered felt too exhausting.

Isabelle focused on learning shorthand for the cooks, how to read the rhythm of the tables and carry four dinner plates. It had been a long time since she had picked up a new skill. After years spent sequestered with her laptop writing thousands of words no one might read, she liked the tangibleness of effort and result, even the physicality of being a waitress. Of course, she understood the novelty of the job was itself a privilege. The hard part was once the diner grew slow, as it often did at dinner—lunch was the moneymaker—giving Isabelle enough time to return to her own thoughts.

At nine o'clock, when she and the manager closed up, Isabelle hung up her apron and put her jacket over the white button-down and black slacks she wore to work. Outside the diner, in the fresh, cool fall air, she was suddenly aware how much she smelled of grease and onions. Fingering the stash of tip quarters in her pockets, Isabelle slowly made her way home to return to the task of writing her book. It was not going well. Isabelle had given up on the draft Fern had rejected, and started over. After nights of thin, restless sleep, she'd wake up at six and make herself a pot of sludgy, overly strong coffee. When she'd had a few cups, she'd begin filling notebooks with ideas, trying to work up an outline of a book she could write well and, more importantly, write quickly, in time for her father. She worked frantically, as if maintaining a frenzied state would itself lead to results. But underneath her mania was a creeping understanding that this was futile. Isabelle believed—she knew—she had a good novel inside her. But she would not write it like this.

Isabelle had often felt that writing was like being on a submarine. She spent years submerged, silent and secret, working toward someday, long in the future, when she would have something to show for all her time underwater. To write her book, Isabelle would need to make peace with this purgatory yet again. But this meant her father might not live to see her book published.

◆   ◆   ◆

Back at home, Isabelle peeled off her clothes, then dumped them on the growing mound of laundry needing to be taken to the basement. Isabelle put back on the ratty Yankees T-shirt she'd been sleeping in for several days. After grabbing an open, flat Diet Coke can from the fridge, Isabelle caught a glimpse in the mirror hanging over her couch and barely recognized herself. Her skin had an unhealthy waxiness and a yellow pallor that accentuated the white tracks of her scar. Her hair had gone so many days unwashed it was a full shade darker. She looked unwell. Isabelle sighed and picked up the yellow pad where she'd been sketching out her latest attempt and resumed writing. She must have fallen asleep because the next thing she knew, her heart was pounding, her cheek wet with drool. She had just begun to dream the dream, her fingers stumbling around the phone dial. She sat up, rubbed her eyes, lingering anxiety coalescing around her chest.

Isabelle looked around the room strewn with papers. Instead of feeling like an artist in the throes of creativity, she felt like a slob. This, she knew swiftly and urgently, was not how she wanted to exist. She got out of bed and began to tidy up, organizing the loose leaf paper into piles, picking up stray laundry. She went to the linen closet and pulled out another set of sheets to replace the dank ones on her bed. As Isabelle cleaned, the frustration always lurking just beneath her sadness broke through to the surface. She was living in a nightmare of disappointments. Her career was failing. Her mother had deserted her. And now her father was sick. If her father died before she published a book, Isabelle would not recover. That much she knew.

When the room was in order, Isabelle showered, dressed, and

sat back down on her bed. Her mother's manuscript was beside her on the nightstand in a neat stack. Isabelle picked up the 182 pages and strummed the side with her thumb like a deck of cards. She'd read the pages over so many times, trying to feel close to the person who'd written it, the person she never quite knew. Instead of her own work, she found herself thinking of her mother's, tweaks she would make to the book, how she would end it. But more than once she'd wished she didn't know anything about the manuscript. It felt close to cruel that her mother had left her with this secret. What good did it do her now when Claire was gone?

And then Isabelle answered herself. The idea came sure and clear, as if she'd just been waiting to be asked the question. It crackled explosively inside her.

Isabelle instinctively pulled her hands off the pages. She couldn't do that. She wouldn't take her mother's book. She quickly got under the covers and turned out the light, desperate to be finished with the day. It was a ridiculous thought, best forgotten. She would never.

But as she closed her eyes, trying to sleep, a question circled: *Why not?*

PART II

21

New York, 1992

Claire

Claire had worked on and off on the manuscript for nearly three years now. Her progress had been stymied by the demands of life and motherhood, and by her tendency to get lost in long, detailed laments about Aiden's behavior. She was pleased with what she had, but she was at an impasse over Livia's fate. In her waking hours, and often in her dreams, Claire considered various scenarios, turning each over like a throat lozenge dissolving into a thin, brittle disk. At the root of her indecision was Claire's discomfort with exposure. She both wanted and feared Livia telling the world what she had done. Claire could not press forward until she had made up her mind. But resolution of this threshold issue would now need to wait until she returned from Jamaica.

They would leave in two days, just before Christmas, and Ward was already crabby. He abhorred being away from his work. And was making up for it by spending every waking moment in his study before they left. Ward did not appreciate the luxury of a full day to write. He did not know what it was like to toil only when it was convenient for others, only when he would not be missed. Time was a different medium for her husband, one that could be bent and molded as it pleased him. It did not need to be stolen, snatched from sleep, traded in exchange for fatigue or hunger.

Her husband's mood was particularly tense because the American Prose Literary Award winners were about to be announced. Ward had already won the award, one of the most prestigious honors in the field, just five years before. Could they really give it to him again? It seemed deluded to expect every book he wrote to win every award there was. But the thing was, Ward did expect this. And by some law of attraction, his over-bloated expectations seemed to work in his favor. But this award, this huge, once-in-a-career award felt truly unlikely. Still, Ward spent his time trying to read the tea leaves, calling up Irving several times a day to find out if he knew anything, and offering prophylactic criticism of other writers who might win, before moving on to the faults of other writers in general. Unlike with most things, when it came to rivals, Ward was undiscerning. He was easily threatened, continually primed to defend his record. It didn't matter whether a writer wrote military biographies or self-help—if they produced pages between two covers available at Barnes & Noble, he was ready to scrap.

Which is why Claire could only imagine how Ward would react to her own book. It was not just her depiction of "Aiden" as an egoist. But when Claire read over the draft again, she saw how much Livia resented her husband, and how quickly she rebounded with another man. This would certainly not be lost on Ward. If he ever had a reason to read it.

Claire looked down and realized she had absently packed up her entire underwear drawer. She threw up her hands and walked out of the bedroom. Isabelle was at school and Ward was out at a lunch with some reporter, so Claire had the house to herself. When she got to the kitchen, she picked up the receiver of the red phone that hung on the wall.

"Oh good, you're still here," she said. "I was worried you'd left for Paris."

"You have me for another ten hours," said Glenda. "You know how I love a red-eye. You can take a truly irresponsible amount of pills in the name of sleep, and no one says a word."

Claire laughed.

"So, are you calling to wish me a merry merry?"

"No, actually . . . I have something I want to discuss with you. Something I haven't told anyone about."

"Oh! Is it about Ward?"

"You could say that."

Glenda squealed. "Oh Claire, I've been waiting for this for a long, long time. Not another word. I want to have this conversation in person. With the proper fanfare. Stay right where you are."

◆　◆　◆

A half an hour later, Glenda appeared at Claire's door with a bottle of Dom Pérignon. Before she could speak, Glenda embraced her forcefully, pressing Claire's face into her fur-covered bosom.

"Oh darling, I'm so glad, I'm just so glad."

Claire pulled away. "Here, come in."

Glenda stepped into the foyer and threw her coat and hat on a chair. "Where's your crystal?" She raised the bottle in the air. "And do you have anyone who can open this?"

"Like who?"

"Staff?"

"No, Glenda, no staff."

"We'll rough it, then." Glenda walked into the kitchen and Claire followed, retrieving two glasses from the cabinet. And Glenda, with much straining, popped open the champagne, foam overflowing onto the floor.

"Cheers," she said, when drinks had been poured. "To your new life."

"My new life?"

"Yes, of course." Glenda beamed at her. "Your new life. *Sans* Ward."

"What?"

"You're getting divorced, aren't you? Isn't that why you called me here?"

"I'm not getting divorced."

Glenda sighed dejectedly.

"Sorry to disappoint you."

"Oh boo. Boo boo boo." Glenda downed her drink.

Claire took a sip of the champagne. "This is good."

"Of course it is," said Glenda. "I've been saving this bottle since your wedding day."

Claire laughed.

"It's worth hundreds by now."

"I appreciate the gesture . . ."

"Are you sure? You really could divorce him. Tell him tonight."

Claire raised her eyebrows.

Glenda sighed. "I don't know how you stand living with that ego on a stick. Someone new would snap you up in a moment. But time is of the essence. You're not getting any younger. Leave him before your ass collapses."

"I'm sure there's wisdom in that, but that's not what I wanted to talk to you about."

"Fine," Glenda huffed. "What is it, then?"

The kitchen phone began ringing. "Hold on," said Claire. "Hello?"

"Mrs. Manning?"

"Yes?"

"It's Mrs. Kingsloving. From Chapin."

"Oh." Claire's heart picked up. "Is everything all right?"

"Fine," she said in her clipped, slight English accent. "Are you able to retrieve Isabelle from school today?"

"Yes, I'll be there at four thirty after soccer."

"Sports were cancelled due to the holiday recess. A flyer went out in the backpacks last week."

Claire was about to object when she remembered. The pink slip of paper. She'd seen it, put it on the kitchen table, and forgotten it. God knows where it had ended up. "I'm so sorry. I'll be right there."

"Crisis?" said Glenda, sitting at the kitchen counter sipping her second glass.

"I need to pick up Isabelle. Want to run with me to East End?"

"Oh darling, I haven't been east of Lex since the Carter administration."

"Of course." Claire leaned over to kiss her friend on the cheek.

"You're going to leave me in suspense?"

"I have to run. I'll call you tonight. Before you leave."

Glenda poured herself another glass. "I'll let myself out."

Claire taxied to the school and found Isabelle sitting on the floor of the lobby, swimming in her gray North Face shell, her knees pulled up toward her chest, exposing the underside of her tight-covered thighs and bottom. It occurred to Claire that Isabelle was probably getting too old to sit this way, and the realization made Claire wistful.

"Isabelle. I'm so sorry."

Isabelle looked up from pulling on the little rubber filaments of her Koosh ball key chain. She stood up, sullenly throwing her backpack over her shoulder. "Mom. What's with you?"

"I forgot, I'm sorry." Claire embraced her daughter and gave her a kiss on the head. When she pulled away, she saw that Isabelle was fighting tears. "Oh honey, it's okay. I was just a little late." Claire had experienced a version of this many times in her life. The flip side of her steady dependability was that she had no margin for error. If Claire forgot a birthday or was five minutes late, it was intolerable precisely because it happened so infrequently. People did not like even small deviations from their expectations.

Isabelle nodded, her bottom lip turned down and quivering slightly. Claire hadn't expected this. At ten, Isabelle seemed so grown up to her, wearing lip gloss, borrowing her mother's Ted Muehling earrings. But Claire could see that Isabelle's maturity was deceiving, like a shiny, hard caramel coating over the soft flesh of an apple. A momentary lapse could still wound her. Well, thought

Claire as they started for home, she would find a way to make it up to her.

When they returned to the apartment, Claire made Isabelle her favorite pasta with peas and pecorino. After she'd kissed Isabelle good night, Claire returned to the kitchen and put on a kettle for tea. As she waited for it to boil, she used the cordless to dial Glenda. Claire reached her just in time.

22

New York, 2018

Isabelle

Isabelle sat in front of a card table that had been set with several dozen copies of the same book. She was halfway through the stacks and her pen moved quickly, "Isabelle Manning" reduced to two jagged lines.

"Doll. Enough with the foot."

"Oh. Sorry," said Isabelle.

"You're jumping around like you're on meth."

Isabelle was in fact bouncing. She heard the buzz in her left ear, the one that tended to flare up when she was stressed or excited. And she had that tickly feeling in her stomach like she had to pee all the time. And though she'd ingested nothing stronger than coffee, she did feel a bit like she used to when she'd load up on Adderall during college exam weeks.

"Why don't you take a break," said Fern. "Go splash some water on your face."

"Good idea," said Isabelle, surveying the sprawling Javits Center, as big as an airplane hangar, filled with the entirety of the New York City publishing world.

"And come back more normal."

Isabelle rolled her eyes. "I'm fine."

"Oh no, doll. You have it bad."

"Have what bad?"

"First-time-author syndrome," said Fern, clucking his tongue. "One of the worst cases I've ever seen."

"The virus had a long time to incubate."

"Touché. Go take a walk. If that doesn't work, I'll wrestle up some alcohol."

When she arrived in the bathroom, Isabelle washed her hands vigorously at the sink. She looked at herself in the mirror, trying out a few different smiles, expressions befitting someone in the throes of newfound success. Which, of course, she was. Her book had sold to Piper Publishing Group—which happened to be her father's publisher—in a two-book deal in the high six figures. At last, Isabelle's name appeared in one of the announcements in Publishers Marketplace, and her debut featured in *Publishers Weekly*.

Six months later, a week away from publication, preparations were in high gear. There had been several well-placed publicity pieces hyping the long-awaited debut novel of Isabelle Manning. Her author photo, in which she appeared in a white chunky-knit sweater, her golden hair hanging in tussled waves around her shoulders, her eyes looking off into the middle distance, her lips somewhere between pursed and a smile, was everywhere. And now here she was at BookExpo America, or BEA, the publishing industry's grand dance. She had previously experienced this gigantic networking event only by scrolling through the Instagram posts of more successful writers, her mouth coated with a bitter film of envy.

Isabelle gripped the sink on either side with her hands and pitched her face closer to the mirror. Maybe if she looked hard enough, her mother's image would appear in place of her own. "We did it," she whispered aloud. "We did it." Another woman entered the bathroom, and Isabelle quickly pretended to fix her hair before she walked out, reentering the fray.

From several yards away, Isabelle could see Fern in conversation with someone. The man was tall with wavy brown hair long enough to be tucked behind his ears. He wore a faded gray flannel shirt, brown twill pants, and leather shoes evocative of moccasins. Closer, Isabelle recognized the thick black acetate glasses.

"Oh good. You're back," said Fern. "Darby, have you met Isabelle Manning?"

Darby Cullman, all caterpillar eyebrows and perfectly cultivated two-day stubble, faced her. "Of course. Isabelle. Great to see you, love." *Love?* He leaned in and gave her a double-cheek kiss.

"Darby and I were at Brown together."

"Ah! Right," said Fern. "I was just telling Darby about your fabulous book."

"Sounds legit. I'm into art."

"It's to die for, Darby!" said Fern. "And it's so timely. You know, women power. And just like the whole 'fuck men in general' vibe."

"Uh-oh." Darby made a mock grimace.

"Oh I don't really think it's an eff men situation," said Isabelle quickly. But maybe it was. And the particular eff-ed man, of course, would be her father. When Isabelle worked on the book, she tried to soften "Aiden," give Livia some morsel of lasting affection, but Aiden was who he was. And so was Ward. The irony was not lost on Isabelle that in her desperation to have her father witness her publish a book, she'd put out what could be viewed as a highly unflattering portrait of him. But she hoped the fact of the book and the status its publication would bestow upon her in her father's eyes would make it worth it. Part of Isabelle believed that her father might be just narcissistic enough to refuse to see himself in Aiden, content to let the fiction that this character was not his doppelganger sit between them.

"Oh you know what I mean," said Fern.

"All right, dig it," said Darby. "Definitely hit me up with a copy."

"Here! Take one." Fern shoved a hardcover at Darby. The design of Isabelle's book was a fuzzy, earth-toned face shape with brush strokes reading *Underpainting* superimposed over it.

"Oh there's Maya Kim." Fern clutched his chest, looking in the direction of the top editor at one of the Big Fives. "I've been stalking her for six weeks. I mean that literally. I think I can corner her." Fern dashed off, leaving Darby and Isabelle alone.

"He's enthusiastic." Darby flashed her a familiar self-satisfied smile. Isabelle had thought many times of what she would say if she ever saw Darby in person again. Mostly she'd imagined giving him a taste of his own medicine, pretending she had only a vague memory of who he was or that he was a writer (even if that was realistic only if she were a troglodyte). But standing there with Darby, she did not want to do that at all. She wanted to revel in their equalness. That she had, at last, entered the world of published novelists. And, in that completely unfair male way, Darby had become more handsome with age. His cheeks were angular, and his jaw had grown pronounced, muscular, with lines on the sides that made him seem substantial. His skin was more weathered, as if he spent a great deal of time outside. Well, he did own a farm.

If social media was to be believed, Darby had just broken up with his girlfriend. Isabelle had spent quite a bit of time researching Chloë, the owner of a meditation studio who posted a lot of pictures of herself draped in scarves, her eyes closed, blissful expression on her face. The scarves made it hard to get a clean look at her, but she was pretty. Very pretty. And very young. But she had not appeared in a post in quite a long time, and Darby had made several allusions to being a bachelor of late.

"Fern must've worked some magic getting your book out so fast," said Darby.

"Yeah," said Isabelle, with a flicker of satisfaction that Darby, despite his aloof, too-cool persona, was in fact paying attention. "He did good." In a normal scenario, her book would not be published for another year at least. When Isabelle asked how he'd done it, Fern waved her off. "Never ask about the sausage." Whatever deal he'd cut, she was glad. The book's early release meant she got paid more of her advance sooner, too. Even so, Isabelle had worked at Three Guys up until press began. She felt simultaneously proud of herself and embarrassed for being proud of herself for doing something that for many people wasn't a brief interlude but a way of life. When she'd taken the job, she thought in the back of her mind, she'd write about it. But she'd changed her mind. It was in some ways the only job she'd ever had that was completely her own. Isabelle believed her father, who was always bellowing about "an honest day's work," would have been happy she had gotten a job. But he was uninterested in discussing it, avoidant of the topic, as if Isabelle being a waitress shamed him. Still, the important thing was she'd published her book. He would not die thinking her a failure. She had that.

"Cool concept for the book," said Darby now. "How did you think of it?"

"Oh, you know, it just sort of materialized."

"Lucky you."

"Yes, very lucky."

"What does Ward think of it?" Darby asked.

"*Ward* hasn't read it."

"No shit?"

"He'll get his hardcover this week."

Darby nodded. "I totally respect that."

"You should come to my book party."

"Oh—"

"It's next Thursday at the Metropolitan Library," said Isabelle. She knew this was, on one level, completely inappropriate. She and Darby weren't friends. But they were now members of the same club. Brian would tease her mercilessly, but so be it. She'd made up to Brian for her hysterical phone call and for going dark for weeks when she'd returned from Sag Harbor. Or at least she thought she had. Brian had been entirely consumed with work. The one time she'd seen him for a drink, he'd seemed distracted, distant even.

She'd need to devote more attention to her friend now that the book was out.

"Cool," said Darby, dropping the *l* at the end of the word.

"Cool." Isabelle watched Darby walk off. She stood at her table at BEA, suddenly in the middle of the life she had worked so hard to create.

Eight months too late, Aiden was finally getting what he wanted. Tonight, *Aiden Connors: Looking Back*, a curated exhibit featuring ten works that had been found postmortem, was opening at the swankiest of swanky SoHo galleries. Aiden had had plenty of shows, but this one, at this place, with this invite list, would have validated him in the fine art world in the way he'd believed was his due.

The gallery was full of obnoxious people who insisted upon double kissing my cheeks, so I was especially glad when I spied Sam arrive from across the room.

"Oh thank god you're here," I said when I reached him. "These art people are brutal."

Sam smiled and offered his arm. "Shall we look around?" We strolled the gallery, admiring Ann-Margret, Sylvia Plath, Frida Kahlo, and Katharine Hepburn. They all had sizeable crowds around them, but nowhere near as big as the portrait at the far end of the gallery. We walked until the packed bodies blocked our way. We stood silently, taking in the image of Zelda Fitzgerald. In the painting, Zelda is not more than twenty. Her look is wistful, yet intense, within her stare a kind of plea.

"Iconic," said a woman next to us. "Aiden Connors was such a feminist."

I quickly turned my guffaw into a cough.

"This one does live up to the hype," said Sam. "Magnificent."

"Yes," I said. "I suppose it does."

"Livia, do you notice someone staring at you?" Sam motioned to a woman standing against the wall, who was indeed eyeing me. She was very young, with hair that sat perched in two little buns on top of her head. She wore a spaghetti-strap dress and had spindly legs punctuated by boat-sized Doc Mar-

175

tens. There was another similarly aged skinny woman standing next to her in a tank top and kilt skirt.

"She's very interested in you," said Sam.

"Oh," I said, "probably some mega fan of Aiden's. Sometimes the fascination trickles down to me."

"I'm fascinated by you," said Sam, kissing my hand.

I felt a tap on my leg. "Yoohoo!" Startled, I turned to see
my mother grinning in her chair.

"Mom!"

"I hope it's okay, she insisted she was up for it," said
Gloria.

"Of course."

"I couldn't miss this," said my mother. "Bring me closer
to Zelda." My mother didn't know her own phone number,
but she had no trouble remembering Zelda Fitzgerald. She
squinted at the picture. "One of your best, sweetheart."

"Oh," I said, heat rising in my cheeks, "it's not mine,
Mom. It's Aiden's."

"Nonsense. I think I know my daughter's work."

I quickly looked at Sam and shrugged.

"It's beautiful," he said to my mother, then softer to me.
"Sometimes it's kinder to go with it."

· · ·

When the show was dying down, we saw my mother and Gloria
into a taxi and then made our way toward an Italian restaurant. As we crossed the street, out of the corner of my eye
I could see the two young women from the gallery, walking
behind us. With them was the sweat suit—wearing man with
the toothpick.

23

New York, 2018

Brian

His boss's office smelled like cigars and freshly printed paper. Brian had only been inside a handful of times before, but he remembered the smell.

He sat in one of the heavy leather club chairs, watching the United States Attorney for the Southern District of New York stand at an antique brass bar cart and pour them each a scotch. Looking around the room, Brian concluded Sherrill Sheehan must've brought the furniture; it was a far cry from the worn, charmless, government-issued stuff the rest of the office used. Sherrill had been in the job for nearly eight years. Before that, he'd been in the justice department for two different administrations and a senior partner at White & Case. He was a rotund figure who favored three-piece suits and a bushy mustache. The look was anachronistic, as if he might have a gold timepiece tucked into his vest.

"Cheers," he growled, offering Brian his crystal-cut old fashioned.

"Cheers."

Sherrill folded his ample body into his chair behind his desk and took a gulp. "Boy, am I glad you didn't fuck that up." He made a noise somewhere between a croak and a chuckle.

Brian smiled. "Me too." He had won his case against the drug cartel. Not only had he handled the key witnesses on the stand, but it was his brief, the one he had been writing the day Isabelle asked him to leave work, the one he'd been toiling over the night she texted him her pseudo apology, that had gotten a key wiretap recording into evidence. It was a moment Brian had been working doggedly toward for his entire career. Winning this case was an essential step to getting promoted to a unit chief. And getting promoted was crucial to an eventual high-level administration job, which would pave his way to one day run for office. Brian had never admitted his ultimate goal to anyone, but Senator Flanagan had a nice ring to it. Sometimes when Brian couldn't sleep at night, his brain would play those words on repeat, soothing him with their syncopated syllables. And Brian knew that this entire fantasy would have been impossible without the intervention of Claire Manning.

A few years before, after clerking and putting in four years at an elite law firm, Brian had been ready to take the next step in his career plan. He applied for a job as an assistant U.S. attorney. The first interview went great. Brian was sure he had it. But just as it was wrapping up, the guy, one of Sherrill's deputies, looked at Brian and said, "I'm going to be honest with you, you're perfect for this job. But we have a lot of other people who are perfect, and they also speak fluent Russian or Mandarin." Brian left the interview understanding that he would not be getting the job and cursed himself for only mastering Spanish. A few days later, at a birthday dinner for Isabelle, he let it slip to Claire that he wasn't bullish on his chances.

"Is that Sherrill Sheehan's office?" Claire asked.

"Yes. Do you know him?"

"His family. Just a bit."

It was more than a bit. Two days later, Brian was called back in and got the job. When Brian thanked Claire, she acted like she had no idea what he was talking about. But she did. Claire was just like that, all class.

"I have two other matters I want you on," said Sherrill now. "No rest for the weary I'm afraid."

"Absolutely, sir. Looking forward."

"That's what I like to hear." Sherrill massaged his mustache with his thumb and index finger. "Keep this up and I think good things will be happening for you."

"Happy to be a part of this team." Brian would be even happier if he were running the team, which is what Sherrill was getting at. The chief of narcotics position had recently become vacant. Brian was a little green; there were more senior assistants who ought to be in front of him. But he'd made himself Sherrill's man. He could taste it now.

"Good," said Sherrill, putting down his empty drink. "Well, I've got a squash game to get to."

"Don't let me be in your way." Brian stood up. "Yale club?"

"That's right."

"Great courts."

Sherrill's eyes brightened. "You play?"

"A bit." Brian knew—from Claire!—that Sherrill would understand this meant he was very good. All Brian's years of squirrelling away the right words, the specific cultural references, even the exact body language did not go to waste. It was because of the Mannings and their world that he understood how to communicate with people like Sherrill Sheehan. He could signal, with small-pattern Hermès ties, easy familiarity with private clubs, and a good squash game, that he was one of them. Even though he was not.

"Well, let's get out there."

"Name a date."

"Tuesday, six a.m."

A few hours later, Brian left the office. He should've been riding the high of his meeting with Sherrill, but it took only a few blocks for the unsettled feeling to resurface. Brian's career was on the rise; this was undeniable. But the soaring of his professional life seemed to only put the failings of his personal life in more stark relief. Brian was thirty-five. At this age, a single man became a bachelor, his unattached status a defining element of personality. While he didn't have a biological clock, there was a creeping urgency hovering at the edge of consciousness. He'd always wanted to get married, have a family. He thought he'd be married with at least one kid by now. He saw his friends with babies and toddlers and felt a tug of not just longing, but a stab of fear that he was being passed by. He knew—of course he knew—that what was holding him back was Isabelle. In recent months, Brian had come to realize that his friendship with Isabelle—no matter how platonic his text messages—was no longer healthy. He would always care for Isabelle, but he needed to put distance between them. Now that the trial was over, he would go back on the apps, make himself go on a few dates a week. It was time.

Brian reached his building, a cookie-cutter high-rise in Battery Park, and went up to his alcove studio apartment. He took off his shoes and jacket and loosened his tie, grabbing a grapefruit-flavored seltzer from the fridge. He sat down on his couch and regarded what lay on his coffee table. Isabelle had dropped it off the day before with a note reading, *Enjoy! XO.* Brian rarely ever read novels; he had trouble with books that were not useful in a concrete way. Currently on his bedside table was *Getting to Yes*, a self-help guide to negotiation. And while he was trying to take a breather from all things Isabelle, there was no world in which he did not read *Underpainting*. He owed Isabelle that much, anyway. And maybe it would bring him closure. Because Brian suspected that within its pages lay the answer to the question that had stymied him since he met her: Who was Isabelle Manning?

24

New York, 2018

Ward

Ward took a left out of the Delta lounge at LaGuardia and headed for the gate. After boarding, he settled himself into his first-class window seat and ordered a drink from the flight attendant. Ward had taken this route before for one book tour or another. On those trips, his publisher jam-packed his schedule with appearances, readings, speaking engagements, radio interviews. But on this trip, there would only be one stop, only one event on his itinerary. There would be no hotels.

And Ward's publisher had no idea Ward was leaving New York. Ward ought not to have been doing anything except sitting at his desk and churning out pages. He'd been late before, a few weeks here and there, but never anything like this, never anything formal. Ward was so late that the novel had been scrapped from the spring catalog and pushed back to next fall.

The field trip to visit Texan uber-fan Diane Dunmeyer had its origins in Riverhead. He should've been elated when the gerontologist diagnosed Ward with nothing more than "normal cognitive decline." But Ward had not fully appreciated how much he needed something to be wrong with him. If there was something wrong, then there were things to do, steps to take. But if his current state was simply who he was, then there was nothing to do. Nothing but wait, observing his own slow march to the grave.

When he had finished with the doctor that day, Ward took matters into his own hands, driving himself to the Sag Harbor Pharmacy and buying every potentially beneficial vitamin in stock. All of the names were ridiculous. Sharp Senior. Elder Acuity! Extreme Ginkgo Biloba. It was humiliating. So he'd purchased one of those days-of-the-week containers to store them discreetly. Ward had been parsing the vitamins out into this container when Isabelle had come into the kitchen. His daughter seemed scandalized, but why should she judge? So he was taking vitamins. Big deal.

So far, the pills had done nothing but give him the runs.

The only thing that made Ward feel like himself was his correspondence with Diane. When Isabelle left Sag, Ward and Diane's email conversation ratcheted up quickly until they were exchanging dozens back and forth a day. They began texting, a medium of communication Ward was previously unfamiliar with. But now he employed it to give Diane intimate knowledge of everywhere he'd gone, everyone he saw, everything he'd watched on television, and everything he ate—which often included a hearty portion of the baked goods Diane was relentless in mailing him. It was very hard to feel lonely when someone else had such a full catalog of his life.

It had been a challenge to get much writing done in the midst of this repartee. He had abandoned his current draft. He should have done it months ago. The story of a secretly murderous Upper East Side doyenne was not his bag. His editor was crazy to have ever pushed him in such a ridiculous direction. Ward planned to give the publisher a full airing of his frustrations at their next meeting. Who were they to shape his work? Ward Manning's was a talent that could not be bridled. And this stallion was heading for Texas.

This trip would be the key to get him writing again. He would go to Dallas and meet Diane, and the trip would spark the right story line for the book. The idea of a melancholy Texas tale, all Venetian-blind motel rooms and crooked small-town politicians—*male* politicians!—appealed to him. He just needed that initial trigger, that first spark, and he would be off and running.

Diane was, of course, thrilled with the visit. The logistics of the plan came together seamlessly. Ward would arrive on a Tuesday and fly home on Thursday. He had to be home by Thursday—Thursday was Isabelle's book party.

Ward's copy of *Underpainting* was tucked into the seat pocket in front of him. He had yet to crack open the first page. He'd deduced from the press that the book was about a jealous wife who takes advantage of her husband's death. The reviews were positive, and in all the right places; Fern and the publisher had done their job. And Fern had done some real funny business getting the book out so fast. Ward didn't like to think too hard about the deal that had been made on that score. Instead, Ward busied himself looking up the reviews of his own first book just to have something to compare it to. (Isabelle's were not as good as his.) He'd planned to read the book on the flight. But as the plane took off, Ward closed his eyes. Just for a few moments.

The landing jolted Ward awake. He rubbed his eyes and looked out the smudged, scratched-up window. The air was thick and wiggly with the steam rising off the runway mixed with engine gas. The land stretched out flat and beige, dotted with cell phone towers and low, slab-like warehouses palpitating in the heat. It was all so ugly. It was a different ugly from the one he'd come from, but the barrenness of it reminded him of Missouri. He'd been back to his hometown exactly once since he'd left for Harvard. Nearly twenty years before, a cousin he barely remembered phoned up and told him his mother had died. There was no one to pay for the burial. Ward hadn't spoken to his mother in two decades. Despite their estrangement, Ward had mailed clippings of reviews and profiles every so often, the paper solid proof of just how wrong she'd been about him. Bobby never replied. That didn't matter.

Upon hearing of her death, Ward's first reaction was only surprise that her liver had lasted that long. Out of some misguided sense of obligation—or maybe just rank curiosity—he agreed to go to her funeral. He did not bring Claire or Isabelle, who must have been a teenager. He had not kept his past a secret—not exactly—but there were different kinds of knowing. If he brought them to Missouri, Claire and Isabelle would see the decaying homestead, they would smell the mold and the sour cigarette stink, they would feel the weight of desperation in the air. And they would understand something about him that he did not want understood.

◆   ◆   ◆

In the Dallas terminal, the air was thin and deodorized. There were crowds of men and women in pastel insignia-ed polo shirts and blindingly white sneakers. Ward followed signs for Ground Transportation, the designated rendezvous spot. Diane had been insistent that she pick up Ward from the airport. But it suddenly felt like a terrible idea, the completely wrong setting. None of Ward's fantasies for this trip involved a Hudson News or an Auntie Anne's.

Ward took the escalator down and scanned those awaiting arrival. No Diane. The surge of distress that perhaps she had forgotten, or perhaps this woman whom he had never met was not actually coming, took him by surprise. Standing there alone at the cavernous baggage claim at the Dallas Fort Worth airport, clutching the handle of his black Tumi, Ward Manning needed this. He had no wife. He had no novel. He did have Isabelle, but he seemed never to be in the right frame of mind for his daughter. Claire's absence sat between them like a deep well. As a parent, Ward had operated like a finishing spice, the flavor that made the dish. The umami. He was never sustenance itself. He felt this inadequacy with Isabelle now, trying to feed her hunger with nothing but salt. Because this feeling was unpleasant, he avoided it. Ward could not take into account anyone's emotional state but his own. At this moment, his own very much depended on the mythical Diane Dunmeyer materializing.

Just then he heard the voice, sweet and lilting like a birdsong, and turned to see the woman with the wavy blond hair he recognized from the photos he'd seen online. Her hair was the same, but everything else was different. She looked older. Pushing sixty. Maybe "from the wrong end" as Claire liked to say. And, though in her picture she had the face of a petite person, in the flesh she was more robust. She wore tight white jeans and a peach sweater with an underlay of sequins. Diane moved toward Ward until they were no more than ten feet apart. Then she stopped, covered her mouth with her hands, and looked at Ward like he was a Beatle.

"Diane, darling."

She fanned her hand in front of her face. "It's you. It's really you."

"Yes, it's me." Ward embraced her. She smelled like baby powder and hair spray. As she pressed her body into his, he could feel her breasts against his chest, large but unnaturally taut, like a trampoline. Well, Ward thought, real breasts in this part of Texas were probably as rare as Democrats. As she hugged him, Ward could feel Diane's shoulders shaking. Was she crying? Diane pulled back and looked at Ward. She had very long—possibly fake—eyelashes and what Ward imagined was painstakingly applied makeup.

Diane clapped her hands. "I still can't believe you're here. I really thought you might not actually be on that flight."

"Really? Why?"

"Oh I don't know. Silly, I guess," she said. "Are you tired? Are you hungry? Do you need to use the restroom?" Raaaste-Roooom.

"No, no, I'm fine."

Diane fished a puffy pink heart key chain out of her gigantic clear plastic purse. "Come on, let's get out of here."

Ward followed Diane into the sprawling parking garage. In the brief outdoor passage, even in April, Ward was confronted with the oppressive Texas heat, thick and sickly sweet.

"I hope you're hungry, Ward. You eat tacos, right?"

"Sure."

"Oh thank the Lord. I was thinking as I came to pick you up,

'Diane, you planned this whole meal and what if he doesn't eat Tex-Mex!'" She threw her head back and laughed.

They kept walking until Diane stopped in front of a black Escalade. The car was shiny and looked recently cleaned. Ward was feeling tickled by all the preparations that must have taken place in anticipation of his arrival.

She clicked open the trunk, and Ward loaded his suitcase before climbing into the passenger seat. Diane started to pull out of the space and then stopped. She put her hand on Ward's arm. "I almost forgot to ask."

"What?"

Diane looked at Ward seriously and asked, as if the free world depended on it, "Ward. Do you enjoy frozen margaritas?"

Sam was having a moment. In honor of his three hundredth Ethical Studies column, a profile had run in this month's *Vanity Fair*, and he was the interview in Sunday's *Times* magazine. Sam was already known to the intelligentsia of New York and LA, but this was a new level of fame. Sam was ever low-key and wanted to celebrate with a picnic dinner in the park, just the two of us. He'd come equipped with a blue-and-white checkered tablecloth and an honest-to-god Little Red Riding Hood basket, from which he produced a bottle of rosé, a Balducci's baguette, and a container of homemade chicken salad with teeny, tiny mandarin oranges. Clearly, Sam's ex-wife should be lobotomized for taking up with the chiropractor.

"Look," said Sam, motioning toward a neighboring blanket. Two women were sitting together, both wearing Aiden's Zelda Fitzgerald on their T-shirts.

I shook my head. "They're everywhere." Aiden's "found women" were all the rage. Sebastian had done his job selling the series to the masses. A new deal with Urban Outfitters had been quickly closed, and Aiden's estate was inundated with interest from galleries and collectors.

"Do you think there are more paintings?" Sam asked.

I swallowed my chicken salad. "Hard to say." On our last telephone call, I'd told Sebastian that the last had been found. I was sick of the lying and terrified that I'd been figured out. The show had attracted too much attention, and that creepy guy following me must have something to do with the portraits—why else was he at the show that night? After a long silence, Sebastian had said, "I hope very much that is not true." When I assured him it was, Sebastian dug in. "Livia, it would be better for everyone, especially you, if you found a few more. Just a few more."

"Who would've thought Aiden could've hidden so much away

in the floorboards?" Sam asked now. "I still don't understand how he got them in there."

"A real twist," I said. My secret sat swollen and heavy in my throat. I'd wondered if I could anonymously write into Sam's column, asking for advice. *Dear Sam, my wonderful boyfriend doesn't know I'm committing art fraud. Help!* But, of course, the fact pattern was too singular. If it came out what I'd done, it would be arsenic to his career. And, even more than that, Sam would never forgive me for lying to him. So I kept lying to him.

We packed up the picnic and headed toward the West Side, making pleasant chitchat. But when we reached the corner of my block, Sam stopped short. I followed his gaze to the strobe of blue and red lights.

"That's your building, isn't it?"

We hurried closer. A cluster of uniformed cops were outside.

"What's happened?" I asked a huddled group of residents.

"Break-in," said Mr. Crandel, the psychiatrist who lived in the building and saw patients in the first-floor office. The others shook their heads solemnly.

"Which apartment?"

"Two apartments—3A and 3C."

My stomach lurched; those were the apartments on either side of mine.

"Was anyone hurt?" Sam asked.

"No," said Crandel, clearly the self-designated speaker of the group. "The apartments were upended, but as far as they can tell, nothing was stolen."

My blood ran cold. All my fears were not imagined. And this break-in was not a random event. I was being hunted.

25

New York, 2018

Isabelle

The days leading up to the official publication of *Underpainting* were some of the busiest in Isabelle Manning's life. When she was not giving interviews, she was working on one of the many personal essays and press pieces that would be timed to come out in tandem with her book. And today, Isabelle would experience the crowning achievement of her life.

Isabelle was running early, so she got out of the Uber and walked down Eighth Avenue toward Port Authority. The temperature and humidity outside felt like a grocery store produce section. A low fog hung in the spring air as tiny green-yellow buds popped up on long-barren trees. When she was a few hundred yards away, she could see the metal scrim that overlay the office façade reading *The New York Times* in signature font. Isabelle walked into the lobby, an atrium built around a plot of silvery birch trees.

"Isabelle Manning. I have an appointment with Eden Jones."

The security guard eyed her with a phone between his cheek and shoulder.

"She's the editor of the Book Review."

"K." The guard typed into a computer embedded into the desk.

He gave Isabelle a playing card–size pass that curled into a C shape.

Isabelle had given many interviews in her life. She'd been just thirteen the first time she'd seen a quote of hers in print. By high school, reporters had her cell phone number. But every interview she had ever done was about her father. Isabelle was enlisted to provide background for a long-form piece or to show the filmmaker around the apartment. She understood her role in satiating the curiosity about what Ward Manning was *really* like. And she dutifully complied, providing what Claire referred to as "family color." Isabelle offered tidbits about what the man liked for breakfast or how he used to play hide-and-seek with her as a child (it was maybe twice, but the anecdote played). She gave fans that little nugget of information, the buried treasure in the three-thousand-word article, the thing that they could rattle off at dinner parties.

But today was different. Isabelle was riding up in the elevator because the *New York Times* wanted to interview the woman who had written *Underpainting*. It was exactly the kind of moment she had fantasized about all those years she'd toiled away unpublished. The doors opened to a large expanse of open-plan and glass-enclosed offices. A receptionist directed Isabelle to wait in a sitting area. A moment later, Eden appeared.

"Isabelle." She extended her hand. "Eden Jones." She was fifty-something in a structured charcoal dress with dramatic full sleeves. Eden was notoriously beautiful. And in person she was even more so than in the headshots and photographs Isabelle had spent much time scrolling through the night before, reading the flurry of press pieces that had come out when Eden had become the first Black woman editor of the Book Review. Her hair was pulled into a dramatic high bun that showcased her cheekbones. The few seconds the women stood face-to-face shaking hands were sufficient for Isabelle to have a full-blooded fantasy of she and Eden as best friends, having long lunches discussing literature, texting each other pictures of their outfits, and drinking wine in whatever fabulous apartment Eden lived in.

"Thanks for coming in."

"Oh it's my pleasure."

Eden beckoned Isabelle to follow her down the hall.

"So I loved the book," said Eden, looking back at Isabelle. She spoke evenly, as if she was stating a fact more than giving a compliment.

"Thank you. That means a lot." Many of Isabelle's interviews had been conducted over the phone, but Isabelle was glad this one was in person. She wanted to breathe the *New York Times* air, to sit on the *New York Times* couch, to absorb the moment with all her senses, devour it like a long-awaited dessert.

"And how's your father?" Eden asked.

Isabelle was caught off guard, though it was naïve to think her father was not going to come up. "He's, uh, he's okay. Working hard."

"Of course. Tell him I said hello."

"Will do." Eden, a literary power player, would probably have better luck getting Ward on the phone than Isabelle. She had seen her father only a handful of times in the past several months. He spent much of his time in Sag Harbor, presumably working. They'd had dinner during one of his scattered appearances in the city, but he seemed barely there. Sitting at the table, he couldn't stop fiddling with the phone, checking it every few moments, claiming it was his editor.

Ward should have received his official copy of *Underpainting* by now, but he had gone to Texas for a "speaking engagement." Isabelle did not know if the book had reached him before he left. When she'd mentioned her father's trip in passing to Irving, Ward's agent had no idea what she was talking about. Of course there was no speaking engagement. Isabelle could only imagine there was some kind of specialist there for whatever it was her father had. Isabelle had pushed thoughts of Ward's illness to the corners of her mind, convincing herself that publishing a book was the best medicine she could give her father. But now the book was about to be out, and it seemed there were practical realities—perhaps desperate realities—she needed to deal with.

Eden opened a door to a small room outfitted like a recording studio. "Here we are," said Eden. "That's your seat."

Isabelle sat and listened as Eden went over the technical details of the equipment and the format of the Book Review Podcast. Eden performed some vocal exercises, which, like everything she did, seemed completely cool. After her introductory remarks, Eden turned to Isabelle.

"With me today is Isabelle Manning, author of *Underpainting*. Thank you for joining us, Isabelle."

"It's a pleasure to be here, Eden."

"For those of you who have not read this book, it is the story of the wife of a highly successful portraitist, who, let's just say, continues the family business after he dies—on her own terms." Eden paused. "Intriguing premise."

"Thank you," said Isabelle.

"You chose to set the book in the early 1990s, which I thought was interesting."

"Yes." Isabelle's heart started beating faster.

"You really nailed the details of that time period." Eden stared at Isabelle for a long moment. Her eyes felt accusing. "I couldn't believe that someone who was a child back then could get it so right."

Isabelle's mouth went dry. At various junctures, Isabelle had considered disclosing the true provenance of the book to Fern. But when she tried to formulate the words to tell him, they never sounded right. He might not get that her mother had given Isabelle the book. *Gifted* it to her. And, Isabelle reasoned, the deception need not extend past this book. She wasn't a charlatan; she could write books on her own. And once she'd published a book, the web of insecurities so thick she could barely see the keyboard in front of her would lift, and she would be able to write. And yet, Isabelle did not relish the prospect of being alone again with her MacBook, the mirror of the blank page held up to her image.

"Well," said Isabelle now, and she gave the answer she'd practiced: The story of Livia's deception was more believable pre-internet age.

"Ah, of course," said Eden, nodding.

Isabelle smiled, her heartbeat slowing.

"And tell me more about the title," said Eden.

"Underpainting is a technique where an image is rendered in a neutral before a full palate of color is applied," said Isabelle. She had learned about underpainting in a college course on Renaissance art. "In the book, photographs serve as a kind of underpainting for the artwork." And there was another unsaid resonance to the title. Isabelle had finished the book, she had edited it, top to bottom, but her mother's work lay underneath, the foundation upon which all else had been built.

"So interesting," said Eden, then looked down at her notes for a moment before she said, "Livia is a pisser. I really enjoyed her character."

"Me too," said Isabelle. "I mean, thank you." Continuing on in the voice her mother had originated, conjuring up scenes and inner monologue for this tortured, yet scrappy character, had been the most enjoyable writing experience she'd ever had. Even in the book Isabelle had been working on about a woman going through a contentious divorce, the voice never flowed out of her the way Livia's did.

"What do you think would have happened to Livia if her husband had not died?"

Isabelle paused. "Nothing?" she said with a laugh. "I think he was such a big star and personality that it was impossible for her to see herself clearly next to him. He sucked up all the oxygen. He was the block to her creativity. Once he was removed, she was free."

◆　◆　◆

After finishing the interview with a discussion of plotting and structure, they exchanged a warm goodbye, and Isabelle left the way she came in. It had begun to rain, and umbrellas hovered over pedestrians. Isabelle hadn't brought one, but she barely noticed. She had been interviewed by the *New York Times*; she could have walked through a hailstorm. There was no question now, she had arrived. By hook or by crook, Isabelle had made it. She wasn't looking as she stepped off the curb, and didn't notice the giant puddle that had formed over the gutter. Her right foot was suddenly submerged up to the ankle in the water and thick, disintegrating black matter of New York City sidewalks.

26

Texas, 2018

Ward

Ward and Diane sat on Diane's couch, which was the consistency of a marshmallow and loaded with silk decorative pillows. Ward held out his wineglass, goblet-sized and patterned to resemble lace, as Diane poured from a pitcher of frozen margaritas. He and Diane had spent the afternoon this way. Sitting together drinking, while Ward read aloud from his own books.

When they'd arrived from the airport, Diane showed Ward into her ranch house, identical to several dozen ranch houses in the development, with a Texas flag outside. The interior was peach-colored and smelled of cinnamon potpourri. Diane's furniture was robust and brocaded. On the side tables were pots of silk plants and cut-crystal bowls filled with Hershey's Kisses and Werther's hard candy. All Ward could think of was how it would amuse Claire to see what happened when Ward was left to his own devices. No matter how famous, rich, and revered Ward became; no matter what he hid from view; all Claire had to do was look at him with that smile at once saintly and mocking, the gleam of a private joke in her eyes, and he wasn't a world-famous writer but a guy in a polyester jacket who ferried beef wellington and Cobb salads. And if Claire could have seen Ward standing in this tacky house with this woman he'd struck up with online, she would have sized him up. *Just look at you now.*

Perhaps this had been an insane idea. Where the hell was he? He could feign some kind of book emergency and get on the next flight back to New York, call off this ridiculous rumspringa. But before he did, Ward caught a whiff of something coming from the kitchen. Tacos simmering in the slow cooker. Ward decided he would stay for lunch. It turned out that Diane was a great cook. And she was also pleasant and complimentary company. Somewhere along the line, Ward's desire to flee melted away, like the ice-slush of his frozen margarita. After lunch, Ward followed Diane into the living room to find his books, all of them, lined up on one of the built-in shelves that surrounded the television.

"Oh," said Diane a bit sheepishly. "I was hoping you could sign those for me."

"My pleasure." Ward picked up her old paperback of *Nightingale Call.* Flipping through it, he saw that there were underlines and notations. "Did you do this?"

Diane nodded. "Yes."

Ward looked at this woman, now wearing the velour pants and matching zip-up hoodie that somehow acted as a bustier that she had changed into after lunch. If he'd seen her passing him by on the street, he'd never have imagined her as one of his readers. He'd certainly never made a single keystroke with a person like her in mind. But standing there with Diane, Ward saw that his writing had the power to reach even those who seemed furthest from him. He was filled with a new satisfaction.

Ward signed all of Diane's books and then read aloud his favorite passages, Diane's head eventually falling into his lap. By the end of the evening, there was no chance that Ward would be joining his suitcase in the guest room. Diane's bedroom had a very ornate crystal chandelier and a canopy bed draped with a fabric somewhere between a wedding veil and mosquito netting. On the floor by her bedside table were several stacks of books. Ward looked closer at the spines. Jonathan Franzen. Tom Wolfe. Philip Roth. Michael Chabon. Ward had assumed that he was the only literary writer she read, though Diane had never actually implied this. It was unpleasant to see the other names. Had Diane written to these writers, these men, too? Was he standing in her bedroom simply because he was the only one to respond?

Diane had dimmed the chandelier and lit the pillar candles nestled together like a little city on her vanity. Then she approached him so they were mere inches apart. Ward had not been with anyone but Claire in nearly forty years. Forty years! He was glad that this woman was so different from his wife that there would be no comparison between them. But still, as Diane inched closer, Ward felt the tug of something inside him, a sadness mixing with pleasure. He wanted no poignancy at this moment. Even with the blue pill he'd managed to discreetly swallow, he knew he needed to act fast before it was all over for him. Ward reached out and pulled down the zipper on her hoodie, and her breasts blossomed toward him. Diane placed one hand on his chest and busied the other with his belt buckle. And Ward rose to the occasion.

◆ ◆ ◆

The next day, Ward and Diane went out for lunch at the Kimbell Art Museum and spent the balance of the afternoon back on the couch with his books. It was good to be with a woman again, to have someone taking care of him, lavishing him with attention, making sure he was never hungry, that he had water by the bedside and the right number of pillows. Such pampering was precisely what had been missing from his life. He had not forgotten a word or felt that gumminess jamming up the gears of his mind. He would soon be ready to write again.

Thursday morning, they had to wake by six for Ward's flight. On the car ride to the airport, both were quiet, overly polite, regenerating their more formal personas as the trip came to an end.

"May I change this?" Ward asked of the high-pitched pop music.

"Of course, be my guest."

Ward jabbed at the button on the dashboard and flipped it to the '60s station, and the strains of Diana Ross singing "You Can't Hurry Love" filled the car. Ward found himself half singing along, thinking reflexively of Claire. His wife had loved the Supremes. Sometimes when he used the car after her, he'd turn the key in the ignition and Motown would come blasting out of the speakers at teenager volume. She often had music on in the kitchen while she cooked, shimmying slightly as she stirred a pot. At least in the early years of their marriage. The house had been quieter as time went on. He blamed the somberness on what had happened in Jamaica, but perhaps it had started long before that. Perhaps it had been his own fault.

Sitting in the car, thoughts of returning to his old life, his writing, his widowerhood, his daughter's book party, filled him with pre-emptory dread. A thought had been germinating. A plan. He was old, but he still had additional acts in him.

Diane signaled and took the airport exit. Ward was running out of time.

"So, Diane," said Ward. "I have a little proposition for you."

"Uh-huh," said Diane, keeping her eyes on the road.

"How would you like to come visit me in New York?"

"Oh, Ward, that's so generous."

"I think we'd have a grand time."

Diane nodded as she drove into the airport proper and navigated toward Delta.

"You could come whenever you like, really—well, I should check my speaking engagement calendar, of course, but I'm sure we can find a time."

"Hm."

"Let's plan for later this month."

She put the car in park and looked down, folding her bottom lip into her top. "I don't think this month works."

"It could be another time."

"It's not that."

Ward was confused. "Then what?"

"Well," said Diane, pausing to sigh. Ah, she was intimidated by his elite New York scene.

"You needn't be nervous."

Diane half smiled. "No. I'm not."

"And I'll come back here, too," said Ward. "I think Texas suits me." He smiled at Diane, but saw that she had a grimace on her face. "What is it?"

"Can I be honest with you, Ward?"

Ward gritted his teeth, nothing good ever came after those words. "Of course."

"After how much I enjoyed your books, I think I felt I owed you a thank-you note. You know, being a proper southern girl and all." Ward looked at Diane, her blond hair perfectly in place, her icy-pink lipstick. "I never in a million years expected you to write me back. Never, ever did I think I would actually meet you."

Ward felt himself recoil. Diane's words touched something tender inside him, like a raw, doughy spot where a tooth had been extracted. Writing back to Diane should have been beneath him. Visiting Diane should have been beneath him. Obsessively reading his fan mail should have been beneath him. A writer of his echelon shouldn't need such petty stroking. All of it debased his status. Some part of him had always known this. But he had not understood until that moment that Diane knew it too.

"And this has been like a fairy tale. To have you in my *home*." Diane drew a hand to her chest. "I will never, ever forget it."

Ward grunted.

"But I think we should quit while we're ahead."

"Fine." He was desperate to end this encounter and begin the process of blocking it out. Diane, however, was not finished.

"I hope I'm not out of line in saying this, but you seem sad. I don't think you've properly grieved your wife."

Ward closed his eyes, feeling his face flush. This was unbearable. Had he even mentioned Claire to her? Maybe a few times, but she had just come up naturally. "Thank you for that insight."

"And this might sound funny, but I don't think I wanted you to be a real person."

With this sentence, a dam inside Ward gave way and sent a rush of blood and bile and heat rising into his throat. "Oh, but my dear," said Ward, his voice vibrating with righteous anger, "I am *not* a real person."

There was a pocket of silence, both of them knowing that these moments, sitting in the Escalade, the smell of air-conditioning and leather around them, *My Girl* playing on the radio, were the last they would ever spend together. Diane moved in to kiss his cheek, but Ward leaned away and opened the door.

"I didn't mean to hurt your feelings."

Ward laughed. "Hurt my feelings? No, I don't think so." He got out of the car and retrieved his bag from the trunk.

When he came back around to the sidewalk, Diane rolled down the passenger-side window. "Good luck, Ward."

He kept his head down, busying himself with the handle of his suitcase, as he raised one hand in parting. He walked toward the oversized revolving door of the terminal. Even though he wanted to, he did not turn around, he did not check if Diane was watching him through the car window, regretting her words. If he had, he would have known that she had already driven away.

27

Jamaica, 1992

Claire

Claire walked toward the water. Seaweed shaped like shredded paper churned in the frothy surf, and the sea felt warm compared to the cool morning air. At just after seven, there was still a biting wind. She had been up for hours. Claire often found herself awake before five, staring at the ceiling, listening to the drone of Ward's exhalations. Alone on the beach, she waded through the shallows and dove in, the noise of the birds circling overhead replaced with the thrum of the water. She imagined this was what the outside world sounded like from the womb. When Isabelle was an infant, the only thing that would quell her screams was the whirr of running water. Claire would take her into the bathroom and turn the bath faucet on full force. The sound of the water pounding the porcelain would lull Isabelle to sleep.

When Isabelle was a baby, Claire sometimes felt as if there was entirely too much time, interminable days marked in bottles, diaper changes, and tummy time. Everyone said children grow up too fast, but time with a toddler could feel entirely too slow. Now Isabelle was ten, with her own schedule, much of it away from Claire, and every hour with her daughter felt like a gift. Maybe Claire was imagining things, but Isabelle had seemed out of sorts ever since the day Claire had been late to pick her up. She was eager to use the week to reconnect.

They were staying at the Full Moon in a little cottage with a white-and-black chessboard tiled floor and a collection of mismatched furniture. Her own family, the Cunninghams, had been coming to this hotel since Claire was a teenager. It was not fancy or slick like some of the newer resorts, and that's what Claire liked about it.

Claire swam back and forth a few more times before she pivoted toward the beach. When the water was too shallow to swim, she stood up, wading her way through the resistance of the waves. Claire did a quick, shivery tiptoe to one of the white mesh lounge chairs and wrapped herself up in a towel. She squinted up at the sun that had broken through the clouds while she'd been in the water. Last night, she'd seen rain in the forecast on the local news. Heavy rain. It was hard to believe looking at the taunting sun in the kiddie-pool-colored sky.

◆ ◆ ◆

They had just settled into après lunch lassitude. Ward was upstairs taking his nap. His usual practice was to lay down on the bed on top of the covers fully clothed, cross his hands upon his chest, and close his eyes, waking exactly forty-five minutes later without setting an alarm. Ward believed his ability to self-rouse spoke to a fundamental strength of his personality. Claire sat on the patio with a crossword while Isabelle lounged beside her, writing in the journal she carried everywhere. She could see the page Isabelle was working on had text but also a number of heavily inked hearts. Being an only child made her daughter simultaneously more mature and more childlike than her sibling-ed peers. Isabelle was fluent in dinner party banter. She was precocious and charming. Claire and Ward recently learned that their daughter knew the exact components in a martini when she'd blurted them out to the waiter. How could this be, when it felt like yesterday that Claire was snuggled up in Isabelle's toddler bed reading *Runaway Bunny*? It would only be a matter of time before Isabelle was too old for the blue gingham bathing suit with ruffles at the hips that Claire had bought for her.

Claire wrote in the answer to 47-down, Wharton's entitled heroine. U-N-D-I-N-E. She heard the phone ringing inside the house and got up to answer it before it cut off. Perhaps Ward had been woken and answered.

"Any interest in a walk down to the beach?" Claire asked Isabelle.

Her daughter shook her head. A few damp strands of hair had blown from her ponytail and gotten stuck in the corner of her mouth. "Maybe later."

"All right." Claire looked back down at her puzzle when she heard a familiar voice calling her name.

"I think Dad's up," said Isabelle.

"I'll go see what he wants." But before Claire had moved, she saw Ward wrestling with the sliding screen door. Even from several feet away and through the dark mesh, she could see the urgency in his eyes. His hair was still wild from his nap, and he was gripping the cordless like a club.

"Goddamnit," he muttered at the screen, which had come off the track. He struggled for a moment and then thrust his weight forward and popped the screen out of its frame. "There."

"Ward! What are you doing?"

"They can fix it," said Ward as he balanced the loose screen on the wall.

"What's going on? Is everything all right?"

"Oh you could say that." Ward smiled at Claire and Isabelle. "I've won."

"Won what?" But as the question escaped her lips, Claire knew. "Oh. Ward. My goodness." The look on his face had not been alarm, but triumph that he had, once again, dominated. "Congratulations."

"Isn't it fantastic? I thought I was a long shot. I was worried they wouldn't want to give it to me again. Not so soon. But I guess they couldn't help themselves."

Claire stood up to kiss her husband, and Ward pulled her into him and danced her around the patio, twirling her as he hummed a tune it took Claire a second to recognize. Carmen. The Habanera.

"How did you find out?" Claire asked.

"Irving just called—the hotel patched him through to the house," said Ward, still twirling, now as if he had castanets above his head.

"Dad," said Isabelle. "You're being weird." But she was smiling at Ward, studying him.

"Isabelle." Ward continued to thrust one hip forward and then the other. "I hope someday you can experience the supreme pleasure of winning a truly important literary award. Twice." Ward inhaled as if he could smell the musk of his success in the balmy air. "And then you will understand why I am dancing around like an utter fool."

Isabelle rolled her eyes, but Claire could see her mouth set into a little knot of intention.

The doorbell to the house rang. Ward stopped and put his finger in the air. "Champagne."

"Really, Ward?" asked Claire, but her husband was already bounding toward the door. His movements and mannerisms were cartoonish, like a 1940s movie star, Cary Grant or Spencer Tracy.

Isabelle and Claire, alone again, regarded each other. She smiled apologetically at her daughter. Claire had chosen this—at least, some of it. She was accustomed to bearing witness to another's success, being caught up in the foamy wake of Ward's accomplishments. Isabelle never had a choice. Ward would never be the sort of man for whom fatherhood was a crowning achievement. He would never put his life on hold for her. His interests would never be subjugated to anyone else's, including his daughter's. At some point Isabelle would understand this, if she did not already. Claire sat down next to Isabelle and kissed her head. She smelled warm, like sunlight and Water Babies sunscreen mixed with grape Bubblicious.

Ward returned and made a grand show of pouring the drinks.

"Here, darling," Ward said to Isabelle. "For a special occasion." And he handed Isabelle her own flute.

Claire was too flustered to protest before Isabelle downed the drink in a large gulp. "Isabelle!"

"What?" Isabelle smiled.

Claire shook her head.

"I need to pack," said Ward once he'd drunk his glass.

"Why?" asked Claire.

"Oh yes, didn't I say? I need to be back in New York. Irving wants to do some publicity. You know, capitalize on the news, trot me around, that type of thing. There's a six p.m. flight."

"You're leaving tonight?"

"Yes."

"It's only two more days. Can't you wait?"

"I'm afraid I can't," said Ward, not seeming regretful in any way.

Claire inhaled. "Fine."

Ward disappeared into the house. Moments later Isabelle's friend Sara, whose family always stayed in the house next door, appeared. Sara was Isabelle's age, but looked like a teenager and had a throaty, movie star voice. Earlier in the week, Claire was sure she was wearing lipstick and perfume. Sara's parents were both therapists and entirely too permissive, not that it was Claire's business.

"Bye, Mom. We're leaving."

"Where are you going?"

"Waterskiing."

"Waterskiing? Does the hotel have that?"

"No, Sara's dad rented a boat," Isabelle said impatiently.

"Oh."

"Come on, we're going to be late," said Sara.

"Bye, Mom."

"All right, bye," said Claire absently, and kissed Isabelle again before she watched her set off down the beach, her little bathing suit skirt bobbing up and down.

. . .

Ward bubbled about the cottage, gathering himself for the flight, involving Claire in urgent searches for keys, the *New Yorker* he was reading, the nose drops he took on the plane. Finally, seated in the back of a luggage-loaded golf cart, waving at her like he was on a parade float, Ward departed. Claire returned to her lounge chair by the pool and lay staring up at the sky filling with light, fluffy clouds. She was restless. She went to her room and got out the notebook where she often jotted down ideas for her book. Claire had planned to take the week away from writing, but she'd found herself drafting out a scene, a version of Livia exposing the truth of what she'd done. Claire was so focused that she did not notice the sun slipping behind the clouds. It was not until sometime later, when a wind picked up, sending goose bumps on her forearms that Claire realized the weather had shifted. And that she had been writing for a long time. She sat up in her chair, putting her notebook aside. Something was not right. Since becoming a mother, she had these Miss Clavel moments, and she felt this one strongly. She looked at her watch. Just after four. She couldn't remember what time Isabelle had said she would return. If she had said anything at all. Claire had been so focused on Ward and his prize and him leaving that she had not been in her right mind. Why hadn't she asked where the boat was from? And exactly when it would be returning? Or, even better, said no.

When it was nearly five, Claire rang up the main desk of the hotel to see if they knew anything about a waterskiing boat. They did not. She walked down to the beach. She used her hand to shield her eyes in the gray glare as she looked back and forth across the surf. The waves that were clear blue that morning had turned opaque, reflecting the pigeon-gray clouds in the sky. The air was heavy with impending rain. The crows circled overhead, calling to one another in a way that felt like a warning. The forecast had been right. But not just rain, a storm.

"Come on, where are you?" Claire said out loud as she scanned the water. "Where are you?" Isabelle had been gone nearly three hours. Could the boat really still be out? Wouldn't the driver have come to shore when the weather turned? He would, wouldn't he? "Please, please, please," Claire heard herself repeating. Out on the horizon, there was nothing. Nothing. Fifteen minutes before, she might have been able to talk herself out of panic. Now, it was coming as sure as the rain.

A drop landed on her cheek. And then another. And in seconds there was a deluge of water, pounding her head, soaking through the white cotton cover-up. With the rain, Claire gave herself permission to cry. The sky turned near black, and zags of lightening with tributaries like pulmonary veins lit up the sky. Another shudder of thunder sent the crows flying off the beach. Arms at her side, fists balled, she began to sob. Over the howl of the wind, and her own cries vibrating in her ears, Claire did not hear the manager of the hotel running down the beach, shouting her name.

28

New York, 2018

Brian

Brian saw Isabelle at the top of the stairs but quickly calculated that she was too surrounded for him to make his approach. He climbed the marble steps of the Metropolitan Library Association—a place he knew from Isabelle as "the libes"—and reached the landing where a jazz quartet played and a table of Isabelle's books had been stacked in a twisting formation like a skyscraper next to a huge arrangement of cherry blossoms. The room was packed. Brian scanned the crowd but did not see anyone he knew. It seemed unthinkable in college, but Brian suspected that Isabelle actually had very few friends from their Brown days. Many of the times he brought up the name of one of her old confidants, Isabelle would stick out her tongue and say something like, *Ugh, she's unbearable since she had kids.* Everyone at the party looked cool to the point of unapproachable. Women with hair cut into razor-sharp edges and bright red lipstick wearing oddly shaped clothes that looked home-loomed but probably cost more than his weekly paycheck. Men with carefully cultivated five-o'clock shadows and very specifically frayed T-shirts. Brian had considered running home to change, but what was the point? He didn't own clothes like this. Brian had only one look: heterosexual lawyer.

Brian had made it two months without seeing Isabelle. The length of time allowed anticipation to build, and being with her now in person felt like an event. Brian was nervous. That might have to do with what he had in his jacket pocket. From several feet away, he took her in. Isabelle wore an iridescent white dress shaped like a chic form-fitting toga. She looked thinner and a bit more drawn in the face. Just then she glanced up from her conversation and saw him, breaking into a smile and giving him a little wink. He swelled reflexively; even among these very hip people, Brian was still Brian.

Brian had made good on his promise to himself. He'd kept away from Isabelle. He'd gone back on the apps, venturing out on dates a few nights a week. He met women who were attractive, women who were funny, women with résumés that far surpassed his own, women who wanted the exact same things he did. But none of them stood a chance. Not after he read *Underpainting*.

After Isabelle's erratic behavior—begging him to leave his office, then barely communicating with him—Brian had convinced himself that Isabelle was not going to change. She would never really give in to the feelings that always simmered tantalizingly below the surface. And it was no secret they envisioned different futures. Isabelle did not share in his fantasy of a big house in the suburbs, a solid, ivy-sprayed structure with a mudroom strung with soccer cleats. She would sooner don a fat suit than drive carpool in Greenwich, Connecticut. Isabelle had always said she wanted a daughter so she could replicate what she'd had with Claire, but Brian could not readily envision Isabelle as a mother. Anyway, she didn't want a sweet, steady life with a sweet, steady guy.

Unless she did.

Underpainting was fantastic. Dark, funny, addictive, just like its author. It was also revealing. The main character, Livia, experiences frustration at the hands of her self-centered husband, and as soon as he's dead, she takes up with Sam, a good, caring, ethical man. A nice guy! Maybe Isabelle couldn't tell Brian how she felt, but she had written it. Brian was Sam. And with that glimmer of hope, the feelings Brian had vacuum-sealed in repression and denial broke free. He'd been kidding himself all these years, pretending he was happy as just friends. Brian didn't want to be friends with Isabelle. He loved her. And finally he could see Isabelle loved him, too.

Not only did Isabelle love him, but she just might be ready to do something about it. Now that Isabelle had published her book, she would be freed from the goal she'd pursued so myopically at the expense of other much-neglected aspects of her life—like having a relationship. The time was, at long last, right.

Brian reached into his jacket pocket and stroked the velvet jewelry box hidden inside. It was a little over-the-top, yes. And it had cost more than he could really afford. But when he saw Isabelle's face, none of that mattered. He just needed to find his moment.

Ward

Ward was late. He had no excuse, since he'd been sitting in his apartment all day, eating pistachios and reading his own books in between watching porn. But somehow the act of getting into the shower and putting on clothes suitable for evening plans was all just a bit much. Now, nearly an hour after he'd meant to leave, Ward was finally dressed. He looked at himself in the mirror. It was as if weighted fishhooks had been attached to his jowls. His hair had grown too thin to support the length. Where his mane had once been sexily unruly, his hair was now reminiscent of the dregs of cotton candy. Had he looked this way a week before? Ward couldn't imagine it, but last week felt like a very long time ago.

Ward considered putting on a tie but decided against it. No one got dressed up anymore. And certainly not for book parties. Not like the old days when he filled up Gotham or Il Mulino with people looking like they were going to the fucking Oscars. That was a different time. A different life. Tonight he was going to a book party, and he'd be lucky if he recognized five people. He hoped to god that many recognized him. Ward wasn't the guest of honor, or the man of the hour, or even a scene-stealing sideshow. He was the has-been. His own daughter had taken his place. Literally.

It was Fern who had come up with the plan to fill Ward's slot with Isabelle's book, to appease the publisher. As if a debut novel could do what his would! Isabelle had no idea, which was fine by Ward. He didn't need that humiliation added to the list. What really bothered Ward was that he hadn't published in over three years, and civilization had marched on. No one had taken to the streets, demanding his work. No one had sent him death threats. Ward hoped George R. R. Martin knew how lucky he was. *His* fans were dedicated. Even Ward's publisher seemed to have lost faith. His editor was no longer knocking down the door, asking for pages. He wasn't giving him a deadline or pressing Ward for a timetable. This silence was the worst punishment. It seemed that the industry had written Ward off. They were taking their losses and moving on.

Ward walked downstairs. He had begun to hate the apartment. He particularly couldn't stand being in his study. The sumptuously done room that had once felt like a haven now mocked him. Sitting in his desk chair he felt the eyes of Napoleon assessing him like a predator might its prey. Maybe Claire had been right about the painting. Maybe it was a pretentious eyesore. But the problem was more pervasive than a painting. In Sag Harbor, Ward could feel comfortable. A house was meant for calm and quiet, an old man shuffling around. But the city was different. A Fifth Avenue apartment should have bustle, crowds, parties, bodies moving with intent among its rooms. The city was for people who were relevant, those at the center of things. It was no longer for him. He should sell.

Ward rode the elevator to the lobby and began walking down Fifth. Ward knew rationally that none of his troubles were Isabelle's fault. Not his inability to write his book. Not the disaster in Texas. Not Claire dying and leaving him alone. And, given what he'd done to her, he should feel nothing but relief that Isabelle finally had her book. His gambit had not backfired. And yet it was difficult for the celebrations for *Underpainting* to feel like anything but salt in an open, festering wound. And as such, Ward had not yet brought himself to actually read the book. This was one thing he could still withhold. And since returning from Dallas, he'd needed to reread his own books, to find proof that he had, at least once, produced great work. He was most impressed by the early books, the first three. He hadn't read them in years and found himself entirely moved by their genius. They had a satisfying tautness, not a wasted word. What he needed was to replicate that. But, of course, he couldn't.

Twenty minutes later, Ward found himself at the steps of the library. He could see the jubilant scene through the second-floor windows. Ward took a deep inhale, walked in, and entered the fray.

Isabelle

The last hour had been a blur of shaking hands, being congratulated, letting people's praise fall over her like the first warmth of spring. Fern worked the party like a rope line, bringing a who's who of editors and publishers over to her one after the other. In a brief reprieve, Isabelle stole into a small enclave by the bathroom. Standing still, Isabelle realized she was trembling slightly. And she was oddly aware of her breathing, as if she needed to focus to get the right amount of oxygen. There was the sound of a toilet flush and a moment later a woman opened the bathroom door, wiping her hands on the skirt of her floral prairie dress. She looked up and her eyes widened. "Isabelle."

Isabelle leaned down and gave Margot a kiss on the cheek.

"I loved it," Margot whispered, embracing her.

"Oh thank you." Isabelle's eyes were suddenly wet. From her post at the library reception desk, Margot had watched Isabelle toil fruitlessly day after day, year after year. She, perhaps more than anyone else, knew what this night meant.

"It's just perfect. Perfect." Isabelle clutched Margot's hands with her own. "So original. I'm so proud of you."

"Better than *Fifty Shades*?"

"Well . . ." Margot smiled, her face flushing.

"All right, I won't be greedy."

A voice came booming from the nearby landing. "What are you doing hiding by the loo?" Isabelle turned to see her godmother, a blur of gold lamé and diamonds, coming toward her. Margot touched Isabelle's arm and gave her a smile before she hurried away.

"Glenda." Isabelle hugged her.

"Oh I'm so relieved. I really didn't know what we were going to do with you." Glenda laughed, and Isabelle laughed too. Now that she had her book out, sad things turned funny.

"I'm so glad you took my advice and used those books I gave you."

"Hmm. Have you read the book?"

"Not yet. Not yet, dear. I've bought hundreds of copies but just haven't had a moment. Jonathan is whisking me to Il Pellicano next week. I'll read it on the plane," she said. "And what an event."

The second-floor reading room, generally taken up with retirees, dozing geriatrics with double-sheets rising rhythmically on their chests, was crowded and boisterous, people's faces flushed from alcohol and raised voices.

"May I borrow you for a moment, doll?" Fern was at Isabelle's side, his thumb and forefinger around the bone of her elbow. "Fernando Ramirez-Clement." Fern extended his hand to Glenda.

"Oh pish, I know who you are," said Glenda, "and you know who I am. Your husband is responsible for this." Glenda put her hands open-faced under her jaw line, like a 1940s pinup girl. "I'm bankrolling all your vacations." Glenda and Fern laughed conspiratorially.

"I was trying to be discreet," said Fern, "but thank you, Sardinia was lovely this year."

"Your husband is a genius. He could charge me double and I'd still be in twice a month."

"I'll pass that along."

"Oh you naughty boy!"

"And how do you like our girl?" Fern put his arm around Isabelle. "Jeez, doll, you're skin and bones. How much weight have you lost?"

"Yes, you look practically ready for Renfrew," said Glenda, running her eyes over Isabelle. "Well done."

Isabelle shrugged. She had no appetite and felt too jittery to eat. She barely slept. She told herself it was just happy nerves, like when she started college or got her story in the *New Yorker*. Though it did feel a bit more akin to awaiting a natural disaster or living on the lam.

Isabelle felt a tap on her shoulder. She turned to see Brian. "Hey," he said softly, and pulled her in for a long hug as Fern and Glenda kept talking. "Congratulations," said Brian. "I have a new favorite book."

"Oh yeah?" Isabelle pulled away to face him.

"Of course, Isabelle. Are you surprised?"

"I just know you're not the biggest fiction guy, that's all."

"Well, this is my kind of fiction." Brian looked at her significantly with a dopey grin on his face. All the coldness from the previous months was gone. He seemed almost high, though that was not a possibility.

"You good, Bri?"

"Great. Really great," said Brian. "Actually I'd love to talk to you."

"Okay." As Isabelle spoke, she saw her father summit the top of the stairs. "Oh, just give me one minute. Sorry."

"Later's good," Brian called after her.

Isabelle wedged herself through the crowd to Ward, who was now taking a smoked salmon blini off a tray. As she got closer, she was alarmed at how tired Ward looked, his entire posture and carriage hunched over. The book was meant to be for her father, but she felt a pang of guilt that she had been so focused on herself, she'd let him deteriorate this way.

"Dad, hi." Isabelle leaned in and kissed him on the cheek. "Thanks for coming."

Ward nodded as he chewed his salmon, holding up a finger. "Pretty good turn out," he said when he swallowed.

"Fern did the invites." Her father's eyes were wandering the room. "How was Texas?"

Ward scowled. "Too hot. Not worth my time."

Isabelle nodded. "Sorry."

Ward shrugged. "Where can I get another salmon thing?"

"I think the waiters are circulating." Isabelle pointed indiscriminately toward the center of the room.

Ward was on his tiptoes looking past Isabelle. "And what does one have to do to find a drink?"

"There's a bar," said Isabelle. "But are you okay, Dad?"

He cocked his head and snapped, "Fine. Why wouldn't I be?"

"No reason." She waited for him to speak. Isabelle did not want to have to be the one to bring it up, but the silence seemed to demand it of her. "And my book, Dad?"

"Oh yes." Ward swallowed. "It was very nice, Isabelle."

"Very nice?"

"Yes. Very nice."

"Oh. Okay. Well, maybe you can tell me more another time."

Fern sidled up to the two of them. "Come, come, time for your toast. And hi, Ward, good to see you."

"Now?"

"No, next week," said Fern. He guided Isabelle by the small of her back to a microphone that had been set up in the middle of the room by the windows.

"Here." Fern offered his champagne. "Liquid courage."

Isabelle took a sip as Fern tapped the inside of his wedding band on a glass, which did nothing. He then put two fingers to his mouth and whistled so loudly several guests put their hands to their ears. The room fell silent.

"I was a crossing-guard in a past life," he said to titters. "It is time for us to hear from the glorious creature who wrote this book." Fern gestured Vanna White–style to Isabelle.

While everyone clapped, Isabelle took one last glance at the scrap of paper with her notes before tucking it in between the first two fingers of the hand holding her flute and taking the microphone from Fern. This was the precise moment she had imagined countless times for so many years. It was the moment when she believed everything would be good and she would feel a pure and true joy, like a child discovering that ice cream exists. She waited for those feelings, but what came were her father's words. *Very Nice.*

The cheering died down and Isabelle was up.

"Thank you so much for being here tonight." Isabelle listed all the people at the agency and the publisher who'd shepherded the book into the world. "As many of you know," Isabelle continued, "this has not been an easy road. For a long time, I was not certain that this day would ever come. There were a few others who were pretty worried this day would never come." She looked at Fern and he mouthed theatrically, *Never.*

"The people to whom I owe the deepest debt of gratitude are my parents. Growing up, my father made writing seem glamorous— thanks a lot, Dad," Isabelle paused to let people laugh. Her father did not smile. The sick jittery feeling was upon her again, the buzz in her ear growing louder and louder. She felt woozy, as if she might be sick. Isabelle swallowed and breathed through her nose. "And my mother, who took care of us and sacrificed more than either of us could understand." Isabelle's throat clenched, and her mouth turned sticky. Her hands were sweating, and the microphone turned into leaden weight. Everything in the room began to get wavy. She looked down to steady herself, but the floor began to undulate. She couldn't remember now if there was more to her speech or if that was it. As the sea of faces began to bleed into one another, the room turning Dalí-esque, she understood that she was in fact falling over. An elbow hit the floor, a cheek scraped the carpet. The last thing she heard was the collective gasp of the crowd.

◆　◆　◆

"Of course there aren't any doctors here. This is a book party."

Fern's face was above her, and he was snapping his fingers. "Oh she's up!" He turned away and barked at a waiter, "Make yourself useful and bring us some juice!"

"Who's the president?" Fern asked her.

"Ha," said Isabelle.

"She's talking!" Glenda was there too, her face still out of focus, a pale circle with dark eyes and a red mouth. Isabelle could feel that she was no longer on the floor but on one of the couches, and there was something cold on her forehead.

"You okay, doll?" said Fern.

"I think so."

Fern turned around. "Someone tell that corn-fed hottie with the dimples to call off the paramedics."

"Brian," said Isabelle, her voice coming out in a whisper.

"What?"

"The hottie. His name is Brian."

"Oh yes," said Fern, and then he shouted, "Someone go down and tell *Brian* we don't need an ambulance. It's all right, people. She's awake. Just low blood sugar. Carry on. Carry on." He shooed away a few people gathered around the couch. He thrust a glass of orange juice in her face. "Drink this, doll."

Isabelle sat up on her elbows, removed the wet paper towel from her forehead, and took a sip of the juice.

"Here." Glenda handed her a potato stuffed with caviar. "Just a warning—it's not beluga."

"How long was I out?"

"A minute at most," said Fern.

Isabelle moaned. "Oh god, this is mortifying."

"Puh-lease, sweetheart. You've given everyone a gift. These parties are usually deadly boring; we're all praying for something like this. And this is guaranteed Page Six coverage. You probably just sold an extra thousand books." Fern seemed positively ebullient. "Here, eat more."

Glenda nodded. "Fainting at your own book party is a small price to pay to look the way you do."

Her father emerged between Glenda and Fern. "You all right?"

"Yes." Isabelle nodded, sitting up all the way.

Ward patted her back. "Fern's right. You just sold a bunch of books."

When Isabelle had eaten several potato caviars, she stood up and walked to the bathroom to splash water on her face. It was all so fucking wrong. She'd published a book. She was not supposed to feel horrible. She was not supposed to faint in front of everyone. And, most of all, she had not been waiting all these years for her father to say her book was "very nice." It wasn't even a phrase she had ever heard her father use before. The dissonance between her expectations and reality left Isabelle disoriented.

Isabelle undid the lock and walked out the door, seeing a ruddy, out-of-breath Brian bounding up the stairs.

"Isabelle!" His face contorted with concern. "Should you be walking around?"

"It's fine, I'm okay," said Isabelle. "Where were you?"

"I went outside to get service to call 911—did you know there's no Wi-Fi?"

"Yes. Writers like it. We need to be protected from ourselves."

"Huh. Well, someone came down and said you were awake. So I ran out and got you these." Brian held up a yellow bodega bag. Through the thin plastic, she could see a Gatorade and a square box. Triscuits.

"Oh, Brian. Thank you." Her friend knew her. And for just a moment, the mask she'd been wearing, the one she'd put on for all these influential, important people, slipped off.

Brian shrugged. He pulled the box out of the bag and opened it up. "Come on, let's go sit. You could use something in your stomach," said Brian. "And I still have something I want to give you."

"Okay." Isabelle was about to follow him when she heard a slow clap behind her. She turned. At first she didn't recognize the man under the brown fedora with what looked like a peacock feather. But when his face came into view, Isabelle saw that ascending toward them was Darby Cullman.

"The writer herself. How lucky am I?" He leaned in and kissed Isabelle on the cheek, smelling of brown alcohol and clove cigarettes. She had forgotten about inviting him.

"Hey, I'm Darby Cullman." He extended his hand to Brian.

Brian grimaced tightly. "I know who you are."

"Thanks, man. Always stoked to meet a fan."

"Yeah, I'm not a fan. We went to Brown together."

"Oh sweet." Darby looked down. "Jeez, I know book party budgets are tight, but are we all sharing a box of crackers?"

Isabelle laughed. "No—"

"Isabelle wasn't feeling well, so—"

"I'm okay." Isabelle shot Brian a look. The idea of Darby knowing she'd fainted was appalling somehow. His presence made it all the more imperative that she pull it together, act like the writer she was supposed to be. The mask slid back on.

"Cool. I actually love these. May I?" Before Brian could answer, Darby reached his hand into the box and pulled out a handful of crackers. "Thanks, man."

"Isabelle," said Brian, closing the box. "Let me walk you home."

"Whaaa? You're not leaving, are you?" Darby asked.

"No, no. Not yet." Leaving her party early was a defeat Isabelle could not stomach. She had to stay, somehow turn this night around, make it untragic.

"Good," said Darby. "Come, let me fete you with a drink." He put his arm around Isabelle and spoke into her ear. "You look amazing." And then his hand moved down her back to cup her butt. Isabelle let out a tiny yelp, and for a moment her eyes met Brian's—long enough for her to see past the disapproval to something very close to contempt.

"Brian, you're coming, right?" she asked.

He stared at Isabelle. "No. I think I've had enough."

. . .

Isabelle managed through the rest of the party with the help of the copious number of drinks Darby was chivalrous enough to ferry from the bar. She needed the night to stand out for something other than her father's stinging words and her brush with unconsciousness. So at the end of the party, when Darby made his move, tripping toward her because he, like Isabelle, was extremely inebriated, she let him kiss her. He leaned in to kiss her, his mouth parched and sour from hours of drinking, and she reciprocated, holding the back of his neck. Isabelle was just sober enough to feel a twinge of shame for sloppily necking in her ostensible place of work. But Isabelle's instinct when she felt lost was to lean in, pile on, make a toxic stew of mistakes. So she closed her eyes, pressed herself into this man—this man with the pretentious fucking vest who did not love her—and tried to pretend he was what she wanted.

I changed my locks, altered my routine, and wore large, face-obscuring hats. I'll admit, most of my ideas came from bad spy movies, the straight-to-video ones that played at two a.m. when I was often awake, envisioning my future in bleak, violent terms.

Mornings were my best time of day. I focused on work and could almost convince myself nothing was wrong. To pacify Sebastian, I managed to complete portraits of Natalie Wood and Bella Abzug. But as soon as I stopped painting, my panic ballooned. What did the man in the sweat suit want? How would he hurt me? And why had he broken into the apartments next door? I couldn't help feeling I'd brought this on myself. Bad things happen when you pretend to be someone you're not.

And now, in front of Sam, I was also pretending to be a stable, non-hysterical person. I still enjoyed our time together, but it was becoming difficult to hide my fragile mental state. I forgot previous conversations, I trailed off mid-sentence, I stared into space. I blamed it on my insomnia, and Sam was patient, forgiving. He was a good man.

Other than to meet Sam, I left the house only to visit my mother. The day I found the note, I left in the late afternoon. I took the elevator down to the lobby and walked outside. I saw the lights immediately. Parked in front of the building across the street, just as they'd been in front of mine the week before, were police cars.

"Another break-in," said a voice. A jolt ran through me. I turned to see John, the doorman. "Can I get you a cab?"

I must've said yes because I made it to my mother's apartment. I managed to tune out the drumbeat of terror long enough to fix her my special tuna salad and watch an episode of *I Love Lucy*. I think I walked home, but I might've taken

221

the bus. Everything is hazy in comparison to what happened next.

As I walked off the elevator, I saw a triangle of paper sticking out from under my door. This was not unusual. There were lots of notices about water shutoffs or building construction. But I picked up the sheet of paper, and there, in cut-out letters from magazines, someone had spelled out the words, I KNOW WHAT YOU DID.

29

Jamaica, 1992–93

Claire

The emergency clinic was just outside the hotel property, in the shopping village, close enough for Claire to be brought over in a golf cart. In her memory, the outside walls had been painted the color of a lemon left too long in the crisper. Whenever Claire thought back on that night, that's what came to her first. That yellow. And the smell of the hallways, sharp and vinegary with disinfectant. But these memories were just coverings, the protective shroud quickly drawn around what she preferred not to recall.

Sara and her father, Randy, stood sheepishly in the waiting area. Claire was given the story. Instead of waterskiing, Randy surprised the girls with rented Jet Skis. They wanted to try it; neither had before. It seemed like fun. Randy had said that with a shrug. Claire would not forget that shrug. Nor the torrent of rage she'd unleashed upon him afterward, leaving him meekly to explain that, when the weather turned, Isabelle had been sent flying off the Jet Ski, and the machine clobbered her in the head. By the time Randy got to her, she was unconscious. No one was sure how much water she'd taken in. Or how hard she'd been hit. "I made sure she was wearing a life jacket though," Randy said, almost proudly, as if this lack of gross negligence made him a hero.

Claire was taken to see Isabelle, who was lying on a flimsy gurney in a treatment room. There was a large oozing wound on Isabelle's forehead, several shades of purple, festering, alive. The blood ran, half-dried, down the front of her blue gingham bathing suit before it spread in concentric circles, streaked and varied like a Georgia O'Keefe flower. Claire covered her mouth. With all the willpower she had left, she swallowed down the contents of her stomach. She walked closer to the table and smoothed her daughter's hair. Isabelle stirred slightly.

"That's a good sign," said a lanky man in a white lab coat. "You're the mother?"

"Yes." Claire was shivering. She'd never changed out of her bathing suit and cover-up.

"Dr. Stanley."

Claire shook his hand, cold and dry like a clamshell.

"Your daughter has suffered a traumatic brain injury," he said. "She has a concussion and possibly nerve damage."

A nurse walked into the room and began hooking Isabelle up to an IV. "We need to suture the wound," said Dr. Stanley. "Then run tests and do an MRI."

A cascade of fears tumbled in half thoughts. "Is this okay? Is this place equipped to treat her?"

Dr. Stanley gave her a look that said, *Ah, one of those.*

"I'm sorry," Claire said. "I'm just—I'm just scared." And then Claire began to sob. "And—And—I should tell you," Claire said, for it was all she had thought about since she'd learned of the accident. "She had some champagne."

Dr. Stanley furrowed his brow.

"Just a glass. It was—a celebration. I tried—" Claire's voice came hiccupping out, faltering on the sob at the back of her throat. "Could it have made her—" Claire could not finish the thought.

Dr. Stanley nodded. "Please. Go outside. Let us take care of her."

Claire listened, understanding she had no choice but to rely on someone else to save Isabelle. She went outside, slumped into a plastic chair and waited. She dabbed at her face with the soggy tissue that someone must've given her, though she had no memory of it. There was a television in the waiting room, showing some kind of game show. The volume was turned high enough to make out who was speaking, but not what they said. Claire looked down and saw that she had torn the tissue into tiny bits, little rolled up pieces the size and shape of mouse droppings stuck to her bare thighs.

This was the first time Isabelle had to go to a hospital. She'd had friends who were always running to the ER for their children's knocked-out teeth, split chins, broken limbs, bee stings. Claire's own brother Hugo had been incredibly accident-prone. He once ran through a glass door in the Southampton house. The doctors at the ER had spent three hours tweezing the shards out of him. Another time, he'd somehow impaled himself on a bocce court in a way that required a two-night hospital stay. At boarding school, he broke his collarbone and dislocated several vertebrae falling out of a bunk bed. And then from college on, there was the sustained and real possibility of him drinking himself sick. Or worse. The stories about Hugo were told to laughs and head shaking, but Claire had never considered how it must have felt to her mother in those moments. Was she terrified? Did she blame herself? Did the frequency make it easier on some level? Claire suspected the fear for one's child could never be calloused over.

Claire's worry over Isabelle had never centered on her physical well-being. Isabelle wasn't one of those toddlers who climbed up on bookcases or fingered electric sockets. She was cautious and skilled on playgrounds. She wasn't the type to try anything unless she thought she could do it well. Claire's anxieties settled on her daughter's psyche. Whether she was content, well-adjusted, too ego-driven, whether it was possible to have a father like Ward Manning and emerge unscathed. A freak Jet Ski accident had been nowhere on Claire's radar, and for that, Claire felt irrationally guilty, as if anxiety over this outcome could have prevented it. Perversely, the randomness of the accident, its unlikelihood, flooded Claire with recriminations. If she had made slightly different decisions—just tiny tweaks—it would not have happened. If she had not let Ward give Isabelle that drink. If she had told Isabelle she couldn't go. If she had accompanied Isabelle on this adventure. If she hadn't lost herself in her writing. As if the cumulative result of those micro failures was Isabelle lying unconscious on a gurney.

It was nearly two hours before the doctor appeared again, walking out of the operating room with an inscrutable expression.

"Will she live?" Claire croaked out. Until she asked the question aloud, she had not let herself think it, but of course this was what had plagued her since she had stood on the beach that afternoon, searching the water for her daughter.

"Yes, she'll live." Dr. Stanley explained that the wound on her forehead required forty stitches. The tests showed significant contusions, or bruises, on both sides of the brain—the ski had hit her hard enough to send Isabelle's brain ricocheting around in her skull. "I've sedated her but I would recommend your daughter be put in a medically induced coma."

The bottom fell out of Claire's stomach, her body stiffened as if to physically resist the information. "A coma?"

"It's the safest option for her right now. An ambulance is on its way to transfer her to a hospital in Kingston. There are specialists there."

Claire nodded, understanding, as she ought to have before, that this nightmare would not end here, but had many more scenes before its conclusion. "Can I see her?"

Dr. Stanley led her into a curtained-off area.

"Take your time," he said, and turned to leave. "By the way," he said, looking back at Claire. "This is the same course of treatment followed by the Mayo Clinic—I trained there."

Claire nodded, a spike of shame breaking through her panic. "Thank you."

Isabelle's head had been cleaned and partially shaved. There was a track of stitches running curved like baseball lacing on the left side of her forehead. Her bathing suit had been replaced by a white gown with tiny blue polka dots, and she was covered by a white sheet. Claire put her hand on Isabelle's stomach, the way she used to when she was a baby to check her breathing. It was a long moment before Claire felt the reassuring swell of her daughter's abdomen.

She stood there looking at Isabelle, completely serene, feeling her breathe until a nurse came in and told her they had to get ready to leave. She was directed to the desk where she filled out paper-work. Claire had thirty minutes to go back to the hotel to pack up their things. In a haze, she threw all of her and Isabelle's belongings into suitcases, retrieved their passports from the safe. She would not realize until much later that the only item she had left behind was her notebook. Hotel staff would find it, abandoned by the pool, its pages swollen with water, Claire's writing reduced to ink-blue tie-dye, and take the notebook for trash.

When Claire climbed into the back of the ambulance with her daughter, she had the thought that Ward did not know. He was still on the plane, obliviously floating above the Atlantic coastline in first class—there was no question that was what he'd booked for himself. The Literary King did not fly coach. But with that realization, another came swift and sure: It did not matter. It did not matter that Ward didn't know. It did not matter that Ward was not there. Even if Ward had been sitting beside her, Claire was the parent. She was the warden of her daughter's well-being. This was, and would always be, her show.

The Kingston hospital was larger with multiple departments. After many hours, once Isabelle was settled in the intensive care unit, Claire got on the phone to her husband. Ward offered to fly back down. She had to give him credit for that. He did offer. But Claire could sense he was also relieved when she told him not to. She was not just martyring herself. Claire did not want Ward there.

He would need tending to. She could see him pacing the hospital, alienating the staff with demands, wanting to know when he would be fed an acceptable meal, and where he would sleep. Claire was a more streamlined vessel without him. She could sleep in hospital chairs, eat cold, soggy cafeteria sandwiches, go unshowered, her focus on Isabelle unbroken.

The first days were horrible. No one could tell Claire what to expect. Different doctors had different theories, and contrasting ideas about treatment. She could tell that all of her questions were irritating the nurses. A few times, doctors argued openly in front of her, which seemed like a horrible sign. Whenever Claire was alone—and sometimes when she was not—she wept. She became shrill and hysterical, and she sensed the staff had begun to resent her. She understood. She could hear what she sounded like. Unhinged. Then she worried that this resentment might affect Isabelle's treatment.

When she wasn't crying or begging someone for information or hope, Claire sat with the machines. She watched numbers flashing on the monitors, learning what each one meant. In addition to blood pressure and heart rate monitors, sensors monitored oxygen and intercranial pressure in Isabelle's brain.

The second afternoon, Claire was curled into a chair, half sleeping, when the beeping started. There was always beeping, but she knew the regular rhythms. This was different, the sound sharp and sustained. Claire opened her eyes to see red flashing on a monitor where it should have been green. Within seconds a squad of people descended on the room.

"What's happening?" Claire cried. "What's happening?"

"Her heart rate is dropping," one of the nurses said without looking at Claire.

More people came in. More beeping. More machines. A countdown, and then Isabelle was lifted onto a gurney and rolled away, Claire trailing behind.

It might have been minutes. It might have been hours. At some point Isabelle was re-stabilized. She was allowed to return to her room. Doctors came in every hour to check her vitals. One said they'd take her out of the coma the next day. Another said it could be weeks. Claire walked out into the hallway. She felt like she was moving in a borrowed shell of skin and bones. Her face was numb except for a persistent tightness around her eyes, permanently swollen from crying and lack of sleep. She walked to the pay phone and dialed her home number. No one picked up the first time. Or the next three that she called. Ward was working and, like always, did not want to be disturbed. But she wanted to disturb him. So she kept dialing until his slightly hoarse, harried voice came on the line. "Hello?"

"Ward."

"Claire, have you been ringing up over and over? Is everything okay? I'm in the middle of something."

"No, Ward, everything is not okay. And you are not in the middle of something. *I* am in the middle of something." Claire could hear her voice rising and sense people sneaking looks in her direction, but she didn't care. "I am in the middle of caring for our unconscious, hospital-ridden daughter."

"Take it easy, Claire. I said I would come down there."

"Yes, you could come down, you and your goddamn gorilla of an ego. What good would that do me?"

"Claire."

"How do you do it, Ward?"

"Do what?"

"Be yourself."

"Claire—"

"How can you even be in New York? How can you write while this is happening? What the hell is wrong with you?" Claire was crying now, sobbing into the phone. "You, Ward, may be the most selfish man to ever walk this earth. You should be studied by science."

Neither of them spoke, as Claire continued to cry. Ward remained silent, allowing her to sob, which felt like the most generous gesture he'd made in years. He understood at least that Claire wanted to cry without interruption. Maybe she wasn't being fair. She had told him to stay away. The accident wasn't Ward's fault. But so much else was.

"Let me book a flight. I'll be down by tomorrow."

"No. I don't want that," Claire said quickly. It was too late. Not just for Ward to show up, but for Ward to adapt into someone who might be helpful in this situation. Maybe he had never been that kind of person, but he sure wasn't now. And it was Claire who had enabled him to become this way. Her understanding of her complicity had always made her loathe to speak. "No," Claire said again. "Stay where you are. I'll call you tomorrow."

As Ward started to say something, Claire hung up the phone. She wiped her eyes, looked up at the fiberglass ceiling tiles and blinked. More crying would do Isabelle no good.

"Mrs. Manning?" Claire looked over at a figure she recognized, standing in the hallway holding a clipboard. It had been just a few days since she'd seen him, the night of the accident, but it felt like another lifetime.

"Dr. Stanley." Claire felt an unexpected flood of relief. "It's good to see you."

"How is Isabelle?"

Claire related to him the frustrating cycle of uncertainty, hope, disappointment, and terror she'd experienced since Isabelle had been transferred. Dr. Stanley, who was beginning a month-long stint in Kingston, listened closely, asking questions and taking notes about Isabelle's condition. From that moment on, Claire had an ally. Dr. Stanley followed up with other doctors treating Isabelle, asking the questions Claire didn't know to ask, interpreting competing advice for her, telling her which doctors he trusted over others.

It took another week, but finally it was determined that the swelling had diminished enough for Isabelle to be taken out of the coma. The doctors warned Claire that the recovery would be long and uncertain. Her brain would need rest and time to heal, but there was hope that her mental faculties would not be affected long-term. Isabelle's hearing, however, was a different story. The damage to her left ear would likely cause lasting deficiency.

"But it's possible she'll recover it, right?" Claire asked Dr. Stanley when he checked in on Isabelle.

"Possible, yes. But, no, I don't think the hearing will come all the way back."

"Never?"

"Never." Dr. Stanley looked at Claire for a moment. "She won't even notice. You'd be surprised how easily people compensate for a loss."

Claire nodded. Even knowing she ought to be grateful it wasn't something more debilitating, she found the hearing loss quietly devastating. The accident would not be erased by time. A faulty part inside her daughter would be its legacy. Claire would have to work to ensure that it was the only remnant of what happened. She would take Isabelle to the right doctors, follow all the rules and therapies about treating post-traumatic stress; she would keep Isabelle's life stable and happy. If she did those things, then maybe the accident would all but fade away. And maybe that she had allowed it to happen would not define Claire as a mother. Because of all things, Claire could not stand that.

30

New York, 2018

Isabelle

After crossing over the Brooklyn Bridge, the car rumbled through several streets of brownstones and small apartment buildings with curved, corrugated metal awnings. The cherry blossoms were at their most luscious bloom, shimmering in the streetlamps. There were glass-fronted coffee places and restaurants without obvious signage, along with a few clothing boutiques and yoga studios.

The Uber pulled up to an unassuming corner. Isabelle checked the name of the restaurant against what Darby had texted, then got out of the car. Despite being strategically five minutes late, Isabelle had arrived first. She sat at the bar with a complicated drink that involved bitters and Aperol. The restaurant was a square with floor-to-ceiling plated windows on two sides. The décor—bare light bulbs, exposed pipes—was industrial, but feminine. Every table was full of attractive people several years younger than her. Isabelle had worn her most millennial outfit: high-waisted jeans with a cropped black T-shirt and ankle booties. Along with the book necklace her father had given her, she chose a chunky resin cuff bracelet and faux-feather earrings. Isabelle checked her phone. Darby was fifteen minutes late.

Isabelle had not expected this to turn into a thing. The night of the book party, Darby and Isabelle had gotten into a cab to Isabelle's apartment together, but at the last minute, Isabelle changed her mind. There was something about waking up the next day with Darby that she suspected would feel much worse than waking up alone. She lied that she had an early interview in the morning and climbed out of the cab before Darby could protest. Not that he was physically capable of protesting. Moments earlier, he'd started to pass out with his tongue still inserted in her ear.

Hearing from Darby again was a surprise. The next afternoon he texted her, a banal missive about being hungover. And Isabelle responded in kind. Throughout that day, Darby and Isabelle exchanged dozens of texts. And the next day, too. None were more than a sentence or two, but they were exhausting to produce. Isabelle spent many minutes choosing her words to hit just the right level of irony, include the right cultural reference, and seem all the while like she didn't give a shit. There was a notable uptick in Darby's texts when the big news hit.

The A-list actress Jenna Dulaney chose *Underpainting* for her book club pick. And Isabelle became a *New York Times* bestselling author. It was what she had always wanted writ large. Her pleasure, however, was undercut by what she was hiding. And her one tepid review. Her father had not bothered to reach out in the week since the book party, nor when her book hit the list. She had called him a few times, but he rushed her off the phone with claims of being busy. Fern mentioned that there was some kind of problem with his book. This was perhaps the most alarming news of all. But Isabelle's hurt—which had a funny way of masquerading as anger—stopped her from pressing harder, trying to ascertain exactly what was wrong with her father and trying to help him.

She took a large sip of her drink to extinguish the flames of guilt rising within her.

"Hey gorgeous." Isabelle felt Darby's stubble rub against her neck. She swiveled in her chair to face him. He was wearing a signature plaid shirt and worn twill pants, and had a thin paperback tucked under his arm. With a subtle gesture to the hostess, they were seated.

Darby let out a giant, theatrical yawn.

"Tired?"

"Depleted. Wrote almost five thousand words today." Darby threaded his fingers through his hair several times.

"Wow. A thousand is a good day for me."

"That's pretty glacial. Your publisher is not going to let you get away with that for long. I mean, unless you sell like Stephen King," said Darby. "Or your dad."

"Right." From the feelers he threw out, Isabelle got the sense that that if she showed receptivity, Darby would be happy to discuss Ward in detail.

The waitress came and more drinks were ordered, then a slew of appetizers and the special orata for two.

"Oh," said Darby when they were alone again. "Can you do me a favor?"

"Sure."

He slid his phone across the table. "Just snap a quick pic."

"Of you?"

"Yes." Darby did a quick shimmy as if he were a dancer loosening up, and then positioned his Manhattan in front of him alongside the book he'd been carrying. It was *Leaves of Grass*. He looked out toward the window, giving Isabelle a three-quarter view of his face, and settled into a pensive expression. "Okay, now," he whispered. Isabelle took a flurry of photos until Darby broke pose. "Awesome, thanks."

"Do you need that for a publicity thing or something?"

"Nah." Darby was focused on his phone, typing intently. "Just keeping the Insta fresh." After a moment, he looked up. "Done." He flashed Isabelle the screen. A post of the picture, filtered to black and white with the caption, **Friday**. Darby held the phone for a long enough time that Isabelle had to verbally respond. "Nice."

When the food came, Darby took methodical shots of each dish, uploading them to his feed. They seemed to have very little to say to each other.

Isabelle broke a long silence with, "So, do you still talk to anyone from Brown?"

"Not really. You?"

"Well, Brian, obviously."

"Brian?"

"You know Brian. He was at my book party," she said. "He's my best friend." At least Isabelle hoped he still was. After her book party, Brian had stopped responding to her calls and texts.

He shrugged.

"I'm also still in touch with some of my girlfriends. But everyone's busy and most of them have kids, so . . ."

"Yeah." Darby rolled his eyes.

"I see Ben Lightman. He writes at the same library as I do."

"Who?"

"Ben. You know, he had, like, really bushy eyebrows. Edited the newspaper."

"Ohhhh. Little guy, right?"

"Yes."

"Totally. He's a writer?"

"I think he's an editor somewhere, but he's working on a book about the history of some kind of comic books. Or something like that."

"Has he sold it?"

"No, not yet."

"So he's not actually a writer."

"Well . . . he goes and writes every day." This was the argument she'd used on herself so many, many times. Being a writer was in the doing. If she sat down at her Word document each morning, then she was a writer. But it had always felt a little like some self-help trope.

"People who publish are writers. No one says, 'I'm a lawyer' because they act out imaginary court scenes in their bedrooms."

"Do people do that?"

"All these wannabes just add to the idea that anyone can do it. Writing is my job, it's not a fucking hobby."

Isabelle felt her cheeks flush. "I'm sure Ben doesn't *want* it to be a hobby either. I'm sure he'd love for it to be his actual job. But you can't just wake up one day and be a professional writer. You have to work at it for a while, just being, you know, nothing."

Darby leaned back in his chair. "Don't get all worked up. You're in the club now."

"I published before," Isabelle said.

"Really? What?"

"Not a book. Just a story. In the *New Yorker*."

Darby's eyes widened at the magic words. The. New. Yorker. "You did? When?" In the look of genuine surprise on Darby's face, it was clear to Isabelle just how much larger he loomed in her life than she in his. He had not tracked her progress obsessively. He'd never had to clear his internet history to cover the shame of an hour-long rabbit-hole session. She wasn't the reflexive measuring stick of his accomplishments. To Darby, until her book was published—maybe even until it was a *New York Times* bestseller—Isabelle Manning was a nonentity.

"Oh, maybe, like a few years ago." April 5, 2013, to be exact, but she was eager to move off the topic.

Darby was not. "What was it about?"

"Well." Isabelle took a long sip of her ice water and motioned to the waitress for more. "It was about a woman who breaks up with her boyfriend," Isabelle spoke quickly, "but then decides she must get him back. So she goes home and tries to call him to tell him she's made a horrible mistake. The first few times, she dials and he picks up the phone, but it's like she has the world's worst laryngitis and she can't speak. The boyfriend hangs up, thinking no one's there. And then her voice returns. It's only when he's on the other end of the line that it leaves her. She gets so upset and discombobulated that she starts misdialing over and over. Sometimes she gets the sequence wrong, other times it's like her mind cannot control her fingers or her fingers are too clumsy to dial."

"Wild. What happens then?"

Usually in Isabelle's dreams, this was the point when she felt underwater, her hands slippery, her voice trapped inside liquid. But it felt too science fiction. And perhaps the drowning feeling was a bit too tender to have the right distance for creative exploration. So she'd diverted from her experience and aimed for a lighter note. "She keeps accidentally dialing her neighborhood Chinese restaurant."

Darby laughed. "Really?"

"Yeah. And on these calls she can speak, which makes her all the more infuriated."

"Huh. How did you come up with all this?"

"I have a lot of dreams about phones. And not being able to speak." Isabelle hadn't needed her therapist to tell her that the dream was related to the accident, the deep sear of panic that scarred her subconscious. The accident was obliquely referred to in her family as "what happened" or "that thing." It carried a sense of fear, but also of shame. Isabelle had known that she shouldn't have ridden the Jet Ski because it was dangerous, but also because it was a particular taboo. When a Jet Ski crossed his precious Sag Harbor cove, her father would retrieve his binoculars, holding them up to the window, shaking with anger. He'd actually gone so far as to petition to have the crafts banned for noise pollution. Isabelle understood that her father's quest was not only about the disagreeable sound. There was something unseemly about Jet Skis, something *low class*. And her father would not stand for anything of that sort to mar his beautiful view. So when Isabelle had mounted that peeling white saddle, she'd understood she was doing something unsafe—and forbidden.

But at this point she'd had plenty of therapy to process that she'd had a traumatic incident as a child. It seemed there were other elements at play, a more pervasive, still-relevant fear pulsing inside the dream.

"That's weird," said Darby now. "In most of my dreams, I can fly."

Isabelle waited for Darby to extrapolate, but that seemed to be the end of his thought. "Anyway," she said, "the character becomes increasingly distraught, feeling as if she's choking, the pressure of the words inside of her unbearable." Isabelle crossed her hands over where her neck met her chest.

"And then? Does she finally call him?"

"No. She can't."

"So, what? She just gives up?"

"She orders lo mein."

"Lo mein?"

"The noodles with vegetables that come with chicken or shrimp or—"

"No, I know what lo mein is. I'm just surprised by the ending."

Isabelle shrugged. She'd struggled with this ending, too. It felt a bit glib. But she had wanted to have certainty. The lo mein was supposed to be funny, but it also represented the fantasy of resignation, an acknowledgement of failure and a moving on. Sometimes Isabelle wondered if she'd be happier if she were better at this.

"I think my next book is going to be about boats." Darby spoke through another yawn.

"Oh yeah? Like a cruise ship?"

"Definitely not a cruise ship." Darby seemed offended, which maybe was what Isabelle had wanted. "Something grittier. Commercial fishing boat. Or an oil rig."

Isabelle raised an eyebrow. There was no way Darby knew jack about oil rigs. Or commercial fishing boats. But men like him—men like her father—had no fear of writing about what was foreign to them. No one had ever told them to keep to what they knew. "How about a garbage barge?" she asked. "That's gritty."

"I'll consider it." Darby nodded seriously.

Being there with Darby suddenly felt exhausting. Talking about her story had ripped away some essential pretense, reminding her that there had been a time when Isabelle Manning had been for real, when her writing sprang from wells deep inside her, when it was hers and hers alone. But she had cheated. She had stolen. She had betrayed. And she had sullied what she loved most in the world. And for what? So she could append "*New York Times* bestselling author" to her name for the rest of her life? So she could go on a date with Darby Cullman at this hip restaurant and listen to his plans to write about a fucking oil rig? Because, really, what else had she gotten out of publishing a book?

Her need to leave was urgent. If she moved fast enough, she could leave behind the part of herself who'd thought this was a good idea. She paid the bill and once they were outside, Darby started to invite her to his place, but Isabelle interrupted before he could finish. "I actually have to get home." Darby stared at her as if she'd spoken in tongues. From the corner of her eye Isabelle saw a lit-up taxi. She backed into the street with her hand raised, away from Darby, and slipped into the cab in a matter of seconds. Before she pulled away, Darby looked at her through the window, confused more than angry, and mouthed, *What the fuck?*

The taxi wound its way through the narrow, one-way streets before accelerating back over the bridge and merging onto FDR Drive. They headed north up the eastern edge of Manhattan. Isabelle had taken this ride so many times for so many years. In high school, she and her friends would roll the windows down and light up their cigarettes, ask the driver to put on Z100 and turn it up. The windows open, eyes closed, she'd floated on the heady mix of wind and music. Now the car was silent, airless. Through the closed window, Isabelle looked down at the river, the black, shiny water moving in swells southward, roiling, impenetrable.

Ward

Ward pulled his car over. He'd missed his turn off Brick Kiln. He took the next left, relying on his knowledge of local geography to make his way toward his house. But the twisting back roads turned alien in the pitch, country night. He got out of the car and peered forward and back, seeking some signpost that would tell him where he was. But there was nothing but oak branches rustling in the wind. With the way people drove out here, walking on the street could be suicide, so Ward slid back into the driver's seat.

He'd gone to a dinner party that evening. Spring had arrived and the Hamptons were waking from a long winter slumber. Ward was happy for the invitation from a well-known political biographer. He needed to get back in the game. Forget Diane. Forget the fucking Texas book. Remind himself that he was Ward Manning. Big Fucking Deal. And these, these other famous, big-deal people, were his people.

The evening was a disaster. Ward had no one to whisper people's names in his ear. To communicate with him through a secret language of light touches on the arm, elbow nudges, and pats on the knee, the dinner party signals he and Claire spoke fluently. He hadn't realized how much they acted as a team at social events. At one point, he completely lost his train of thought in the middle of a story. He felt something akin to jet lag, as if his mind was filled with a gelatinous substance. He drank more than he should have and got quiet. "Are you all right, Ward?" the hostess had asked him out on the front porch when he was leaving. On her face was a concern that was inching toward pity. Ward brushed her off and got in the car. And now, twenty minutes later, here he was, lost and alone on a deserted road.

Ward's phone was dead. Not that it mattered. He probably had some kind of map application, but the chances of him finding it and operating it correctly were slim. He sat listening to the repetitive drone of crickets and the periodic sigh of the leather as he shifted in his seat. He considered just reclining and going to sleep in the car. He was tired. And he probably ought not to be driving. But something in him rejected the idea as surrendering, not just to being lost but to everything he was fighting against. So Ward started up the engine and steered the car back onto the road, his headlights guiding him in the velvety dark, hoping he could still find his way home.

Brian

Brian was planning to throw it away. Keeping it was out of the question. And there were no returns on a custom item like this. So he'd tucked the box back into his pocket that morning. But he had not tossed it into one of the street wastebaskets on his way to the office. The box remained inside his jacket pocket, pressing against his chest as he worked at his desk, as he argued at a motion to dismiss hearing, and as he attended a plea bargain conference with the Federal Defenders office. And there was not one moment during which he forgot its presence.

His promotion to chief of narcotics had not officially gone into effect. That wouldn't happen until the ceremony on Friday, an event his whole family was flying in for. But for all intents and purposes, he'd already taken charge, and his workload had doubled. Brian wasn't complaining. This was what he'd wanted. This was what was necessary. But his afternoon had blown up as it did almost every day, and it was after ten p.m. when he'd finally finished with his deliverables.

From his office he headed west, but instead of making the turn south toward the financial district and his apartment, he continued toward Tribeca. The idea of throwing the box into the Hudson River had formed over the course of the day somewhere between Brian's awareness and subliminal thought. But by the time he walked out of his office, it had hardened into a concrete plan. This kind of dramatic gesture wasn't really Brian's style. It was over-the-top. And pointless; he wasn't the type of person who got involved with symbolism or ritual. Yet he continued toward the water.

Since Isabelle's book party, Brian had thought a lot about the time Isabelle came to Minnesota. It was over a decade ago, in those hazy postcollege hangover years. Brian had just graduated law school and moved home for a year when he scored a clerkship with a federal appellate judge in Minneapolis. Isabelle volunteered to come visit, buying her plane tickets before she'd consulted him. She had never been to Minnesota—of course she hadn't—and thought it would be "fun." The weekend was horrible. Isabelle arrived at his parents' house bearing a box of truffles, tiny square confections painted with scenes of the French countryside she'd purchased in SoHo. "My father knows the owner," Isabelle explained. The significance was lost on his parents, whose palates were unprepared for the bitterness of two-hundred-dollar chocolate. Isabelle was full of overblown, theatrical enthusiasm for her "tour of the Midwest," but on some level it was all a joke. His town, his family, even Brian, were there to amuse her, a pleasant distraction when she was bored of her elitist New York life.

Isabelle seemed oblivious to basic normal person guest etiquette, oblivious that she was supposed to offer to chop vegetables for salad and do dinner dishes and make her bed. These failures were no doubt tabulated, cataloged, and stored in his mother's long-term memory. In his family's space, Isabelle's quirks soured into rudeness, and he could barely meet his parents' gaze. It was useless to make excuses; they would never understand. Isabelle could be mercurial, thoughtless, selfish, but it could not have been easy growing up with a father like Ward Manning. And there was a kindness inside her, the part of her that took after Claire. Isabelle was never one of those popular girls who thought she had to be mean to maintain her status. Isabelle made friends with odd ducks and learned people's names. She could be wildly generous in critical moments. When Brian took the bar, Isabelle had insisted on accompanying him to Albany, spending two days at a shitty hotel, where she befriended the staff and got them upgraded to the "Presidential Suite." When he finished the test on the second day, there she was, waiting in a long, flowered dress with a bottle of good champagne she'd secretly smuggled from New York and a bakery cake with *da da dun-dun-DUN* written in gooey red icing.

Brian looked at the cake for a few moments and then smiled.

Isabelle lit up. "I knew you'd get it!"

"*Law & Order.* Obviously."

"The woman at the bakery thought I was nuts."

Brian laughed.

"I braved the mean streets of Albany to procure it for you."

"You drove?" Driving was Isabelle's kryptonite. She hated it and became uncharacteristically flustered and insecure behind the wheel. She claimed it was everyone else who was crazy to be so casual about it.

"Yup," said Isabelle. "That's how much I love you."

They sat outside the hotel, drank champagne out of Solo cups, and ate the cake, which he still remembered as chemically saccharine and delicious. When she wanted to be, Isabelle was perfect.

And Brian thought once her book was out, this good inside Isabelle, the part of her he was sure was there, would rise to the surface. Underneath it all, Isabelle loved him. She had put it in her book, hadn't she? But if, at the end of the day, Isabelle was interested in a screaming asshole like Darby Cullman, if she couldn't see what was right in front of her, then Brian had been wrong. The person he'd seen in Minnesota was who Isabelle really was. And it was time to move on. Everyone has limits. Even him.

Brian crossed the West Side Highway. He walked out onto the pier, deserted save for a guy sleeping on a bench. At this time of night, there was no good reason to be out here. There was wind, and water lapped at the pier's thick, graying wooden poles. The river was dark, no doubt teeming with a biblical level of filth. Years ago, when he was still at a law firm, Brian had represented an insurance company defending a lawsuit brought by the family of a man who dove down into this water to fix bridges and piers like this one. One dive, his tank had malfunctioned when he was deep underwater. He was deprived of oxygen too long and, within minutes, he became a vegetable. He was twenty-nine years old. It had been the job of Brian's firm to give the man's wife and child as little money as possible. The case settled after Brian had left the firm. He never found out what the family got. Whatever it was, it wasn't enough.

Brian thought of the man every time he saw the river, and lots of other times too. The bravery it took to dive in, to work submerged for hours on end, with no sunlight, no air; to endure conditions not fit for a human, all to make a living. It required a kind of primal courage that was unfathomable to Brian—and he felt, with a shiver of shame, that, because he was white, educated, and well-off, it was a kind of courage that was unlikely to ever be required of him.

Brian walked right up to the edge of the pier. He removed the box from his pocket. Holding it in his fist, Brian stretched his arm over the water. All he had to do was let go.

31

New York City, 1993

Claire

Claire took the box of crackers out of the cupboard and arranged a dozen on a plate alongside the wedge of brie, as the news gurgled at low volume on the kitchen television. She poured pistachios into a bowl and set aside another for shells. Then she went for the vodka. Claire kept the handle of Stoli in the freezer, liking the liquor cold enough for the first sip to give her an ice-pick headache. She stirred in the vermouth and, with a paring knife, cut off two twists of lemon peel. Claire paused for a moment as she often did now and felt glad and slightly incredulous at the privilege of focusing on mundane details, the proper ratio of vodka to vermouth, the right amount of pith in her twist.

◆ ◆ ◆

Claire and Isabelle had returned from Jamaica nearly six months earlier, after a three-week stay at the Kingston hospital. When she first woke up, Isabelle was alarmingly weak, unable to speak or sit up, a frail, incoherent replica of herself. Each day she got a little bit stronger; words returned, expressions, laughter. Isabelle, it came as no surprise to Claire, was a fighter. When they returned, Isabelle spent another week at Mount Sinai under observation. There were consults with the ENT. Several MRIs. A plastic surgeon was brought in for her forehead. "It's too late for me to do anything," he said to Claire outside of Isabelle's hospital room. The doctor was tall and wore those woven loafers stitched with martini glasses from a shop on Madison Avenue. They struck her as inappropriate, and wool as an unsanitary material for medical footwear.

"Are you sure?" asked Claire. "Nothing?"

"The healing process has already begun. I'm not going to disrupt that." He seemed eager to leave Claire and get back to the face-lifts and tummy tucks that were paying the mortgage in East Hampton. But he was not wrong; other doctors agreed. So Isabelle was left with her scar.

When Isabelle returned to their apartment, her concussed brain still needed to rest. There was no television or excessive stimulation. She spent a few weeks in her bedroom, shades lowered, still lethargic, and napping much of the day away. Claire read *Pride & Prejudice* aloud to her, and eventually they played Scrabble and did the homework the school had sent to the house. Claire was relieved that Isabelle showed that she was still Isabelle when her daughter began to enjoy the benefits of her convalescence. Friends from school stopped by to pay homage, with dramatic concern over Isabelle's injuries as if she were an ailing member of the royal family. Isabelle ate it up, regaling everyone with stories of the accident, accounts that got longer and longer with more and more details she couldn't possibly remember.

Ward tried in his way to be helpful. He tried. He treaded more carefully after Claire's blowup. At least for a while. He went out and bought a beautiful, old-fashioned bed tray from Gracious Home, and ordered Isabelle lavish meals from Quatorze. He and Isabelle read *To Kill a Mockingbird* together, and he stopped by her room each day to discuss their progress. Isabelle always brightened at Ward, summoning the energy to discuss the book. Ward was not so chastened as to lose sight of his own desires. Still riding the high of his award, Ward answered every invitation to speak or be celebrated in the affirmative. Ward would always do Ward.

Claire was vigilant for signs of lingering trauma, of some fundamental shift in her daughter. Isabelle was curious about what had happened to her, but her interest was removed, intellectual. Claire was careful to assure her that what had happened was a freak accident and nothing more. By April, after months of coddling, Isabelle emerged a particularly vivid version of herself. Things resettled into regularity, and Claire found that she once again had days to herself, no daughter to read to, no doctors to call, no medical bills to pay or insurance claims to file.

Claire's manuscript had hovered at the back of her consciousness for months. Even in the midst of crisis, Claire had not fully tuned out Livia's siren call. Finally, on Presidents' Day weekend, thinking she might have a moment to reacquaint herself with the draft and reconjure the ideas she'd put down in the forsaken notebook, Claire tucked the manuscript in her duffle and brought it to Sag Harbor. But when she got the pages out, read them over, something had changed. Writing had once brought warm excitement, like thinking of the answer to a crossword clue, but it came to her now with bitterness, something very close to guilt. Her book had nothing to do with the accident, certainly. And yet. Claire had been writing when Isabelle was hurt. An unpleasant link had been formed. More than that, Claire had recently realized something. From the start, Claire had been very aware that Livia was an alter-ego who would do, and even think, the things Claire could not. The book was her fantasy of all that she could become without Ward. But Livia was also childless. Was this too her fantasy? Though she hadn't given it a second thought before, Claire was gripped with the idea that her choice spoke to some horribleness inside her, a desire to be unburdened from motherhood. And after the accident, this was intolerable. Livia was a dream she could no longer indulge. Claire put the manuscript in a drawer, shutting away what had once brought her pleasure. She thought often of what Dr. Stanley had told her: *You'd be surprised how easily people compensate for a loss.*

Claire took up a new project. Over the course of Isabelle's illness, Claire had spent a great many hours in hospitals. She understood in a concrete way what a horrible thing it is to be a parent of a hurt or sick child, the slog of hospital life, waiting for doctors, hoping for good news, the anxious monotony of it all. And Claire was one of the lucky ones. But what about the families there day after day, week after week, month after month? When Isabelle went back to school, Claire missed the hours she'd spent reading to her daughter. She called up the director of the Mount Sinai children's hospital and asked if she could start coming with books and reading to the children there. They agreed, and quickly Claire was a regular presence. She instituted a weekly schedule, she brought other friends with her. They wanted to bring their friends. She formalized the program. And suddenly her days were full of planning and phone calls and running up to the hospital to volunteer and for meetings. And she had very little time for her mind to wander to things like the book. Or to Ward.

• • •

Claire put everything on a tray and carried it into the library where Ward was already seated watching *MacNeil/Lehrer*.

"Thank you, dear," Ward said when Claire handed her husband his drink and put the pistachios in front of him. Claire took her seat on the couch. Ward began shelling nuts and tossing them into his mouth. Whatever small fright Claire had put into him had passed. He did not—or chose not to—see through the flimsiest veneer of politeness that shrouded Claire's true feelings. It baffled her that a man who lacked such basic awareness could write characters. Claire had noticed when she perused his more recent books that he relied more and more on flourishy prose—gorgeous tangents that went on for pages and pages but said nothing at all. Perhaps these weren't just showing off but covering up something, too, a finger that had slipped off the pulse of the human soul.

Despite her feelings, Claire would not leave him. The last thing Isabelle needed was upheaval. And she would keep her thoughts to herself. She had said all there was to say from that pay phone in Jamaica. Her barbs might soften him around the edges, but they would not change him. She did not want to "work on" the marriage. Ward would probably enjoy couples' therapy, co-opting the process as yet another venue to verbally expound upon his gifts. And good luck finding a shrink in this city who wasn't a fan. Claire could just see it, sitting in the office with some PhD off Park Avenue, who'd probably ask Ward to sign books after the session.

She would not be the first or the last woman to stay with a man she resented, Claire thought as she looked at Ward. His eyes fixed on the screen, lips slightly parted. He held a handful of shelled pistachios aloft in his non-drink-holding hand. After a moment, he tossed all of them into his mouth at once. His lips smacked vulgarly, the semi-macerated nuts visible as he chewed. Feeling her eyes on him, Ward turned toward her and smiled. She smiled back, imagining him choking. It would start slowly at first, her husband pointing at his throat. His face would turn crimson, every vein and tendon in his neck and vast forehead straining. His eyes would implore her. He'd stand up, trying to move closer before he fell to the ground. Would she help him? Or allow her husband to succumb?

Claire drank the last, watery sip of her vodka and saw that Ward's drink was also in need of refreshing. She stood up and took the empty glasses.

"Thanks," said Ward, his eyes not leaving the television.

"My pleasure." She started to move toward the kitchen but stopped. She walked around to Ward's other side and picked up the bowl off the coffee table. Ward looked up at her. Claire looked at him. "More nuts, darling?"

My life had been reduced to a single question: Who wrote the note? The most obvious answer was a buyer of one of Aiden's found paintings, angry at being duped. But I had an unsettling feeling that Sebastian was part of what was happening to me. This did not entirely make sense. He was in just as deep. If it were revealed I'd done all the portraits since Aiden's death, we'd both be in hot water. Maybe this was his trick to spur me onward, force me to continue our scheme. Each found portrait sold for more than the last. And money had always been Sebastian's primary agenda; the only thing that motivated him. Despite knowing what I'd done for Aiden, Sebastian had been more than happy to cut me out for the sake of financial gain. Now the situation had changed. Sebastian needed me, his cash cow.

But would Sebastian turn criminal if I abandoned our scheme? Hiring muscle to follow me felt oddly consistent with his capabilities.

After I found the note, I spent two addled, desperate days inside my apartment debating what to do and whether I could bring the note to the police without also admitting my role in the portraits. But my deliberations were mooted when I opened my door on the third morning and found another sheet of paper, same as the first.

ALICE IN WONDERLAND. TOMORROW. NOON.

Alongside the note was an envelope, and inside it were photographs taken of a woman through a window. A chill ran down my spine as I recognized myself, standing at Aiden's easel, painting the portrait of Natalie Wood.

32

New York, 2018

Isabelle

Two days after her date with Darby Cullman, Isabelle walked the twenty-five blocks from her apartment, up the ramp and into the hospital's main entrance. She'd been there many times, but as she passed through the automatic door, one memory rose to the surface. It was years ago. Isabelle had come to see her friend Eugenie and her newborn baby girl. Eugenie had married a much older man and had been the first to have a baby. From depictions of maternity wards in TV and movies, Isabelle had braced herself for chaos, speeding gurneys, frantic OBs, howling women in the throes of labor. But it wasn't like that at all, just regular rooms, whisper-level quiet, broken only by fragile, catlike mews. Her friend explained that the actual birthing took place on a completely different floor. "And everyone has C-sections, anyway." Eugenie's daughter slept in a clear plastic bassinet, while the two friends ate the pastries Isabelle had brought and watched whatever daytime talk show was playing on the ceiling-mounted television. Baby Serena awoke just in time for Isabelle to hold her. Impossibly small, Serena was swaddled in a blue-and-pink hospital blanket from which a tiny, reptilian hand had broken free. On her head was a hat of the same

251

fabric, which had been fashioned into a bow at the center. Isabelle was glad when Eugenie took Serena to nurse, not because Isabelle didn't enjoy holding her, but because she did.

Not long after that, Isabelle and Brian had made a pact that if neither were married by thirty-five, they would have a baby together. Neither of them mentioned this when these contingencies matured. She wondered if Brian even remembered. Of course, now this idea was absurd. Brian wasn't speaking to her, much less fathering her child. Isabelle didn't blame him. She'd been horrible to him at the book party, going off with the inane Darby. While Brian and Isabelle both dated other people, it was an unspoken rule of their friendship that neither waved it in the other's face. Her display must have seemed to Brian nothing less than an unprovoked cruelty. He couldn't understand that it was her own misery that drove her. But this wasn't the first time she'd treated Brian badly, taken him for granted, put her wants above his own.

In all the hoopla from the book, Isabelle had received more attention than ever before in her life. Old friends and acquaintances from all facets of her life had gotten in touch. She was invited to the exclusive literary parties she'd always dreamed of and was written up in the right publications. But instead of lifting her up, it only made Isabelle understand that there were only two people who loved her just as she was—or had been. Two people who did not care whether she wrote a book or became famous or that her father was Ward Manning. Now that her mother was gone, there was one. And Isabelle had done everything she could to drive him away.

Her regret was made all the more bitter by the fact that Isabelle did not just miss Brian. She longed for him. She hated how the little things she used to tell him now piled up unsaid inside her. She'd tried to watch a *Law & Order* episode, and started sobbing. Images of him kept popping into her head, and then images of them together, Brian holding her, telling her it would be okay, the specific way he would run his hand along her hair. In Isabelle's fantasy, he'd then take her face in his hands, lifting her mouth to his, and kiss her. It was vintage Isabelle to excavate her true feelings just as Brian had turned away from her.

Isabelle was finding it increasingly difficult to pretend that anything was okay. She was riddled with guilt, haunted by various imagined scenarios in which her duplicity and lies were unveiled. Her father would understand at long last who Isabelle really was. Not a writer, but a fake. She'd promised herself that she would right the situation or at least confide in someone and get counsel. But the twin forces of ego and fear would lobby persuasively for silence. Then the cycle would repeat itself. Over and over and over, many times a day. It was untenable to carry on like this. And yet, divulging her secret was perhaps the only worse course of action.

Isabelle called up her publisher and told them she was sick and could not complete the West Coast leg of her book tour. Over the phone, she could hear the judgment in her editor's silence, her mentally labeling Isabelle as a "difficult author." It was painful to cancel what was meant to be her victory lap, but Isabelle knew it would feel like anything but. She didn't deserve to be celebrated. So instead of boarding a Jet Blue flight for Los Angeles, Isabelle woke up that morning and walked to Mount Sinai hospital.

The clerk at the desk waved her in, and she rode up in the elevator to the children's hospital. For nearly twenty-five years, at least two or three times a week, her mother had taken the path Isabelle was now walking. She started Project Story not long after the accident. The program now sent volunteers for a daily story time as well as several private readers who visited children in their rooms. Her mother had raised enough money for the construction and maintenance of a library, a thousand-square-foot, softly lit carpeted area, filled with bookshelves and cozy reading nooks. Most recently, her mother had funded an offshoot program that paid New York City teachers to come and tutor children who were trying to keep up with schoolwork. At the hospital, Claire was a celebrity. Everyone loved her. And no one cared that she was Ward Manning's wife. In a place filled with children fighting serious illness, Ward was irrelevant.

Isabelle walked through the library's glass doors just before eleven. A woman in a Mr. Rogers–style cardigan and a long, flowered skirt was refiling books from a rolling cart. She turned around at the noise of the door and removed the glasses that hung on a chain around her neck.

"Well! Isabelle!"

"Hi, Cecily."

Cecily walked over and gave Isabelle a hug, before resting her arm on Isabelle's shoulder. Isabelle remembered how being in Cecily's presence had a calming effect, like the feeling of having one's hair brushed. "How are you?"

"You know, getting by."

Cecily nodded, her lip beginning to quiver. "We just miss your mother so much over here." She tilted her head down, closed her eyes and pinched the top of her nose with her thumb and forefinger. Isabelle felt tears springing to her own eyes.

"Oh gosh, I'm sorry," said Cecily.

Isabelle nodded. She used to go read about twice a month, but she had stayed away from Project Story since her mother died, feeling it would be just too fucking sad. But today it felt almost good to just stand there with Cecily and be sad.

"Look at us." Cecily took Isabelle by the shoulders. "Here, let's pick out a book for you to read." Cecily led Isabelle over to a shelf. "I'll leave you to it."

Isabelle's eyes wandered over the titles, which always filled her with a warm nostalgia. Isabelle took out a few and perused their pages. *Where the Wild Things Are. The Carrot Seed. Make Way for Ducklings. Tikki Tikki Tembo.* Isabelle kept scanning the titles until she settled on the familiar red spine. It was the one she'd known she'd pick all along.

"Did you find something?" Cecily asked.

"Yes," said Isabelle.

"Oh, a classic. Good choice."

A few minutes later the children arrived, half a dozen patients with some siblings and parents mixed in. They ranged from four or five to somewhere in the tweens. Some had lost their hair, others had oxygen tubes that ran underneath their noses, behind their ears, connected to the fire extinguisher–sized tanks they wheeled beside them. Isabelle walked around with a vague awareness that she was lucky, and on a macro-level, essentially problemless. Her angst about her book was an ailment of the entitled, a trouble one could only focus on because the real things that mattered—food, shelter, health—were taken care of. She remembered learning about this in a psych class in college. Maslow's hierarchy of needs. Only people unconcerned with the basic elements of survival could afford to be neurotic. Isabelle could spend years myopically worrying about whether she was a real writer and when her book would finally come out, because she didn't have to worry about anything real. Her crisis was a privilege.

Reading to the children at the hospital had always been a good reality check, but as Isabelle sat there, she was struck with a deep sense of shame at her own self-involvement, her obliviousness, for all the mornings she woke up feeling the world owed her something, for the times she genuinely believed in her own tragedy. The intensity of her self-reproach was only amplified by the children who seemed happy, despite all odds, and earnestly excited for the simple pleasure of being read to.

Isabelle had wondered since the moment she found the manuscript, how her mother could have put it away and let it languish unfinished. How could she have withstood never knowing if it could be published? Isabelle did not think she herself could've ever passed that up. But her mother had other considerations. The obvious ones like maybe not wanting to trash her marriage or hurt Isabelle. But perhaps Claire, a woman who chose to be regularly confronted with her own luckiness, to make a life out of helping people experiencing genuine crisis, thought of writing entirely differently. Maybe publishing had not been the point for her. Maybe things like Amazon rankings and *Kirkus* reviews, the markers by which Isabelle so desperately measured herself, were less important to Claire. Maybe a person could choose to make them not important.

The children sat cross-legged in front of Isabelle, and quieted, looking at her expectantly. *Once there was a little bunny who wanted to run away . . .* Claire had read the words of *The Runaway Bunny* to Isabelle time after time. Isabelle remembered having to replace one copy because it became so dog-eared, the pages sticking together, touched too many times by hands coated in jelly and pancake syrup. She loved the pictures, especially the one of the mother bunny fishing in the river, still with her purse hanging off her shoulder, at once fearless and practical. The unwavering tenacity of the mother had once been soothing to Isabelle. But now it broke her heart. The bunny mother was Claire, forgiving, steadfast, unconditional. Isabelle knew that even if it had not been Claire's grand plan for Isabelle to take the book and publish it herself, Claire would not have abandoned her for what she had done. Claire might be the only person in the world who would have understood and forgiven her. And this was what made Isabelle feel worst of all.

After she finished, Isabelle took requests from the audience. Then she walked around talking to the children as they picked out their own books to read. Before she realized it, an hour had gone by and it was time for them to go back to their rooms. Isabelle said goodbye to Cecily and walked out of the library, promising she'd be back.

She followed a different route out and got turned around, unable to find the elevator. She had been to the hospital so many times, but its labyrinthine structure could still confound her. Isabelle followed one hallway that led to a set of double doors labeled I Wing. She pushed them open. The walls were no longer painted bright, primary colors as they had been in the children's hospital, but drab and beige. The rooms were different, too, with large glass windows in front. The patients inside were not children. And they were not reading or watching TV; they were unconscious, hooked up to many serious-looking machines. Isabelle walked more quickly, sensing this was not an area where visitors were welcome. But as she passed one window, she looked in and stopped in her tracks, staring at the wild white-gray hair, the large head. The resemblance was uncanny. And for one horrifying moment, Isabelle believed she was looking at her father, motionless with tubes coming out of his mouth, a machine doing the work of breathing. Isabelle walked closer, lingering at the window even after she knew that it was not really him.

"Excuse me, can I help you?"

Isabelle flinched, then saw a scowling nurse approaching her.

"I'm sorry, I'm just looking for the lobby."

"Elevators to the left. How did you get here?"

"I—I don't know."

♦   ♦   ♦

Isabelle walked home, the image of the man she'd seen filling her thoughts. She entered her building and was about to step into her elevator when her doorman touched her arm.

"This came for you," he said, and handed her a yellow-beige padded square envelope with her name on it. The return address read **United States Attorney, Southern District of New York**. She could feel there was something solid and block-shaped within it, the size of a golf ball.

"Oh. Thanks," said Isabelle. She waited until she was in her apartment. Then she peeled open the envelope, reached inside, and retrieved a black jewelry box. Her rational mind could not work fast enough to pull back a nanosecond fantasy that this was an engagement ring. Of course this was insane. She'd done nothing to merit such a gesture, and Brian would not send an engagement ring in a U.S. government envelope swiped from work. But even this idea—as fantastical as it was—filled her with something she had not known she was still capable of, something a lot like joy. Isabelle pried the box open. There was no ring. What sat inside the silk-lined, cushioned box was a necklace. Isabelle felt the blood drain from her head. On a delicate gold chain hung a single charm, a tiny replica of a book, just like the one she'd worn since she was seven years old. Except this one wasn't of her father's book; it was of *Underpainting*. This was what Brian had wanted to give her when she'd blown him off for Darby Cullman. Isabelle felt a wave of nausea at her own wretchedness. She pawed around in her bag for her phone. She would call him as many times as it took until he answered. She would show up at his doorstep. She needed to tell him that she was sorry. So, so sorry. She was a fool and an idiot and a complete and total asshole, and she'd spend her life trying to make it up to him. But just as she drew her phone out of her bag, a text came through. Isabelle stared at it for several seconds. There it was, the thing she'd been waiting for since the day *Underpainting* came out. A single line of text. But, she needed no further context. *I KNOW WHAT YOU DID.*

Isabelle Manning was caught at last.

PART III

33

New York, 2015

Claire

Claire inspected the fouled bed of geraniums. The flowers lay in a tangled mess of churned-up dirt, many fully decapitated, others still with a few bruised peach-pink leaves, nearly all the stems had been de-rooted. There was no mistaking that what had been done had been done with hostility, even rage. It was a feat of willpower to accomplish this level of destruction without the aid of opposable thumbs. But in the center of the pot was the true message. In a shallow hole, flowers pushed away, were four finger-length turds stacked on top of one another in a neat pyramid. The cat had made moves before, peeing on the lawn, stalking the birds at the feeder until Claire took it down, not wanting to play accomplice to avicide. But this was a bona fide escalation.

Claire put on her thick, padded gardening gloves and used her trowel to remove the excrement into the garbage bag she'd brought outside. Years ago, when Isabelle was five or six, this part of Claire's garden had been where she and Isabelle planted their fruit and vegetables. The two of them always spent the whole summer in Sag Harbor, Ward coming and going, making cameo appearances into the family. Together, Claire and Isabelle grew tomatoes, snap peas, strawberries, and carrots. Everything had grown well except for the carrots. Despite following the instructions diligently, and watering the soil, Claire found the leaves limp and shriveled. She kept reassuring Isabelle that it would turn out just like in *The Carrot Seed*, but nothing came up. Day after day, and it looked as if the tops were dying.

"It's so odd," Claire mused as she and Isabelle made the rounds with the watering can.

Isabelle nodded seriously. "Especially since I've been checking on the carrots."

"Checking on them? What do you mean?"

"Every day I come out here and pull them up to see how they're growing, and then I put them back."

Claire shook her head at the memory. She'd explained to her daughter that checking on the carrots had done them in. The tiny seed needed time to marinate in the soil, away from the sun, so the roots could take hold. Some things can only grow out of view. "It requires patience," Claire had explained, "but it's the only way." They replanted the carrots. Isabelle waited this time, but Claire could tell that it was torture.

Perhaps instead of flowers she'd plant vegetables again, Claire thought as she finished shoveling the tainted dirt into the bag. She and Isabelle could do it together as a lark. A comforting little regression into the past. God knew Isabelle needed it. She'd heard from her daughter that day that her agent had advised "shelving" the book. Apparently there were no more publishers to try. And there was a "blind" item in the paper about a famous writer's daughter not selling her book. Isabelle was distraught. Claire was livid.

Claire had hoped that Isabelle's literary aspirations would lead to happiness. But she'd long feared for her daughter. Claire had read enough of Isabelle's work to know her daughter was a gifted writer, but Isabelle had no clue how difficult it would be to write her way out of Ward's shadow. And Isabelle had a completely unrealistic sense from Ward of what the profession was like. He had hidden his own struggles from her—from everyone—so Isabelle believed that anything less than immediate blockbuster success was failure. Claire tried repeatedly to gently express to Isabelle that this was not, in fact, a normal trajectory, but her advice sat like oil on water.

In order to give herself credibility, Claire would need to explain what had never been explained. And this she could not do. Claire could imagine few things less pleasant than explaining that it was Claire to whom Isabelle owed her identity as the famous writer's daughter. She could imagine how quickly she'd be reduced to shrilly insisting—to a disbelieving Isabelle—that Ward's career had almost ended before it began, that it was really *she* who had written the ending to *American Dream*, she who had saved *Urban Idols*, and provided the entire plot line—and plenty of the prose—in *Manifest Destiny*. But what proof did Claire have anyway? She could almost hear her daughter laughing: *Oh please, Mom, that's a likely story.* Well, there was the one way to prove it.

The manuscript lay hidden underneath layers of nightgowns, just waiting for the right moment. But Claire had to tread carefully. Isabelle might be angered at Claire's depiction of Aiden, her idol desecrated. Or it could come off as Claire competing with her, and Isabelle certainly had enough familial rivals as it was. While trying to start her own literary career, Isabelle might not be heartened to think that Claire had failed in her own. She would show Isabelle the book when the time was right, when she could be sure it would do more good than harm.

For now, Claire would provide Isabelle with an emotional soft-landing. Maybe she'd have Isabelle out when Ward was away for something or other, so that he couldn't hijack the weekend, turning it into a Ward-fest as he was so skilled at doing. Isabelle would be only too willing to indulge him. Ward needed to be kept out of it. Especially since one of her most urgent reasons to see her daughter was to give her a check. Claire knew that Isabelle had been counting on selling this book, not only to launch her career, but because her daughter needed the money to cover even basic expenses.

It was ridiculous, given Ward's piles of money. If they had just set up a trust for her years ago—nothing extravagant, but something to support her through her writing—Isabelle would have been comfortable instead of financially precarious. But Ward was adamant. And, as he liked to thread into the discussion, it was *his* money. Be that as it may, Ward had no patience for financial minutiae. It was Claire who handled their accounts, and he had no clue about the thousand or two that disappeared from their checking every month.

A plan formed in Claire's mind. She would have Isabelle out to the house, reassure her that she was still there for her financially or otherwise, and they would plant carrots again. Maybe she'd even invite Brian. This could be Claire's opening to finally get her daughter to see reason.

Isabelle's boyfriends were typically boarding school types with pretentious facial hair and delusions of their own import. But Brian. Brian was different. He was good and down-to-earth and had values and character. He was just the type of person to keep Isabelle grounded, make sure that if Isabelle did ever see success, she wouldn't become unbearable. And Brian was an Adonis, for heaven's sake. Claire always wanted to take him aside and tell him that if he were less available he might stand a chance. But Isabelle and Brian were over thirty now. How long before another girl—any girl in her right mind!—made a move? If Isabelle missed her chance with Brian, she could end up with someone like Ward. Or—and Claire didn't like to fully articulate this, even in her mind, but— Isabelle might end up alone.

Before she could start working Brian into this as-yet theoretical weekend, however, Claire had to deal with the cat who'd despoiled her geraniums.

Miss Muffins's sojourns onto Manning property had begun as a minor nuisance, but when she began using the lawn as a litterbox, Claire had asked their neighbors to kindly keep the cat in their own yard. Kimberly Swanson shrugged and looked at Claire as wide-eyed as her Botox would allow. "She's a cat. What do you want me to do?" she demanded in her clipped, high-pitched chirp, as if fences were an entirely alien concept. At one point Claire had even offered to split the cost, but Kimberly was not interested in losing the "open feel" of her lawn. Kimberly was a recent addition to the neighborhood. She and her husband hosted lavish, tented affairs in their backyard, and Claire had heard Kimberly was once on reality TV. It used to be that women like Kimberly, women with golf ball–sized diamond rings who plastered themselves with overt designer labels, wouldn't deign set foot in Sag Harbor. These women wanted their trophy house to be south of the highway so they could spend the rest of their natural born lives dropping those four words into conversation. But times had changed. Sag Harbor was trendy. And now Kimberly Swanson and her bedazzled-collared cat were there to stay.

Even without the crystal collars, Claire was not a cat person. The Cunningham family had dogs, big, loose-skinned black labs with thick ropes of drool hanging from their muzzles. Their fur smelled of salt and damp and they left fetid, gooey tennis balls all over the house. Labs were simple, lovable creatures. Her preferences aside, Claire felt bad for Miss Muffins. The name, for a start. And Kimberly was hardly a conscientious pet owner. She had admitted to Claire that sometimes she didn't know where Miss Muffins was for days at a time, apparently unconcerned about her cat roaming the raccoon-infested landscape late at night. Perhaps Miss Muffins frequented their yard so often as a means of escape, her hostility and destruction some misplaced frustration. A cry for help.

Claire heard the gravel-crunch of a car pulling in. Ward was home from tennis. She stood up, took off her gloves and dusted the dirt on her knees, then walked around the house toward the shed, intersecting Ward standing in the driveway. He raised his eyebrows at the trash bag slung Santa-style over her shoulder.

"Miss Muffins. She got at the geraniums."

Ward shook his head and made a *tsk tsk* sound. "She knows how to wound you." He bumped the heel of one shoe against the other, knocking off the sea-green clay.

"This can't continue."

"Is this your way of telling me we're moving?"

"We're not. But Miss Muffins may be relocating."

Ward smirked. "Uh-oh." Ward found her feud with the Swansons and their cat amusing. On the one hand, Claire did too. It was ridiculous, the plot of a sitcom episode. "Mom Goes Nuts over Cat in Yard." But there was another part of Claire that felt a legitimate, coursing anger. Why should she suffer, her home defiled, the things she loved debased? It was not right. If the cat had been defecating all over Ward's manuscripts, he might not find it so funny. Claire had absorbed enough indignities for a lifetime. And now she had decided she would tolerate no further abuse from the fecal feline.

Claire walked with her husband back inside the house. She checked her watch. It was nearly four. That night they were hosting a couple who'd made a substantial donation to Project Story. Ward's behavior at Claire-driven social events was unpredictable. Best-case scenario, he would play the magnanimous celebrity, overly and histrionically warm. Worst-case, he would grow sullen and withdrawn if he wasn't given sufficient attention and lauding.

"Did you see this?" Claire asked, pointing at the *New York Post*.

"No. Why?"

"There's a mention on Page Six. One of those blind items."

"About me?" Ward was fixing himself a glass of seltzer.

"No. Not about you." Claire picked up the paper and read aloud: "'*What daughter of a famous scribe can't seem to unload her manuscript? Word has it she's been turned down all over town.*'"

"Ah."

"Blind item my foot."

"Hm," said Ward, not looking at her.

"Fern wants to put the book aside. Seems to feel it's snakebitten at this point."

"Probably right."

"Isabelle is distraught."

Ward moved to the refrigerator and got out a block of cheese.

"Cut neatly. We need that for tonight."

He continued to unwrap the cheese.

"Do you have anything to say?"

"About what?"

"Isabelle's book, for crissakes."

Ward whacked off a chunk of cheddar and stuffed it in his mouth.

"You don't seem terribly bothered by this."

"What do you want me to do?" he said through a mouth of cheese. "Cry?"

"Our daughter is struggling, Ward. Her misery is being poked fun at in the paper."

"Maybe that's not a bad thing."

"What? What are you talking about?"

Ward put up his hands. "Not the *Post*. But a little adversity will be good for her. She's had it too easy all these years."

"Oh don't start with that. Please."

"She didn't sell her first book. She'll have to work it out. This is a much-needed dose of reality."

Something cold and heavy settled inside Claire. She looked at her husband. "You know, it's strange, Ward. You don't seem surprised by what's happened. In fact, you don't even seem disappointed."

Ward snorted. "Forgive me for not thinking this is a tragedy." He popped another piece of cheese into his mouth. She saw that he had not in fact cut the wedge cleanly and she would have to find something else to serve to the guests. In that moment, Claire hated him. Given everything that had happened, it was a miracle she didn't feel this way more often. There were still times, despite all the odds, that she actually could enjoy her husband. But now she was filled with the urge to take the block of cheddar and smash it pie-like into his face. Claire stared at Ward until he broke her gaze. "I'm going to shower," he said.

"Fine," said Claire. "Be ready by six thirty." She picked up her bag off the kitchen table and walked toward the door.

"Where are you going?" asked Ward.

"Out."

"Why?"

"I need a cat carrier."

34

New York, 2018

Isabelle

Isabelle read the text again. *I KNOW WHAT YOU DID*. She turned around, walked out of her apartment, rode the elevator back down to the lobby. Her heart was pounding hard, blood rushed in her ears, and the world shrunk away as she focused on typing a reply. *I'm on my way. I can explain.* The former sentence was true; the latter was a more aspirational statement.

Isabelle walked west to Park Avenue. That Glenda knew something of this book did not come entirely as a shock. Isabelle had taken the risk that Glenda might know, because by the time it occurred to her, she was so far down the path of self-justification that it did not matter. And because Isabelle had needed her book in a way that made her immune to things like reason, judgment, and good sense. She'd needed her book because it was the thing she'd wanted since before she could remember. No, that wasn't true. She knew exactly when this had all begun. She'd set off on this ruinous path when she was seven years old, the night of her father's book party, the night she got her necklace, whose new sibling now sat inside her purse. Sometime since that evening at Gotham decades ago, her ambition had slid into entitlement, which curdled into desperation, revealing something inside Isabelle that was unhealthy. Even a little bit scary.

Isabelle passed the doorman unnoticed, rode the elevator to Glenda's private landing, and found Glenda's door wide open. "Hello?" She stuck her head in, but there was no one in the entryway. It occurred to her that her godmother might not, in fact, be home. Glenda could easily have written her from some remote European locale. One of the staff could have left the door open for a delivery. But as Isabelle turned around to leave, she heard the all-too-familiar husky voice. "Well, well, well."

She looked up and saw Glenda standing at the top of the staircase. She was wearing a scoop-neck black leotard over black leggings. Her hair was tied up in a silk turban. On her feet were soft ballet slippers, and in her hand she was holding *Underpainting*. "Don't stand there like an imbecile—come in."

Isabelle stepped into the circular marble foyer.

"I read your book on my flight home yesterday."

Isabelle was suddenly aware that she was sweating and had been for a while.

"I was enjoying it," said Glenda. "I prefer my literature with some steam, but it was energetic enough. And then around—I don't know—page twenty-five, I begin to think, *this is familiar*." Glenda had made her way down the curved staircase and was now standing under the massive crystal chandelier, her eyes trained on Isabelle. "I kept thinking, but I couldn't place it. Then somewhere over the Atlantic, it came to me. The realization shocked me out of my sleep. And, mind you, this was despite my cocktail of three Ambien and half a bottle of Shiraz. I was wide awake, and I knew it like I know my net worth: This is Claire's book."

Isabelle opened her mouth, but Glenda put up her hand. "Don't even think of denying it. Claire told me about this book years ago. She outlined the entire plot to me."

A voice in Isabelle's head screamed to give in, prostrate herself on the floor and admit her wrongs, end this deceit here and now, but something else in her gripped at the slippery edge of the cliff from which she was now hanging pendulously. Isabelle had one card left to play. She cleared her throat. "Well, Glenda, after we had lunch, I thought a lot about what you said about being inspired by other authors. I took your advice to heart."

"Ha! I did not tell you to steal someone's book. Much less your mother's."

"I didn't steal it," Isabelle said, her voice quivering. "My mother told me where to find it before she died. She wanted me to have it."

Glenda snorted.

"It wasn't finished when I found it. So I finished it and I edited it. I made it my own."

Glenda folded her arms over her chest.

"So I should thank you for the idea."

Glenda looked at Isabelle for a moment, her face softening the slightest bit. There was no limit to the power of flattery. Glenda smiled at Isabelle, and Isabelle felt herself exhale. Her godmother took a step toward her. She made a movement that Isabelle read as the start of an embrace, but Glenda drew her hand back and slapped Isabelle across the face. "You manipulative little cunt."

Isabelle staggered backward, almost falling, her hand to her burning cheek. She looked at her godmother, dazed, "You hit me?"

"You're lucky it wasn't a right hook. I've been taking cardio boxing."

"Jesus," said Isabelle, rubbing her jaw.

"After all your mother did for you, this is how you repay her? This is how you honor her memory? I always thought you were too much your father's daughter. But the difference is, people put up with Ward because he has the success to back it up. What do you have? Nothing. You're just a wannabe."

Isabelle closed her eyes. "I've made a mistake," she said. "I know that."

Glenda shook her head, disgusted.

"But I'm a good writer. I am. I can write more books myself."

"The facts suggest otherwise, sweetheart."

"I just wanted—" Isabelle paused, then continued more softly, "I just wanted to have a book published, to feel like it was real. That's what I've wanted my whole life. Just to be a writer."

"Wrong," said Glenda, sharp as a buzzer.

"Wrong?"

"Wrong. That's not what you want."

"I can assure you it is."

"No, dear, what you want is to be *famous*. For everyone to praise you, tell you what a good job you did and fawn all over you like you're the second coming of Shakespeare. That is what you want. And that is an entirely different can of soup."

Isabelle opened her mouth, then closed it again. Of course, Glenda was right. She had decided to be a writer the night of her father's book party. But when she saw her father climb up on that banquette, when she saw how the room swelled for him, when she saw the adoring, dopey way people looked at him, she had also decided *I want that*. Isabelle wanted to be the center of every room she walked into. She wanted to be important. She not only wanted it, but an assumption took root in her mind that this was what it meant to be successful, this was what it meant to be worthy, and all other kinds of lives were inherently inferior. And she believed if she ever wanted her father to see her the way she saw him, if she ever wanted him to deem her a valuable human being, she would have to achieve that celebrity factor too. Writing and these beliefs had gotten impossibly tangled up together until they were one sputtering mass of toxic ambition.

Glenda looked at Isabelle now. "Do you need ice?"

"No."

"Come sit down." Glenda led her into a classic library done in lavish red wallpaper with carved marble spaniels on either side of the fireplace.

"When did my mother tell you about this book?" she asked once they were sitting.

"It has to be more than twenty years ago, maybe twenty-five," said Glenda. "Let's see, I remember I thought she was finally kicking your father to the curb. Prayers answered." Glenda raised arms bent at ninety-degree angles and shook them to the sky. "I was crestfallen when I found out that wasn't the reason. We got distracted, and somehow or other I ended up drinking the lion's share of a bottle of champagne . . ."

"And?" Isabelle said finally.

Glenda was looking up at the ceiling, mentally calculating. "That's right, Claire had to go, but then she called me up later and told me about the book. Right before you left for—" Glenda stopped herself.

"Right before we left for what?"

"Well, I'm remembering now, this all happened just before that business in the Caribbean."

Isabelle felt her stomach turn. She'd suspected this. Her mother had decided to abandon the book around the time of—or, more likely, because of—Isabelle's accident.

"And then what happened? What happened when we got back?"

"Claire didn't want to pursue it. I encouraged her to, of course. But she was firm. And I would have pressed, but it was around the time I met Jonathan. And I was too busy being swept off my feet. I forgot about the book until the plane ride." She sighed and, after a moment, said, "I failed her then, but I won't now." She straightened up and pursed her lips before she spoke. "Here's what you're going to do. Call up your publisher and make clear exactly what you did."

"Oh Glenda, I don't know if I can do that. I hate all this lying; it's driving me crazy. I can't sleep or eat. But—"

"Ah, so this is the miracle diet you've been on? It's worked wonders, I must say."

"Do you understand what will happen to me if I tell my publisher?"

"Nothing good, I'd imagine. But, Isabelle my dear, you should have thought of that before."

"I should've. I know. I should've. But what good will telling now do?" Isabelle had used this argument on herself dozens of times. Claire was gone. How would telling help? Glenda's expression suggested she found this reasoning about as persuasive as Isabelle did.

"Oh, you ungrateful beast. If you can't see why your error needs to be corrected, then I'm not going to waste my breath explaining it to you." Glenda paced the room for a moment. "I have half a mind to call up the *New York Times* this minute."

"Please, please, Glenda, do not do that," Isabelle said, her voice turning gravelly and desperate. "My life will be over. Please."

"It's all about you, isn't it?"

"There's something else."

"What?"

"My father is sick."

Glenda turned to face Isabelle more fully. "Ward? What are you talking about?"

"There's something wrong with him. I don't know exactly what yet, but he's ill. Maybe very ill."

"I'm sorry to hear it," said Glenda perfunctorily. "But I don't see how that has any bearing on you coming clean."

"He can't die knowing this." This was the rub that chained Isabelle to her fraud. Whatever she had to endure as a closeted plagiarist could not be worse than her father's eternal disappointment.

Glenda's lips were twitching. "That's who you're worried about? Your father?" She made a dramatic show of laughing, clutching her stomach and keeling over. "Oh darling, haven't you learned yet? Your father isn't thinking about *you*. Your father isn't thinking about anyone but Ward Manning." She set a hand on Isabelle's shoulder, a first gesture of tenderness since she'd arrived. "Listen. I'm not a monster," she said. "Because you're Claire's daughter, because I'm your godmother, and because, despite popular belief, I am a very tolerant person, I'm giving you the opportunity to speak up for yourself." When Isabelle didn't answer, Glenda took her chin in her fingers. "But Isabelle, you have a simple choice. Tell, or I will."

"That doesn't seem like much of a choice."

"You started this. Now finish it." Glenda stood up and smiled slightly. "And if what you say is true about writing the end of the book, you ought to have known this would happen. It's right there in your pages. I took the script from you, darling."

Isabelle closed her eyes. She should have seen it before. *I know what you did.* Glenda's text had used Isabelle's own words, mocking her. Now she, like Livia, would face the prospect of revealing her secret. But the parallel between them ended there. Livia was hiding her identity as the true artist; Isabelle was the fake masquerading as the genuine article.

"All right," said Glenda, "you've interrupted my barre session, so off with you."

Isabelle got off the couch. "Can I have some time? There are people I need to speak to."

"You have two days."

Isabelle nodded. Glenda walked back upstairs. Isabelle made her way to the door, still unsteady. Her objectives had turned small: leave the house, end the scene. Isabelle found herself standing back on the street. She stood still a moment, the cityscape suddenly immense, the spring sunshine too bright. She looked around, trying to choose a direction to move. Whatever path she took, there was no escape.

As instructed, I sat down on the park bench at noon sharp. I scanned for Sebastian or his underworld minion. But there was only a woman pushing a shopping cart brimming with cans, and a gaggle of toddlers with their handlers. Children usually put me on edge, as if I owed them an explanation of why I never had any, but today the sight of them calmed me. How much harm could be done in broad daylight among three-year-olds eating Lunchables?

I was considering this when two young women sat down next to me. I scooched away huffily. Couldn't they have picked one of the many other open benches? I was about to get up when I heard, "Thanks for coming."

I turned my head. "What?"

"Thanks for coming," said one of the women who couldn't have been more than twenty-five. And then I saw the two tiny buns on her head, her friend with the spaghetti strap dress, the Doc Martens on their feet. The women from the gallery, the ones who'd followed me, the ones I'd seen on the street with my stalker.

I recoiled. "Who are you? What do you want?"

"I'm Anna; this is Jennifer," said the one with the buns. "And, isn't it obvious?"

"We think you should stop pretending to be your husband," said Jennifer.

"How did you figure it out?"

Anna raised her eyebrow. "Come on. Aiden Connors doing a set of historically significant women—"

"With all with their clothes on?" finished Jennifer.

"Good point," I said.

"Plus, your technique is better," said Jennifer. "When you look closely, it's much cleaner, more precise."

"Thanks." A small jab of pride punctured my panic.

276

Jennifer and Anna explained that they were both artists, but working as gallery assistants to pay their rent. They picked up the buzz about Aiden's new works and became interested. When they saw pictures of the paintings, it raised their suspicions. They began investigating, looking for definitive proof. They followed me. Called my apartment to see when I was home. Believing that Aiden's studio was adjacent to our apartment, they broke into 3A and 3C. When that didn't work, they broke in across the street and took photographs from the fire escape with a long-focus lens.

"You're quite mad, aren't you?" I said.

Jennifer shrugged.

"And what about the thickset guy with the toothpick who was following me around?"

Anna and Jennifer looked at each other and laughed. "Tommy's my brother," said Anna. "He was just helping us keep an eye on you. He's not really employed right now, so he had some free time."

"Sweetest guy in the world," said Jennifer.

"Well, he scared me half to death."

"Sorry," said Anna.

"Why is this so important to you anyway?" I asked.

Jennifer narrowed her eyes. "Do you know how many women get shows at that gallery?"

"Not many."

"No. Almost none," Jennifer spat. "And here you are, your work getting rave reviews, and you're pretending to be a man."

"You have to tell," said Anna.

"You don't understand. I need the money. My mother is ill. I'm the only one taking care of her."

The women looked at me, unmoved. They were too young to understand.

"And I have this boyfriend. And he's amazing, but also the most ethical person alive. Literally."

"Aw, that guy in the old-man sweaters?" Anna asked.

"Yes. You can see it's complicated."

"Not really," said Jennifer.

We sat there unspeaking for a moment before I said, "Why did you come to me? You could've just told."

"Because," said Anna. "We think you're very good. If we tell, it might trash your career—if you tell the story yourself, you could save it."

As if on cue, both women stood up. Anna threaded her skinny arms through the straps of her mini backpack.

"But," said Jennifer, "we won't wait forever. If you can't find your spine in the next two days, we'll find it for you."

"It's true," said Anna. "My boss has the *New York Times* on speed dial, and I'm really good at impersonating her voice."

35

New York, 2018

Isabelle

Isabelle pushed through the revolving door on Worth Street. She stood on the security line before stepping through the metal detector and placing her bag and suit jacket on the screening belt. Isabelle had found nothing right for the occasion, at once conservative and celebratory, in her own closet, so she'd gone to the bag she'd packed up from her mother's closet many months before. The suit was navy bouclé with a pencil skirt and collarless jacket with three-quarter sleeves. She'd recalled her mother wearing it to Easter brunch at the Met one year. The weight was almost too heavy on the balmy May morning, but Isabelle put it on anyway, hoping it imbued her with the strength she was going to need.

The courthouse had an antiseptic smell and cold that reverberated off the marble walls. Serious, briefcase-carrying people passed her on the way to the elevator. Yesterday, when she'd gotten home from Glenda's and recovered a small shred of her wits, Isabelle remembered the significance of today. She'd done some pointed internet searching, placed a call to the Southern District information line and figured out where to go and what time to be there.

When the elevator doors opened at the ceremonial courtroom,

she was greeted by a legitimate mob of people. This was, Isabelle realized, a very big deal. Not knowing anyone, Isabelle didn't loiter, and quickly found a seat. She spotted Brian's parents in the front row, his mother in a teal suit, standing up to greet people, seeming to levitate with happiness, and his father, next to her with his characteristic stoic half smile. It was nice; they were clearly thrilled. This was the legal equivalent of writing a bestseller. Isabelle had to remind herself that there were trophies in noncreative professions, and, for some people, there were things more meaningful than writing a book. Most parents would celebrate a child becoming a successful U.S. attorney. Ward Manning was just not one of them.

When she saw Brian several yards away, up near the stage, he did not see her. Isabelle watched him talking to people who looked government-like and official. He looked pretty official himself in his charcoal suit, white shirt, and red tie. Isabelle squinted and saw that it was the one with tiny yellow penguins on it, the one that she had given to him years ago. That had to be a good sign. Brian wouldn't return her calls or texts, but he didn't hate her enough not to wear that tie on his big day. His hair was longer, and he looked like he'd been working out even more than usual. A new gravitas surrounded him. Brian was in his element.

In the next few moments, the seats filled up and the program started. The judge that Brian had clerked for in Minnesota spoke first, recounting what a diligent, hard-working clerk Brian had been; one of the best, he'd said. "I've had lots of smart clerks," said the judge. He looked close to eighty, imposing yet grandfatherly, the type of person you'd really hate to disappoint. "Brian, though, had judgment beyond his years. I trusted him with the thorniest of legal issues. And I hope that one day he will decide to take a seat on the bench. Maybe back in Minneapolis?" Brian's mother cheered a bit too loudly.

After the judge, a number of other lawyers spoke, including a partner at Brian's former law firm, two colleagues at the U.S. attorney's office, and finally, Sherrill Sheehan, Brian's boss, a hulking man who loomed over the lectern. Everyone said some version of the same thing: Brian was of unassailable character. With each iteration of the sentiment, Isabelle slumped a little lower in her seat.

At last Brian got up to speak. He accepted his new position and then gave a short speech thanking lots of people. He couldn't have spoken for more than five minutes, but Isabelle absorbed almost no substance of it whatsoever. She was too busy thinking, *Who is this person?* He was completely self-assured. His voice was deep and calm, with no trace of nerves or embarrassment, the audio equivalent of a firm handshake. A chill pricked up the downy hair on her forearms. The Brian she saw—*her* Brian—was an anachronism, a regression, a relic from his youth. In their nearly two-decade-long relationship, Isabelle had been the dominant one, the alpha. Brian had always seemed happy—lucky even—to play the role of her best friend. But now she saw with blinding clarity that this was all wrong. *She* was the one who was lucky to get Brian. He was better than her. He was perfect. This was not an opinion; it was an uncontroverted, objective fact now testified to by fine, upstanding members of the bar.

It was not until Brian was almost finished when their eyes locked. Brian looked startled, but in the tiny curve of his lips and a flash in his eyes, Isabelle thought she also detected something else, something pleased. He fumbled for a moment, glancing down at his notes for the first time since he'd taken the podium, before he refocused and continued, looking away as if he'd never seen her.

After, Isabelle waited in the back of the room while Brian was crowded with well-wishers. She did not want to be intrusive, but she had to speak to him. Isabelle had around thirty-six more hours before Glenda would expose her. She could not stand the thought of Brian hearing what she'd done from anyone else. Or him not knowing how she felt about him.

Finally, he broke away and walked toward her. Isabelle stood up, her heart hammering in her chest.

"Hi," he said, not smiling, "how did you get here?"

"The subway?"

"No, I mean how did you even know about this?"

"You told me a while ago," said Isabelle, adding, "I stalked you, basically."

Brian raised his eyebrows.

"Congratulations. You were fantastic. I mean, this is really amazing—what everyone said about you?" Isabelle put her hand to her chest, and that's when Brian's eyes were drawn to her collarbone and he saw the necklace.

"Thanks."

"I've been trying to get in touch with you. And I wanted to say thank you for the gift. And also say I'm sorry—"

"This really isn't a good time, Isabelle."

"Yes, of course, sorry."

"My parents are here."

"I saw, that's so lovely."

"And there's a lunch thing."

"No, no, I totally get it. Go, do you."

Brian nodded. He started to turn away, and Isabelle had the urge to grab his hands, to pull him toward her, to hug him and press her face into his shoulder. She always teased him about his man perfume, but now she wanted to inhale his smell, have it soak into every pore of her body. "Hey, Brian?"

He turned. "Yeah?"

"Do you think there's another time we could talk?"

Brian rubbed the back of his neck with his hand. "I gave you the necklace because, I don't know, I wanted you to have it. But I wasn't really trying to start up our friendship again."

Isabelle blinked. The coldness of Brian's voice, that he'd made peace with giving up their friendship, knocked the wind out of her. But she could not give up. "Okay. I understand. But could we just meet and talk for like a few minutes?"

Brian's mother had begun calling him. If his parents recognized

Isabelle—and of course they did—they had made the conscious decision not to say hello.

Brian sighed. "Okay," he said. "Let's get a drink tonight. Downtown."

"Great. Perfect. Wherever you want."

"Odeon. Six thirty."

"I'll be there."

As Isabelle stood still, Brian went to join his family and the other friends who'd been invited to mark this moment with him instead of her.

36

New York, 2018

Brian

He should have known. If Brian wanted to be done with Isabelle—really, truly, irrevocably done—he would've thrown the necklace into the Hudson, letting it be carried with the current to its final resting place, washed up alongside used condoms and Poland Spring bottles somewhere in industrial New Jersey. But he hadn't done that. He could not perform the simple act of opening up his fist. Instead, he'd put the necklace back in his pocket and had it delivered to her apartment the next day. He might as well have sent an engraved invitation back into his life.

And now here he was, thirty minutes from meeting Isabelle, trying to decide which polo shirt said "unavailable." He decided on the navy and put on a pair of khakis. He brushed his teeth and Listerined. He put on extra cologne. Brian was done editing himself to please her. And yet, he still felt the specific anticipation he'd felt since he was eighteen years old at the thought of soon being in the presence of Isabelle Manning.

Brian waited to leave until he was sure he'd be ten minutes late. The last thing he wanted was to sit at the bar twiddling his thumbs so she could arrive twenty minutes later, breathless with some story of the stalled subways or a psychotic cab driver. This time had to be different. When Brian was a few steps from the restaurant, he could see Isabelle sitting at the bar. It had been one of the first truly warm days of the year, and she was wearing a short, sleeveless dress. When he walked in, she turned toward him, her face lighting up. If he didn't know better, he'd believe she loved him.

"Hi," he said, choking down an apology for being late.

"Hi."

Brian slid onto the barstool next to her. Isabelle was having a glass of white wine. He wanted something stronger. Something worthy of his status as the new chief of narcotics at SDNY. He looked at the drink menu and ordered the most expensive bourbon they had.

"Nice," said Isabelle.

Brian shrugged.

"You look different, Bri."

He cocked his head. "Oh yeah?"

"In a good way. Quite handsome, actually. You have this whole fresh-off-the-lacrosse-field glow."

He took a large sip of his drink, tamping down the warm feelings for Isabelle that were straining inside him. "Thanks."

"No, thank you for meeting me."

Up close, Isabelle looked exhausted, but she managed to be beautiful, in a stark, angular way.

"How's Darby?" Brian asked.

"Oh. I don't know. I'm not in touch with him."

"You seemed pretty in touch."

"I'm sorry. It was a bizarre night. I was drunk."

Brian rolled his eyes. "Really, Isabelle? You were drunk? It's not 2003. I don't think that works anymore."

"You're right." Isabelle rested her chin on her fist. "You're right. I was a complete asshole. I have no excuse. I'm so sorry, Brian. But nothing happened, not really, and nothing will ever happen between me and Darby ever again."

"Good for you." Brian finished his drink and motioned for a second one. "So why did you want to meet me?"

"Brian, I've really missed you."

He looked down at the newly poured glass. He was not saying it back. He was not.

"I have, Brian. And I'm just so sorry about the book party. And lots of other things. I know this all sounds trite—realizing what I have when it's gone and all of that. But I mean it. I've been incredibly selfish and stupid. I'm so ashamed. I could have been a much better friend to you. And I want to be."

"Oh yeah?" Brian looked up to face her. He was feeling the effects of the bourbon on an empty stomach. "Is that what you want, Isabelle? To be my friend?"

"If you'll have me."

Brian shook his head. "No."

"No?"

"No. No, because that's not what I want."

"I'm sorry, Brian. I'm so—"

"I don't want to be your friend anymore. I don't want that at all," said Brian. "No, what I want is for you to be mine, Isabelle. I want us to be together. For real. No more fucking bullshit. And if you don't want that, if you don't—if you won't admit that you love me, then I never want to see you ever again." Brian saw that Isabelle had started to cry, tears were streaming down her face, and her shoulders were shaking.

"I do want that," she choked out.

Brian closed his eyes, allowing the words he had been waiting his entire adult life to hear to wash over him like the warm, Hibiscus-scented breeze of paradise. At last, Isabelle was his. Brian leaned over, took her face in his hands and brought it to his own, his lips warm against hers.

Brian then rested his forehead on hers and wiped the tears off her cheeks with his thumbs. "Why are you crying?"

"I love you, Brian," she whispered. "I love you so much."

"Good," he said, her face still in his hands.

Isabelle turned away. "I do, but I don't deserve you."

"Yes, you do. You do. I know you, Isabelle."

Isabelle started to speak, but he pressed on. "Please, I want to make you happy. We can both be happy. You have your book now." She began to sob harder. "What did I say?"

She sat up straighter in her chair and looked at the crowd that had grown around them. "Can we go outside?"

"Sure." Brian paid for the drinks, and they walked out onto the street.

He put his arm around her. It felt good to stop holding himself back, to touch her this way, this way that wasn't "just friends." "So. What's the problem?"

"My book."

"What about it?"

Isabelle looked down. "It's not what it should be."

"What? Isn't it a huge hit?" Brian braced himself for Isabelle to launch into some tirade about a bad review or some other author she vaguely knew whose sales were better than hers. Was she really going to let some little petty grievance ruin this moment?

Isabelle pulled away from him as she said, "My mother wrote it."

"Wrote what?"

"*Underpainting.*"

"I'm not following."

"When I went to clean out my mother's closets in Sag Harbor, I found an unfinished manuscript that she wrote years ago. So I edited it and finished it. I sent it to Fern. And he sold it."

Brian put up his hands. "Wait. You didn't write the book?"

"I wrote a lot of it."

The brown liquor roiled menacingly inside Brian's stomach. "But it was your mother's book? It was all her ideas?"

"Well, I mean, yes, I guess so. Except the last third or so."

Brian's chest constricted. He couldn't look at Isabelle. He realized with the hard thud of certainty that what he believed was not the truth. The words he was so sure proved Isabelle loved him were not Isabelle's at all. They were Claire's. And Sam was Claire's too. Beneath what had given him hope, there was a noxious underpinning of lies and deceit. "Why are you telling me this?"

"Because—because I hate living this way. It's awful. I'm racked with guilt, and I'm scared. And it's going to come out. Glenda knows. She's threatening to expose me."

A ripple of understanding ran through him. Of course. He shook his head and laughed joylessly.

"Why are you laughing?"

"I'm laughing because you had me fooled. I thought you came to my event, I thought you reached out because you cared. Because you actually loved me." He shook his head again. "But no, of course not. You came because you need something."

"It's not like that. Brian, I do love you. I do love you." Isabelle's voice was hoarse and shook with desperation.

"No. No. You don't. You love me being your fucking puppy. You love that you snap your fingers and I'm there. You love that you can say 'jump!' and I'll say 'how high?' You want me to help you, to be your dance monkey, like always."

"That's not true. Please. I know how it looks. But I was calling you and texting you before I knew anything about Glenda. I wanted to talk to you because I've missed you. Because I do love you. Not because I wanted something other than your friendship—and more, if I thought you would be remotely interested in that." Isabelle tried to take his hand, but Brian pulled it away. He was sick of listening. He was sick of the excuses. He was sick of playing her games. He was sick of it all.

"Stop. Just stop."

"Please, Brian. Please don't hate me. You are literally all I have."

Brian shook his head. "I want to hate you, Isabelle. I really fucking want to. But what I really feel is sorry for you. Because I think you're right about that. I am all you have. And I'm sorry for me, too, because I love you, but you're so mired in your own bullshit, you are so completely fucked up, that it doesn't matter." Brian shook his head and looked down as he added the thing he'd thought, but never said. "Your father did a real number on you."

"My father?"

"Yes. He convinced you that you're only worth as many stars as you get in the *New York Times*—"

"The *Times* doesn't give stars—"

Brian threw up his hands. "See? This is my point. You are damaged, Isabelle. You are warped. The point isn't the fucking stars. The point is there is more to life than publishing a book. And deep down inside I don't think you get that."

Isabelle stared at him, her lips quivering, but Brian pressed on. "He ruined you, Isabelle. Your father raised you to treat him like a deity. He made you completely incompatible with any other human being because they'd have to compete with The Great Ward Manning. And no one—oh no one—can compete with him. Look at you. You're thirty-five years old and your primary identity is being your father's daughter."

Brian knew he'd been mean, cruel even, but he wasn't sorry. "Good luck, Isabelle." He turned and started walking away.

"Brian." He kept walking. "Brian!"

He turned around. "What?"

"That's it? You're leaving?"

Isabelle stood in the middle of the sidewalk, her bare arms dangling at her sides, shoulders shaking slightly, suddenly appearing tiny despite her height. A light, misty rain had begun to fall. She looked pitiful, crying in the street like a child who'd lost her balloon. Any impulse to comfort her was kept in check by the boulder-like weight of his own hurt. Enough was enough. If Brian had any chance at lasting happiness, he needed to get straight, quit the drug that was Isabelle Manning. But even as he stood there, he didn't think he would ever love another woman the way he loved Isabelle. And maybe that was as it should be. Love like this was not healthy. He would choose contentment over despair. Stability over passion. Good enough over perfection. There was a life for him to lead without Isabelle Manning. At some point, maybe he'd even start believing in it. Brian looked at Isabelle, knowing that in the months and years ahead, this image would endure each time he wondered whether he should have said something other than, "Yes, I'm leaving."

"Are you fucking crazy?" Sebastian thundered.

"I can't go on this way."

"You can and you will," he barked. "Do you know what would happen if you told anyone you're behind the latest paintings? We would get sued, sued up to our eyeballs. You realize you've committed fraud, right?"

I closed my eyes and shook my head. When I finished John Cusack, I thought I'd eventually come clean about the portraits and the pivotal role I'd played in Aiden's career. Even after I'd met Sam, I believed I might figure out a way to tell. I could see now how naïve I'd been. Of course buyers wouldn't just be displeased to learn their expensive Aiden Connors had really been painted by his wife; they'd be litigious.

I hung up the phone with Sebastian without telling him about Jennifer and Anna. I didn't like to think about what he might try to do to them. Given my new understanding of the catastrophe of disclosure, I'd talk to them myself, make one more plea for silence. I was thinking of how to make my case when my telephone rang.

"Hello?"

Gloria spoke so fast I could hardly understand her, but when she'd finished speaking, I said, "I'll be right there."

Gloria was rattled when I arrived. "She hasn't eaten in over a day. She barely speaks at all."

I nodded and walked over to my mother, sitting in the living room.

"Hi, Mom," I said, putting a hand on her shoulder and kissing her head. My mother stared at me blankly for a long moment before she smiled in recognition.

I sat down on the couch next to her. Neither of us said

anything, as I debated whether to put her through the ordeal of the ER yet again.

"Bring me that one," my mother said suddenly.

"What one, Mom?" She pointed at the built-in bookcase.

"That one."

I went to the shelf and lifted off the pastel drawing I'd made of her when I was still in art school. Her hair was a vibrant red then, and I'd accentuated her large green eyes. When I brought it over, she took it in both hands, beaming. She tapped the picture with a curved finger. "This is me."

"Yes, Mom."

My mother looked at me, a sudden clearness in her eyes. "Remember me this way. Just like in your picture."

"Mom . . ."

She batted her hand as if warning me not to get sentimental. She handed me the drawing and quickly retreated back into her own fog.

37

New York, 2018

Isabelle

The next day, for a brief half second when she opened her eyes, Isabelle did not remember what had occurred the night before on that Tribeca sidewalk. Then the memory cascaded through her like the chills and pangs of a stomach virus. Isabelle wanted to hide in a dark room, but the clock was ticking, and she had unfinished business. She got out of bed and tried to book herself on the Jitney to Sag Harbor. They were all full. Friday afternoons this close to Memorial Day required "advance booking," according to the rather smug phone operator. There was construction on the Long Island Rail Road, and trains to Bridgehampton were being diverted through Patchogue, creating a six-hour sojourn. This was out of the question. As was taking a $250 Uber, given that once Isabelle did what she was planning to do, she would inevitably be broke again. Telling her father on the phone was too awful. And anyway, he wasn't picking up her calls. So Isabelle called her garage and told them to get the Volvo ready. She was driving.

Isabelle left her apartment without bothering to pack a bag, since worrying about changes of underwear and her toiletries seemed entirely beside the point. She was like one of those religious zealots preparing for end of days; everyone she loved had left or been pushed away, and after she told her father, she will have lost him, too, and the world would essentially be over. So, you know, eff flossing. She picked up a comically giant coffee from Starbucks, and mentally got ready to drive on a highway for the first time in over a decade.

"Isabelle!"

Isabelle looked around for a moment before she saw the woman waving from across the street. *Oh god.* Isabelle closed her eyes. There was nowhere to escape.

"Hi!" said the woman, slightly out of breath when she'd crossed to Isabelle's side of the street. "Funny seeing you outside the library!" Margot was wearing floral overalls, carrying a canvas tote that stated in bold, pink letters, *I'D RATHER BE READING.*

"Hi, Margot. Great to see you."

"You too! You haven't been in lately." As she looked at Isabelle, Margot's face crinkled with concern. "Are you okay, Isabelle? You look a little peaked."

"Oh yes, I'm fine," she said. "It's just been, you know, busy."

"I can only imagine. It's so exciting! The *New York Times*! You're a star."

"Oh not really."

"No, you are. Don't forget us now that you're big and famous."

Isabelle smiled, a lump forming in her throat. "I need to run, Margot. But thank you."

Margot cocked her head. "For what?"

"Just, you know, just being a good friend."

"Aw, always," she said. "Come back soon. We miss you!"

Isabelle watched as Margot walked away, and she thought of the awful disappointment Margot would feel when she learned the truth.

• • •

The gray-blue 1999 Volvo was parked right outside the garage. The car was technically Ward's. If anyone asked him what he drove, he would say this one, his chest puffed out. But Ward enjoyed the idea of driving an old, beat-up station wagon more than the actual expe-rience. His real car was a sleek, black, brand-new Mercedes E-class, just like a thousand other rich men in the Hamptons. So the Volvo was kept in the city.

Isabelle climbed in. She adjusted the seat and mirrors, put her foot on the brake, turned on the ignition. Just as she was about to pull out onto Eighty-First, her phone buzzed: Glenda calling for the millionth time. Isabelle had been sending her to voice mail, but her godmother would just hang up and call again. Isabelle picked up. "Glenda, I'm going to Sag Harbor to tell my father. Please stop calling me." Isabelle could hear Glenda saying, "Wait," but Isabelle powered off her phone altogether. She needed all her focus now as she steered herself out into traffic.

Isabelle did not identify as someone who feared driving. But there she was. She jerked her way up First Avenue, eliciting a few sustained honks. City driving was unpleasant, but it was not terrify-ing. It was the speeding of the highway that made her palms go slick with sweat on the wheel. It seemed to her that there was a trick, some magic to driving that Isabelle had never unlocked. She felt particularly close to death in cars, and marveled that more people did not feel the same way.

Isabelle now lined up for entry onto the FDR. The car three spaces in front of her went, then the next, then the next. It was her turn. Isabelle inched closer. A car whizzed past, not letting her in. And then another. The cars behind her began beeping. But Isabelle felt frozen in place. A truck driver down the line stuck his head out the window and yelled, "Come on, lady!!!" The heat of panic rose within her. She grit her teeth together and pushed it down. There was a small break in the traffic, and she pressed the gas pedal, gathering speed, until, *whoosh*, Isabelle was on the highway. She let out a gasp of relief, feeling as she always did that her survival in the car was due to some divine intervention rather than the product of physics and human skill. She realized her breath was coming out in trembling sighs. Isabelle kept her eyes trained in front of her. She had no choice now but to keep moving forward.

Isabelle drove one mile and then another without incident. With much breathing, talking to herself, and wincing as other cars merged into her lane, she guided the car onto the LIE. When she saw signs for Ronkonkoma, Isabelle knew the trip was more than halfway over. On one of these drives long ago, Isabelle had remarked to Brian that Ronkonkoma was a wonderful word. She said it aloud several times, gargling its consonants. Brian had kind of shrugged, uninterested. It was a moment in which she thought of him as small, uncreative. Isabelle had taken it as a sign that Brian shouldn't be her boyfriend; she should keep looking for someone else, someone who'd get her on a phonetic level.

What an idiot she was.

What was also idiotic was thinking that she could just walk into Brian's event and expect him to pick up with her where they'd left off. Isabelle had wildly underestimated—and undervalued—him. Brian had his own life, his own needs; he was not there to simply absorb Isabelle's troubles, to be the netting that caught her time after time. And yet it still came as a shock that within his kindness, his Midwestern politesse, he saw all her faults in vivid color. The force of his vitriol, the spite in his tone, was a hot rake over her tender psyche. His words circled her head in a toxic loop. One point in particular had stuck with her: Isabelle Manning was *ruined*. Not just ruined. Ruined by her father. This barb had found a mate inside her, fusing with the unspoken insecurity lying in wait.

Isabelle had always viewed her veneration of her father as inevitable. Anyone with a parent as brilliant and famous as hers would hold them lofted above all others, anyone would do whatever it took to please them. This was not a choice. She did not like to think about this, but ever since she'd read her mother's book, Isabelle had to entertain the possibility that she had been wrong about her father. He was not the god he held himself out to be. But if Ward was not who she thought he was, then who was she?

She drove down the ramp at Exit 70. She passed the bank that once, long ago, had been Grace's, where she and her family stopped for hot dogs and deliciously synthetic lemonade. She could see her father sitting on a red picnic table with peeling paint, eating his hot dog piled high with sauerkraut, an unguarded family moment that only she and Claire got to experience. Except that when Isabelle was in college, she'd given a quote about it to a reporter at *New York Magazine*. She'd wanted the reporter to like her; she'd wanted to seem cool. But she immediately felt slimy about it, not so much for her father's privacy, but because of how easily, and for so little, she'd sold her childhood memory, making it just another tidbit for public consumption.

Isabelle pulled into the driveway just after four o'clock. She saw with relief that her father's car was not there; she would have time to prepare. When she walked through the unlocked door, the first thing she noticed was the sweet, sulfurous garbage smell. And then she saw the mess. Sheets of newspaper lay on couches and under the coffee table. There were plates on the counter caked with congealed scrambled eggs. A nibbled-at muffin lay on the dining table, its paper sheath halfway peeled off, alongside a Cove Deli takeout coffee, a topography of brown stains on its plastic top. Shallow reservoirs of water sat in the drinking glasses crowded on every free surface. Flies circled over unwashed dishes in the sink.

"Jesus, Dad," she said aloud.

The detritus spoke to a truth of how her father was living out at the house, sick and untended. Isabelle took out the putrid, overflowing garbage to the bins by the shed. She gathered up the sections of paper, some dated in the previous month that had begun to yellow with age, cleared the water glasses, and scrubbed the dishes. She threw away the muffin. In the closet, she found a roll of paper towels and some Fantastik and began spraying the counters and coffee table down.

Growing up, her father had always demanded order in the house, chastising Isabelle if she so much as left a sweater draped over the couch or a glass in her room. "Mess begets mess," he liked to say. He seemed almost fearful of disorder. Claire had told her once it reminded him too much of his house growing up. Then immediately told Isabelle not to mention to Ward that she'd said this. But knowing his background made it all the more troubling that her father had succumbed to living this way.

When Isabelle had finished cleaning, she walked out onto the deck and saw that the dinghy was in the water. It must have stayed out all winter, and now looked worse for the wear. Isabelle hadn't been in the boat in years. She was shocked that her mother had kept it after the accident. Afterward, there were no more beach trips, no waterskiing. There was a particular way Claire would stiffen when anything potentially related came up in conversation, her hackles raised, ready to shepherd the conversation in another direction. For as long as she could remember, silence had a presence in the Manning home, the air charged with the unsaid. Isabelle had blamed the accident, and by extension, herself. But she knew now secrets had nested long before.

Isabelle walked from the deck, down the hill and toward the water, the thick tufts of crabgrass roughing her bare feet. She went out onto the dock and stepped into the cold, damp bottom of the boat. When she'd gained her balance, Isabelle unspooled the rotting rope from the hook on the dock. Wet immediately seeped through the thin material of her clothes as she sat on the wooden plank in the center of the boat. She had to pull the cord enough times to wonder if there was gas in the tank, but then the engine roared to life. Isabelle steered away from the house, the wind slicing through her hair. Perversely, boats had never scared her the way cars did. Out in the center of the cove, she slowed the dinghy down and turned off the motor, allowing herself to drift out by the opposite shore. Staring down at the water Isabelle saw a jellyfish, plump and translucent just beneath the surface. This early in the season, it must've come in with a storm. Then her eyes caught others undulating in the water that had been clear a moment before. It was always this way, the creatures seeming to appear all at once by magic, though they'd been there all along.

Sitting in the boat, she felt Claire's absence, the balance of her now-motherless life stretching out before her. Isabelle floating alone, a tiny silhouette against the darkening sky, turned terrible metaphor for her life. Whatever else happened to Isabelle, even if there was some second act, Claire would not be there. This truth would endure day after day, month after month, year after year. Isabelle did not resist her sadness. She did not keep it at bay, blunting its impact with trite little defenses. She let it in. Her mother was gone, and her life would be less for it. Isabelle put her head in her hands and let herself cry. Soon she was shaking, her face wet with big, blustery tears, choking on her own sobs. The pain was visceral, an aching hollow in her chest. She knew there would be no "getting over this," no healing with time. She was broken without her mother and would not be fixed. This was the grief she'd been awaiting. This was what she had not let herself feel as she busied herself with the book. This was the center of the onion.

◆ ◆ ◆

Back at the dock, Isabelle tied the boat up hastily. As she walked toward the house, there was a rustling in the reeds by the shore. Isabelle stopped and peered through the dusk. A shock of fur rippled through the grasses. The size of a raccoon but the wrong color. The animal emerged into open space, trotting confidently along the shoreline toward the Manning lawn, its fur unmistakably marmalade. Isabelle tiptoed down the stairs to the sand. Miss Muffins turned around, and Isabelle came face-to-face with her mother's white whale.

"It's okay. I'm not going to hurt you."

The feline gave Isabelle a withering gaze, licked its paw, and trotted away. Isabelle lunged after her. Startled, Miss Muffins ran. The cat stopped just a few feet ahead, under the shelter of a bush, scratching an ear with her paw. Isabelle sprang forward again, tackling the animal, this time managing to get ahold of her rump and hind legs. Miss Muffins thrashed and kicked, her head turning around with a contemptuous hiss. "Easy there." Isabelle held on tight, as if everything rode on capturing this animal. But Miss Muffins was strong, and she was feisty. When Isabelle got a grip on the animal's torso, Miss Muffins ratcheted up the fight, landing several scratches on Isabelle's face and bare forearms, yowling as she swiped rapid-fire. But Isabelle did not let go, and she forced the cat into her arms, cradling Miss Muffins like an infant.

Inside the house, the two of them left a train of water and sand. Isabelle took the cat into the spare bedroom on the first floor and left her shut in there. She got a towel to dry them both off and found some milk in the refrigerator. This was what cats liked, wasn't it? Isabelle opened the door to the room gingerly. The cat was nowhere to be seen, and for a moment Isabelle wondered if she'd escaped. Then, out from under the bed, Miss Muffins was all over Isabelle's feet and ankles. "Fuck, that hurts!" The cat kept nipping with her stinging little teeth until Isabelle placed the milk on the floor. Then Miss Muffins stopped, regarded the bowl, and drank greedily, giving Isabelle her chance to slip out.

38

Sag Harbor, 2018

Ward

As he drove toward his house, Ward could see the lights on in the kitchen and living room. He didn't remember leaving them on when he'd gone to play tennis. But who was he to be trusted? Maybe they'd been on for weeks. He turned into his driveway, registering the parked car just in time to slam on the breaks and avoid a rear collision. "Christ!" Ward's head jerked violently against the headrest. He backed up and then pulled into the spot next to the Volvo. His Volvo. For a moment, he considered that a deranged fan had stolen his car, driven to his home, and was now there to make violent literary demands.

Ward rushed inside the house, throwing open the front door, hollering, "Hello! Who's here?"

There was silence before, "In the living room, Dad." Ward slipped off his sneakers and walked from the entryway to find his daughter sitting on the couch. She was barefoot in a flowery yellow sundress, holding a glass of wine, as if at a garden party, but she looked dazed. It was clear now; he had forgotten something.

"Isabelle! When did you get here?"

"A few hours ago."

"Forgive me. Did we have an engagement?"

"No, no engagement."

"You looked dressed to go out. Was there an event? I feel as if I'm missing something."

"Oh. No, this dress was the only thing I had here. It's totally wrong for the occasion, but whatever."

"What occasion?" Ward looked closer. He saw that there were scratches on Isabelle's face and arms, fresh wounds still oozing blood.

"Isabelle, what's happened to you? Are you hurt?"

"I'm fine."

Ward looked around and noticed for the first time that the house had been tidied, but the carpet had several damp spots encrusted with sand.

Isabelle saw him surveying the floor. "I went out in the boat."

"The dinghy?"

"Yes."

"Did that thing even have gas? Why?"

"Yes. I don't know. I wanted to." Just then there came several loud thumps from the guest room, and a low, mournful yowl.

Ward turned. "What is that?"

"Miss Muffins. I captured her," said Isabelle, pointing to her face. "Hence, the scratches."

"I can see them. Do they hurt?"

Isabelle shrugged. "I have bigger problems."

"This is all very mysterious. Did you *drive* here, by the way?"

"Yes. I did." And in his daughter's pale, marred face, he saw a glint of satisfaction.

"But why?"

"I needed to talk to you. You wouldn't return my calls. So here I am."

"I'm sorry, I've been—"

"It's okay, Dad. I know."

"Know what?" But of course. Ward had slipped up to Irving, and gossip of his trip to Texas had reached his daughter. "Well, there's nothing to tell because it's over."

"You mean you're cured?"

"Cured?"

"Dad, I know that you're sick."

"Sick? What?"

"It's obvious."

"Where are you getting this?"

"The state of this house, for one thing."

"I hadn't had a chance to clean up for a few days." Ward had not in fact cleaned up for weeks. He was revolted with the place. He was using the mess to overcome his writer's block. Every day, he wouldn't let himself clean until he'd written two thousand solid words. But he never came close to that. Most days he wrote absolutely nothing. So the house remained a sty, and his book remained unwritten, Ward telling himself that at some point his disgust would spur his creativity. But all of this felt very complicated to explain. "I didn't know you were coming."

"It's not just the house. I saw you with the medications."

"I don't know what you're talking about, Isabelle."

"In the kitchen, the last time I was here. I came downstairs and saw you with your meds."

"What?" And then he remembered. "Oh, no, no. Those weren't medicines, they were vitamins."

"Vitamins? Please. You've never taken vitamins. Come on."

"Isabelle, I promise you." Ward was getting irritated with this line of questioning. "I bought the vitamins to help with my memory, which apparently is just going to continue deteriorating. They didn't do a damn bit of good, but that's what I was doing. Taking my fucking vitamins."

Isabelle scowled. "Dad. Stop. You went to Texas to see some doctor. Don't make this worse by lying. I'm so sick of the lying."

Ward sighed. He could have come up with an excuse. But maybe his daughter was right. "I went to Texas because I began a, um"—Ward coughed—"correspondence with a woman. A fan of my books. And I went to visit her."

Isabelle scowled. "What?"

"I went to visit a woman. A fan."

Isabelle's eyes narrowed. "The pie lady!"

"Yes," Ward said tiredly. "The pie lady." He paused and looked up at the ceiling. "But there's nothing going on. I am alone."

"So why is your book late?"

"My book is late"—Ward clenched his teeth—"because I'm having trouble writing it."

"Oh. So you're really not sick?"

"Unless you count writer's block, then no."

Isabelle closed her eyes and breathed in.

"I might rather have cancer."

"Stop, Dad, don't say that. You'll make it work. You always do."

Ward grunted. "I'm not so sure," he said. "And if I might offer some advice to you, young writer. Enjoy those highs, my darling girl. Ride that wave of success you're on for as long as you can, because it will come crashing down sooner or later."

Isabelle blinked at him. "It's going to be sooner for me."

"I wasn't saying that—"

"No, I am. My career is about to implode. That's why I'm here."

"What do you mean?"

"The book—*Underpainting*. It's not all my own."

"Oh, Isabelle, you didn't hire someone, did you?"

"No, worse. I took the book from Mom."

Isabelle explained what she had done. "Glenda figured it out. She's threatening to expose me. It's probably for the best. I'm going to tell my publisher tomorrow morning. But I wanted to tell you first." She spoke robotically, like a kidnap victim reciting the terms of the ransom.

Ward sat down on the arm of the couch. "My god."

"You knew about Mom's book."

"No, I didn't."

"Didn't you suspect something when you read it?"

"I—I haven't actually read it."

Isabelle's eyes widened. "You haven't read it?"

Ward shook his head. "I tried, Isabelle. But I just . . . I've been having a hard time."

"Wow. Okay."

"How much had she written?"

"Around two-thirds. I finished it and edited it."

"I see."

"So you really knew nothing about this? She wrote a book in complete secret?"

Ward rubbed his face. He hadn't known. But, of course, should've. Claire was a good writer. A great one. And there had been a time when she was always hiding herself away with that computer in the kitchen. Walking around in the clouds, forgetting things, but dopily happy. He had ignored it—then blocked it out—because he did not want to know. But now, much too late, it was undeniable. "No," he said, "I didn't know."

Isabelle looked out the window at the cove now gleaming in the residue of daylight. "I don't know what Mom wanted me to do with the book. I thought maybe she wanted me to, you know, have it. But maybe she never thought I'd be so desperate."

"Hm. I think I'll join you in a drink." He went into the kitchen, alone. Ward leaned his hands on the kitchen counter, closing his eyes, overcome with a feeling he could not place. But as it lurched from his gut into his throat, he knew its bitterness. What he felt was shame. Pure, blinding shame for his catalyzing role in this whole godforsaken mess, shame for being the person who'd sacrificed his own daughter at the altar of his ego. "Who am I?" Ward whispered into the empty kitchen, his knees buckling from the weight of his self-loathing. A searing pain throbbed at his left eye socket. He was tempted to bludgeon himself with the wine bottle on the counter, escape from consciousness. But instead, Ward poured its contents into a glass, and prepared to rejoin his daughter. There was only one thing to do now.

• • •

Isabelle had gotten up and was peeking into the spare bedroom.

"I don't hear anything," she whispered, before walking back to the couch. "Maybe she's asleep."

"What are you going to do with it?"

"Take her to the shelter, I guess. Kimberly Swanson clearly isn't taking care of her."

"Good for you." Ward sat in the Eames chair opposite his daughter.

"The least I could do." They sat in silence a moment, Isabelle looking into her drink. Ward opened and shut his mouth several times; what he had to say sat clogged inside him. He leaned over in his chair, his hands smoothing back his hair.

"Dad, are you okay?"

"No. This is all my fault. I did this to you." Ward finally looked up at Isabelle. "I made you this way. I did this."

"Dad, you don't have to say that. Yes, maybe you weren't the most present father, but—"

"You don't understand. I—how can I explain this?" Ward heard his voice crack. "Oh darling, I'm so sorry."

"Sorry? For what?"

Ward cupped his face in his hands, giving himself one last moment before Isabelle knew his secret.

"Isabelle, I had Fern tank your first book."

Isabelle looked at her father quizzically. "You did what?"

"I told him to soft pitch editors who were a bad fit, so it wouldn't sell."

"What are you talking about?"

"I wanted you to understand the reality of this profession."

"And he agreed to this?" Something steely and angry had slipped into his daughter's voice.

"Irving didn't give him much of a choice. Keeping me happy is a priority for them. Was a priority."

"Keeping you *happy*?"

"It was meant to help you in the long run. Not selling a first book is a valuable lesson."

Isabelle's eyes widened and a large vein running down the center of her forehead was suddenly visible. "Are you fucking serious?"

"I didn't know it would become so public. I didn't know there'd be those nasty press pieces. I swear to you."

"Oh my god."

"Your childhood, Isabelle. You were too coddled; you had no understanding of how the world works for most people. And then you got that story published in the *New Yorker*, just like that. I didn't want you to get the wrong idea about how this works. If success came too quickly, you'd never value it. And I thought you'd write another, and it would sell right away."

"But I didn't. I couldn't write another." Isabelle had finished her wine and set the glass aside. Her hands were in her lap, gripping the fabric of her cheery yellow dress, her eyes narrowed to slits. "Did Mom know?"

"I didn't tell her, but she suspected something." Ward paused. "I think she figured it out."

Isabelle shook her head. "Do you have any idea what you've done to my life? Do you have any fucking idea? I have put everything on hold to write a book. Everything. I have given all I have—including my character and self-worth—into publishing a book."

"Isabelle—"

"You've ruined me. You've ruined my life." She spoke quietly but with conviction, as if this conclusion had been settled on with some deliberation. Ward looked at his daughter, searching for some softness behind the hard shell of anger that had frozen on her face.

"Darling, you have so much ahead of you."

Isabelle shook her head. "You're a monster."

"I was trying—"

"All I ever wanted was to be like you. To be a great, big writer, just like my daddy," said Isabelle, trembling. "And now I see that I am. I'm a monster, just like you."

"No. Please, stop," said Ward, moving closer toward his daughter. He tried to take her hands, but she refused him.

"Look at us. We're both liars. We'll do anything for public adoration, for someone to tell us we're special, including plagiarism and following some psycho fan to Texas. It's sick. And it's pathetic. We're pathetic."

"Isabelle. Maybe that's true of me, but not you. You could never be pathetic. I never said it enough, but, but I am so proud of you." Ward could feel heat behind his eyes and a tightening in his chest, but he pressed on. "So proud. You have the gift, Isabelle. You have it. You notice what other people don't. Your sentences have always been beautiful, even in those little crayon books. You are a writer. A very good one. That *New Yorker* story knocked me off my feet; you know that, right?"

Isabelle looked at her father, then closed her eyes before she said, "It's too late. It's way, way too late. None of what you say makes a difference. Not anymore. I'll never write again. It's poison now."

"You are so young still—"

There was a loud thump, and both Ward and Isabelle looked toward the sound.

"I think it's coming from outside," said Isabelle.

Ward walked to the front door. He peered through one of the frosted glass side panels and could make out a figure. Ward opened the door, and there, standing in front of him, swathed in a moneyed-gray cashmere shawl, was his wife's best friend.

39

Sag Harbor, 2018

Ward

"Well, let me in, for crissakes." Glenda wrestled her way past Ward. "Do you know how many 'Birch Groves' there are in Sag Harbor? There's a street, a lane, a circle. And the signs here are shamelessly dilapidated. It gave my poor driver a devil of a time with the GPS." Glenda took off her scarf and pressed it into Ward's chest. She sniffed, surveying the entry before concluding, "Place looks a bit worse for the wear, doesn't it?"

"Glenda, to what do we owe this honor?"

"Your daughter refuses to answer her cellular phone," said Glenda, as she walked deeper into the house. She looked back and said, "I suppose she's told you about her little scam?"

Ward frowned. "I wouldn't call it that."

Glenda did not hear what Ward said because she had begun shrieking. "Isabelle! What the devil is wrong with your face?"

"It's nothing," said Isabelle, now standing.

"It looks like you've been in a street fight."

"Something like that. Glenda, you didn't have to come all the way here."

"I had no interest in coming all this way. But you hung up on me before I could speak, silly girl," said Glenda. "Sit back down. You too, Ward." She pointed to the couch, and Isabelle and Ward tiredly complied.

"You're here to goad me into confessing—but it's not necessary. I've already decided to come clean."

"No, dear, I did not upend my entire schedule to *goad* you. I've come here because I have changed my mind. I do not want you to tell anyone about this." Glenda put up a hand to keep Isabelle from speaking. "What you've done is positively vile. And I'd have little compunction about letting you face the music." Glenda paused as if to underscore her seriousness. "But last night something occurred to me." She stopped again, as if she'd rehearsed her pauses for maximum dramatic effect.

Ward had always found Glenda to be an insufferable blowfish of a woman. She was thoroughly self-righteous, enthralled with her own import, and lived in a fantasyland where everyone had yachts, family crests, and rolling emerald lawns set for croquet. Glenda had made no secret of her disdain for Ward and made sure to remind him she thought him an ill-suited match for her Claire. But Claire was charmed by her, and loyal to her old friend.

"Claire would not want you publicly punished." Glenda looked at Isabelle. "She'd be mortified to be involved in any kind of sordid literary scandal. Mortified."

"Fuck the spectacle," Ward interjected. "Claire wouldn't want this because she loved her daughter, Glenda. And she wasn't some vindictive harpy."

"True. Claire was always too kind for her own good. Too giving, I always told her," said Glenda, now facing Ward. "But you never understood how strong she was, the toughness underneath that size 2 J. McLaughlin sheath."

"Be that as it may." Ward was not going to get sucked into Glenda's game of who *really* knew Claire. "I think we can all agree that there is no reason for the origin of the book to leave this room."

"Precisely."

Ward nodded. "Nothing good comes from telling."

"How about the fact that I'm miserable?" said Isabelle. "And isn't there always an inherent good in truth?"

"There's an inherent good in not giving up on your career," said Ward.

"And what about Mom? Doesn't she deserve to get credit? The book is a big hit."

"Mom is not here, Isabelle. You'll write another book, and this will all fade away." Ward well knew this to be true. "I promise you." Isabelle sat very still, looking intently at the bookcase, making no sign that she could hear what Ward was saying.

Glenda smiled contemptuously. "I'll leave you two to stew in whatever other self-justifications you have up your sleeves."

As if to punctuate Glenda's sentiment, a sustained yowl came from the bedroom.

Glenda started. "Is that an animal?"

"Don't worry about it," Isabelle said.

Her godmother clutched her chest. "I've heard the raccoon problem is terrible in this area, but an infestation inside the house?"

"Glenda, my daughter and I are tired," said Ward. "Unless you have anything more to add, you can go."

"Oh I'm leaving. I'm leaving before I need a rabies inoculation."

Ward rolled his eyes. "Excellent."

Glenda began to walk toward the door. She'd always operated like a windstorm, kicking up dust and debris, then disappearing as fast as she'd come in. The pressure in the room began to resettle with her impending exit, but then she paused. Glenda looked at Isabelle with what might have passed for real concern. When she spoke, there was kindness in her voice. "Don't tell, Isabelle. Don't ruin your life. That is the last thing Claire would want."

◆　◆　◆

The next day Ward was awakened by morning light shining through the diaphanous shades. He rubbed his eyes and fumbled for his

Patek Philippe on the bedside table. Just after eight, the latest he'd slept in decades. He didn't remember dozing off, only staring into the darkness as the hours went by. He hoisted himself out of bed, rinsed his mouth, and put on his bedroom slippers.

He and his daughter had barely spoken after Glenda left. It was as if Isabelle was in a trance, and he did not know the magic word to bring her back. Ward was heartened that she seemed to have given up the idea of exposing herself. It would be a huge mistake to soil her burgeoning career. Especially after the start she'd had. The start he'd given her.

When Isabelle sent out her first book, Ward was gripped with a vicious, consuming envy that his daughter was at the precipice of her literary career. She got to be the new, shiny thing. Ward—no matter how much of a legend, no matter how many more best-sellers he wrote—would never be that again. And this fact filled him with a near physical pain. So he did what he did. He was accustomed to operating this way. A career like his, filled with chart-toppers and literary trophies, did not just happen. It required a fierce, unyielding strategic defense. How else could he keep going? How else could he fend off a new, hot Iowa MFA's splashy debut written entirely as text messages? How else did he convince readers to keep coming back again and again? The work, yes, but it was so much more than that. He had to tie up his books with self-image, self-worth. People had to become scared that if they missed one, it would mean they were lesser intellectuals, left out of the conversation. He had to cultivate a respect that tinged on fear. He couldn't do this by being nice, by helping others up the rungs, by giving any-one else credit, by admitting fallibility, even humanity. Yes, Ward could write. Yes, he was good with details. But Ward knew that his true talent was not the actual writing. No, his true talent was being a merciless defender of his celebrity. Just look at what he'd done to Claire.

Ward rarely thought of the real role his wife had played in his career. He'd spent the years convincing himself that even if he'd never met Claire Cunningham, *American Dream* would have happened. His next two books would have happened. His life would have happened.

But underneath the layers and layers of ego, built up thick and hard like a callous, was the truth, raw and pink, that without Claire, Ward would still be waiting tables.

Ward had cloaked what he'd done to Isabelle in good intentions. He was trying to teach her a lesson. It would help in the long run to toughen her hide. But no wrapping could fully obscure the hideousness of betraying his daughter. Ward ought to know. Despite all he had done to escape his own origin story, Ward was just like his mother, a parent who cut down their own child. A monster. If Isabelle had not been gone when Ward woke up, he might have told her this. He might have continued the long process of apologizing. But Isabelle was not in the kitchen. She was not in her room, either. The house was still. It looked immaculate. She must have cleaned after he was in bed. Ward checked the guest bedroom. It, too, was empty; Isabelle and Miss Muffins were gone, a cat-sized depression in the duvet cover and a soft shedding of downy, marmalade fur the only things left behind.

Ward opened the front door, his thin pajamas no match for the still-nippy May morning. The Volvo was, of course, missing from the driveway. Ward ambled out into the yard. He looked up, watching the white wispy clouds drift together and then apart. Ward lowered himself to the ground and lay down in the grass, the damp soaking into his clothes, arranging himself like a snow angel. He'd had a lot more hair the last time he'd done this, and he was startled by the cold of the dew on his scalp. But Ward did not get up. He did not move. He lay there, alone in the yard of a house far away from the place where he'd begun, and he tried to lose himself in the sky.

He stayed in this position until the rising sun burned astringent upon his face. Ward knew what needed doing. He coaxed his body upright, walked into the house, and climbed the stairs to his office. He pulled the book off the shelf where he'd left it. He situated himself in his leather club chair. When he was comfortable, he opened to the first page of *Underpainting*, and Ward began to read.

40

New York, 2018

Isabelle

Isabelle drove back to the city at first light, Miss Muffins riding in the cat carrier her mother had bought, wedged on the floor behind the passenger seat. Given the gusto with which she'd carried on during their cove-side skirmish, the cat was oddly serene. Miss Muffins did not seem to care that a relative stranger was putting her in a box and taking her in a car. Isabelle supposed at some point she'd have to call up Kimberly Swanson and let her know that she'd stolen her pet. If Claire was to be believed, Kimberly was unlikely to mind. Isabelle did not want to wait for the shelter in East Hampton to open. She couldn't stand another moment with her father. She'd take the cat back to New York and figure out what to do from there.

Since Miss Muffins might be in her apartment for a day or two, Isabelle stopped at King Kullen and bought some cans of food and a litter box. The grocery clerk on the graveyard shift mistook Isabelle for a new pet owner, had gotten overly excited, and tried to sell her a scratching post and a little felt mouse that bounced on the end of a wire.

Back in her apartment, Isabelle took a long, scalding shower. The water stung the still-fresh scratches on her skin. The pain, in its definiteness, was a kind of relief, a crystallization of the many things that were wrong. When Isabelle had left the city, she'd planned to come clean regardless of Glenda. But things felt different now. Very different. Her feelings of guilt and self-loathing had been over-ridden with some new ones. Anger. Resentment. Self-pity. Her first book should have sold. She should never have been in the position to steal *Underpainting*. None of this would have happened if it were not for one person. Ward Manning. Her father had taken from her the thing she wanted most in the world, the thing she was trying to do to please *him*. Her love and admiration in all its intensity had been changed into a thick, molten hatred. It was so automatic, like flipping a switch to convert Fahrenheit to Celsius, that it was almost as if Isabelle's love had been hovering at this threshold for years, just waiting to cross over to the other side.

Knowing now that it was her father who'd stymied her book, Isabelle was filled with a renewed sense of her capabilities. In a way, it was flattering that Ward found her so worthy an adversary. Of course, she could write another book. Many books. There was nothing now to hold her back. Unless she told what she'd done with *Underpainting*. If she told, she'd never have the chance to write again. And this seemed a little too unfair.

Isabelle lay down on the bed in her robe, letting her wet hair soak her pillow. She heard her phone buzzing and saw it was Ward again. She sent him to voice mail. There was nothing he could say to her now. Still, Isabelle had to work to bat out of her mind the praise he'd given her, at long, long last. The person Isabelle wanted to talk to was Brian. But he was gone, and she didn't blame him. Isabelle had to take whatever steps she was going to take by herself.

At that moment Isabelle felt something tugging at her duvet from the bottom of the bed, before the cat leapt into the air and landed on her legs. Isabelle shrieked. She'd forgotten there was an animal in her apartment. The cat advanced toward Isabelle with her purposeful, stalking walk and then curled herself up, so her back was up against Isabelle's left side. Isabelle stroked her fur, and the cat began to purr aggressively. When Isabelle paused, Miss Muffins thumped her tail and glared back at Isabelle, so she'd start again. They sat this way together for several minutes until Isabelle's exhaustion overtook her and she felt her eyes begin to close.

She dreamed not of phones and water, but of Livia. Since writing the book, Isabelle's thoughts often came out in Livia's voice. In this dream, Livia was standing on the sidewalk in what looked like Isabelle's neighborhood. Livia beckoned her over, and Isabelle followed. When they were face-to-face, the other woman remained silent, reaching out and taking Isabelle's hand, interlocking their fingers. Isabelle opened her mouth, and this time, her voice came out clear and strong. "We'll go this way," she said to Livia. And the women walked together.

When Isabelle awoke, she felt the wet of tears on her cheeks. She got out of bed and went to the bathroom. In the mirror she looked alarmingly haggard, with circles under her eyes and a heavy gravity around her cheeks. She splashed water on her face and looked again, into her own eyes, as if she could stare long enough and understand, finally and magically, who she really was. After a few moments, Isabelle sighed. She knew. Maybe she'd always known.

Isabelle walked back into her room and got her computer. She had the woman's email somewhere; she'd used it just after her mother died to send the pictures for the obituary. Within minutes, she found it, composed her message, and sent it off.

41

New York, 2018

Brian

Brian arrived at the gym by six every morning. He'd done CrossFit for years, but in the last few weeks, it had been different. Today, he gave his usual wave to the other early-morning diehards. They often stopped to chat between sets; Brian never joined in. He went over and got on the bike, immediately pushing hard through heavy resistance, feeling the blood flow into his hamstrings and calves, sweat prick up on his forehead. Quickly he was breathing heavily, his body slick. After twenty minutes, Brian moved on to the long, heavy ropes that lay on the floor, attached to one wall. He raised his arms up and down so the ropes undulated like a sine wave. Then he lifted weights. He'd added ten pounds to his bench press in just the past week. He was getting stronger. As he worked out, Brian blasted music in his headphones. He usually liked pop, lots of nineties rap, even some eighties stuff, but he'd gotten rid of all that. Music like that—music that she liked—no longer existed. He listened to hard rock, the Beastie Boys, Metallica, stuff he didn't enjoy. It wasn't about that.

Brian got back on the bike for another round. When he was done, he went to pull-ups, thirty in a row. Then he went to the tires, picking out the biggest one he could find and then rolling it along the floor, pushing it with the entirety of his weight. He liked to imagine scenes from *Gladiator* during this part. Or pretend he was an ancient Roman townsperson transporting a boulder to a coliseum site. This was what he was doing, straining with all his might, when he felt a tap on his shoulder.

Startled, Brian whipped around to see one of the trainers, an older ex-military guy who ran an evening class Brian used to take. Mike was his name. It was always Mike, wasn't it? Brian saw Mike's lips moving and took out his earbud.

"You okay?"

"Yeah?" said Brian breathing heavily.

"You were just screaming."

"Oh. Was I?" Brian looked around and saw that everyone in the gym was watching this interaction.

"I've noticed you pushing yourself really hard."

"Yeah."

"Don't overdo it, okay? Results will come."

Brian smiled tightly. He wanted to tell Mike that he wasn't working out like this, like a fucking feral-ass animal, because he wanted more defined pecs. He wasn't trying to sculpt his abdomen. He was doing this because he needed to be numb right now, because making his body strain to the absolute physical limit was the only way he could stop feeling. And he could not let himself feel. But instead he said, "Got it, Mike."

Mike patted him on the back, "Just looking out for you, man." Brian put in his earbud and went back to pushing his tire.

•   •   •

Brian showered and changed into his suit at the gym. There was a possibility he'd come back for another session after work, depending on how late he stayed at the office. If he left before eight, he often did two-a-day. As he passed her desk, Rachel, the gym receptionist, grinned, half stood up, and leaned over the desk as she said, "See you soon!" Rachel, who was twenty-five—one day there'd been number balloons and some kind of Keto cake—had a tight body and a beauty contestant smile. He waved back and gave a nod. She was desperate for Brian to ask her out. Maybe he would. Maybe next week.

He walked to the subway, drinking the Muscle Milk shake he'd packed in his duffle. It had an off-putting greasy texture and tasted of synthetic vanilla, but whatever, it made him not hungry. On the platform, the display still showed the train as six minutes away. Brian started looking at the *New York Times* on his phone. His boss loved to quiz his deputies on arcane news stories, so he might as well use the time. Brian was skimming the home page when the link caught his eye.

What I Stole from My Mother

Brian felt his breath catch. He knew before he read the byline.

Last month, I published the novel *Underpainting*. The book has enjoyed success and I, as the author, have received numerous accolades and positive reviews for this work. But I can no longer stand by and falsely take credit. I am not the writer of this book; I am the writer's daughter.

Let me explain.

Isabelle went on to detail Claire directing her to the dresser drawer on her deathbed, finding the manuscript among childhood mementos, and then selling it as Isabelle's own work.

When the book came out, I did not believe that anyone knew of my mother's writing. Subsequently, I came to understand that my godmother had known of the book's existence when it was written in the late 1980s and early 1990s. My godmother initially threatened to expose me, but ultimately reversed herself, believing that my mother would not have wanted me to ruin my own career. She may have been right about that. However, my mother was an immensely talented writer, and though she kept this largely to herself, she deserves that recognition, even in memory, whatever the personal and professional consequences to me.

I am deeply ashamed of my actions. I apologize to all of those whom I've hurt in this process, and there are many, including people I love very dearly, who now understandably will want nothing to do with me.

This was him, right? It had to be him. Or was she talking about her father? Was it always actually her father? It felt like it was him, though. Brian was so engrossed that the train's doors opened and closed without him getting on. Isabelle finished the piece explaining that she'd returned her advance and would no longer receive any financial benefit from *Underpainting* and urging people to honor her mother's memory by reading the book. Brian read the whole piece again and then dropped the hand holding the phone to his side, staring into space. He'd blocked her number and her email, he'd thrown himself into work, he'd pushed her out of his mind with grit, sweat, and determination, but he had never been fully secure. His system was vulnerable. Isabelle had found a way in.

It didn't matter. None of it mattered. None of this changed what she had done. Or who she was. So she'd confessed. So what? Isabelle said she was confessing voluntarily, but could she really be trusted? No. Fuck her. Just fuck her.

Right?

Another train pulled into the station. The doors opened, offering Brian a second chance. This time he was ready. He stepped in, gripped a pole, and the train barreled into the tunnel.

42

New York, 2018

Isabelle

Isabelle could see no reason why they couldn't end things with a short phone call. What good would it do to formalize the breakup in person? It was over. Sitting across from each other at Le Charlot— where he'd cleverly made the reservation so Isabelle could not beg inconvenience—would bring only pain, an unnecessary confrontation of what they might have shared if things had not gone so terribly wrong.

She walked down Park Avenue toward the restaurant. She was in yoga pants and a fleece, her unwashed hair tucked into a baseball cap, her unofficial uniform for the last two weeks, ever since her *Times* editorial. The scratches on her face were healing but visible. Her forehead would sport a new scar that bisected her old wound. Isabelle opened the door and was greeted by the model-level-pretty French hostess, who was nice enough to pretend Isabelle was not woefully underdressed. He was already seated at the corner table by the window, awaiting her.

"Hi."

Fern looked up from his phone. "Oh, Isabelle. Are you hiding from someone?" he said, kissing her on the cheek.

"Everyone."

"Ah."

After she'd outed herself, she'd gotten a few tepid texts of support. A lot of once-friends and acquaintances stayed silent. Darby posted a photograph of himself in an unbuttoned flannel with the caption **Plagiarism . . . so uncool**. She had been hoping she'd hear from Brian. But she should have known; he was a man of his word. Isabelle still had not spoken to her father. He had responded with his own editorial, explaining what he had done with Isabelle's first book. There was a muffled public outcry that quickly ran out of steam. And the new notoriety had only helped Ward's sales. Though no one was outselling Claire. *Underpainting* had climbed to the number one spot on the *New York Times* bestseller list.

Ward's version of a mea culpa had brought Glenda back around to Isabelle's side of things. Her godmother did not hesitate at the chance to pin everything on Ward and was eager to kindle with Isabelle an us-versus-him dynamic. Isabelle was glad to have Glenda back, but what she really wanted to do was not talk about her father at all.

"I took the liberty of ordering you a glass of pinot," said Fern.

"Thanks."

Fern nodded. "So. How are you holding up, doll?" After his initial freak-out, Fern's shock had given way to a surprisingly genuine empathy. He stood by her as she navigated her disclosure, and he seemed to have more than a superficial interest in her well-being. The animating force behind his kindness was no doubt guilt that he'd played a critical role—under duress, but still—in leading Isabelle down this ruinous path. But even guilt had limits. Fern had his own career to consider, and Isabelle had no illusions about the purpose of this lunch. In the politest way possible, Fern was about to make clear that they'd never see each other again.

"Like you'd expect," Isabelle said now.

There was a silence after the waiter had come and taken their salad orders. Isabelle took a sip of her wine. "We don't have to do a whole thing, Fern. I get it."

"Get what?"

"I didn't think that this"—Isabelle motioned with her fingers back and forth between them—"was going to continue. I mean, obviously."

Fern regarded her, a slyness creeping into the set of his lips. "Maybe there is a way . . ." Fern sat up straighter in his chair. "Look, I've done a little work behind the scenes, and I may have found a solution."

"A solution?"

"A way to get you back on track."

"Fern, I'm not interested in writing."

"You don't even know what I'm going to propose."

"All right. Tell me."

Fern fanned out his hands dramatically in front of him and said in a faux Hollywood announcer voice, "Memoir."

"You're kidding."

"Hear me out. You're probably done in fiction, at least until everyone forgets about this. But I have a way to make that happen sooner rather than later. In the midst of doing damage control at the publisher, I floated the idea of you writing a tell-all about being Ward Manning's daughter, and they were into it. *Very* into it. It's a perfect palate cleanser. You'd have to work fast, of course, to catch the momentum of the firestorm around your family, but I have no doubt you can do it." Fern paused expectantly. "You're looking at me blankly. Are you wondering about money? I probably can't wrench an advance out of it, but we could get you something on the back end. You'll have to tide yourself over until it comes in or you wrangle *Underpainting* money out of your mother's estate."

"I'm not doing that."

"Even more reason to write the memoir."

"And Irving is okay with this?"

"Yes. His loyalty to Ward—what's left of it—can't beat a commercial opportunity like this. And the mood is right for shifting the blame to your father, you know. An entitled white man? Forget it."

"I've never done memoir."

"It's not rocket science. All your material is right there. You don't even have to make stuff up."

"Huh."

"This is good, Isabelle. I'm giving you a chance at redemption."

Isabelle looked out the window at a woman walking by, smoking a cigarette, talking on her phone, smiling, invincible.

"Hello? Isabelle?"

"Sorry."

"You don't have to answer me now," said Fern, drumming his fingers on the table.

"Okay."

"You'll think about it?"

"Yes."

"But not too long. The iron won't stay hot forever."

◆ ◆ ◆

Isabelle woke up early the next day. She got dressed and put on sneakers before walking outside, intending only to grab a deli coffee and return home. But the June day was warm and sunny, and she found herself heading toward the park. She entered on Seventy-Sixth Street next to a playground where she'd often met her friends with children to *ooh* and *ahh* over their toddlers going down the slide or give a few pushes on the baby swings until it felt too poignant and she released herself out of the playground's iron gates. Isabelle continued, walking past the steep hill where there was sledding on snowy days but which was now a vibrant green, and then back behind the Met until she stepped onto the elevated path that circled the reservoir.

The water sparkled cheerfully in the sunlight, looking the same as she remembered it from years ago. It felt that morning, walking in the sun, with vitamin D soaking into her skin, that one layer of the deep, opaque sadness had lifted. She was not happy, but she was no longer confused. Nothing would be easy. But for the first time,

Isabelle understood in more than the most theoretical way that she would endure.

* * *

Back in her apartment, she dialed his number. After a few minutes on hold, he came to the phone.

"I've been waiting for your call."

"Hi, Fern."

"I'm in the middle of a million things, but let's talk timing. How soon can I see a draft?"

"I'm not going to do it."

"What?"

"I'm not going to write the memoir."

Fern sighed loudly into the phone. "Well fuck, Isabelle. Why not?"

"Because I'm done, Fern."

"This isn't cute, doll."

"You don't understand. I can't write about my father. I'm done just . . . just being the daughter, the barnacle."

Fern was silent, and Isabelle could almost hear him scowling. "No, you don't understand, Isabelle," he said at last. "I'm going to put a fine point on this: If you want to write again, this is it."

"I believe you. But I'm still not going to do it."

"Give it a day or two. You'll change your mind."

"No, I won't. Thank you for trying to help me. But I'm sorry. I have to go."

Isabelle slipped off her shoes and walked to the window. The day yawned out in front of her. What she made of it was entirely up to her. Isabelle had come to realize that, until very recently, she had not been the protagonist in her own life. Her story had always belonged to her father. Isabelle felt grateful to have been given the role of daughter, and she never broke character. Even writing had been Ward's. Her books were born of desire to please him, to provide her father with the comfort of a literary legacy. It was always Ward driving the plot.

But Isabelle could see now that the story had been more complicated than she understood. It was never about a man, even one as imposing as Ward Manning, but a family. Isabelle and Claire were not bit players in Ward's story, but the pillars that held up the structure. They needed each other to tell their stories, and without Isabelle, the narrative broke down.

Isabelle was now faced with the terrifying prospect of being the catalyst for action. It was up to her who she was and what she wanted to say. She would learn to speak with the elusive voice of her dream, the one that was hers and hers alone. Isabelle had spent her life moving through darkness, down a single illuminated path, but now light shone all around her, and trails sprouted in every direction. All she had to do was pick one. Isabelle Manning had nothing to lose.

43

Sag Harbor, 2017

Claire

Claire hung up the phone and stared out at the cove. Hearing the sound of one's own child crying never got easier. Even after thirty-four years. Nearly thirty-five. It had been over two years since Isabelle's book had been rejected by every single publisher it had been submitted to, and her daughter had not recovered. Isabelle was still cycling through recriminations, her failure hanging over her as she tried to write something new. She was stuck, unable to let go. Claire couldn't blame her. There had always seemed something off in what happened to Isabelle's first book. She couldn't prove it, but Claire suspected foul play.

How Claire sometimes wished that Isabelle would move on to a different career, or better yet, had chosen a different one to begin with. She was smart and capable. Isabelle could have been good at a great many things. Claire knew that any suggestion of the sort would be met with hostility. And perhaps rightly so. Isabelle was a real writer. She ought to have a career in what she loved. But Claire could no longer stand by, watching Isabelle flounder this way. The time had come for her to step in.

Claire got out of her chair, bringing the box of tissues with her. She had been trying to rid herself of a nagging cold for over a week without success. One of the vestiges of her upbringing was Claire's approach to illness, which was to ignore until full-blown emergency. In the Cunningham family, doctors were viewed as an indulgence, and illnesses to be combated instead with iron will and strong drink. Claire had done nothing about her lingering symptoms, and in the last day, she felt increasingly miserable and as though she were spiking a fever.

Up in her bedroom, Claire removed a thick card of stationery from the pile on her desk and wrote Isabelle's name on it. She went to her drawer and excavated the manuscript from beneath the nightgowns and the little trove of treasured items from Isabelle's childhood.

There it was—the book she had written two decades before. Claire paused to thumb through the opening chapters. It had been so long since she'd read over what she'd written, but seeing her words was like looking at the photo of a long-ago lover, the one that could never be fully left in the past. Sweetness seared by the burn of regret. She chuckled at some of the lines, remembering how wonderful it had been to inhabit Livia's mind instead of her own. Though really, they were one and the same. For decades, Livia had felt too revelatory. Molded out of Claire's quiet rage, she revealed a truth about Claire best left hidden. As much as Livia strained to be heard, Claire always asked herself, to what end? But the answer to that question had changed.

It wasn't Claire who needed Livia, but Isabelle. Claire was always searching for a tangible way to help her daughter, and now she had it. Claire affixed the card to the manuscript. She'd bring it into the city next week, but for now, she put it back in its hiding place. She did not need Ward happening upon it in the interim.

Claire felt a calm she had not experienced in months, years even. For the first time, she had a plan. It was unusual, perhaps even crazy. But that's what people always said right before something worked. Claire was certain now her temperature was elevated. Even in the grip of fever, she felt sure that Isabelle could finish what Claire could not.

I sat at my table for one outside Cafe Lux, sipping a crisp Sancerre while I made my way around a plate of oysters. Beausoleil. The name was fitting for a day with not a cloud in the sky. I lingered over my wine and bread basket before paying the check. When I was done, I started up Broadway for home. The streets were full of people, all ages, colors, and types, enjoying the unseasonable warmth. I stopped to put a dollar in the cello case of a street musician playing Bach's Cello Suite no. 1. It was one of those afternoons when the combination of being alive and being in New York City filled me with an intoxicating sense of my own luck.

My secret was out. The day after I saw my mother, I called up a reporter and revealed my identity as the artist behind Aiden Connor's "found women." I later gave a more fulsome account in a *New York Magazine* interview, describing my role in the genesis of Aiden's portraits. Some buyers were irate. But thanks in large part to the efforts of Jennifer and Anna, there was a groundswell of support among women. It wouldn't be an exaggeration to say I became a kind of female folk hero. The value of my paintings soared. The buyers decided they weren't so mad. At least at me. Sebastian's perpetuation of the fraud solely for his own financial gain had not gone over as well.

My mother lived only long enough to inspire me to do the right thing. A few weeks after my revelation, she passed away. But even if she did not understand what had happened, she knew before she went that I was happy. And I was.

Sam had not left me. He was shocked. Gobsmacked is more like it. And angry. But after taking some time, he decided that we could work through it. Our problem became fodder for his column, which spun out into a series responding to readers with long-held, life-altering secrets. They were his most popular writings yet.

When I reached my building, I went upstairs and straight into the studio. Except for that god-awful couch, which my new pal Tommy was nice enough to remove for a very reasonable fee, I left the studio mostly as is. I didn't mind working in the space that had been Aiden's. After all, it had once been art that tied us together. I continued with the portraits and was now working on a long-neglected project, one that had been percolating for years. I didn't expect a market for this one, but that was fine by me. I approached the canvas, regarding the image from several angles. I picked up my brush and added a shadow to one side of the face and highlighted around the cheekbone. I stepped back, considered the changes. I was pleased. There, staring back at me from the canvas, was a face at once familiar and completely inscrutable. My own.

EPILOGUE

New York, 2018

The meeting spot was Isabelle's idea. He undoubtedly would've preferred the cozy environs of one of his Carnegie Hill haunts, but the days of him dictating the terms were, as he well knew, over. "Exactly where am I looking for you?" Ward asked over the phone, an unfamiliar nervous pitch to his voice.

"You'll find me," said Isabelle.

Isabelle arrived early and settled herself on a bench near the water. It was still just warm enough to sit outside. Isabelle looked out at the boat pond, dark and murky in the shadows, empty of sailboats. The view was the whole point, the water providing a familiar cloak of distraction.

She spotted him as he came down the hill from Fifth Avenue. Isabelle raised her hand, and he lifted his in return. Ward walked around the edge of the pond, coming closer. He seemed smaller, less imposing than she remembered. He was half a year older since she'd last seen him, and maybe at his life stage people aged like infants again, every month significant. Or maybe the Ward in Isabelle's mind remained the father of her childhood, youth still clinging to him, imposing in size and presence, a Ward that had not existed in decades.

Ward sat without saying anything, hands still in his coat pockets, and for a moment they just looked out at the water, like two strangers who'd happened to find the same bench.

"So. How are you?" he said.

"I'm well." Isabelle waited to feel anxious, the way she always did around him, scared he would ask a question and she wouldn't have the right answer, scared she would bore him.

"What have you been doing with yourself?"

"Working, mostly."

"I've heard something about this."

Isabelle had started writing content for Whole Cloth, the feminist fashion site founded by Asta Grunwald, a twenty-six-year-old who'd become famous Instagramming her cat in outrageous outfits that she hand-sewed in her Barnard dorm room. Two years later, she was one of the most powerful women in fashion. After Isabelle wrote a piece for the site on the oddities and indignities of being a childless woman in her thirties, Asta took Isabelle to lunch and offered her a staff writer job.

"Are you sure?" Isabelle had asked. "I mean, after everything?"

Asta seemed confused, and then said, "Oh. Right." She then looked at Isabelle through her vintage 1950s crystal-encrusted glasses and said, "Just own it, you know? Yeah, I did this. Move on." So Isabelle tried to take her advice.

"Is that enough for you?" Ward asked. "A fashion blog?"

"It's not just fashion, actually."

Ward raised his eyebrows.

"It's a chance to write. They pay fine. And, Dad, you know I sold the apartment."

Ward nodded slowly. "Herb told me. He also told me you've given away the proceeds from *Underpainting*, which is lunacy. Claire wanted you to have them. She put it in her will."

Isabelle had learned that when a feverish Claire had asked for her computer, it was to write a clause into her will directing any future earnings to Isabelle. Of course, this referred to the book. It suggested that a part of Claire did envision the book published.

Isabelle had donated the money to her mother's charity, Project Story.

Ward sighed. "I want to help you out financially, Isabelle."

Isabelle shook her head. "No. No thank you."

"It's the least I can do."

"I don't want your money, Dad," she said. "But there is something else."

"What's that?"

"Start coming with me to the hospital to read to the kids."

Ward shifted uncomfortably. He'd never participated in Claire's endeavor. Claire had not seemed to want him to when she was alive, but now it was different.

"I've been going. Mom built something amazing. I want us both to go."

"Well . . ."

"We can do it together. Every week."

"Every week?"

"Yes."

Ward raised his eyebrows. "All right, all right, Isabelle."

"Good."

They sat in silence for another moment, watching the water.

"Have you read it?" Ward asked.

She reached into her bag and slipped out a pile of pages bound together with a large clip. "Yes."

"And? What did you think?"

Isabelle looked at her father. "I don't think you need me to tell you that it turns out you can write a good memoir."

"Hm."

"Why did you write this?"

"I didn't think Dale Horowitz should get the last word on my life," said Ward, pausing to clear his throat. "And because there were things I needed to say to you. Things I needed you to know."

Isabelle breathed in. This was the part of the conversation she had waited for, the part when she was sure she would crack. She could feel the tightening in her throat. Instead of a novel, her father had written his life story. In it, along with the full truth of his low beginnings, he had laid down on paper what Claire had done for him, her responsibility for his career. He'd looked at his failings as a father, too. The book was a love song to Claire and Isabelle.

"I meant it, you know. I'd have been nothing without the two of you. This year without your mother and these months without you have been the bleakest of my life. I'm hollowed out. I was a fool to believe that I did anything on my own. It's too late for your mother to hear how utterly lost I am without her. But it's not too late for you."

Isabelle nodded, crying now.

"I know it doesn't make up for what I did to you. But . . ."

It didn't. But there was a "but." And from that conjunction would flow the rest of their story. Ward handed her a crisp folded handkerchief. He put his arm around his daughter, and Isabelle leaned into him. He was not a perfect father. He wasn't even a good father by any usual measurement. He had wounded her. And he could again. But only if she let him, only if she forgot that her father was just another human, a man who needed her as much as she needed him. Isabelle buried her face in her father's soft coat. He still smelled the same, like pine, expensive loose-leaf English Breakfast, and library books.

"I love you very much, Isabelle."

Isabelle let out a sob. Neither of them moved for what felt like a long while.

"When does it come out? Your memoir."

Ward shook his head. "I've told my publisher I won't publish this unless they publish your first novel. Which they ought to have bought the first time around."

"Oh."

"Or another book you write. It's up to you."

"And what if I say no? You'll really not publish it?"

"I've already reached my intended audience. I'll lock it away in a drawer."

"That always ends well."

"Ha."

"I appreciate the gesture. I'm not sure I want to write any more books."

"You'll change your mind."

Isabelle shrugged. "Did you ever read it, by the way? Mom's and my book?"

Ward looked at the water. "It was brutal," he said finally. "And I've never been prouder of my family."

• • •

She got home to her fifth-floor walk-up on the Upper West Side in the late afternoon, after they'd taken a long walk around the park. Isabelle sat down at her desk, feeling an insistent nudge against her ankle. She reached down and scratched the cat's chin. Most days Miss Muffins sunbathed in the windowsill, her tail absently lolling over Isabelle's laptop screen. Isabelle resumed an essay about the joys of eavesdropping that she was working on. Her work for Whole Cloth did not require as much heavy lifting as a novel did, but it was, despite what her father believed, enough.

Isabelle had spent so much time wondering why her mother put the book away, why Claire had kept it secret. Isabelle would never know the precise reasons, but as she turned it over and over in her mind, Isabelle circled in on an essential truth: Whatever had happened, Claire had chosen being a mother over being a writer. This sacrifice filled Isabelle with a profound sense of responsibility. She would keep writing. She would not squander what had been given up for her. But she would not take her father up on his offer. Isabelle had a feeling her father still would find a way to get his work into the world.

Isabelle checked her watch. It was time to leave. She went down the stairs and out onto the street. She walked the two blocks to where she'd parked the used Mini Cooper convertible she'd purchased with funds from her apartment. In the driver's seat, Isabelle turned on the ignition. Traffic was light on the West Side Highway, and she was quickly navigating the corridors of Tribeca. She pulled up outside the squat, brick office building near City Hall. The streets were quiet. Not many civil servants went to the office on a Saturday. But there was one.

In a few moments the building doors opened, and Brian appeared. Isabelle felt herself swell at the sight of him and gave a wave. Brian walked to the car and got in the passenger seat, kissing her on the cheek.

Two months earlier, Isabelle had written Brian a letter spelling out exactly how she felt about him and exactly how much she knew she'd fucked up. Isabelle was done keeping things unsaid. She and Brian had spent the last several weeks easing back into their friendship, getting to know each other for the first time as adults.

"So," said Brian. "Where to?"

"I thought we'd take a drive."

Brian smiled. "Let's do it."

Isabelle pulled out and navigated east to the FDR. She got on the highway, picking up speed. A salt-spiked wind whipped her hair. Brian turned the radio up and put his arm around her. It was in the car that she'd learned that what lay beyond her fear was exhilaration. With a steady hand and steely determination, she had come out the other side. Now, with no destination in mind, Isabelle pushed down on the gas, continuing north, feeling that she could drive this way forever.

ACKNOWLEDGMENTS

The first note of thanks goes to Stefanie Lieberman, my wise and steadfast agent. My admiration for her knows no bounds. And I owe Stefanie big-time for bringing Molly Steinblatt and Adam Hobbins into my life. The encouragement, honesty, and conviction of these three people sustained me as I wrote this book. I'm so grateful for all they did to bring it into the world.

It is my pleasure and privilege to work with visionary editor Loan Le, who took this story and its characters to places far beyond what I could have imagined. I am indebted to the dedicated team at Atria: Libby McGuire, Lindsay Sagnette, Dana Trocker, Nicole Bond, Gena Lanzi, Maudee Genao, Paige Lytle, Liz Byer, and Stacey Sakal. And thank you to Daniella Wexler for her belief in this book.

Much appreciation goes to Mindy Steinberg, Natalie Edwards, Jaime Winkelman, Rachel Schechter, and Camilla Velasquez whose early reads, keen eyes, and perceptive feedback did much to shape and improve my narrative.

For sharing her knowledge of the early 2000s Brown bar scene, I'm obliged to Maisie Hughes Lamb. Thank you also to Mindy Utay for interpreting my dreams, and to Marty Seif for coaxing me into the left lane.

For their expertise, efforts, and enthusiasm, thank you to my publicist Kathleen Carter, Olivia Blaustein and Bianca Stelian at

Acknowledgments

CAA, and Michael Steger and Lianna Blakeman at Janklow, and Nikki Terry at Orange Custard.

I'm continuously appreciative for what I learned about writing from the Honorable Colleen McMahon, aka TJ. Thank you for telling me I had "a way with the facts" all those years ago.

Thank you to my first ever "writer friend," the brilliant Judy Batalion for her always spot-on reactions and shoulder of support. And I'd be lost without my writer girls, Lauren Smith Brody and Elyssa Friedland, two fantastic writers who make this solitary profession a whole lot less lonesome.

Thank you to my mentors, inspirations, and confidantes: Alana Newhouse, Annabelle Saks, Bret Gutstein, Alexa Geovanos, Danielle Stein Chizzik, Joan Jacobs Brumberg, Judy Batalion, Julia Edelstein, Nadia Klein, Lara Crystal, Melissa DeRosa, Patricia O'Toole, and Stephanie Butnick. To Liz and Chris Bunnell, thank you for the light of friendship in the darkness of a pandemic. For allowing me to be a working mom, a big thank you goes to Tasha Sankar.

I'm so lucky to have my Abramson family—Patti, Alan, Sami, and Josh—who managed to live with me as I struggled to write during those first months of quarantine.

Thank you to my parents, Kate and Jim McMullan, for showing me the possibilities of a creative life, and always believing I would find my way here.

To my master storytellers, Arthur and Lily, I couldn't love you more.

And, most of all, Adam. To say I couldn't have written this book without you is a comic understatement. Thank you for listening to all my bad ideas. You'll always be my best one.

ABOUT THE AUTHOR

Leigh McMullan Abramson lives in New York City with her husband and two children. Her writing has appeared in *The New York Times, The Atlantic, Tablet,* and *Real Simple.* This is her first novel.